# Collected Cat Stories

# Collected
# Cat Stories

## Stella Whitelaw

*Containing*

CAT STORIES
MORE CAT STORIES
TRUE CAT STORIES

ARROW BOOKS

*To Mavis,*
*a very good friend and cat lover*

Arrow Books Limited
62-65 Chandos Place, London WC2N 4NW

An imprint of Century Hutchinson Limited

London Melbourne Sydney Auckland
Johannesburg and agencies throughout
the world

*Cat Stories* first published in volume form by Hamlyn Paperbacks 1981
*More Cat Stories* first published in volume form by Hamlyn Paperbacks 1984
*True Cat Stories* first published 1986
This collection first published 1988

'Esmeralda' first published in *Woman's Realm* 1959
'This Man is Mine' first published in *Mother* 1965
'Tufty's Horse' first published in *Parents* 1966
'Xinia and the Witch' first published in *Favourite Story* 1975
'Travels with Inky Packer' first published in *Woman's Realm* 1978
'The Cat from Next Door' first published in *Woman's Realm* 1980
'Curtain Call' first published in *My Weekly* 1981
'The One-Eyed Angel' first published in *Woman's Realm* 1981
'The Window-Dresser' first published in *Woman's Realm* 1982
'The Cat That Could Fly' first published in *Grimalkin's Tales* 1983
'Nine Lives' first published in *Grimalkin's Tales* 1983
'Arbuthnot Road' first published in *Grimalkin's Tales* 1983
'The Great God Mau' first published in *Grimalkin's Tales* 1983
'Independence Brown' first published in *Woman & Home* 1984
'Walkabout' first published in *Woman's Weekly* 1984
'The Vanishing Act' first published in *My Weekly* 1984
'Lucky's Story' first published in *More Cat Stories* 1984

Illustrated by Lesley Craig and Marilyn Day

Printed and bound in Great Britain by
Anchor Brendon Limited, Tiptree, Essex

ISBN 0 09 961150 3

# Contents

# BOOK ONE
# Cat Stories

*To Diana,*
*daughter dear*

# Travels with Inky Packer

Inky was an extraordinarily beautiful, pure white, long-haired, pedigree Persian. She had vivid blue eyes and exactly the right short nose, full cheeks and broad muzzle. She lived at Russets, Culimore Crescent with the Packers. It was a large, comfortable house, the kind estate agents describe as 'a highly desirable residence'.

Inky could have lived a pampered existence with a cushion to sleep on, daily grooming, limitless minced chicken, and nothing more exhausting to do than stretch herself luxuriously at the occasional cat show.

But Inky, right from kittenhood, developed some odd habits. For a start she preferred to be thought human and rapidly developed a liking for many human-type occupations. She regularly went shopping every morning, paying a call at each of the various establishments in the High Street, leaving the Chinese take-away and the fish and chip shop until last.

Twice a week she went to the Public Library and browsed round the shelves. She particularly liked the crime section which had quite a different smell. She soon became addicted to the television in the evening, but turned her back and went to sleep if a repeat was being shown.

She knew her way round the neighbourhood and there was hardly a building with an open door or window that she had not visited. Exclusiveness did not deter her. She preferred eating out, and several times strolled nonchalantly into a very posh restaurant, though she was soon lulled to sleep by the warmth of the place, and curled up on a stool at the cocktail bar.

She also liked a good play, and the bright lights of the local theatre lured her to an evening performance. It took two programme sellers ten minutes to coax her out from under the seats. Inky took umbrage at this total lack of understanding and retreated to the cinema where she sat through *A Hundred and One Dalmations* for the third time, which is saying something for a cat.

But she was a happy wanderer, and the Packer family became quite used to telephone calls from a faintly bewildered librarian.

'Miss Packer? We've got your cat here at the library again. Could you come and collect her? We don't like to just turn her out into the street.'

Elaine Packer would take the car down to the library and scoop the errant book-lover into her arms.

'Inky Packer,' she would say severely. 'Stop looking so lost and helpless. You know your way home perfectly well.'

Of course Inky knew her way home. She knew her way everywhere. But she would never pass up the chance of a ride in the car. She stood on the front seat with her paws on the dashboard ledge, her vivid blue eyes alert for any jay-walkers.

The other Packers, that is, George Packer and his daughter, Elaine, were resigned to Inky's wanderings until the episode of the hospital.

Inky could not have gone off at a worse time. George Packer worked for an advertising firm which had alternately grown and been taken over, grown and been taken over again. With this last takeover, he had an uneasy feeling that his style did not fit the trendy image of the present organisation, New Views Inc. George always believed in the products he advertised, and some of his accounts were very long-standing. He could not see himself promoting some tasteless product simply for a fast profit.

The word redundant had not exactly been mentioned but it hovered over his iron-grey head like a neon sign. Redundancy would not be that disastrous, but Russets cost a lot to run, there was still the mortgage to pay off, and jobs were not easy to find at his age. Fortunately Elaine was a thrifty housekeeper, and never thought of eating out or spending money on clothes.

Elaine, too, had her problems. But she did not say a word to her father for fear of hurting his feelings. She had taken over the reins of the household at seventeen when her mother died of an unexplained virus infection. Then it had seemed the right thing to do. She had no career in mind and was content to run the house and garden. But now she was almost twenty-eight, and when the children next door suddenly grew from Brownies into brides she began to feel restless.

There was very little she could do except run a household. She had not been trained for anything. But the urge to get away and do something on her own was certainly part of the reason for her restlessness.

Mr Packer invited Clive Hilton, Managing Director of New Views Inc. to supper. He had some strange idea that if he could show the young man the solid background and comfort of his home, Clive Hilton might feel less like casting him out into the street.

But it was also the day Elaine had arranged to go for an interview for a job. She had answered an advertisement for a housekeeper to a wealthy titled family with a large estate in Norfolk. It meant a long drive there and back. She wanted to look her best, so much of the evening beforehand was spent washing and setting her hair and pressing her best dress and jacket.

It was no wonder Inky decided to explore further afield. There was simply no one to talk to, and certainly too much fussing going on for one visitor. It was best to keep out of the way on such occasions.

Elaine did most of the meal before she left. The chocolate mousse was put to set in the refrigerator, the sauce for the prawn cocktail was ready mixed, the chicken casserole and vegetables sat in the automatic oven waiting to be switched on electronically.

'Now Inky, you've got to be a good girl while I'm away,' said Elaine to the white Persian. 'No going off anywhere.'

Inky looked at Elaine with blank astonishment. What me? Never. She pounded a little circle on Elaine's dressing stool and curled up for a snooze. She had every intention of remaining there for as long as it took Elaine to drive down the road.

The interview went well, and despite her lack of references Elaine felt she had a good chance of getting the job. But she hit the evening traffic and the return drive took far longer than she expected. She flew into the house. She had very little time to get everything ready.

The chicken casserole was definitely overcooked; the chocolate mousse slipped as she took it out of the refrigerator to decorate and slid untidily up the sides of the cut-glass bowl; and the mayonnaise, made in haste, had curdled. She was just making some more when Clive Hilton arrived.

Clive Hilton was a quiet young man in his early thirties, his horn-rimmed glasses hiding the determination and burning ambition in his eyes. He had built up New Ideas Inc. himself and was set on success. He had no room for old-fashioned operators like George Packer, and he was going to have to tell him tonight.

'I'm terribly sorry,' said Elaine, tucking wisps of hair behind her ears. 'Supper's going to be a bit late. I was delayed. Would you like to have a glass of sherry first?'

Despite the generous schooners of dry sherry, Elaine's supper was not memorable. George Packer could not think what had happened to his normally efficient daughter. The table was not even laid properly – no side plates and not so much as a daisy for a floral centrepiece.

They were trying to take Clive's mind off the dry chicken with conversation, when the telephone rang. A loud voice resounded against Elaine's ear-drums.

'One of my nurses tells me that this flea-ridden creature padding round my wards belongs to the Packers in Culimore Crescent,' she barked. 'Would you please come and remove it at once.'

'Inky hasn't got fleas,' said Elaine, not caring if Clive Hilton did hear.

'Anything that has fur and moves has got fleas,' said the

matron. 'You've got fifteen minutes to come and collect your animal, or I will telephone for the vet.'

The matron's voice was indeed threatening, and Elaine found that her hand was trembling slightly as she put the telephone down.

'That was the hospital,' said Elaine. 'Inky's visiting out of hours. I'll have to go and fetch her. I hope you don't mind having your mousse without any cream on top . . .'

And it was that evening the family car went on strike and refused to start. Try as she could, Elaine could not get any life out of it. The engine turned over with an unresponsive whine. She began to panic, remembering the fifteen-minute deadline and the fate that awaited her fluffy beauty.

Elaine felt the perspiration breaking out as she struggled with the starter.

'Having trouble?' inquired Clive owlishly.

'I've got to get to Inky,' said Elaine desperately. 'They're going to send for the vet.'

'We'd better go in my car then.'

The ward sister had shut Inky into the sluice room. Inky was quite indignant about it. She had come to visit the patients, not an unresponsive collection of bedpans. Still, it was clean. She sat on the floor licking her fur into place, waiting for Elaine to collect her in the car.

'So this is Inky,' said Clive, amused.

'Inky Packer,' said Elaine, lifting the cat up with one hand. Inky hung there, eyes closed, feigning a dreadful incurable illness. 'You bad, bad thing. I'm fed up with having to come and rescue you. Why can't you stay at home and catch mice?'

Inky shuddered at the word. However, she recovered when she saw the size and make of Clive's car, and forgot her indisposition enough to purr ecstatically while exploring the innards of the vehicle.

'Can't you get your cat to keep still?' asked Clive. 'It's a little unnerving having to drive with that thing leaping about.'

'She's enjoying it,' said Elaine. 'She likes your car. She's never been in a Mercedes before.'

'I'm glad she likes it, but I'd rather she sat on your lap.'

Elaine managed to extract Inky from the glove compartment and sat her forcibly on her knee. Inky trampled enthusiastically, her claws going through the thin material of Elaine's dress. Elaine gritted her teeth . . . after all, Clive had been very kind.

'Does your cat go wandering often?' Clive asked.

'Yes, but I know why she does it,' said Elaine with feeling. 'She just wants to get out and see the world.'

'Do I detect the stirrings of a rebellion in the homestead?'

'You do,' said Elaine, glad to have someone to tell. 'I've looked after my father for over ten years. I just feel it's time I started doing something of my own. I've got to get away.'

Clive Hilton was ruthless when it came to decisions, but even he could not see a man losing both job and daughter on the same evening. So he said nothing to George, but accepted Elaine's invitation to return for supper another evening before she took up a post.

This time her preparations were well in advance, and she set the table perfectly with matching candles and flowers. She also looked very pretty. A letter that morning confirming the job had given her a new sparkle. But she had yet to tell her father.

Just as Elaine was about to serve the salmon soufflé, the telephone rang. It was the local librarian.

'Oh dear, not Inky again,' said Elaine, exasperated. 'Would you mind keeping her for another ten minutes or my soufflé will collapse?'

'Oh, she isn't here,' explained the librarian. 'I just thought I ought to let you know that I saw her boarding a 507 bus to Kestram.'

Clive was very understanding about the supper. 'This is getting to be a habit,' he said, starting the Mercedes. 'Do you know the 507 route?'

'Vaguely,' said Elaine anxiously. 'I do hope she's all right. She'll be so frightened. She's never been on a bus before.'

'If I know Inky at all, she won't be in the least put out.

14

She's probably sitting up with the driver by now.'

'I hope she doesn't jump off anywhere.'

'What, and miss seeing the terminus? You bet she won't. That little lady can take care of herself. She'll land squarely on all four feet.'

Inky landed all right. They found her in the drivers' canteen sampling bus company milk. She'd had a lovely time. Buses were far more fun than that Mercedes. However, she was tired and quite happy to curl up on Elaine's lap for the drive home.

Seeing the contented look on Inky's face gave Clive an idea.

'I'm going to put Inky into advertising,' he announced.

Elaine stared at Clive in horror. 'Not cat food,' she said, appalled.

'Of course not. Tourism. I've a series of television ads to make for the American market to promote package tours to England. Who better than Inky, our happy wanderer, to show them around? Imagine . . . Inky at Edinburgh . . . Inky at Stratford-on-Avon . . . Inky at the Changing of the Guard . . . Inky meeting Concorde. . . !'

So Inky went on the box. She took to it like a duck to water. Filming held no terrors for her. And it meant lots of lovely travelling. George Packer became her business manager and Elaine, after sending a letter of regret to Norfolk, was Inky's personal assistant and travelling companion.

Clive supervised the American advertisements himself so it meant he saw a lot of Elaine. She grew prettier and prettier. One evening when they were at Land's End he asked her to marry him. She did not say yes at first, though she knew she would eventually. She had a little wandering of her own to do first. . . .

# Xinia and the Witch

Xinia was small, fluffy, predominantly marmalade in colour and inclined to be overweight. She did not know this as she was completely colourblind and disinclined to face facts. She thought herself to be a sleek cat, black as a raven's wing and destined by Fate to ride forever on the back of a broomstick.

It was the broomstick fixation that led Xinia to wander. She had had four homes in three years. They were mostly on lonely, isolated hill farms where you might expect a witch to lurk. But each time Xinia's hopes of finding one were doomed to disappointment, and so she decided to move on once again.

She moved on to Tupminster, a small village tucked away in the Cotswolds, green and growing, but still full of charm. There was a row of old farm labourers' cottages by the road leading into the village which had been turned into trendy weekend homes. The end cottage had more garden than the rest, and on her knees in the middle of the front path was a gorgeous female creature.

She was slim, willowy, with skin like fresh cream, cheeks flushed with her exertions at gardening, and a cascade of glossy black hair hanging down her back. At least Xinia thought it was glossy black hair, but really it was amber-blonde, with red and gold streaks that were a photographer's delight.

The young woman put down a trowel and began to leaf

through a clutch of seed packets. 'Virginia stock, Godetia, Candytuft, Gloxinias . . . ' she began to chant in a low voice.

As soon as Xinia heard her name called she leapt into action. Hello, new home! She threw herself enthusiastically into the young woman's arms, purring, pawing and generally making a nuisance of herself.

'Hello, pussy. Where did you come from?' the woman asked, removing her gardening gloves in order to give Xinia a friendly stroke.

Between purrs and chin-licking with her small, rough tongue, Xinia noted this refinement with some satisfaction. This was obviously the very nicest kind of witch. Xinia trampled happily over the scattered seed packets and then threw herself back into the witch's arms. Home number five was settled.

'Heavens, keep still, you funny little thing,' the young woman laughed, trying to free her hair from Xinia's claws. 'I'm not a bed and I don't need a bath. But I do think it's coffee time, don't you?'

Coffee might have magical properties but any time was milk time, so Xinia followed the young woman indoors, carefully keeping her long fluffy tail out of the way of the girl's bare feet. Bare feet, thought Xinia, were quite an improvement. Most witches wore the most awful heavy black boots with sharp, painful heels.

Sally Jenkins put her percolator on the stove and then opened the refrigerator door to get out some milk.

Xinia's amber-flecked green eyes widened with astonishment. Inside the door the milk was actually standing up, all by itself, in tall round shapes! It was quite amazing. Xinia was used to watching milk squirting from those stupid brown animals and being slopped around in pails. But here it was actually standing up in regular shapes inside this cupboard. Xinia held her breath, expecting the milk to suddenly collapse and spill all over the floor.

Sally poured some milk into a saucer and put it down for the cat. 'There you are, pussy,' she murmured absent-mindedly. She took a letter from her pocket and began reading it as she stirred her coffee. The letter looked as though it had been read many times. Sally gave a small quivering sigh. 'He says he's found somebody else and that it's all over,' she said. 'I can't believe it . . . everything was so wonderful . . . '

Xinia listened, but only to be polite. She began a swift inspection of the cottage, climbing over books, skidding along oak window-ledges, sniffing at pot plants and greatly admiring the soft patchwork bedspread in Sally's bedroom. She was not yet entirely certain that Sally was a witch, but she thought she would hang around for a few days to make sure.

There were many things about Sally that were very witch-like. She had only to touch a small black box and the room was instantly full of discordant music like banshees let loose. She had a strange kind of crystal ball, square shaped, which again she had only to touch and people were captured on it, much smaller in size but actually in the room. Xinia often sat with her nose only inches away from the screen, mesmerised by a round black blob that whizzed about like a flying insect. Sometimes she would shoot out a paw to catch it, but she couldn't penetrate the magic.

'What are you doing?' Sally would laugh. 'Playing goalie?'

Sally seemed to spend a lot of time talking down a long, flexible cord, which, although clever, appeared pretty pointless to Xinia. She did not have a cauldron, but there was a grey pot she often put on the cooker which hissed ferociously in the most alarming manner.

What almost convinced Xinia that Sally was a witch was the discovery that Sally sometimes took off her hair. Xinia nearly jumped out of her fur the first time she found Sally's hair sitting on a stand on the dressing-table with no Sally underneath it. She sniffed at the wig cautiously, patting it with a tentative paw. It was real all right. It was even curly, whereas Sally's other hair was straight. Xinia was most impressed.

Sally was pretty lonely, even for a witch. She never seemed to go to any covens to meet other witches. She did a lot of gardening and talking to herself and reading letters and experimenting with spells that she called cooking. But often she sat in the evening gloom of the little sitting room, not bothering to put on the lights.

'I'm going to be an old maid,' she said one night, hugging Xinia tightly. 'They'll call me Sally the Spinster.'

Xinia thought this a very odd remark to make, especially when there wasn't a single spinning wheel in the house. She made a quick reconnaissance of upstairs and downstairs to make sure that Sally hadn't sneaked one in, but there was nothing more mechanical than a bag of crochet which Sally wasn't making much headway with.

Sally didn't sleep much, but then witches don't need much sleep. She often wandered about the cottage in the small hours of the morning, coming into the kitchen to make herself some hot milk.

Xinia didn't really mind being woken up by the light being switched on. Any time was milk time. But she did think all that crying on the kitchen table was taking things a bit far. Witches didn't usually shed tears, but this one did and Xinia objected to being used as a superior sort of paper tissue to mop up the tears trickling down Sally's cheeks.

'I do miss him so. What am I going to do?' she sobbed into Xinia's fur. 'Whatever am I going to do? I can't go on like this . . . I can't work . . . I can't think . . . it's awful.'

Xinia did a quick lick to rearrange her damp fur and agreed wholeheartedly. It certainly couldn't go on like this. They were both losing their beauty sleep, and Sally hadn't cast a really good spell all the time she'd been there.

Xinia went for a long, thinking walk, snapping at dragon-flies, chasing ants and terrorising the stone dwarf who fished all day long in their neighbour's goldfish pond.

Of course, what Sally needed was another man so that she would stop missing this other one and start knowing what she was going to do. But she would never meet another man staying in the cottage all day reading sad books and trying to find out where she'd gone wrong in her crochet.

Xinia only knew one man. She'd met him at those four farms she had lived on. She remembered the nice polished smell of his boots and the gentleness in his voice as he tended a sick cow or a mare in labour. She even knew his name – Gavin Jones. But mostly people called him 'the vet', whatever that meant.

She knew where to find him, too. He had a rambling red-brick house where people brought all their sick animals – dogs with hot noses wrapped in blankets, and fractious cats in baskets, spitting straw. Xinia took to sitting in the middle of a flowerbed outside the surgery, waiting for Gavin Jones to come out.

'Hello, thing,' he said quite kindly several times as he got into his estate car to start on his rounds.

One morning he came out talking to a plump woman who was carrying a bandaged poodle.

'You'd better keep him warm, and make sure your husband's workshop is locked in future. I think life is getting more and more dangerous for our pets,' said Gavin Jones. Then he spotted Xinia among the French marigolds. 'Hello, thing,' he said.

Xinia gave him a long, cool stare, flicked her tail haughtily and then deliberately scratched up a geranium.

But what she had overheard was food for thought. Obviously being the vet had something to do with looking after pets in danger. Perhaps if she did something dangerous, then Gavin Jones would arrive at the cottage, meet Sally, and before you could say 'Mary Poppins' they'd be speeding down the M1 on a broomstick.

So that night Xinia made her bed in a box of old jam jars that Sally had been saving for the blackberry season. She trampled energetically, sliding and clattering jars about, making a great fuss and being terribly dangerous.

Sally fished her out and held the marmalade cat at arm's length. 'You great goof,' she laughed, her pretty dimples showing for the first time in days. 'You can't go to sleep on jam jars! Let me find you a nice new piece of blanket.'

The next day Xinia climbed on to the roof of the cottage, then leapt on to the chimney stack and pretended that she couldn't get down.

'Dinner time!' Sally shouted from the garden, banging a fork on a tin of cat food. Xinia tried to look pathetic and frightened. Then she did a little bit of pretending to jump and being overcome with terror at the brink.

'Oh, come on,' said Sally, exasperated. 'It's getting cold out here. I won't let you watch any telly!' she threatened.

Xinia crouched down and prepared to sit it out, hurt that Sally could be so ungrateful. Still, witches were unpredictable. It wouldn't do to upset one. She didn't want to be turned into a toad.

About half-past ten, Xinia picked her way down in the dark and pushed open the kitchen door. Sally was mashing some sardines in a saucer.

'Did you enjoy the view?' Sally asked sweetly, putting the saucer down on the floor.

But she had been crying again, and although Xinia was starving, she could not help twining herself round Sally's ankles a few times.

'Oh, pussy,' Sally sighed. 'You don't know what being in love is like . . . ' and she ran out of the room, forgetting to give Xinia any milk.

Xinia sat there, licking her paws, her mouth as dry as old fish bones. She couldn't open the cupboard where the milk stood up by itself. She jumped on to the draining-board but there wasn't a drip of water to be seen.

She wandered into the pantry and leapt up on to the marble shelf, jumping awkwardly because she was stiff from sitting on the roof all day. Normally she would never have knocked anything over, but something new was there – some contraption of tubes and funnels. Sally edited cookery books for a living and all sorts of strange things were always going on.

The contraption crashed to the ground, shattered, and a pale liquid spread all over the floor. Water, thought Xinia joyously. She leaped down and began to lap it up. Well, it wasn't quite water, but beggars couldn't be choosers. She drank her fill, but soon began to feel quite odd. Something was happening to the kitchen walls . . . perhaps Sally was doing a twirly spell?

Her head was muzzy and her legs felt as if they did not belong to her. Xinia looked down carefully and was relieved to see that they were still joined on. But what . . . on earth . . . was happening?

She staggered round the kitchen, suddenly quite merry

and happy. Of course, being such a young witch, Sally couldn't be expected to get everything right the first time, but still she was trying and that was a hopeful sign.

She was vaguely aware of Sally coming into the kitchen, all floating and misty in a white nightgown. Really this was getting better all the time. Levitation now.

'Whatever's the matter?' she heard Sally exclaim. Then Sally was talking in the hall. 'Hello? Hello? This is Sally Jenkins, six Elm Cottages. I'm so sorry to call you out so late, but I'm terribly worried about my cat. She's staggering about in the most unnatural manner . . . thank you very much.'

Xinia was clambering unsteadily up the stairs – or was she coming down the stairs? – when Gavin Jones arrived at the cottage. Sally opened the door to him, a large shawl wrapped round her shoulders, her amber hair clouding her pale face. He looked uncertainly at the vision of white and gold in the doorway, and coughed. 'Miss Jenkins?'

'I think she's drunk,' said Sally.

'You've got a sloshed cat?' he asked, wondering if he was dreaming.

'Please come in and have a look at her.'

'What was it? A drop of mother's ruin?' asked Gavin.

'No, my elderflower wine. It's been fermenting in the larder and she must have knocked it over and drunk some . . .'

'Ah . . . the raw stuff. Elderflower, eh? Can have quite a kick,' he said pleasantly.

Xinia saw two Gavin Joneses coming towards her. She didn't much mind which one picked her up. He held her very gently and stroked her in an understanding way.

'I think it might be best if we just let her go away and sleep it off somewhere safe,' he said a little later.

When Xinia eventually woke up around midday, Gavin Jones was in the kitchen having a cup of coffee with Sally.

'Hello, here comes the patient,' said Gavin, going down on to one knee. 'How are you feeling this morning? A bit groggy?'

'Will she have a hangover?' Sally asked anxiously.

'I've really no idea,' said Gavin, his eyes twinkling.

'Perhaps we ought to put her in touch with Alcoholics Anonymous before she gets a taste for elderflower wine. But first, a little warm milk . . .'

After that, the nice looking young vet was always at the cottage, whether Xinia was thinking up dangerous exploits or not. He either popped in on his way to somewhere, or on his way back from somewhere. Sometimes Sally grabbed a coat and went with him which was very promising. In fact, soon she had stopped crying, and the pile of letters on her dressing table were gathering quite a dust.

'The office phoned today to see how I was,' said Sally one evening as they were strolling in the garden. 'I only took a month's leave and it's nearly up. I shall have to go back to my editorial chair before they give my job to someone else.'

'I shall miss you,' said Gavin quietly.

'I'll be back most weekends,' said Sally, apparently pretending that she had not heard him. 'It's not really that far from London.'

Xinia sat in a tree half listening. She couldn't understand why Sally had to go . . . there were plenty of chairs in the cottage. What was so special about this editorial one? Perhaps it had some kind of magic.

Xinia stood on a branch and arched her back. She supposed, reluctantly, that it was time to move on. She'd never been absolutely sure that Sally was a witch, anyway.

Having decided, Xinia left without further ado. She walked straight down the road, across the fields and began to climb the hilly country. Before darkness fell it began to rain, lightly at first but soon it developed into a steady downpour. Then, after a low far-off rumbling, the sky suddenly burst with a clap of overhead thunder; lightning flashed across the dark clouds with crazy fingers. Xinia thought at first it was Sally's doing, making a spectacular fuss. But how could it be? All the time she had lived at the cottage, Sally had never once been angry. No, it must be some other lot.

Xinia tried to find a dry spot to shelter until the storm was over, but the hours of steady rain had soaked everything. Eventually she gave up the hills and found a road to walk on; the ditches were running with rain, and even the road was covered with deep, slopping puddles. Xinia stopped and shook the drops off her paws fastidiously.

Suddenly she was blinded by the headlights coming towards her along the road. Her wits vanished and she froze, petrified, convinced that it was a she-wolf, eyes flaring, jaws ready to crunch her into oblivion . . . The car screeched to a halt within yards of her. Both doors were flung open and a man and a woman got out, running through the torrential rain.

Xinia found herself being scooped up and crushed against a wet raincoat. Sally cradled the bedraggled cat like a baby.

'Whatever are you doing out here in the wilds?' she cried in amazement. 'You're miles from home and absolutely soaked. You'll get lost wandering off like this.'

'And run over . . . sitting in the middle of the road to tidy up,' said Gavin. 'Let's get back into the car. We were going out to dinner, but I suppose we can hardly take a drowned cat with us.'

Suddenly he put his arms round Sally and kissed her, standing in the middle of the road in the pouring rain.

'Don't you realise I love you?' he said, almost roughly. 'You've bewitched me and I'm utterly under your spell. You're beautiful . . . a beautiful witch.'

Xinia, squashed between two raincoats, forgot her discomfort. So Sally *was* a witch after all, quite definitely a witch. Gavin Jones couldn't be wrong. He knew everything.

'Let's take this scruffy thing home first,' he went on tenderly, 'and then we must have a talk . . . a proper talk.'

Sally nodded, smiling. 'That's a good name for her,' she agreed. 'Scruffy.'

Xinia went completely limp. She practically died with mortification. Scruffy! She would never get used to it . . . never, never.

She closed her eyes, nursing her wounded pride, as she was carried back to the car. Sally wrapped her in a warm knitted scarf and settled her comfortably on her lap.

'I hope she won't be frightened of the car,' said Sally. 'I don't suppose she's been in one before.'

But Xinia wasn't frightened. She wasn't frightened of anything. Soon she sat up and took an interest in her new surroundings, fascinated by the rivulets of rain and the windscreen-wipers chasing them, and the dark countryside flashing by.

'I'll put the heater on,' said Gavin. Then he touched another switch and the air was filled with soft, melodic sound.

Xinia was most impressed. This must be some sort of updated version of a broomstick, she thought. Well, it was certainly an improvement on the old type. . . .

# The Commuter

When Great-Aunt Hannah died she left all her worldly possessions to her nephew, Philip Newton. These consisted of a small, wisteria-clad, red-brick house on the outskirts of a town tucked away among the few remaining heaths and hills of Surrey, a frighteningly-depleted bank balance and a very large broad-shouldered silver tabby called Darby.

'We're just like Darby and Joan,' she used to tell the cat as they took their daily walk together past the old water-mill. 'Just you and me left now, pussy. And dear Philip, of course, although we don't see much of him, do we? He's working somewhere in Senegal, West Africa . . . dear me, I do believe I've never even heard of the place . . .'

Neither had Darby, but it did not bother him too much. Great-Aunt Hannah always talked to him as if he were a person and the actual content of her conversation was not important. He always listened attentively and then curled himself round her arthritic ankles to show that he understood . . . even when he didn't.

He knew when Great-Aunt Hannah came back from the hospital that she was not going to live long. From that moment he barely left her side. He gave up hunting. His only excursions into the garden were brief but necessary. He made sure that she was never lonely, and at night took to sleeping at the foot of her bed.

'You're better than a hot-water bottle,' she used to say, but was more glad of the sound of his even breathing when

26

she woke in the early hours and waited for the dawn light.

He was there when she died, watching her face with his fathomless green eyes. Afterwards he sat like a large grey shadow outside the door of her room and would not move.

'I'm right glad you've come at last,' said Mrs Bevins, the next door neighbour who had been taking care of the house and Darby till Philip's return from West Africa. 'I've been real worried. I've done my best but he seems to be pining badly for the old lady.'

Philip swung himself out of his two-seater sports car, a lanky brown man, his face bronzed by the tropical sun. He was overcome with gloom as the empty house brought back memories, and he turned and unloaded his golf-clubs, his back-pack and his typewriter before answering Mrs Bevins. All three items had travelled the world with him as he earned a living and made a reputation as a freelance journalist. Now an international magazine had offered him a staff post, and the sad, unexpected windfall of a house within commuting distance of London had made up Philip's mind. He had accepted the job and was due to start on Monday.

'Who's pining?' he asked, his mind a dozen years away. 'Who's this? Some friend of my aunt's . . . ?'

'Not exactly a friend, Mr Newton. It's Darby. You know, her cat.'

'Of course, Darby,' said Philip. 'But it's only natural that he should mourn for her. I expect they were close companions.'

'But I didn't know that cats . . . er . . . did that,' Mrs Bevins said awkwardly.

'There are many mysteries in this life,' said Philip. 'And cats are one of them.'

Despite the profundity of this statement, Philip did not know how to solve the problem of what to do with Darby. The cat had not eaten for days and his beautiful black and silver fur hung loosely on his large frame like an empty bag. He sat quite still, wrapped in melancholy.

'Hello, old chap,' said Philip, tentatively scratching the cat behind his ears. 'Missing Auntie, are you? But life has to

27

go on. Try a little drop of milk. . . .'

But Darby sat staring into the distance, as still as the Egyptian Goddess Bast, only the occasional twitch of a whisker betraying that he even breathed.

'I don't know what to do with you,' said Philip, sitting back on his heels. 'I can't make you eat. Auntie would hate to see you like this – she would be most upset.'

An answer-phone recording told him that the local vet was on holiday and that emergency calls only should be referred to the next county. So Philip hunted through the shelves at the local library, and took a pile of cat books to the girl at the counter. She had a mass of light brown hair tied back with velvet ribbon and wore large owlish glasses.

'You like cats, then,' she commented as she date-stamped the books and filed away Great-Aunt Hannah's tickets.

'I have inherited a depressed cat,' said Philip.

'I hope you'll find something that will help,' she said with a sweet smile before turning to the next borrower.

Philip put the books on his kitchen table and sorted through the indices for all references to 'Cats, sick.' After reading harrowing descriptions of infectious enteritis, abscesses, bites, worms and ear trouble, Philip found a paragraph which seemed to have some bearing on Darby's present condition.

'Nursing is very important because sick cats give up easily. They must not be left alone. They should be visited frequently and talked to cheerfully . . . tempt with tiny morsels of favourite food . . . ' Philip read aloud. Tempting with tiny morsels was not exactly how Philip had planned to spend his first weekend back in England, but he would give it a try, for Great-Aunt Hannah's sake. But what was Darby's favourite food, he wondered?

Philip assembled a tray and went to join Darby in his silent vigil outside her door. If Darby did not like any of the selection from Great-Aunt Hannah's larder, then Philip could see himself with a very odd menu for supper.

'OK buster, here we go,' said Philip, twisting the opener on a slim, flat tin. 'The first item for your delectation is A for anchovies . . . now what do you think of these?'

Not much apparently. Darby regarded Philip's offering with apathy. With an air of polite indifference he also refused to look at bread and butter, biscuits, crab and corned beef, dripping, egg, fishpaste, gravy, ham, ice cream, jelly, kipper fillets and a slice of liver sausage. Neither did he show any interest in the proprietary brands of cat food waved under his nose.

'Whatever am I going to do with you?' sighed Philip, forgetting to sound cheerful. It was already dusk and a hundred small tasks were waiting to be done. Still Philip persevered. He unscrewed a small sticky jar and held out a teaspoonful of malt extract with cod liver oil.

Darby's nose twitched. His memory went into reverse and, as if re-enacting an old dream, he sat back on his haunches and gracefully rose into a begging position. His paws captured Philip's wrist lightly and a rough tongue came out to lick at the thick brown goo. At that instant Philip remembered it was Darby's party trick. Great-Aunt had taught the cat to beg, but the contents of the spoon with which she rewarded him had always been a closely kept secret.

'So malt and cod liver oil is your weakness,' said Philip with some relief. 'But it's hardly a balanced diet, Darby.'

Darby licked the spoon clean and sat back. There was a gleam in his eyes as he turned to the tray of food. He was going through an emotional struggle, torn between loyalty to Great-Aunt Hannah and this new man to whom she had obviously entrusted the secret of his party trick. That must mean he was someone special, in which case a transference of allegiance might be the wish of his dear mistress . . .

Once having made up his mind, Darby was practical as well as loyal. He knew that crab would not come his way often, so obligingly finished it up along with a few other items so that Philip would not have to eat a supper of fishpaste hash. After a saucer of warm milk to wash it all down, Darby fell into an exhausted sleep right in the middle of the stairs.

Philip stepped carefully over his body. He felt sure that Darby would recover now. With that problem solved, he could concentrate on his career, building up a decent social life and putting down a few roots.

Philip and Darby settled into a routine. They did not see very much of each other as Philip left early in the morning to catch his commuter train, often working late or staying in London for a show or a party. But whatever time Philip returned home, Darby was always there in the front porch, under the wisteria, waiting to jump down and greet him with a friendly rub round the ankles.

Slowly Darby regained his former size and handsomeness. The black rings on his long tail showed up like glossy bracelets, the pale softness of his tummy like swansdown, the distinctive M mark on his forehead giving his big round face a faintly thoughtful expression. For some unknown reason, Darby continued to sleep half-way up the stairs, stretched right across the tread. It was a curious place to sleep, as if he were waiting to meet someone or needed to be aware of the exact movements of the household.

At the weekends Darby was content to sit and watch Philip tinkering with the car, or gardening, or painting the outside of the house. If Philip went to the golf course he would accompany him, sitting on the perimeter of the greens and waiting to see if the tantalising little white ball would roll his way.

'No, Darby. Don't touch,' Philip commanded as Darby crouched ready to spring. Darby obeyed reluctantly. Great Aunt Hannah had brought him up well.

'How's your depressed cat?' asked the girl at the library when Philip returned the books.

'The crisis is over,' said Philip. 'He's on the road to recovery.'

'I'm so glad. It must have been quite worrying. My sister's got a cat but he's never ill. In fact quite the reverse, he's a bundle of energy. He's a stray but nonetheless we would be really upset if anything happened to him. I'm afraid there's a sixty pence fine. The books are overdue.'

'Sorry,' said Philip, searching in his pockets for odd coins. 'I've been busy . . . working late rather a lot.'

'That's all right,' she smiled again. 'We need your

money. I see you are also interested in golf,' she commented, noticing the titles of his new batch of books.

'My recipe for keeping fit,' said Philip, wondering what she would look like with her hair loose and without those big glasses. He thought the effect would be strangely disturbing. She had an unworldly air that made one think of hazy summers long ago, half forgotten lines of poetry, a lingering melody . . .

It was not that Philip minded paying fines, but he found himself going to the library more frequently. He needed assistance on such topics as Flemish painters, orismology and the history of field sports, and Lois Brooks was quite willing to search for helpful books.

'What a lot of reading to get through,' said Lois, date-stamping Philip's weekend research. 'Don't you ever feel lonely?'

'On the contrary,' said Philip. 'As Martin Tupper wrote more than a hundred years ago: "A good book is the best of friends, the same today and for ever." And besides, I have my cat for company. He's a quiet, sedate sort and sits beside me for hours. He's probably getting on a bit.'

'Not at all like our cat!' said Lois. 'Ours never keeps still for a moment. He's always dashing about all over the place chasing his own tail, playing catch-me with the children, scampering up and down trees. A regular bundle of energy.'

It was when Philip stayed at home for a few days to write a difficult feature on the future of nuclear power that he noticed Darby had a habit of disappearing for long periods of time. Occasionally the cat made a lightning visit back to Philip's side at the typewriter, vanishing again before Philip could even offer some light refreshment.

But in the evening Darby returned for good, threw himself down near Philip's chair and immediately fell into a deep whisker-twitching nap before supper. He was still quite a small eater for such a large cat.

'Not going off your food again, are you, Darby?' Philip asked, offering the cat his daily teaspoonful of malt extract. Darby caught Philip's wrist in his usual gentle, well-mannered way and licked at his treat, a low, throaty purr starting up. 'You seem a bit worried about something these days . . .'

Darby was definitely in some sort of a state. When Philip began his writing each morning, Darby would hover, padding around, watching Philip with some puzzlement. Then he would suddenly leap out of a window and disappear for half the day. This happened every morning, but as soon as Philip returned to commuting to London, the tension in Darby vanished. He became the relaxed cat he had been before, and his welcome home to Philip in the evening was genuine and touchingly reliable.

'I'm blessed how you know what time I'm coming home,' said Philip late one night. It was nearing midnight and he had come off the last, empty, bleakly rattling train. The big tabby was waiting in his usual place under the wisteria. 'You must have been waiting hours. By the way, old chap, I've brought you a present.'

It was a narrow leather collar with 'Darby' engraved on the name plate. Philip fastened it round the cat's furry neck, making sure it was comfortable.

Philip stepped back to view the effect. 'It makes you look a bit like a dog,' said Philip, not quite sure.

Darby was perfectly willing to look a bit like a dog if that was what Philip wanted. He knew his own superiority. The comparison did not worry him. He knew that his fur was like silk, that his muscles rippled like those of a wild tiger, that he could leap over the moon, be as silent as a shadow, and was descended from the Caffre cat of Egypt. He knew all these things yet didn't possess an ounce of vanity.

The first thing Philip noticed about Darby the next evening was that an ordinary brown luggage label had been tied to his new collar. Philip lifted the cat and squinted at the dangling label, trying to read the writing on it.

'My name is Fuzzy-Bear. I lodge at Keats Cottage and my owners would like to know where I go at nights,' Philip read aloud. 'Fuzzy Bear?' he repeated. Darby pretended not to hear, struggling a little as if objecting to being held aloft like a parcel.

Before he left to catch the 8.17 am train the next morning Philip wrote out a fresh label and attached it to Darby's collar: 'FUZZY BEAR? What a ridiculous name! Great-Aunt Hannah christened me Darby, and Darby I remain.'

He pushed the cat gently outside and locked the front door. Darby sat on the step, totally unconcerned, and began to wash his ears. A fresh breeze scurried through the branches, ruffling his fur, making him look bigger than ever.

Commuting doth not always run smoothly, as Philip was to discover that day. The derailment of a goods train outside Clapham Junction threw the whole region into chaos. He only managed to get home by leaving the office early, queuing for a series of buses and then hitching a lift for the last few miles. The driver dropped him at the end of the leafy lane by the now-deserted station.

The wind was still blustery as Philip walked along the lane, his coat collar turned up against the chill, feeling thoroughly disconcerted and out of humour. Travelling to London was just about bearable when everything went right, but at this moment he felt a surge of longing for the freedom of his back-pack and his wanderings through Africa under the blazing sun.

He could hear the voices of children laughing in one of the gardens that backed on to the lane. The sounds carried high and clear in the evening air. Several small figures in dungarees and anoraks were chasing a cat. It scrambled up a tree, danced tantalisingly along a branch, then hung from the furthermost end, for all the world like a striped monkey.

'Darby!' Philip shouted, astonished.

The cat froze, almost in mid-swing.

'Fuzzy-Bear,' called Lois Brooks, coming out of the cottage. She was no longer wearing her glasses and her hair was loose and blowing across her face. And she looked every bit as disturbing as Philip had imagined.

Darby looked from one to the other, and if a large tabby cat hanging from a tree can look embarrassed, then Darby looked embarrassed. He slithered a few inches, digging his claws into the bark, his long tail dangling like a rope.

'So this is your lodger,' said Philip.

'Who dosses down at your place,' said Lois. 'For the night.'

'And weekends.'

Lois nodded. 'Quite an arrangement.'

Darby knew they were talking about him. He was facing a dilemma. He had to decide what to do when he could not hold on to the branch for a moment longer. The children had disappeared indoors, bored once the adults appeared. There was no easy way out.

'A bundle of energy, eh?' Philip went on. 'Plays with the kids . . . dashes about all over the place.'

'Hardly the antics of a sedate, elderly cat,' said Lois demurely.

Darby could hang on no longer. He fell to the grass, picked himself up, shook the bits out of his fur, walked over towards Philip and Lois and sat down exactly halfway between them.

'Ah, a born diplomat,' said Lois.

'Part of Great-Aunt Hannah's training,' said Philip. 'It seems that while I have been commuting to London, Darby has also been commuting.'

'And it's easy to understand why,' said Lois, going down on her knees to rub Darby's nose. 'He was used to Great-Aunt Hannah at home for company, and when you went out all day he was lonely. So, very sensibly, he looked around for someone to spend the day with and walked into my sister's house. It also explains why he would suddenly disappear in the evenings. From here he could hear the trains coming into the station. I suppose when he saw you coming along the platform, he knew it was time to go home.'

'And raced ahead of me through the back gardens, to be sitting in my porch waiting for me,' Philip chuckled. 'And all this dashing about . . .'

'. . . is merely feline second childhood,' Lois finished for him.

There seemed to be no good reason to curb Darby's sensible arrangement, though now Darby could walk openly along to the station with Philip before going on to Keats Cottage for his second breakfast.

In the evening, Philip called to pick up his cat and somehow it seemed natural to stay and talk to Lois and her sister and the children.

Darby basked contentedly in the warmth and love of his two homes, watching with approval as a certain relationship developed. Quite soon he might not have to do so much commuting. It made it almost worth being called Fuzzy-Bear.

# The Cat from Next Door

It was so undignified and that's what really got Herbie about living with the ever-expanding Robinson family. Sometimes he felt he must have been delivered in a Christmas stocking, gift-wrapped, but far more durable than the other playthings.

He knew if he saw six-year-old Katy donning her nurse's outfit then he was due for a blanket bath, and that meant being swathed in towels and ignominiously anointed with water. It meant having his face and ears washed which he particularly detested, but for the sake of Katy's gentle crooning and cuddling, he put up with these atrocities.

Eight-year-old Jane had thought up a torture of a different kind. He suffered being dressed in a matinee jacket, long nightie and bootees with a satin-ribboned bonnet flattening his ears. He endured being ridden up and down the road in the basket on the front of her bicycle. This was far worse than being pushed in the pram, because at least in the pram he could take a nose dive down to the foot of the cover and leave only his tail showing, whipping the pillow.

But in the bicycle basket, he was exposed to public glare and comment. He could not even have a good scratch. At the first sign of a slackening of Jane's attention, he would leap out on to the pavement, fly through gardens and across the fields to a secret place where he would hide long enough to divest himself of the hated garments.

This went on until Jane ran out of baby clothes.

Thomas, two years her senior and lanky with it, had a habit of putting Herbie on the top of doors. Just why, Herbie did not have the slightest idea. One minute he would be curled up happily on some abandoned school blazer, then . . . whoops! He would find himself being born aloft by Thomas and deposited on the top edge of an open door, scratching and clawing to gain a balance. Once there he could remain lying along the edge with complete indifference until rescued by some adult Robinson.

Herbie was a Bi-coloured Shorthair. He could be described as a black cat with white splodges or a white cat with black splodges. It depended on the angle of viewing which colour was predominant. He had a small, alert face with intelligent eyes and neat ears. No one was quite sure of his age. He came sort of before Katy and after Jane. His birthday was celebrated on the date of the Battle of Waterloo, 18 June, when he was encouraged in vain to blow out the candles on a nice piece of cod fillet and all day it was cream, cream, cream in his saucer.

He ate well with the Robinsons. They were always saying he was the only cat in Great Britain who got meals on wheels. This was because Grandma Robinson was too old to have new teeth fitted, and anything she fancied but couldn't manage went into his bowl. Herbie was game to try anything from trifle to spaghetti bolognese. He was not fussy.

Herbie loved boxes. They were his all-consuming passion. He would get into any box, trying it out for size. He would investigate the depths of paper bags, plastic carriers, handbags, suitcases, typewriter lids . . . you name it, he would get into it.

When the crates arrived he was delighted and curious. But when he made a few tentative forays, there were immediate shrieks of 'Mind the china!' 'Off that linen!' 'Help, that one's full of glasses!' and eventually, 'Will somebody put Herbie out, *please?*'

So Herbie sat in the garden and watched. There were no blanket baths and rides on bicycles these days. Everyone was so busy. He did not quite understand what was going on.

One morning the Robinson family assembled outside with bags and parcels and he was being passed round for hugs and wet kisses. It was all very messy and he still did not understand what was happening. He hoped it didn't mean that he was going down the road. Several of his elderly friends had told him that hugs and wet kisses meant going down the road and not coming back.

So Herbie was quite relieved when it was evident that the Robinsons were not intending to put him in the car as well as all their family and the mountain of luggage. He rubbed his head against Katy's new ankle socks to show that he forgave her all the medical ministrations.

'We don't really want to leave him behind, but what else can we do?' said Mrs Robinson. 'One is always hearing about cats that walk back to their old homes and how could Herbie cope with all that ocean? We're so grateful for your kind offer.'

'Shall I have a new kitten in Australia?' asked the fickle Jane.

'Of course, darling.'

'Don't worry, Mrs Robinson, I'll look after Herbie for you,' said a new, sweet young voice. 'He'll be perfectly all right with us. I'm sure he'll soon get used to us and we'll take great care of him.'

Katy wept more water all over Herbie's ears. 'Goodbye, darling Herbie,' she whispered. 'I'll never forget you, never, never, never . . .'

It was very disturbing, and then amid a great deal of noise the Robinsons drove off, leaving Herbie and the sweet voiced young woman on the front lawn. He looked at her, wondering what was going to happen next. She was very young and quite tall. He hoped she was not going to put him on top of doors. She regarded him a little uncertainly, her fairish hair brushing her cheek like a breeze stirring a cobweb in the moonlight.

'Come along,' she said, trying to sound brisk. 'You live next door now.'

He did not move for two reasons. Firstly he did not know what next door meant, and secondly he was a mite worried about the door bit. Chrissie picked him up carefully and gave him a few little pats. 'Come along,' she said, again, more cheerfully. 'This way . . .'

The next door house was joined on to the Robinson's house and it was exactly the same, except that it was all the other way round. He discovered that Chrissie and Alan Marshall were newly-weds, that they lived in empty rooms and went out all day. It was very strange. Sometimes Herbie thought he had gone deaf.

It was an odd house. There was nothing to jump on, knock over, hide behind, sit on, scratch at, sniff at, trample on or investigate. Most of the time Herbie sat in the middle of the kitchen floor, polite and distant, grooming himself and slightly nauseated by the pervading smell of paint. He missed the Robinsons and all the noise and activity. He missed being talked to and included as part of the family.

'Herbie doesn't seem very happy,' said Chrissie for the hundredth time. 'He behaves like a visitor.'

'Perhaps we ought to show him round,' Alan suggested. 'That might make him feel at home.'

'It's very difficult when you've never had a cat before,' said Chrissie. 'I never know what to do.'

'Don't worry, darling. They are very independent creatures, aloof and stand-offish. It's probably just his way.'

Alan hoisted Herbie off the floor and carried him up the stairs. He flung open the first door with a flourish.

'Now, this is the spare room,' he announced, putting Herbie down on the lino. Herbie was amazed. It had been impossible to move in the Robinson's spare room when they had one. It had always looked like a central sorting depot for Oxfam. But this spare room was totally without interest . . . he prodded the two tennis rackets with some apprehension.

'Careful, old chap,' admonished Alan. He steered Herbie out of the spare room and into the next room. 'And this is our bedroom. We sleep here,' he added unnecessarily.

Herbie made a flying leap on to the rose-patterned duvet. It sank most satisfyingly, but before he had even done half a turn, Chrissie had whisked him off again.

'Sorry,' she said. 'Not on the bed.'

He was not allowed on the two armchairs either, or on the draining board, or in Chrissie's shopping basket, or in the linen cupboard or under the television set. So he took to staying in the middle of the kitchen floor, quiet and withdrawn, sometimes pretending to be asleep or watching a bee buzzing against a window-pane trying to get in.

The garden was immaculate and everything was in measured rows. Herbie learned to tread carefully. He found it hard to stalk tigers in an organised jungle of Tom Thumb lettuces, or scare birds who were already wary of all the flapping labels.

The best spot was the greenhouse, baking warm and out of the draught. But Alan was growing grass in trays and kept shutting Herbie out.

'Shoo . . . mind the cuttings. Off my seedlings, old boy.'

Herbie lost weight despite the fact that the Marshalls were kind to him and fed him. But Herbie's heart began to fail when he saw Chrissie reaching yet again for the tin opener. He longed for a bit of fruit cake and some cold cocoa.

He made one visit to the Robinson's old house but never again. A horrible sloppy dog with ears hanging down like soup plates had moved in. Herbie shuddered and kept to his side of the fence.

Sometimes he sat on the pavement outside and watched people go by on bicycles and in cars. One young woman with red-streaked hair always stopped and stroked him, knowing the special place under his chin just above where his purr started.

Sometimes he followed children along the road, but he was afraid to go too far. He was less trusting than he used to be. Especially after the field-mouse episode. He had only meant it as a gift for Chrissie. It was such a tiny thing and was paralysed with terror. Yet Chrissie had shrieked as if being attacked by a rampaging bull elephant. Herbie simply did not understand her and brought no more gifts.

The situation improved somewhat when Chrissie stopped going out every day. She started to sing around the house and that was rather nice. However, although she sat around quite a lot Herbie was never invited on to her lap. He now learned that he must not sit on her sewing or try to get into her knitting bag. The tennis rackets were moved into the back of the broom cupboard and some furniture was delivered for the spare room. Alan began hammering in the evenings and Herbie watched the shelves going up with interest.

'Off you come, Herbie. They won't take your weight,' said Alan, lifting him down.

'He's just testing,' said Chrissie with new perception.

Alan kissed her tenderly.

'Funny girl,' he said, ruffling her hair.

One day a new smell arrived in the house. Herbie recognised it immediately. It was the thin, sweet smell of milk. Something stirred and breathed in the pram parked in the hallway, and made small mewing sounds.

Herbie pricked up his ears. Surely it was not another cat? He stood up on his back legs and peered in, but the mesh of the cat-net obscured whatever lay under the mound of blankets.

'Say hello to Timmy,' said Chrissie, picking Herbie up with a growing confidence. It was the first time that Herbie had felt safe and not about to be dropped. He trembled slightly with a small rush of emotion.

Now the improvements began to accelerate at a rate of knots. Chrissie left things on the floor and was far too busy to notice if Herbie sat on them. All sorts of boxes and pails and bins began to appear in the kitchen.

'What on earth shall I do with this cereal?' Chrissie wailed one breakfast time. 'Timmy won't touch it.'

'Give it to the cat,' said Alan.

Baby cereal! One of Herbie's favourites. His rough little tongue could hardly lap it up for purring. Then at teatime it was marmite soldiers dropped all over the floor in various stages of squashed disintegration.

'Oh, you are a messy baby,' said Chrissie, hurrying to clear up, but Herbie was there before her. It seemed like years since he'd had a marmite soldier.

The baby soon began to crawl and then there wasn't a thing Chrissie could do about life at floor level. It became a glorious landscape of wooden bricks, round-eyed ducks, chewed crusts, lost shoes, sticky spoons and a fat yellow teddy bear who kept falling over. Herbie sat amid the chaos, keeping an eye on the baby, keeping his claws sheathed and never getting in the way. He was still rather like a visitor.

One afternoon Chrissie was sewing while her baby played on the floor with some empty cotton reels. Herbie was sunning himself by the window when through half an eye he saw the baby reaching up towards the flex of a reading lamp.

No one really knew whether he remembered the occasion when Katy Robinson did the same thing and brought the whole contraption crashing down on her head, but in a split second Herbie leaped off the windowsill and sent the baby flying back on his bottom on the carpet. The baby howled in surprise and one chubby fist shot out and grabbed at Herbie's long waving tail.

It hurt. It hurt very much. Herbie was almost transfixed with pain. He dug his claws into the carpet.

Then Chrissie was down on her knees, scolding the baby, hugging Herbie. Or was it hugging the baby and scolding Herbie? It did not really matter for Herbie's heart was leaping up into a joyful rumble of happiness.

For in that moment Herbie had looked into Timmy's eyes, and had seen a faint but unmistakable vision of blanket baths, and bicycle rides and door tops, and perhaps even worse. But it meant Herbie had a home. The move was complete. Next door had become home. At last.

# Esmeralda

Esmeralda lay lazily in the garden soaking up the warm sun. She yawned daintily, showing her small pink tongue.

Then she stretched out her limbs and abandoned herself to sun-worship. A small fly buzzed nearby but Esmeralda did not twitch a whisker. The heat was glorious and nothing bothered her.

Esmeralda was a large long-haired marmalade cat. The colours of her fur ranged from the rich rust of autumn leaves to pale top-of-the-milk cream. Her eyes were almond-shaped pieces of glinting amber that could change from pleading, bewitching or being scornful in seconds.

Esmeralda lived with Joelle. Joelle Martin was a very up-and-coming ballerina with the New London Ballet Company. She was slim and beautiful and even in jeans she walked like floating thistledown. All her movements flowed like liquid, and Esmeralda, who was a great lover of beauty, would often watch Joelle just for pleasure.

Sometimes Esmeralda would settle herself on Joelle's bed and watch her mistress brushing her long raven hair, or drawing on those incredible gossamer tights. Or she would sit on the windowsill, still watching, as Joelle moved round the kitchen, reaching up to put away the blue-spotted china in the cabinets.

There were times when Joelle and Esmeralda seemed strangely akin to each other. Often Joelle stretched like a cat, and Esmeralda was all ballerina when she twirled on her toes to pat a fluttering butterfly, or ran lightly along the top of the garden wall.

They lived in a tiny converted cottage on the outskirts of Westerham – for Esmeralda's sake.

'I couldn't bear to have Esmeralda shut up all day in a flat,' said Joelle when she told her friends of her move.

So Joelle travelled every day to London by train. Night after night she returned home very late from the theatre on the last train, carrying her weary body like a dispirited faun. She often slept late into the morning, and Esmeralda would find it necessary to jump on to her bed and pat her mistress's face so that she would wake up and provide breakfast.

'You're better than any alarm clock,' murmured Joelle sleepily, throwing a bare arm over the fluffy cat. Esmeralda was flattered but still hungry enough to nudge her mistress's ear.

'All right, all right, bully-puss. I'm getting up . . . '

Esmeralda and Joelle agreed on almost everything. They agreed on whether to go out or stay in, whether to eat or not eat, whether to clean or not clean, whether to garden or not garden. It was all most amicable. They agreed on mostly everything, that is, except about men.

Esmeralda did not like men. Men totally, full stop. On the whole they had big feet and she did not like big feet. They had loud voices, clumsy ways, smelt different and were a race apart. A few she would tolerate – at a distance – but the rest she disliked wholeheartedly.

But Joelle, being both beautiful and sweet-natured, gathered men-friends in droves. They descended on the cottage in cars, on motorbikes, on mopeds, or more rarely by train and then by foot.

Suede Shoes was a train person. Esmeralda tolerated Suede Shoes because he stroked her gently and did not disarrange her long fur. But she could never hear him approaching in his suede shoes and he often gave her a fright.

He too was a dancer. A choreographer in Joelle's company. He and Joelle would talk dancing for hours. Sometimes Joelle would float off into the garden and try new steps to music from the stereo, while the choreographer improvised and made suggestions. Esmeralda sat on a step and purred. It was all quite beautiful to watch from a distance, but his sudden flying leaps were very alarming. One sign of a leap and Esmeralda was off.

Suede Shoes did not like the journey from London. 'I don't know why you've buried yourself in the country, Joelle,' he would say in his thin, high voice. 'It makes it so difficult to come and see you at weekends. The train service is abysmal.'

Joelle would smile at him and try to explain.

'Esmeralda likes it here, and so do I. It's so peaceful.'

Grey Pin-Stripe was altogether a different matter. He came in a flashy car. He wore shiny black shoes, and fastidiously picked off all the long hairs that Esmeralda left on his turn-ups. 'Shoo . . . shoo . . . scat,' he would say sharply when Joelle was out of hearing.

Esmeralda was a naturally polite cat and only went to greet visitors, male or female, out of good manners. But when she got to know the sound of Grey Pin-Stripe's car, she sat on the wall with her back to him.

Once he left his overcoat on the old rocking chair in the hall. Esmeralda trampled happily all over it and made a bed right in the middle. After that, he was always careful to hang up his coat.

Grey Pin-Stripe was a banker and he bought beautiful and expensive presents for Joelle. His car was low, sleek and powerful. In desperation to win Joelle's love, he brought Esmeralda a wicker travelling basket. It took her several weeks of chewing to demolish the edges, then she totally ignored it.

'Devil of a drive out here,' Grey Pin-Stripe complained for the hundredth time. 'That turning before the village is a real bottle-neck. And the traffic's nose to tail once you reach the outskirts of London. Heaven knows what time I'll get home tonight. And I've a heavy day tomorrow.'

Joelle picked up Esmeralda and hid her amusement in the tawny fur. 'Esmeralda and I hardly hear the traffic from our little garden,' she said.

But just now, with the sun warming her deliciously,

Esmeralda was not thinking about Joelle's various men friends. She was dozing, half watching an ant running about on a smooth stone . . .

She heard a car slow down and stop at their gate. It was a small, noisy car and one she had not heard before. She decided it was too hot to go and see who it was. She did open one amber eye when a tall young man walked down the garden path. He had the reddest hair she had ever seen – Esmeralda felt quite a pale ginger in comparison. He had a kind brown face and eyes as blue as the sky. He stooped a little as though he were weary or the small car had left him with cramp.

Suddenly Esmeralda found herself lifted into the air. She struggled frantically, waving her velvet paws like windmills.

'Why, hello gorgeous,' said a deep, friendly voice. 'I didn't know there were two beauties in the family.'

Esmeralda stopped waving and stared at him, one paw suspended in mid-air. She rather liked being thought gorgeous. Joelle came out of the back door. She had on her old faded jeans and a loose sweater, but even in those clothes she walked like a dancer. She smiled hesitantly at the stranger holding her cat, then her smile warmed as she recognised him.

'Hello. You're the doctor who came and looked at my ankle last night, aren't you?'

'That's right. I was wondering how my patient was this morning,' he said, stroking Esmeralda behind the ears. 'I hope you don't mind my coming out here to your home. The stage doorman gave me your address. Only, of course, when I explained my medical interest,' he added quickly.

'It's very kind of you to bother. It's a long way.'

'It's not far really. Besides, a spin in the countryside is rather refreshing after night duty.'

Both Joelle and Esmeralda looked at the young man with red hair again. He was the first man not to mind the journey, they noted, even after a night's work.

'I hope you weren't taken away from anything important last night,' said Joelle quickly, a little alarmed by her thoughts. 'It was such a slight accident. I didn't really want them to go and fetch a doctor.'

'The hospital is only a few doors away from the theatre so it was no trouble to come and see what was the matter. You managed to get home all right?'

'Oh yes, it was really a lot of fuss about nothing.'

'No injury, however slight, is a fuss about nothing. Especially for a dancer.'

Joelle could not believe her ears. She asked him to stay for some coffee. While she went indoors to put on the percolator, the young man carefully put Esmeralda down on the spot where he had first found her. 'Just go on promoting that tan of yours, my beautiful,' he said.

After that, Esmeralda saw quite a lot of the young man with red hair. Every time he had a day off from the hospital he came down to the cottage and made himself useful. He trimmed the hedge and painted all the window frames bright yellow. When autumn came he swept up the leaves and carted them to the rubbish dump in a wheelbarrow, with Esmeralda hitching a ride on top. But when he chopped wood for the open fire, she kept to a safe distance, eyeing the flying chips with caution.

Joelle cooked him nourishing meals and he began to look less pale and tired. She was glad to see the change in him.

Suede Shoes still came down, and so did Grey Pin-Stripe, but Joelle never looked happier than when she was with the young man with red hair.

To Suede Shoes, she was always foremost a dancer. He never allowed her to forget that or her career. To Grey Pin-Stripe, she was a famous name it was flattering to be seen with. Neither of them saw her as a real person. But when the young doctor came, she was able to forget her career and her fame. He saw her as a shy, vulnerable person, beautiful and talented and way out of his reach.

Esmeralda knew that he wanted to marry Joelle. He often told her about it as she watched him working in the garden.

'You know, Esmeralda,' he confided in her one day. 'I'm wishing for a bright star, a star so bright that I haven't the nerve to pluck it from the sky.'

Esmeralda wound herself round his ankles to comfort

47

him. She knew he was not very rich. Anyone could tell that from his shaky old car; and Esmeralda, from her viewpoint, could see that his nicely-polished brown shoes had been mended many times and the turn-ups of his good tweed, comfortable suit were showing signs of age.

Red was determined to take Joelle to his hospital ball. He bought the tickets, cleaned his car, sent Joelle a single camellia and arrived at eight o'clock looking incredibly handsome in a hired dinner jacket.

'I'm almost ready, Red,' Joelle called from her bedroom.

Of course his name was Red. Esmeralda had guessed that all along. It had come as no surprise when Joelle had whispered that his name was Dr Red Carter.

Red bent down to say hello to Esmeralda. 'I can't pick you up this evening, my beauty. You'd just ruin this suit, I'm afraid.'

Then Joelle swirled out of her room, clouded in midnight blue chiffon, with her dark hair gleaming. On the single diamond-studded strap of her dress she had pinned the camellia.

'Oh Joelle,' Red murmured, unable to take his eyes off her.

They went off into the night, leaving Esmeralda in the kitchen like Cinderella.

When they returned in the early hours of the morning, the air was warm with love. Theirs was a secret happiness and their hands touched as they moved about the room, drawing the curtains, switching on the electric fire, putting a romantic record on the stereo.

Then, as the gentle sounds floated through the room they were drawn into each other's arms. Their lips met in a kiss that lifted them to the stars. Suddenly Joelle broke away and ran to the french windows. She flung them open and ran on to the lawn, the folds of her blue chiffon dress streaming behind her. She danced like a fairy on the grass, light and beautiful, till she flew back to Red's arms and his words of love.

However, the next morning Esmeralda found her mistress weeping into her pillow, her hair tangled and wet.

'I've told him I can't marry him, Esmeralda. I can't, I really can't,' she cried into the cat's long fur. 'I can't give up my career, my dancing, just to be a doctor's wife. And it would mean leaving London when he becomes a GP. No . . . I just couldn't . . . it's too much to ask . . .'

Esmeralda jumped on to the windowsill and licked her fur back into place as her mistress went on crying. For many days Joelle wore a tired, lost look on her face, and Esmeralda knew she was not sleeping for Joelle often crept into the kitchen in the small hours to make a warm drink of milk.

Dr Red Carter came no more to the cottage, the garden drifted into neglect, and Esmeralda missed his friendly company. Every time she heard a noisy car, the cat went flying down the path to meet him. But she was always mistaken and would arch her back as the offending vehicle went by.

Joelle became more and more absent-minded and withdrawn. Four times she ran out of cat food, and Esmeralda's daily brush and comb stopped being fun because Joelle was so quiet and unhappy. Once she locked up at bedtime without letting Esmeralda in and the cat spent a lonely night under a hedge.

Esmeralda watched her mistress with narrowing eyes. It was these men who had brought unhappiness to Joelle and discomfort to Esmeralda's orderly life.

One day, as Esmeralda lay sprawled on the path in her favourite spot, contemplating the busy fussing of a colony of ants, she decided that Joelle needed something to rouse her from her unhappiness. Some kind of shock. Dried cat snacks were no substitute for a nice piece of fresh coley.

She stood up slowly and stretched, her fur prickling with sensuous delight as her limbs quivered and relaxed. She stalked down to the end of the garden, eyeing the different trees with apparent unconcern.

Joelle had risen late, heavy-eyed and listless. She was brushing her hair by the window when she first became aware of a plaintive miaowing. She put on her blue dressing-gown and ran out into the garden. High up on the topmost branch of a spindly ash tree she could see a small blob of orange fur.

'Esmeralda!'

The cat answered with a faint miaow. Her fluffy tail swung erratically. A breeze moved the slender branch and Esmeralda dug her claws into her precarious perch. She had climbed higher than she had intended.

'Oh poor Esmeralda . . . don't be frightened. Try and climb down. Come on, Esmeralda. Puss, puss, puss . . . fish, fish, fish . . . '

Joelle called and coaxed but Esmeralda clung to her swaying branch like a sailor to rigging in a storm. She would have to get help, thought Joelle desperately. As she ran indoors to the telephone, Esmeralda watched her disappearing figure with hope.

Joelle dialled the number of the theatre. It was some minutes before Suede Shoes came to the phone.

'My dear Joelle, I'm in the middle of a rehearsal,' he scolded gently. 'Do be brief. You know how I hate to be disturbed. It simply ruins my emotional flow. Esmeralda? Up a tree? Well, I don't see what I can do about it. Now, now, don't take it like that, Joelle, of course I'm fond of Esmeralda . . . Try waving a piece of fish tied to a broomstick. Surely you're not expecting me to climb up after her?' His voice rose to a higher pitch. 'Why, I might fall!'

Joelle slammed down the receiver, trembling with disgust. The man was a coward.

She dialled a city number and after speaking to two secretaries she eventually reached the great executive himself.

'Joelle? How nice to hear from you,' said Grey Pin-Stripe, full of his usual charm. 'I've been meaning to give you a ring ever since I got back from Zurich. How are things, darling?'

When Joelle explained Esmeralda's plight, Grey Pin-Stripe exploded.

'Up a tree? Do you mean to say that you've phoned me at my office to tell me that your idiotic cat is marooned up a tree? How do you know it's marooned? Perhaps it likes being there. Look here, my dear Joelle, I'm devoted to you. You are an exquisite woman, but I have a board meeting in a quarter of an hour and my time is valuable. Surely you are not expecting me to come down and rescue your feline companion myself?'

Joelle began to weep quietly.

'Now, now, don't take it so badly. Here's what I'll do. I'll phone the fire brigade. They'll rescue your perishing cat in a jiffy.'

'Esmeralda's not a perishing cat,' Joelle retorted. 'And don't bother to ring the fire brigade. You might waste two minutes of your precious time. I'll ring them myself. Goodbye!'

She rang them immediately and was told that the tender was already out but that the officers would be given the message when they returned.

Slowly she dialled a fourth number. She did not know what she would say, or what to expect, so it was with relief that she heard that they were unable to contact him. Dr Carter was busy, would she leave a message? Joelle sighed. There was nothing she could say. Red's job really was important.

'No, thank you. There's no message.'

An hour later the fire brigade arrived. Joelle was still wandering round the garden distractedly in her dressing-gown, coaxing and pleading with the errant Esmeralda. The fireman began to unload their equipment in the lane.

'Don't worry, miss. We'll soon have her down.'

The young fireman gave a cheerful grin and began to climb the extending ladder that stretched up into the highest branches of the tree.

'Come along, Ginger,' he called to Esmeralda. 'Nice pussy.'

The nice pussy arched her back like an outraged porcupine and hissed.

'Now then, Ginger-nob, I won't hurt you,' he coaxed.

Every one of Esmeralda's hairs stiffened at the insult. Ginger, Ginger-nob indeed! She backed further out of reach along the swaying branch. As she eyed the fireman with distaste, Esmeralda heard a familiar noise coming along the lane. The car stopped at the gate and Red Carter hurried down the garden path, going straight to Joelle.

'I came as quickly as I could,' he said. 'I knew there must be something wrong.'

'Oh Red, I didn't mean you to come. But I am glad, so very glad that you have.'

'I had to finish Casualty first, or I would have been here sooner.' His keen blue eyes swept over the scene, missing nothing from the soft flush on Joelle's cheeks, her wild-eyed desperation, to the waving fireman perched at the top of the ladder.

'I'd better go up there,' he said, taking off his coat. 'Esmeralda won't come down for a stranger.'

The fireman descended and wiped his brow. 'Coo, proper little tartar, that one. Mad as a hatter, spitting and hissing. You'll get more than a couple of scratches if you manage to get hold of her.'

'At least she knows me,' said Red, trying to sound confident. The rungs of the ladder stretched upwards into nothingness. In all his years of hospital work, he had never faced anything more terrifying. He hated heights and the thin, waving ladder only made it worse.

Red gritted his teeth and put his foot on the first rung. Slowly he forced himself to climb. His feet felt like lead and the palms of his hands were slippery with sweat. He did not dare look down, and suddenly his fear communicated itself to those watching down below.

Joelle ran to the foot of the tree. He did not look at all safe. She realised how much he meant to her, and always had. 'Come back,' she shouted. 'Please, Red, come down. I can't stand it. You'll get hurt. Please, darling . . . '

Esmeralda peered out between the leaves. Her small, crinkled face looked worried. Suddenly she knew what she must do.

With a tremendous leap, she left her high perch and sank her claws into a lower, sturdier branch. Then, sliding, scratching, clawing wildly at anything within grasp, she slithered down the tree, landing at Joelle's feet amid a shower of leaves and twigs. But before Joelle could pick her up, she was off like a bullet across the garden, disappearing through the hedge and away to the meadows.

'Well, I'm blowed,' said the fireman. 'These damned cats . . .'

Shakily Red descended to earth. Joelle went up to him and put her arms around him.

Not far away, Esmeralda sat under a hawthorn, licking her disarranged fur into place. Now perhaps she would have some peace at home. And with that comforting thought she swatted at a fly and started to purr rapturously.

# This Man is Mine

She had been living with him now for almost a year. The time had flown and neither of them had really noticed the months passing. He was a man worth loving, a man with his head among the stars, dreaming and thinking and plucking ideas out of the bright dark night with long, slender fingers. He was an author, writing under the name of Graham Marsh, but she did not know if this was his real name.

They lived in quiet, rural happiness with never a quarrel to mar the peaceful days in that small Devonshire cottage. He asked nothing more of her than that she should always be there. And so she was, ready to greet him on his return from London, or from the nearby market town – waiting to welcome him home.

He asked that she should be quiet and undemanding when he was writing, but that she should be ready with affection during the long evenings. The perfect lover. And how she loved him on those evenings, waiting for the moment when he would push aside his papers and smile at her. Then she would come into his arms, and his soft words of love were music to her ears.

She rarely left the cottage, partly because she was still a little nervous of the outside world. He had given her a home when she was most lonely and afraid. He had offered her a haven.

She did not like travelling in his car because it made her feel sick, nor did she like fishing with him in his little boat because she was afraid of the dark blue sea. So she stayed at home, happy to wander round the little cottage and its sunny, flower-filled garden.

But she also liked it when they walked together into the surrounding countryside. Sometimes his long legs tired her and then, if there was a field with poppies and butterflies, she would sit and daydream and wait for him to return.

There was no doubt that Graham adored her. 'You have beautiful eyes, my love,' he would say, staring into their amber-flecked depths as if seeking some truth there. Then he would run his hands over her face and rest his cheek against the softness of her neck.

And she loved him till sometimes she thought her heart would burst, and she just had to go over to him where he sat at his desk and touch his sleeve or make some small gesture of love. But when he was working, he had little time or thought for her.

'Go away, Susy,' he would say, not unkindly. 'Leave me alone, there's a good girl.'

She did not sleep with him but had her own bed in another room. Once she had come to him in the middle of a cold, wintry night when the temperature had fallen and frost was biting the air with icy needles. She had stood in the doorway of his bedroom. But he had been angry with her and had escorted her back to her own bed. She had heard his door shut firmly and had not been able to understand his harshness.

Then one day – a day in early spring – when the garden was full of nodding daffodils and the long green pods of unopened tulips, Graham came home early from seeing his publishers in London. He stood in the porch and Susy ran to him, wanting him to take her into his arms as he always did. But today he stepped back, and she saw that his arms were full. In them he held a small bundle wrapped in a blanket.

Susy faltered in her approach and looked up at him questioningly.

'I've brought a baby home for you, Susy,' he said softly. 'A little baby for you to look after.'

He turned so that she could see what was in the blanket,

and the small blue eyes that regarded her were startlingly clear and unafraid.

'This baby has no home,' he added, 'and you and I are going to look after the poor little mite.'

Susy saw the baby look up at him with adoring eyes, and anger began to smoulder in her heart. He was her man. He belonged to her, and no one else. She did not want to share him with anyone – not even a baby.

She backed away sullenly, not even welcoming him as she usually did, then suddenly it was all too much and she turned and ran upstairs, her heart turning over and over in a turmoil of jealousy and love for him.

'Oh, come on, Susy. Come downstairs and don't be such a silly girl,' he called out after her.

But she did not answer, nor did she come downstairs. She heard him talking to the baby then preparing its food in the kitchen, and she began to hate it. Oh, why did he have to do this to them, she cried to herself, when they had always been so happy together?

Hours later, feeling hungry and desolate, she crept downstairs. The door to his study was ajar. She stood silently in the shadows and saw that he was holding the baby on his lap and it was sleepy with milk. His papers lay on his desk, untouched.

Susy fled out into the garden, not caring where she went, running wildly through the flowers, shaking with a storm of rage. She ran to her favourite tree, a lilac, and climbed a little way, sitting and plotting against this newcomer. She heard Graham come to the door and call her name, but she took no notice. She did not return to the cottage until she saw the lights go out, then she trod softly into the kitchen.

She was very hungry by now, but was almost too angry to eat or drink anything. It would have choked her.

She wandered round quietly, looking for the baby. Where was it? She stood outside the door to his bedroom and her senses quickened. The baby was in his room! She could hear its small movements. She crept away, cowed and beaten, but loving him still despite the misery in her heart.

So the baby came to live with them, and they were three.

It was female and for the time being its name was just Baby. Susy refused to look after her, and once Graham had accepted her decision, he was not angry any more but simply laughed and teased her about it.

'Why, Susy, I do believe you're jealous!' he would say. 'Fancy being jealous of a scrawny little mite with a screwed up face, when you are beautiful and I love you.'

But Susy was still and unrelenting in his arms. It was not easy to forgive him.

So Graham took care of the baby and saw to her small needs. He loved to encourage her unsteady efforts to walk and gave her a soft, woolly ball to play with. When she was tired, he carried her in his arms, while Susy sat and watched from a distance, hatred in her narrowed eyes.

Now in the evenings it was the baby he cuddled on his lap, and Susy slunk sadly away for she could not bear the sight of them together. However, if he wanted to smoke his pipe, he put Baby down, frightened that hot ash might fall on her. It was then that Susy crept back into his arms, burying her face against his neck, trying to ignore the swirling puffs of smoke from his pipe for the sake of being with him again.

'Just like old times, Susy,' he would say to her, and she would soften with love for him all over again.

One day he had to go up to London, and he asked her to look after the baby. He stood in the doorway, tall and handsome in his city suit and polished shoes.

'Now will you be a sweetheart and take care of Baby for me?' he asked. He turned her face so that she had to look straight at him. 'Can I trust you?' he added seriously. Susy turned away so that he could not see her eyes, and in answer she went over to the baby and began to wash her half-heartedly.

He sighed with relief. 'That's a good girl. I'll be home tomorrow, but there's plenty of food for you both.'

Susy waited until she heard his car going down the lane, then she stopped washing the baby and shook her rather roughly. She hit her, quite lightly at first, then harder a second time. Baby cried out with surprise and looked at her with hurt eyes.

Susy walked away, pleased. She went into the kitchen and deliberately spilt the food which he had prepared for Baby – some special mushy stuff that had no taste.

She went into the study, finding those typed sheets that were so precious to him, and she tore them and scattered the bits over the floor. The baby crawled in after her and began to chew the shreds.

Susy stepped over the baby, not caring now, bent on her path of destruction, all her unhappiness boiling over in a torrent of uncontrollable hatred.

She smashed vases, cups, a jug of water, trampled on his bed, wrecked a pile of clean shirts just back from the laundry, tore at the curtains, swept his photographs off the bureau. She was like a wild creature, her eyes gleaming, her pulse thudding, her breathing sharp and shallow.

The baby was at the foot of the stairs but Susy ran down, knocking her over in her flight. The baby started to cry but Susy did not care. She turned on her, wanting to hit her again. One of her long nails caught the baby's face, making her squeal in pain.

'Here! What's going on?'

Graham stood in the doorway, the key still in his hand.

Susy froze. His eyes went round the scene of destruction, finally taking in the baby who was still crying pitifully.

He turned to Susy. 'You wicked, wicked girl,' he said angrily, lifting his hand and striking her.

'Thank goodness I came back for my wallet. You might have killed the baby. I'll take her to Mrs Simons down the lane. She'll look after her for me while I'm away. I'm ashamed of you, Susy.'

He picked up the baby and began to soothe her.

Susy did not move. It was the first time he had struck her. She thought the world was falling to pieces around her. She stayed quite still, thinking perhaps he would hit her again and then she would die. But he did not touch her – he simply turned and walked out.

She ran away into the woods, and when he came back from London he called and searched in the garden and the woods beyond, but he could not find where she was hiding.

At last she could bear it no longer. She would accept his terms, share him, if only just to be with him sometimes and to love him.

She was thin and cold and hungry, and she went back to the cottage to ask him to take her back. He swept her into his arms, overjoyed that she had returned.

'Oh, Susy darling, I've missed you so much,' he said.

The weeks passed and the baby grew, and Susy still hated her, though now she hid this hatred inside, growing thinner as the baby grew fatter.

One day Graham came home from the market with someone and there were happy, laughing voices in the hall.

'Well, Val, this is it,' Graham was saying. 'What do you think of it? It's certainly not a palace, but at least Susy keeps it wholesome.'

'I think it's perfect,' said a woman's voice. 'Just the kind of cottage I've always dreamed about.'

'And you don't mind about Susy and Baby? Susy might break out again, you know.'

Curious, Susy came out of the kitchen and saw a tall young woman with loose, fair hair standing in the hall, close to Graham, holding his arm. Susy withdrew slightly, suddenly afraid, wondering what this man she loved was going to do now.

'Of course they hate each other,' the young woman said with a laugh. 'It's only natural. It's like having two women in one kitchen. They never get on.'

'Am I to take that as a hint that you don't want any other female in your kitchen?' Graham asked. They were smiling at each other.

'Nonsense,' she said. 'We'll keep Susy, of course. She obviously adores you. But the kitten will have to go. I'm sure my sister would have her.'

At that moment, the young woman caught sight of Susy behind the kitchen door and went to pick her up.

'Why, you beautiful thing,' said Val gently, stroking the long black fur. 'You are a lovely creature. Now you have two adoring females to spoil you,' she said to Graham, her eyes shining with happiness.

And Susy stretched deliciously in the young woman's arms, curling and uncurling her claws among the loose fair hair, purring a loud, rapturous welcome.

This was a woman after her own heart. Susy quite agreed. The kitten would have to go.

# Curtain Call

It was not that Titus was stagestruck or came of a theatrical family, but rather that he came upon the warm, steamy stage door entrance on a chilly October night when he was at his lowest ebb.

The Titus of that moment was far removed from the majestic creature that now greets patrons in the foyer of the plush Wellington Theatre as they arrive for the evening performance. He always sits a little to the side of the first step of the grand staircase leading to the Dress Circle, his brilliant lemon eyes scrutinising each new arrival.

But on that wet autumnal night, Titus slunk his emaciated body towards the stage door, drawn like a magnet towards the light and warmth. His black fur was matted, his white vest caked with Thames mud, one ear tattered and bloodied after a fight with some Soho cats over the debris from a restaurant dustbin.

Titus had been on the London streets for twenty-seven days. It had been a terrifying experience, and one for which his suburban upbringing had not prepared him. From kittenhood he had been housed by the Carson family, fed, milked and comfortably quartered in a specially designed cat-bed lined with foam cushions. Life had been uneventful apart from pouncing on the odd bird, or an occasional night-out caterwaul.

As Titus sunned himself in their back garden, he gathered vaguely that the Carsons were going on something called a holiday. He sensed change in the bustle of packing and kept out of the way. Then the Carsons discovered that the cat kennels had closed because of a flu epidemic.

This seemed to throw everyone in a panic, and Titus, who somehow felt responsible, kept very quiet and withdrawn. Then an old aunt appeared with an equally old wicker basket and said why couldn't they take Titus with them to the house they were renting in Cornwall?

Titus had sniffed the basket with apprehension. It smelled of long gone cats, ill cats, bored cats, tired cats. When they put him inside it, he fought and scratched and it took two adults to fasten the lid.

All the way to London in the car Titus spat and howled and they had to turn up the volume of the radio to drown his protests. Nerves began to get frayed and the children started to quarrel about silly things.

Titus scratched and chewed between howls. Suddenly the lid flew up and he scrambled out, perched for one petrified moment on the back of the driver's seat and then leaped out of the open car window. The cacophony was terrifying – buses, cars, coaches, hooters blaring from all directions . . . Titus fled along Westminster Bridge, careering between people's legs, dashing across the road, slithering down stone steps and racing along the Embankment, tail high, fur on end.

The Carsons could not find him. They spent an agonising two hours searching and calling his name. Eventually they gave up, reported their loss to the police, and continued on their way to Cornwall, both children crying noisily in the back of the car.

Titus crawled out from his hiding place under a fruit stall near Embankment underground station and surveyed the busy street scene. It was nothing like the town he came from. At first he felt a little heady and elated with his new freedom, and he strolled the streets, taking in everything like a tourist. He was somewhat bewildered by the sheer volume of traffic, but continued sight-seeing, curious and wondering.

However, three days later the excitement of city life had

worn off. He was cold and hungry, and had come across unexpected hostility from other vagrant cats. If he found a restaurant dustbin with some fish or chicken scraps in it, within seconds some huge alley-cat would turn up, hissing and spitting and claiming territorial rights.

The weather changed and it began to rain, and warm, dry places were difficult to find. The pavement was hard on his paws, and his pads grew callouses. The foam-cushioned bed began to fade from his memory.

Titus was not built for jungle warfare. His plump good looks quickly disappeared and he became scrawny and untrustful. No one spoke to him and he missed human companionship. No one stroked him with affection. His heart shrank with emptiness. Sometimes his only human contact was a boot kicking him out of a doorway.

He roamed the mud flats of the Thames shore, wondering if they might lead him to this place called Cornwall.

He had had nothing to eat all that twenty-seventh day except a rotting fish-head he had found in a gutter near Billingsgate Market, where the language addressed to him had not improved much since the sixteenth century.

He crouched against a wall where the overhanging stonework gave him some protection from the weather. His tail was curled under him, his ears flattened against his head. He watched the lights of the stage door entrance, and the orange-red glow from within. It looked warm and he could hear cheerful sounds.

People were coming out now, chatting and laughing, wrapping scarves round their heads and putting up brightly coloured umbrellas.

'Night-night. Sleep tight.'

'On my diet? See you tomorrow.'

Titus was wondering if he might be able to slip in unnoticed when the next group of people paused in the doorway before venturing out into the grey street. He slithered forward, his dark fur merging into the shadows of the night.

'Just look at that poor creature,' said one of the young women suddenly. She came out of the group, not conscious of the rain on her dark, curling hair. She did not touch

Titus, but went down on one knee, approaching him respectfully like a true cat lover.

She made small encouraging noises so that he would not be alarmed, and when he made no move to escape or bite, she put out a careful hand to rub his forehead.

'There, there, puss. My goodness, you are wet. And so thin. Look, Nigel, you can see his ribs. I don't think the poor thing has had a decent meal for weeks.'

'Oh, do come along, Lindy. Stop messing about with that revolting creature. You know we're meeting the others for supper, and we're going to be late as it is.' Nigel strolled over, a tall, elegant young man turning up the collar of his trench coat.

'It doesn't seem fair,' said Lindy, straightening up. 'Here we are, going out to supper when we're not really hungry, leaving this poor cat who is starving. It's cruel.'

'What do you propose to do? Take the cat out to supper with us? Do you think it would prefer Chinese or Italian?' he asked with a calculated degree of sarcasm in his voice. He was a very promising actor.

'That's a splendid idea,' said Lindy with some spirit. 'You go ahead and join the others. I'm taking him across to Joe's for a square meal. Don't wait for me.'

'You must be joking. Lindy, for heaven's sake, you're not going to pick it up? It's filthy and it's probably got fleas. It'll bite you and then you'll get tetanus. We've no one to replace you if you get ill,' Nigel warned gloomily.

'Nonsense, he's not going to bite me. He's got the look of a perfect gentleman. And you'd be filthy too, if you were living in the streets. He's a gorgeous cat really. Look at his eyes. They're beautiful . . .'

Titus did not struggle. The young woman's arms were holding him confidently, and her voice dripped words which were honey to his soul. Her eyes were a dark hazel, flecked with amber, warm, caring and unafraid.

Joe's Café was on the point of shutting, but when Joe saw Lindy approaching, he hastily reversed his closed sign.

'Hi,' he said, casually stacking his accountancy books out of sight under the counter. He was taking a correspondence course between customers. 'What can I get you?'

'One coffee and one warm milk straight away please, Joe. Then one cottage pie with plenty of gravy and I think I'll just have a cheese omelette,' said Lindy, choosing a table away from the door and the draughts. She settled the cat on her knee, calming his nerves with gentle strokes.

'Eating alone?' asked Joe, slightly confused by the order.

'No, just me and Titus,' said Lindy, making an equally puzzling reply.

How Titus.enjoyed that first meal with Lindy! The warm milk was nectar, the cottage pie ambrosia. He could hardly eat for the deep, rhythmic purrs that threatened to choke him.

Afterwards Lindy took him back to the theatre, explaining that he could not live in her high-rise flat, but that he was welcome to doss down in her dressing room. She found him an old props box and lined it with a towel. She thoughtfully left open a small top window so that he could get in and out.

Titus fell asleep immediately, hardly able to believe his luck. He felt his dignity returning. He soon warmed to this strange, rambling building where people seemed to live during the day but went away at night when it became all his. Not only did he adopt the Wellington Theatre, but he appointed himself Lindy's guardian and mentor, too.

Taking charge of the theatre was a gargantuan task. He swept it clean of mice and no rats dared to come within a whisker of the place. He checked security, superintended the cleaning women, attended rehearsals, and was in the foyer every evening to welcome the patrons.

His appearance improved out of all recognition – he was not only clean and well-fed, but he had grown in magnificence with his new status. His black fur gleamed like darkest velvet, his white shirt front was whiter than pure snow and as soft as swansdown. He held his head proudly, his shoulders haunched haughtily, his tail curved over his toes with precision and delicacy. His lemon eyes watched everybody and everything: nothing escaped him, from a spider taking up residence behind a marble pedestal to a programme wedged between two seats.

Titus ate at Joe's Café and Lindy insisted that Joe gave her a weekly bill. Joe was reluctant about this, saying that Titus mainly ate leftovers, but Lindy was adamant. What about all the extra milk, she argued? Titus guessed that Joe did not charge Lindy enough because there was often a nice piece of fish or some steak for him. So he took on the café as a side line and the mice got a salutary eviction.

However, Titus had a curious attitude towards the cats who scavenged the dustbins. He did send them flying, but not, Joe observed, until after they had found something to eat.

'It's as if Titus remembers,' Joe told Lindy, one evening over a late coffee. 'He seems to have a certain sympathy for them.'

'Of course he remembers,' said Lindy, rubbing Titus expertly under his chin bone. 'Cats have memories, and are most intelligent creatures. Why, the Egyptians even worshipped a cat-goddess called Pasht.'

It was in Lindy's dressing room that Titus overheard Lindy and Nigel having a fairly heated discussion about the play. It was a classic thriller and assured of a pretty long run with the tourists and coach parties. But Lindy was unhappy about one scene.

'The letter incident really is my best scene,' Lindy was saying as she sat at the mirror taking off her make-up. 'And I would appreciate it if you would not fidget so much, Nigel. Somehow it destroys the tension I'm trying to build up.'

Titus was only half listening. He was curled up in his prop box which by now was lined with Lindy's shawl.

'I'm not fidgeting,' said Nigel, lighting up a cigarette. 'I'm merely being natural and at ease.'

'I don't regard that messing about with the decanter this evening as being natural and at ease. How can I be tense and emotional, reading the letter, when you are wandering about doing different things? It wouldn't be so bad if you always did the same things, then at least I could time my pauses.'

'I'm improvising, darling,' said Nigel, casually. 'You should be able to cope.'

66

Lindy turned, the amber in her eyes starting to spark. She crunched the tissue in her hand and tossed it into the wastepaper bin.

'I don't rush about madly during your confession scene,' she retorted. 'I keep still, I blend, I merge. I leave it to you. It's your scene.'

'But that's your style,' said Nigel, getting up to leave. 'You blend, merge . . . I just naturally dominate.'

'Oh!' The crash as she slammed down the jar of cleansing cream made Titus almost jump out of his box. 'How can you be so selfish?' Lindy stormed at Nigel. 'You're spoiling my best part. People will stop believing in me, and then when the c-contracts are renewed, they'll get s-somebody else . . . and I'll be out on the streets.'

Titus did not understand about contracts, but he knew all about being out on the streets. He had had twenty-seven days of it and he would not wish one half-minute of the experience on his beloved Lindy.

The following evening, once the audience was seated and he had checked the stalls, the dress circle and the upper circle, Titus sat in the wings, keeping well out of everyone's way.

It was true. During the letter scene, Nigel very craftily took the tension out of Lindy's reading. He stretched, he got up to close the curtains, he smoothed his hair in a mirror . . .

Lindy's hand was trembling as she held the crucial letter but Titus could tell that the audience had been diverted and the atmosphere in the theatre had lost its electricity.

In the interval he went back to Lindy's dressing room but he did not go in. From inside he could hear the sound of weeping. He quickly nipped over to Joe's Café to try and seek help there. Joe looked up from the text book he was studying, surprised, since Titus never usually left the theatre during a performance.

'Hello, you're early,' he said. 'What's the matter?'

Titus could not tell him, but he tried. He rubbed against Joe's ankles, miaowing desperately. Realising he wasn't having any luck with Joe, he returned swiftly to the theatre.

The confession scene was near the end of the play. It was

well-written and Nigel made the most of it. He began the speech with his usual confident skill.

At about line four, Titus casually strolled on stage. He sniffed carefully around and then decided that the upholstered arm of the settee was the best vantage point. He leapt up gracefully and got into position. Then he turned and stared at Nigel.

He stared. He kept still. He remembered what Lindy had said about blending, but it was a little difficult for a magnificent black and white shorthaired cat to blend successfully.

He sat there throughout the whole speech, staring, dignified, enigmatic, ears pricked at such an angle that he looked as though he were listening politely to a vaguely amiable idiot.

Nigel fought back. His voice grew louder, his projection more deliberate. The sweat glistened on his forehead.

Then Titus yawned, a small pink-mouthed yawn of delicate boredom. The audience collapsed in laughter.

It did not ruin the play but it did ruin Nigel's scene. He stormed off after the curtain calls in a furious temper.

'I'll kill that cat,' he raged. 'Get it out of the theatre!'

But the management refused. Everyone liked Titus. The producer thought the change of emphasis actually improved the finale. He was wondering if Titus could be persuaded to do it again.

Meanwhile Titus took refuge under a table at Joe's, exhausted. Acting was definitely tiring work. And those blinding bright lights. . . the experience had been quite unnerving.

Of course it was in all the newspapers the next day, and soon the box office began to break records as people flocked to see Titus. He did not always go on. It seemed to depend on how the letter scene went, observed Joe, who came over regularly to watch the phenomenon.

Eventually Nigel's nerve broke. He could stand it no longer and he left the cast. Lindy got her contract renewed, Joe passed his exams and a few months later they got married.

Titus was guest-of-honour at the wedding reception. He

decided wedding cake was overrated but champagne was delicious. Lindy looked as pretty as a picture with white roses entwined in her dark curls, and he hardly recognised Joe in a suit.

'And where are you going for your honeymoon?' someone asked.

'Cornwall,' said Lindy. 'We've been lent a very romantic fisherman's cottage. We thought we might take Titus with us.'

Titus did a standing leap which took him out of the window on to the balcony of the restaurant. He fled down the Strand, through the back streets of Covent Garden, down an alleyway that led to another alleyway that led to the back of the theatre, up through his window into Lindy's dressing room and into his prop box.

He loved Lindy. He was prepared to follow her to the ends of the earth. But there was one place where he would not go.

# Tufty's Horse

Seven-year-old Howard eyed his lunch with distaste. Casseroled chicken, carrots, onions, creamed swede, potatoes, there was nothing there he really liked except the spuds. He looked calculatingly at his mother, not appreciating her young dark looks and fresh yellow dress, but trying to size up from her expression just how much she would allow him to leave on his plate.

Howard knew there was the most delicious apple sponge to follow because he had seen her making it that morning. He also knew that he would not get any if he left his first course.

He sighed. Life was hard. He dug his toe into the soft fur of his kitten, Candy, who was asleep under the table, and wondered if he could slip her any of the chicken without being noticed. Candy liked chicken.

His sister, Jane, four and solemn, with stubby slow-growing pigtails, sat opposite him at the table, plying her knife and fork with the concentration of a gourmet.

'For goodness' sake,' said Lisa, exasperated by her son's unwillingness to eat. 'Do get on with your lunch. It's getting cold and you know we're going to see Grandma this afternoon.'

'I don't like it,' Howard mumbled, pushing morsels relentlessly round his plate with his fork.

Candy awoke from the prodding toe, stretched herself and padded daintily over to Jane's kitten, Tufty. The

70

children had two kittens, both black. But Candy was small, appealing and pretty, while Tufty was already growing into a big clown, always falling over his own paws, chasing his tail idiotically, boxing his own shadow on the wall, his long black fur sticking out wildly at all angles.

'You don't know what's good for you,' said Jim, his father.

Jane let the argument flow over her. She was watching the kittens playing on the carpet, rolling over and biting into each other's soft necks. When the kittens had arrived, Mummy had given the girl kitten to Howard and the boy kitten to Jane, which was all very sad for secretly it was Candy she loved, the sweet little female.

How Jane loved and longed for her, with her dainty doll-like ways, tiny blue-eyed face and minute whiskers. And yet she was supposed to love and look after Tufty, a great fool who just rushed about the house like a mad thing, with stuck up fur and big ears and nothing pretty about him at all.

Jane felt the tears of her unspoken love welling up and burning her eyelids. She blinked hard. She had tried to persuade Howard to swop kittens, but he had refused. He too preferred the appeal of the smaller one.

'Swop? Of course I don't want to swop,' he had said firmly, stroking the neat little Candy under her chin till her tiny, melodious purr threatened to engulf her throat. 'For that untidy old Tufty? He looks more like a hedgehog than a cat. Me, swop? Not likely.'

Jim put down his knife and fork and looked first at his watch and then at his stubborn son. 'You have exactly five minutes, my boy. Now eat your lunch or go hungry.'

Howard stared at his chilling plate. 'Chicken – white and stringy and horrid,' he mumbled.

Jim was about to burst into a lecture when he caught Lisa's eye. She hated scenes, especially at meal times. He decided to ignore the challenge.

'Chicken? But that's not chicken,' said Jim casually. 'Don't you know the difference? That's elephant meat.'

'Elephant meat?' Howard's eyes went round and incredulous.

71

'Yes, elephant meat. Caught it in the garden this morning.'

'You didn't. . . '

'Well, no, I didn't personally catch it,' said Jim with a shrug. 'I was busy with the bonfire, but along came this elephant. Quite a small one, actually, and. . . er. . . '

'Tufty caught it,' said Lisa quietly.

Jane looked up in surprise. 'Tufty?'

Lisa nodded. 'Mmm. Tufty. You know Tufty's a great hunter. Well, this morning he went out and caught an elephant.'

Jane stopped eating to think about this for a moment. 'But an 'nelephant's 'normous,' she said suspiciously.

'Tufty shook out his fur until he was twice his normal size, growled fiercely at the elephant and chased him all over the garden. He never gave up. He's such a great hunter,' said Lisa.

Jane thrust out her lower lip in disbelief. 'Tufty couldn't run after 'nelephant. 'Nelephant got 'normous legs,' she said loudly.

'That's true,' agreed Lisa. 'We all know that elephants are enormous. That's why Tufty went on his horse.'

'On his horse?!' Howard's voice spiralled up to a squeak. 'Tufty on a horse?'

Howard's face was agog, a forkful of hated carrot halfway to his open mouth. Jane sat straight and still, an inner battle going on inside her against the tiny seed of admiration sown for Tufty.

'I don't believe Tufty's got a horse,' she said at last.

'Oh yes, he has,' said Lisa airily. She glanced across to her husband. He was silently choking. 'He keeps it in the cellar.'

Jim coughed and spluttered, and then Howard saw the way his parents were smiling at each other, and suddenly, to his intense delight, he knew. His face went pink with pleasure.

'You're tricking me,' Jane protested to the other three.

'No, we're not!' Howard shouted, his eyes bright with excitement. 'He keeps it in the cellar. Didn't you know that? I knew it all the time, silly.'

Jim tried hard to control his laughter. He leaned over to his small solemn daughter. 'You know every time we see Tufty flying past the window?' Jane nodded slowly, uncertainly. . . 'Well, really he's sitting on his horse. Because of the window-sill, and the horse being low down, it's only Tufty we see. But actually he's sitting on his horse.'

'And he's got a cowboy hat,' added Howard, almost convulsed by his own wit. 'With two holes in it for his ears to poke through.'

Jane shot a venomous look at Howard. But she was not sure about her father. . .

'Tufty keeps his horse in the cellar, Jane,' Lisa explained quickly, 'because he's very shy about having a horse. After all, it's not every cat that's got a horse, is it? Candy doesn't have one. Girl kittens don't have horses.'

'I see. . . ' said Jane, who didn't. 'And girl cats aren't great hunters, are they, mummy?'

'That's right, so they don't need a horse. But Tufty's a great hunter and he needs a horse.'

The great hunter espied a mote of dust floating in a ray of sunlight and hurled himself at it, skidding on the polished floor, landing in a big clumsy heap hard up against the foot of the bookcase. He blinked his large surprised yellow eyes and shook out the ruff round his neck. He caught sight of the crumpled rug and stalked it slowly, stealthily, his long fluffy tail thumping the floor in mock rage. . .

Jane finished her dinner thoughtfully. 'Can I see this horse in the cellar?' she asked.

Jim raised his eyebrows fractionally. Get yourself out of this one it signalled to his wife.

'Now that might be a little difficult,' said Lisa. 'You see, we can only see this horse in the dark. It's extremely shy, and as soon as we put the light on in the cellar, it disappears, as quick as a flash, into the coal hole.'

'Into the coal hole?' repeated Jane, with all the scorn that a four-year-old could muster. 'But a horse is much too big to go into the coal hole.'

'Don't you know anything, stupid,' crowed Howard triumphantly. 'It's not an ordinary horse. It's a cat's horse, of course!'

Everybody started to talk at once. Jane wanted to know the truth but how could she? It was all too confusing. Lisa began to clear the plates, not commenting on Howard's passable effort in that direction. She brought out the well-risen apple sponge and a jug of custard, and smiled at the puzzlement on her small daughter's face. She wanted to believe in the horse; she wanted to believe that Tufty was a great and intrepid hunter. But she was a sensible child and her brain cells were working overtime telling her all this couldn't possibly be true. . .

After the meal, Jane got down and went round to her mother. She put her arms round her.

'Will you show me Tufty's horse?'

Lisa opened the cellar door as quietly as she could, feeling Jane's small fingers gripping her hand tightly. It was not fair, she thought with compassion, to tease the little girl to this extent. But it was too late to turn back now. It had to be acted out. She did not want the episode to end in tears.

'I can't see anything,' Jane whispered, peering down the steps into the darkness. 'Where is he?'

'He's usually in front of the boiler,' Lisa whispered back. She put her hand on the switch and suddenly the cellar was flooded with light. 'Oh dear, he's gone,' said Lisa casually. 'Too late. Never mind, Jane.' Lisa drew back. 'Let's get ready to go out. We're going to Grandma's, remember? That'll be nice.'

Jane thought about Tufty's horse all the way to Grandma's, and she even told her Grandma about it.

'My kitten, Tufty, has got a horse,' Jane informed her.

'Oh, how lovely for him,' said Grandma, who couldn't hear very well.

It was dark and very quiet in the house when Jane woke up and wanted to go to the bathroom. She padded sleepily out of her room on to the landing in her striped pyjamas and thought how lonely the house was in the middle of the night. It must be very, very late.

But there was a gleam of light from under Mummy's bedroom door which meant that Daddy was probably reading in bed as he often did. It was comforting to think

74

that they were both there, and if she wanted anything she only had to call.

The old house rustled and creaked, and on her way back to her room Jane suddenly thought of Tufty's horse. Of course! This was the very time to catch it there in the cellar. It would be asleep and wouldn't have time to wake up and dash into the coal hole. She would be sure to see it this time!

She crept down the stairs, her heart beating furiously. The cellar door creaked as she opened it. A furry softness touched her bare ankle. Jane jumped back with a frightened gasp, but then in the moonlight from the window she saw that it was only Tufty. She picked him up, grateful for some company.

She felt her way carefully down the wooden steps, and put her hand slowly over the cold metal lightswitch at the bottom. She was trembling, her mouth dry with fear. The kitten, suddenly feeling unsafe, started to struggle, and as she tried to hold him still with one hand, his claw flashed out and drew a long scratch down her hand.

Quickly she switched on the light.

There was nothing. Nothing at all. Only the boiler, a pile of chopped wood for starting the boiler, Mummy's empty jam jars, and an old kitchen table that they no longer used.

Relief swept through Jane. She hadn't really wanted to find a snorting, stamping, pawing four-legged horse, however small, in their cellar. She hugged Tufty to her, stroking his funny big ears.

'But I'm sure you could catch an elephant if you wanted to,' she whispered into his soft neck. She felt all the tickly softness of his ruff on the end of her nose. He began to purr. It was an enormous, joyous sound and Jane's heart began to swell with love for him.

At breakfast the next morning, Jane waited until there was a break in the family chatter to announce her news.

'I've seen Tufty's horse,' she said at last, rather loudly.

There was an astonished silence while Jane held out her hand. It was bound with a ragged piece of pink sticking plaster.

She waggled her hand proudly.

'And he bit me,' she said.

# A Catastrophic Person

It always took Grace a considerable time to walk along Oakleigh Road because she had so many friends to say hello to on the way. She would never dream of slighting an old friend, or a new one, even if it made the difference between catching the 8.15 am to Victoria Station and missing it.

First there was Mabel. Mabel was a smoky grey Persian with tabby markings, the prettiest little face and BO. She waited permanently on the pavement for the admiration and caresses which she considered her due.

A few houses further down was Susie, who was black, sleek and had three legs after a road accident. She was pathetically grateful for attention and would hop frantically through the flowerbeds at the sound of Grace calling her name. Susie made little of her disability but she never attempted to cross a road again. She stayed on her own side, her world reduced to a few acres of garden surrounded by a border of tarmac.

Titch was also black and sleek, but with four legs and a velvet sheen on her coat that spoke volumes about her well-fed, pampered life. However, Titch came of a theatrical family and her favourite role was that of a homeless, starving waif thrown out on to the pavement. Her acting was pretty good, and she managed to fool a lot of people.

'Poor Titch,' Grace would murmur, sympathetically

stroking a forlorn ear. 'Have they all gone out and left you again? And did they forget to give you your breakfast? You'll have to catch yourself a mouse.'

Thomas was a thug-faced ginger tom who spent most of the day guarding cars. He sat on a car roof top, barely acknowledging Grace's friendly greeting although his timid heart yearned to respond. He was too shy even to run away. Whereas Sheba, the pale Siamese next door, spoke to no one, not even other cats, and hid in hedges perfecting her vocal imitation of a baby.

Grace never ignored any cat and this left her breathless by the time she reached the station and stumbled into a carriage. Hugh held the door open with an expression of amused tolerance on his handsome face. He helped her aboard.

'Nearly missed it again,' he said. 'All those damned cats, I suppose.'

'Susie can't hurry,' said Grace. 'And I'd hate to miss her out. It's a miracle she's still alive.'

'Ridiculous to go to all that trouble for a cat. They should have had her put down,' said Hugh complacently.

'How would you like it if you had a road accident and someone decided not to bother to patch you up?' asked Grace, with a trace of anger in her low voice.

'Don't be silly,' said Hugh, only half listening. 'People aren't cats.'

But cats are like people, Grace thought. 'And I'm cultivating Thomas,' she said aloud. 'That takes time.'

She was between cats at the moment, and that meant she had a special need for the unconditional affection so generously offered by cat friends. Even the distant Thomas and the vanishing Sheba were reassuringly themselves and a challenge for Grace's incurable ailurophilia.

Grace sighed as she settled back into a seat and Hugh opened the *Financial Times*. She had been going out with Hugh for nearly a year. He was good company, intelligent, successful at his job as an accountant, and, for some reason totally unknown to Grace, he had singled her out from all the other local girls.

Grace never really could understand why. There was a

shortage of men in their area and Grace had felt it more acutely because of her height – her five feet eight inches immediately put off half the male population. Hugh was an easy six feet and she had been captivated from the moment she fell over his feet getting on the train one morning. His dark eyes seemed to radiate warmth and sensuality; his hand steadying her arm had sent shivers down her spine; his dark brown voice rendered her speechless.

'Are you feeling all right?' he had enquired as he dusted off his hand-stitched brown shoes.

'Oh yes. . . ' Grace had breathed. She had never felt better.

However, Grace soon discovered that she had a price to pay for Hugh's favours. She had to conform to the kind of behaviour Hugh expected from a young woman. She had to tone down her disco dancing from its normal wild abandon, put away her outlandish gear and wear restrained dresses and skirts. She had to go lightly with the kohl round her eyes – Hugh thought that too much make-up was vulgar.

Grace played a good game of tennis and Hugh liked having her for a partner. She had the height and reach, but Hugh soon discovered that she lacked concentration, particularly if a certain tabby kitten was around the tennis club.

'Hello, Little Mo,' said Grace, stooping to stroke the little stray who had attached herself to the club for the season. Little Mo seemed to live on bar food, crisps and cold sausages, so Grace often brought her the odd tit-bit in a margarine tub.

'It's your service,' Hugh hollered.

'Sorry,' said Grace, throwing the ball into the air. 'Little Mo feels hurt if I don't speak to her. She gets quite lonely at times.'

The kitten danced across the court, bouncing after the ball, her tail a streaming banner. Hugh missed his return shot.

'You're the most impossible person I have ever come across,' said Hugh, removing the kitten. 'How can you tell if a cat's feelings are hurt? Tell me that.'

'She looks hurt,' said Grace defiantly.

'With all those stripes on her face, I fail to see how you can detect any expression. Really Grace, it's time you grew up.'

'Please stay off the court,' Grace whispered to Little Mo, wrapping the kitten in her cardigan and putting her on a sunny chair. Her blue eyes blinked lovingly and she immediately went to sleep.

They played well and won the match. Hugh was pleased.

'That's my girl,' he said, throwing an arm round Grace's shoulders and bending to brush the lobe of her ear with his lips. Grace almost stopped breathing. This had to be what she had been waiting for all her life. It was chemistry, magnetism, sex-appeal, any word would do. . . but it was still a magical something that made Grace try to change in order to please Hugh.

However, there was nothing much she could do about the cats. She had loved cats all her walking days, and she could not ignore them even to keep Hugh.


'For goodness sake, come along Grace,' said Hugh, as they hurried along Oakleigh Road. 'We'll miss the beginning of the film.'

Grace caught him up, a little breathless. 'I will not pass Susie without saying hello,' she said. 'She has a very uneventful life with only three legs.'

'And you think your two-seconds worth makes a difference to her?' Hugh commented wryly.

'It's a human contact. Without this vital contact, her life would become dry and empty.'

'Nonsense,' said Hugh. 'I've never yet met a cat that wasn't snooty and offhand.'

Grace almost said that was because he was snooty and offhand, but she bit back the words. Sometimes she wished he was not quite so perfect for her in every other way.

It was with these sobering thoughts that Grace walked to the station the next morning. She was not sure that she wanted to change the way Hugh proposed. She could change herself on the surface, but beneath her lady-like exterior she would still be the girl she had always been.

Thomas, the thug-faced ginger tom, was sitting on the

roof of a soft-topped sports car. She stopped and reached up to scratch his furry ear. He arched his back, embarrassed.

'Don't be shy, darling,' she said gently. 'I want to make friends.'

'And I'd like to be your friend, too.'

'How extraordinary,' said Grace, recovering her composure. 'I didn't know Thomas could speak.'

A tousled head of unruly hair appeared from beneath the car, then a face streaked with grease grinned up at her. The young man looked at Grace with admiration in his bright blue eyes.

'We don't tell everyone,' he said. 'Not even the neighbours.'

'I was actually talking to your cat,' Grace explained formally, her hand resting lightly on Thomas's furry neck. He moved imperceptibly, half an inch forward.

'My mother's cat. I'm Pete Hardy. I'm home on leave from the army. I don't think we've met but we should have. Thomas is slipping – I rely on him for introductions.'

'He's very shy,' said Grace. 'It's taken me months to get this far.'

Pete scrambled out from under the car and brushed the bits off his jeans. 'I promise I won't be so slow,' he grinned.

'I shall have to go,' said Grace. 'If I talk to people as well, I shall miss my train.' She noticed they were the same height.

'Hop in. I'll give you a lift to the station.' He scooped Thomas off the roof and deposited him on a flowerbed. 'Do some gardening for a change,' he suggested to the cat.

Grace was not late for her train that morning. Hugh noted her even breathing. There was not a strand of red-streaked hair out of place. She looked almost serious.

'No cats this morning?' he enquired.

'Only one,' she said. 'The shy one.'

He squeezed her hand encouragingly. 'That's my girl,' he said. 'You're showing some sense at last.'

The last dance of the season was a special evening in the tennis club calendar. Hugh and Grace danced together all evening. She floated in his arms, very aware of his close-ness, the spicy fragrance of his aftershave, the smoothness of his cheek so close to her own. It was a wonderful evening and Grace began to think of a lifetime of such bliss. Perhaps Hugh was right when he said she was immature . . . per-haps it would be easy to change if she could always be so happy . . .

Then the music quickened to disco and Grace promptly broke a heel dancing to the latest chart success. She hob-bled off the floor, the offending spike in her hand.

'You're hopeless,' said Hugh, putting the heel in his pocket. They walked outside the clubhouse, their arms entwined. The music was still playing, the air full of pale blossoms swaying in the silvery moonlight. It was a perfect evening. The last of summer. Hugh took Grace into his arms and her mouth was warm and sweet as he kissed her.

As Grace soared in the heady sensation of his embrace, far away she heard a small, faint sound. At first it hardly registered, but then she heard it again and moved hesi-tantly away from his seeking mouth.

'Grace . . . what is it?' he murmured against her face. 'Don't go . . . please.'

'I thought I heard something. It came from over there . . .'

'It was nothing. An owl, a mouse . . .'

'No, it wasn't. I think something is hurt . . . I must find out.' She twisted out of his arms and began to search the darkened car park, limping with her shoeless foot.

'Grace . . . come back. You can't do anything.'

'But I can hear something crying . . .'

Grace almost stumbled over a small dark shape stretched out on the driveway. It was Little Mo, the stray kitten. She had been hit by a car and her back legs were unnaturally still. There was blood in her nostrils, and she was crying piteously and uncomprehendingly.

Grace crouched over the injured animal, her heart pounding. 'Poor baby,' she moaned. 'Poor Little Mo.'

The little creature looked smaller than ever, its face pointed and bony with pain. She tried to drag her back legs but there was no support in them.

'We must do something,' Grace shivered. 'It's the little tabby kitten,' she called to Hugh. 'She's badly hurt. Some stupid driver . . .'

'It's only a stray. She'll be dead by the morning,' said Hugh, strolling over and looking down at the mutilated animal. 'Come back to the clubhouse. I'll buy you a drink. You look pale.'

Grace was aghast. 'We can't just leave her. She's in terrible pain, poor little thing. She's suffering and she doesn't understand what's happened to her. All she knows is something's not right and she's frightened.'

'It's only a cat,' said Hugh, exasperated. 'You make her sound like a human being.'

'I'm going to find someone who will help if you won't,' said Grace fiercely. 'Someone with feeling. Someone with a heart and not just a handsome face.'

'You're impossible,' said Hugh, his profile immovable in the moonlight. 'All this fuss over a stray cat. I don't understand you.'

Grace limped up the steps into the clubhouse. She knew who she was looking for. Pete was not dancing, but talking in a crowd by the bar. He looked tough and dependable, the aggressive line of his jaw softened by the humour in his eyes. He was still in jeans, a cleaner pair perhaps, with an old, faded combat shirt. He saw Grace and left the group immediately.

'What's the matter?' he asked.

'It's Little Mo. She's been run over and she's very badly hurt. I don't know . . . perhaps we could take her to a vet, or something.' Grace swallowed hard. 'She's in such pain . . .'

'Show me,' said Pete.


The world shrank. Grace could only think of the pain, the small heartrending cries, the stillness . . . Grace hid her face. She could not look. It was all over in moments. The crying ceased.

The music was playing again and the soft, balmy air was filled with the scent of blossom. It was all unreal, the music, the dancing, the passionate kisses she had shared with

82

Hugh. Reality was the pain and bewilderment of a little cat.

Grace knew she could not change. She would always be this kind of person, a little impossible to live with but not if the man really loved her. And if there were not enough men to go round, then she would make her own home and live by herself . . . well, not quite by herself. There might be a cat or two . . .

'Would you like to walk home?' said Pete. 'I can fetch my car in the morning. You can borrow my tennis shoes.'

'Yes, I would like that,' said Grace, hardly audible.

They did not talk. They walked slowly through the coolness of the night, the street lamps throwing their orange glow on to the pavements. A small grey shadow detached itself from the darkness and wound itself round Grace's ankles.

'Oh, Mabel,' said Grace, with instant recognition. 'You do need a bath. Hasn't your best friend told you?'

Susie leaped off a low wall and landed a little unsteadily on her three paws. She was delighted and surprised to see Grace so late and purred loudly.

'Hello, Susie,' said Grace in a trembling voice. 'You survived all right, didn't you? Not like Little Mo.'

'Little Mo was too badly hurt. No one could have done anything,' Pete began.

'Yes, I know,' said Grace, walking on.

Titch was sitting on the top step outside her house. She had only been out five minutes but she managed to make it look as though she had been there hours. Grace had to smile.

'Cheer up, beautiful,' she said. 'They'll let you in again soon.'

They stopped outside Grace's house. She turned to Pete, wanting to say something.

'I'm between cats at the moment,' she said. 'I was going to bring Little Mo home for the winter.'

'I know. I know . . . ' he said.

He did not take her hand or touch her. There was no magic or chemistry. But there was something else. . . a tiny feeling of awareness that had nothing to do with sex and everything to do with love.

Thomas was sitting on top of a van. He had been trying to make up his mind all day. But here she was and she had not seen him. If he did not hurry, she would be gone and then it would be too late.

He leaped off the van and ran across the road, his heart pounding. Even now he dared not come too close, but hesitated some yards away with a little sidestep.

But Grace had seen him. She went down on one knee and held out her hand. He sniffed it cautiously. Grace did not move or speak, knowing that they had come to the moment of trust. And trust was the beginning of love.

# The Princess and the Pauper

As soon as she came into the compound, he realised that she was not among the ordinary run of visitors. There were no children tugging this way and that at her hand. She was not making various cooing noises. She did not flutter ecstatically by the first large cage of adorably fluffy kittens . . .

Purposefully the young woman approached the row of cages housing adult cats, her air of calm efficiency only slightly impaired by the tension in her slim neck. She was pretty in a flower-like way, but with strength in her delicate features, a contradiction that gave her face character. She looked along the line of cages.

'Oh heavens,' she murmured, somewhat distraught.

There were dozens of cats. Fat ones, thin ones, old ones, young ones. Pairs of green, blue and yellow eyes swivelled away from her. They ignored visitors. She was merely part of the daily procession.

But he knew she was someone different. He sensed the hidden distress as the young woman swiftly progressed towards him. She stopped and looked into his cage, a sudden gleam of hope coming into her clear hazel eyes.

'Now, you might do,' she said. She turned to the kennel maid who had been following her. 'Can you tell me anything about this one?'

The kennel maid, who was a sturdy youth of nineteen, had all the facts. 'For a start,' he said, 'we get very few

Seal-points. Most Siamese owners take good care of their animals. But the circumstances here are a little unusual. The owner was an elderly lady, a Mrs Ferguson from somewhere in Australia. She left the Siamese in six months' quarantine when she came back to England, presumably to spend her last days in this country.'

'An Australian Siamese. How interesting!'

'Well, apparently they must really have been her last days, for no Mrs Ferguson ever turned up to collect her cat.'

'Have you tried to trace her?'

'Of course, people have tried, but with no success. There's a bill of several hundred pounds outstanding at the boarding establishment.'

'What's the cat's name? Have you got its papers?'

The youth coloured slightly. 'Er . . . unfortunately, no. The relevant papers became detached from the cat during its transfer to the refuge.'

Fiona was inspecting the animal closely. It had a cream-coloured body, shading to a pale, warm fawn on the back, with mask, ears, legs, feet and tail of dark brown. There was a good width between its eyes, its ears were well pricked. It gazed at her fathomlessly with its brilliant blue eyes, oriental in shape but with no squint.

'The mask is a little dark,' she murmured.

'We usually only keep 'em seven days, but this is such a beautiful cat.' It was blatant sales talk.

'OK. I think she'll do.'

'He's a neutered male.'

'Oh heavens!' The young woman was torn, then something in the Siamese's dignified expression made up her mind. He was too proud to remind her of the six months already spent in lonely quarantine, or of the fate that awaited him soon if he remained homeless. But it was there in his eyes. He looked intelligent and she desperately needed intelligent help.

'Do I have to sign something?'

'Come to the office,' said the kennel person, thrusting his hands into the pockets of his overall. 'You've got a good 'un there.'

The Siamese was put into a cardboard cat box and Fiona took him out to her car. Once inside with the windows closed, she opened the lid. He stepped out cautiously.

'I don't like these boxes,' said Fiona. 'Do you think you could manage to keep still while I drive us home?'

He listened. He'd been in a car before, couldn't she tell? He sat down on the front seat and began to groom himself meticulously. He did not turn a hair when she switched on the engine and drove slowly out of the compound.

'I have to tell you that your name is Princess Mila,' said Fiona with some trepidation. 'I know it sounds a stupid name, but it's only a collection of syllables after all. If it's all right with you, I think I'll call you Prinny. Perhaps you'll get used to it. But I wish we knew your real name. If only you could tell me.'

Prinny sat very still awaiting events. He was so damned glad to be out of that cage that he did not really care where this nice young woman took him or what she called him.

'We live in a house near Kensington Gardens,' she went on. 'I think you'll like it. At least, it's not my house. I work there as a sort of housekeeper-come-secretary. It's my responsibility to see that everything runs smoothly. The main advantage of the job is that I have my own small flat at the top of the house, and in these days that's like gold dust. I couldn't afford to live anywhere in London at today's prices.'

Prinny gave a low miaow to show his understanding. He was enjoying the ride and his driver's gentle voice. He noticed that the delicate spring leaves were bursting out on the trees again and little clouds were chasing each other across the sky. He liked seeing children skipping along the pavements, the other cars flashing by with powerful roars, the lumbering red buses towering overhead while he sat safe and contained in this funny little square car. He trusted Fiona implicitly. There were some people that could be trusted straight away. Yet she had not touched him once yet. It was all in her voice.

'Poor puss,' she was saying. 'What a long time to be shut away. It must have been horrid. I suppose you have almost forgotten Mrs Ferguson by now.'

He felt compelled to tell her that he had not forgotten Mrs Ferguson, nor ever would. But Fiona did not know him well enough to understand or recognise his different vowel sounds.

Prinny looked curiously at his new home – an elegant Georgian town house in a square of other elegant Georgian town houses, very different from the rambling Australian ranch on which he had once lived. He padded over the priceless Persian carpet in the polished hallway, and sniffed at the burst of bright yellow daffodils arranged in a crystal vase on the Sheraton table. He felt sure the young woman had put them there.

Is this it, he yeowelled?

'This is it,' said Fiona. 'And, believe it or not, you have a sitting room of your very own. Now how many pussycats can boast of that? See what you think of it.'

Fiona opened a door to one of the ground floor rooms. It was furnished like a normal sitting room, but there were a few feline refinements. There was a cushion-lined cat bed on four short gilt legs. A grooming table. A china bowl of water standing on a king-sized mat. A cat litter-tray was discreetly hidden behind a screen. The room was centrally heated and the double-glazed glass doors lead out on to a small but richly-green lawn. On the wall hung a cabinet containing a collection of satin rosettes and several silver cups.

Wow, said Prinny, impressed.

He also immediately knew a lot about the other cat that had once lived there. She scratched and sharpened her claws on the legs of the grooming table. She adored minced chicken and warm milk. She was lazy and sat about a lot, especially on the chair with the satin cushions. The doors to the room had not been opened for a long time.

'I want you to stay indoors for a few days,' said Fiona. 'I'm sorry about it, but I'd hate you to run away or get lost.'

Prinny shrugged his compliance. He would have agreed to anything at that moment. Anyway, there was plenty to look at around the house.

'You can roam all over until she comes back. Would you

like to see the kitchen and my office? Then I'll get you some milk. Come along, Prinny.'

Prinny followed her neat ankles along a mirror-lined corridor to the back kitchen. He did a complicated little side step as he crossed over the threshold – a sort of celebration dance. It was a very modern room, not at all like the kitchen at the ranch, but nevertheless it had a more lived-in atmosphere than the rest of the house. In a room leading off the kitchen there was a desk and a typewriter. The room smelt of flowers and the young woman.

'This is my office. You can come and see me anytime.'

He leaped up on to the desk and walked all over her papers, which rustled delightfully. He smelled the mysterious innards of her typewriter. His ears pricked as he heard a thrush somewhere in the garden singing loud and clear, a tantalising sound. He turned and gazed longingly at Fiona. Can I, he asked, please . . .

She shook her head. 'Sorry, Prinny. No birds allowed. It's a rule. Come and have some milk while I make myself a cup of tea.'

Prinny sat beside the saucer she had given him. He had no taste for English milk; now Australian milk, that was different. He waited patiently then he tapped her arm. She was stirring her cup of tea.

'Why, I do believe you would rather have some tea,' she laughed. She got a clean saucer and poured him some from the teapot. He began to paw the ground as she put it down for him, but he still did not touch it.

'Sugar?' she inquired.

That night he did not sleep in the cushioned bed. He chewed a corner thoughtfully, then decided to curl up under the radiator. He had also ignored the chicken dinner, preferring to share Fiona's scrambled eggs and bacon in the kitchen.

The next morning he was exploring the rooms on the first floor when he heard a car draw up outside the house. He peered down from the windowsill and saw a large purple-ribboned hat being helped out of the car and then coming up the front steps. The ribbons wobbled as the hat laboured up the steps.

Fiona rushed into the room, her brown hair flying, picked Prinny up and hurried downstairs to his sitting-room. He lay stiffly in her arms, like a bundle of brown sticks. Did he have to go back to the refuge? It could only be bad news . . .

'Now you've got to be very, very good,' she whispered urgently. 'Mrs Armitage is back and you know what she's like.' Then Fiona did a very peculiar thing. She patted his face with some fine white stuff that made him sneeze. 'Don't fuss,' she pleaded, shielding his eyes with her other hand. 'It's only talcum powder. Your muzzle is a little too dark.'

She put him on to the satin cushions.

'Sit,' she hissed. He was so surprised, he did.

Under the large purple-ribboned hat was a large purple-ribboned woman, and suddenly Prinny found himself clasped and squeezed against ample folds of purple bosom. He was too astonished to resist.

'Princess, my darling Princess. Mummy's back! Has my darling Princess missed her Mummy while she's been away in America?'

Prinny yeowelled politely. What a strange woman!

'Beautiful little girl, Mummy's beautiful little girl,' Mrs Armitage cooed. 'Mummy's brought a lovely present for her beautiful baby.' She turned excitedly to Fiona. 'Bring in my small leather travel bag, will you, Fiona? I want to give Mila her present. I hardly knew what to choose. They have such marvellous things in America. Dear little jackets, and wellington boots for her little paws. I could have bought and bought.'

Prinny lowered his ears. He hoped he wasn't going to get any damned fool wellington boots.

Mavis Armitage took a long leather box out of her travel bag and opened it. Lying on velvet was a soft suede collar, intricately shell-edged and finished with a butterfly-shaped buckle studded with bright blue stones. She fastened it lovingly round Prinny's neck.

'There, doesn't she look absolutely gorgeous. It matches her eyes. She must wear it to the cat club show next month.'

Mrs Armitage took her spectacles out of her handbag and put them on her matt-powdered nose. She peered at Prinny.

'Have you been keeping to Princess Mila's high-protein diet sheet?' she asked, frowning. 'She looks a different shape. A bit thinner . . .'

'She's been pining for you,' said Fiona quickly.

'Ah, yes . . . of course, that would explain it. Now my baby must have a nice rest so that she will look beautiful for the cat show.' Prinny sat back on the cushion, speechless. But he would definitely have plenty to say later.

When Mrs Armitage had disappeared upstairs and Prinny was sure the coast was clear, he made his way to Fiona's office and put his paw on her lap. He tilted his head so that Fiona could see the buckle fastening.

'Do you want me to take it off? I thought you wouldn't like it. No, you can't have it to play with. Or bury. Mrs Armitage would be angry. It's probably very valuable. Nor can you sit on my lap, silly. How could I type? And I've got masses to do. Look at all this work she's given me . . .'

But Prinny insisted. He pushed his way on to the chair, sitting behind her like a cushion. He did not particularly like the whine of her electric typewriter, but the flying keys and the fast carriage return were entertaining.

Mrs Armitage was not exactly suspicious, but certain things puzzled her. Princess Mila had always been content to sit on her chair and doze, but now she seemed to have developed a rampant vitality and curiosity, streaking up and down stairs so fast that no one ever really knew where she was. She refused to eat any of her special foods, preferring a helping of whatever Fiona was eating, and her appetite ranged from downright earthy to the quite sophisticated at times.

Princess Mila had never played before, but now she boxed the tassles on the curtains, skidded across the polished floor on the Persian carpet, trampled on the piano keys, and chased everything chaseable, even her own shadow.

And she insisted on telling everyone about it. Mrs

Armitage simply wasn't used to so much vocalising.

'Will you be quiet?' said Mrs Armitage irritably when Prinny was trying to tell her that tea was late. 'I shall shut you in your room if you don't leave me alone. Fiona, for the last half an hour I've been trying to make some telephone calls but Princess insists on pushing in and miaowing down the telephone. My friends can't hear a word I'm saying. You'll have to take her away.'

'Siamese do love to talk,' said Fiona gently.

'Nonsense. Princess never used to be so noisy.'

'Well, Princess was always shut in her room.'

'And that's her place now,' Mrs Armitage snapped, putting on her spectacles and thumbing through her engagement diary.

Fiona carried Prinny away to the kitchen. The cat's cool azure stare told her what he thought of that conversation. He would not be shut in his room, he warned her.

'Please don't be difficult,' she pleaded, swiftly powdering his nose. It was the oddest habit, but one which he had got used to. 'Jobs are hard to find, especially ones with flats, and Mrs Armitage does pay me well.'

But Prinny had a will of iron. He was determined now that he would not go into that room at any cost. He dared Fiona to put him there.

'I said put Princess in her room,' Mrs Armitage called sternly from the hall. 'And I mean now, Fiona.'

Prinny's tail began to whisk. A low growl rumbled in his throat, his ears pricked forward as if stalking, the prey in this case being large, bossy, and, to his eyes, always purple-ribboned.

'Oh dear,' said Fiona, trying to obey.

It was blue murder. It was all hell let loose. Prinny exploded into the most deafening protest of outrage Fiona had ever heard. She stood outside the room with her hands over her ears. She would never have believed that one cat, even a Siamese, could make such a frenzied row.

'I'm going out to Harrods,' said Mrs Armitage, sweeping through the hall with her mink coat over her arm, her face creased with annoyance. 'I trust Princess will have calmed down by the time I return.'

But Prinny had no intention of calming down. The uproar reaching a shattering crescendo . . .

'What on earth is all this racket?'

A man strode into the room – he was tall, solid, dark-browed and unflappable. He scooped Prinny up out of the wreckage of the cushioned bed which he had been violently demolishing. The man held Prinny out at arm's length and gave him a slight shake.

'Stop this fuss at once,' he said firmly, in the kind of voice he used for raw recruits on deck.

A fine cloud of talcum settled on the lapels of his naval coat. Lieutenant Nicholas Armitage looked Prinny straight in the eyes – deep-sea blue met brilliant sapphire blue, and locked instantly.

'This isn't Princess Mila,' said Nicholas to Fiona. 'This Siamese has a wider muzzle, and look at those bright, mischievous eyes. It's younger, slimmer, healthier . . . and male.'

Fiona smiled apprehensively. She put a hand on Prinny's soft cream fur to still the pounding of his heart. He immediately quietened, changed down gear to a lower tone. He was on her side, but he did not know what he could do to help.

'It's a long story . . .'

'I have five days leave.'

'Well, you see, while your aunt was abroad, somehow . . . er . . . somehow I lost Princess Mila,' Fiona confessed. She moistened her lips as she remembered the desperate days that had followed. 'I don't know what happened. I suppose she got out somehow . . . I can't believe she was stolen. Anyway, I reported it to the police, and I went to every home for strays in London, but no Mila. If she had been run over I'm sure someone would have found her and reported it. So I think she must have found herself a new home. But how could I tell your aunt, when she had entrusted Mila to my care? She would have fired me instantly.'

Nicholas agreed. 'She would.'

'Then as it got nearer and nearer to the date of your aunt's return, I was nearly at my wit's end. I decided I would have to find a replacement . . . a look-alike adult Siamese to take Mila's place. And I found Prinny. The markings were so alike . . . '

'But not the character,' said Nicholas, stroking the now-docile cat. Prinny was calmly accepting a new fate. He had met his new master. He loved Fiona, but she was his slave. This man Nicholas was his master.

'Did I do something terribly wrong?' asked Fiona, still stroking the soft fur. 'They told me at the refuge that they would not have kept Prinny much longer. Seven days is usually the maximum, but because he was such a lovely cat. . . ' tears welled into her eyes and Prinny was immediately worried. He patted her cheek sympathetically with his beautiful oval paw. He did not like to see her cry.

'My dear, sweet maiden in distress,' said Nicholas, shifting the cat into her arms, then putting his arms round both of them. 'The solution is at hand. I think it's about time you left my aunt's employment and took on a more interesting and permanent occupation.'

'Prinny's an Australian,' said Fiona incoherently as Nicholas began to kiss her.

'Good on you, sport,' Nicholas drawled.

And good on you, Prinny purred deeply. He did not add pommy-bastard. It would not have been nice.

# A Thoroughly Bad Lot

You only had to take a good long look at Jasper to know that she was a thoroughly bad lot. Her answering glance was always scornful, with only a flicker of interest in the depths of her almond-shaped green eyes. Her long black tail thrashed the ground in perpetual anger. She walked alone. She cared for no one. She refused to conform.

'I don't understand why you're such a bad cat,' said Jennifer. 'You have a good home and you are well fed. And yet you steal. I don't like cats who steal.'

She marched to the back door with Jasper under her arm. She hung there like a limp fur stole, only a minute flick of her tail betraying her inner fury. She did not care if she was not liked. It was quite immaterial to her.

'Stealing Candy's fish, indeed. Ungrateful thing. And it's not the first time I've caught you.' Jennifer tipped Jasper out on to the doorstep. 'Reflect and reform. You can come back when you've repented.'

Repentance. She did not know the meaning of the word. She was uncontrite, even if it was raining. She had not one fleeting whisker of regret. That Candy was going to get exactly what was coming to her.

'Is the delinquent in the stocks again?' asked Edward. 'You know it's raining, don't you? It's not like you to be unkind.'

'I've got to teach her a lesson,' Jennifer insisted, wrestling with her conscience. 'She's been stealing Candy's supper again. Of course, Candy is a perfect lady and won't stand up for herself. Jasper gets away with it every time.'

The perfect lady sat under a chair in a corner of the kitchen, velvet-gold eyes half-veiled, waiting until it was safe to venture out.

'Come on, beautiful,' coaxed Jennifer. 'I've put that bad cat out.'

Candy broke out into a low, passionate purr. Her love was embarrassingly vocal. She could be heard on the telephone, and the mere mention of her name was enough to start the throbbing, quivering, claw-retracting fluffy black Persian on her dauntless track to the nearest soft lap. Nothing deterred Candy in her quest. She was blind to newspapers, sewing, even coffee cups in her way. She would place herself roundly on top of the lot, drooling moist words of love into the nearest ear.

Outside on the windowsill sat Jasper, balefully watching the tender reunion. Although she was nearly full grown, she was still small and sleek – sometimes she thought that one of her ancestors must have been a witch's cat . . . of course, there weren't such things now, what with radar and computers.

The rain settled on her short spiky fur like pearl onions on cocktail sticks. Her attention was caught for a moment by a shining trickling raindrop, and she licked the wet window with a small, inquisitive tongue.

Jasper looked into the kitchen at the bundle of four-inch long Persian fluff now being lovingly brushed and combed by Jennifer, and she felt almost naked by comparison. Electric sparks prickled up her spine. Her tail swung to and fro. She could not stand the nauseating sight any longer.

She jumped down and walked deliberately across a freshly raked flowerbed. Further down the garden tiny shoots of lettuce were peeping through the earth where none had been the day before. She scratched at them curiously and chewed on a tender thread of root.

The bluetits and sparrows were fighting noisily round the bird-bag that swung from the Japanese maple tree. They hung upside down, pecking at the nuts, dropping from a precarious hold, fluttering and squabbling.

Jasper watched them with narrowed eyes. Stupid, irritating things. She could not even be bothered to catch them. She had bigger prey. That long-haired layabout: the precious Candy.

Any good psychiatrist would have sorted Jasper out in a trice. Beneath that smouldering hatred lay a deep-seated inferiority complex; an unconscious distaste for her own black sleekness; a repressed wish for a coat of four-inch long Persian fluff.

Jasper did not understand this. She did not need a motive to be mean – it came naturally. She could not remember a time when she had had a pleasant thought. She had the vaguest memories of a half-wild mother, a crowded cage of stray kittens, of being handled by many strange hands.

Neither did she know that she had been chosen by mistake, nor that she was a profound disappointment to Jennifer. In kittenhood she had looked remarkably like a Persian, and Jennifer had picked her out of the selection at the animal refuge as company for Candy. But it never worked out. The sleeker she grew, the more Jasper disliked the Persian. She brooded for hours on her animosity, plotting horrendously sticky ends for her rival.

'Hello,' said Edward, scooping Jasper up against his shoulder. 'Put you out again, has she? You really will have to learn to behave.'

Jasper reared away from him, back arching, elongating her long neck like a snake. Edward scratched her smooth, almost hairless chin.

'Now you're what I call a real cat,' he said. 'Not like that other overgrown fur mat, all fuzz and fluff.'

Jasper replied with a piercing yeowl and leaped out of his arms. She could not bear all that petting and fuss. Yuck. She shook out her crumpled fur and stalked disdainfully down to the stream.

She trod daintily over the pebbles and thought wicked thoughts. She knew that by engineering something simply terrible for Candy, she would revenge herself on the humans and the pampered Persian at the same time.

She sat on a broken piece of concrete and thought. Death

by drowning was a delicious possibility, but in a mere two inches of slow moving stream? Another tragic road accident – but Candy was as nimble as Jasper in dodging the traffic. Starvation? But the humans were too wily. They had seen through that one.

Jasper thought treacherously of the big golden retriever who lived down the road. Could she, without endangering herself, convince him that Candy, beneath all that fur, was a chewable proposition?

Jasper looked at her own quivering reflection in the shallow water, her eyes darting and flashing among the round pebbles like a shoal of minnows. Perhaps she could get Candy into trouble, then they might get rid of her.

She sauntered back to the house, her tail held high. She watched from the camouflage of a rhododendron bush as Candy was put out of the back door.

'There's a good Candy,' said Jennifer. 'Have a lovely run-round.'

Jasper felt sick. Have a lovely run-round . . . to a cat. It was nauseating.

Candy had a favourite sleeping place. On a rack across the ceiling of the garage were some ladders and Edward had stored the cushions of the garden swing on top of them.

It infuriated Jasper to see Candy up there on her Dunlopillow. It made her deliberately seek out the most uncomfortable box of nails to curl herself up on and go to sleep. She was no softy.

Out of slit eyes Jasper watched Candy go into the garage and climb up the shelves to her throne. She trampled it into order, settled blissfully and began her throbbing vocal appreciation.

Jasper fled down the garden. There must be some way, something that would choke off that awful racket for ever. Her claws caught in some flimsy stuff that was hanging from a shrub. It seemed to have fallen from Jennifer's washing line, and the wind had carried it away. The stuff ripped as Jasper jigged sideways trying to unmesh her claws. She bit and scratched at it, strands catching in her teeth and setting them on edge.

Wildly she leaped about, determined to rid herself of the

hellish stuff. It trailed after her everywhere. She rushed into the garage where there were sharp things and it caught on some logs . . .

Some hours later, when Jasper had almost forgotten the incident, she heard Jennifer saying quite crossly: 'Candy, you naughty thing. Those were my best tights. They're absolutely ruined.'

The days that followed were almost pastoral. Jasper's animosity seemed to mellow into a kind of saintly reserve. She no longer spat at Candy. She deigned to allow Candy her half share of the nourishment provided. She would sit in the same room for several minutes without provoking a squabble.

'I do believe Jasper and Candy are making friends at last,' said Jennifer with relief. 'It's a miracle.'

'Don't be too sure,' said Edward. 'This sudden change of heart doesn't ring true.'

'Jasper's being a good pussy now, aren't you?' Jennifer crooned. 'There's a darling . . . ' The darling good pussy stiffened as Jennifer stroked her sleek black fur. It took immense self-control not to leap out of a window and escape to the woods.

'I think I'll go down to the shops and buy the cats some really nice fish for a treat,' said Jennifer.

'You can go into the newsagents and tell them that the new delivery boy is being highly erratic. And will you pay the gas bill? We've got a final demand. All red print and threats,' said Edward, opening his cheque book. 'You know,' he added thoughtfully, 'perhaps Jasper doesn't like her name. You must admit it sounds very masculine.'

'Nonsense,' said Jennifer. 'It means a kind of quartz, an opaque kind.'

'I know what jasper means, but does she?'

'Or something taking a high polish. Very suitable for a highly-polished cat,' said Jennifer firmly.

'I suppose it doesn't actually make any difference, but I just wondered,' said Edward, signing the cheque with a flourish. 'I suppose it's just a sound to her.'

Jasper remained unmoved. She trod a tightrope of

deception with cool aplomb. She slipped through the waving grasses in the garden, her sharp ears alert for the unexpected. She roamed the area, peering into sheds, nibbling the odd stalk.

The cuddly Candy relaxed into perpetual Elysium; her home was the enchanted fields of Arcadia; the walls vibrated with her ecstatic purring. Her complacency grew with her plumpness.

Jennifer was more surprised than alarmed when one afternoon, she found a uniformed policeman ringing the door bell. He was youngish, fresh-faced and very slightly embarrassed.

'Mrs Jones,' he asked. 'Mrs Edward Jones?'

'That's right,' she said, puzzled.

'I'm making a few inquiries and I'm wondering if you can help me,' he began.

'Yes?'

'We've received a number of complaints in this road about missing items. These complaints cover a period of several weeks. The latest was this morning when a builder working on number 23 reported the loss of a tin of emulsion paint, shade Radiant Blue.'

'I'm afraid I don't understand . . .' said Jennifer.

'There are paint tracks, shade Radiant Blue, leading into your garage.' The young policeman looked even more embarrassed. 'I wonder if you would allow me to have a look . . . er . . .'

'Of course,' said Jennifer briskly. 'Look all you like. This is absolute nonsense, you know. It was probably some children larking about.'

There were some spots of fresh blue paint on the driveway, and a larger splash by the garage window. Jennifer opened the garage doors, the policeman close behind her. They peered into the gloom. Jennifer switched on the light.

At first all seemed normal. Edward went to work in his car so the garage was empty, apart from the usual flotsam of suburban garages. Jennifer turned to the policeman, triumphantly, but then followed his gaze to the floor. A small pool of Radiant Blue was forming. They looked up at the ceiling, where the drips were coming from.

'Oh dear,' said Jennifer in a small voice, not knowing what to expect next.

The policeman climbed on to the workbench at the end of the garage and reached up among the ladders and cushions from the garden swing. Candy looked down into his youthful eyes and began to purr rapturously, soft fluff a-quiver.

'Oh dear,' said Jennifer again.

'I wonder if you would mind helping me,' he said, sounding quite apologetic.

He passed down the pot of paint, glistening with slopped Radiant Blue. Then he solemnly handed her one child's red wellington boot. Next, three copies of the Radio Times, one unopened gas bill and a dead rose bush. Dried earth showered his uniform.

Jennifer put the items on the floor. 'Is there any more?' she asked hopelessly.

'It's like a jumble sale up here,' he said cheerfully.

The pile on the floor grew . . . a knitted rabbit, a silk scarf from Liberty's, two pairs of bikini panties, one marked Tuesday and the other marked Friday, a man's vest, a brand new pair of secateurs still in their shop packaging. Jennifer went from bright pink with acute embarrassment to pale with horror.

The policeman stretched further into the robber's trove . . . a length of washing line, three odd gloves, a garden trowel, an ordnance survey map of south-west London, a tennis sock and seven pairs of sunglasses.

'I don't understand,' said Jennifer, shaking her head.

'I'm sure there must be some explanation,' the young policeman said.

The explanation sat in the middle of the garden path quickly trying to lick Radiant Blue off her paws. On the path beside her was a carton of yogurt with teeth marks denting the lid and a muddied copy of *Teach Yourself Arabic*.

'Caught red-handed,' said the policeman, almost disbelieving his eyes.

'You mean blue-pawed,' Jennifer remarked, eyeing the cat levelly. 'A serious case of kleptomania.'

Within minutes Jasper was in the kitchen sink up to her middle in warm water, struggling like a demented fiend, as Jennifer tried to wash off the paint before it dried.

'You are a very naughty pussy,' said Jennifer, unable to stop herself from laughing. 'And trying to put the blame on poor Candy. I'm ashamed of you. You're a thoroughly bad lot.'

Jennifer wrapped the cat in a towel. Jasper scowled, knowing she looked a fool with her fur all wet.

'Just you wait until I tell Edward what you've been up to,' said Jennifer, towelling her briskly till her fur shone like silk. Jasper dug her claws into Jennifer's knee. She could not understand what had gone wrong with her plan – they ought to be scolding Candy. She jumped on to the floor and shook off the towel . . . immediately in her way stood the big black Persian. She met Candy's yellow stare. There was no sympathy in the older cat's knowing eyes. Instead there was a distinctly chilly authority.

Candy sensed a momentary weakening in Jasper's fierce spirit, and stepped forward, a long hiss coming from her curled lips, her fluffy tail hoovering the floor with steady sweeps. She lifted a round velvet paw and boxed Jasper smartly on the ear.

Jasper sprang back, astonished. It hurt.

Jennifer gathered both cats up into her arms, still laughing, and buried her face in their soft fur.

'Now stop it, both of you,' she admonished. 'I won't have any more of this nonsense.'

Jasper veiled her slit eyes and arched her slender neck away from the mass of vibrating Persian almost smothering her. Then she remembered the accuracy of that unexpected wallop, and thought hard. . . perhaps there was room for negotiation after all.

# The Honourable Member

Conscious life for this kitten began on the mudflats of the Thames, or rather in a plastic bag on the mudflats. The family had five children to feed on supplementary benefit and a kitten was beyond their means. The man took a 159 bus from Brixton and dropped the plastic bag with the kitten in it over the parapet of Westminster Bridge.

There was no human rescue at hand, for the days of the Roman ford and medieval ferryman had long since vanished into the mists and fog, but the bag floated for a few moments then was caught in the wake of a passing coal barge and washed up on to the mud. With the frantic strength of fear, the kitten tore at the bag, its tiny claws perforating the plastic and pushing through until there was a hole large enough for its head. It wriggled out, its fine baby fluff clinging to it like wet rats-tails.

Unsteadily, trembling, but with a primitive instinct for self-preservation, it negotiated a set of slimy stone steps. It was an alien world, freezing cold, dark and wet. The parapet above loomed gigantic and foreboding; the water below swirled by black and smelly; the evening air curled dank fingers round the helpless creature. It shivered, crawling along endless slabs of pavement, going it knew not where. It squeezed between some tall iron railings that reached to the sky like trees. It found an overturned wire litter basket full of discarded newpapers. The newsprint was warm and nest-like. After licking up fragments of potato crisps from a crumpled bag, the kitten curled into a small ball and went to sleep.

In the morning, the kitten wandered round the outside of the empty building, mewing piteously, but no one saw or heard her. The place seemed to be deserted. She wandered through stone courtyards and cloisters, awed by the grim size of everything towering above her, grey and dingy, flecked with bird droppings, statues crumbling and sinister without faces.

Her nose led her to the kitchen waste. She was too small to eat most of what was there, but a messy slop of cold sago pudding filled her empty stomach till she staggered away, pot-bellied and tired. She found another warm place to sleep, and for the first time a glimmer of hope entered her world.

But the next day she crouched, terrified, in her hiding place. An army had invaded the precincts. Noisy cars, vans, people wearing black shoes and walking with heavy measured treads, rattling trollies laden with crates, clanging bells . . . it was bedlam. Everywhere she crept she was surrounded by hordes of tramping people. Feet appeared from all sides. It was very frightening. She retreated still further into her hiding place. It was only when it began to rain, and the drops bouncing off her tiny nose became a continuous trickle, that she made a wild dash for shelter and found herself indoors.

Now the floor was wood blocks, then a carpeted stairway that went on and on. She climbed the endless green mountain, pausing on each landing to pant and make little lost mewing sounds. Then it was polished wood again and she slid along helter-skelter to the next place, where the carpet was thick and grass-coloured. It was like a great corridor stretching into the distance with high wood-panelled walls; a sensuous warmth oozed from the grills under the dark green padded seats.

Stern portraits gazed down from the walls . . . Sir Marc Brunel, Field Marshal Smuts, Joseph Chamberlain, Sir Isaac Pitman, John Pym, Ramsay Macdonald . . . their eyes followed her, and she gazed innocently back.

The doors to some of the rooms off the corridor were

open. She heard voices coming and hid behind the heavy green curtains. The warmth and darkness were overpowering and she could no longer keep her eyes open. When she awoke all the noise had gone and she could hear herself breathing in the stillness of the night air. Her fluffy coat had dried out and puffed round her like a ginger and white poncho.

She crept out again, with more courage now that she was dry and warm. She found a crumpled ball of paper and patted it curiously. It bounced away from her along a tiled floor and she ran after it, dancing like a wind-blown dandelion clock. The crumpled paper rolled down a wide stone staircase and the kitten bounced after it, sliding and skating on the smooth worn marble, her tiny claws unable to gain a grip of any kind.

She tumbled past marble busts of Gladstone, Palmerston. Pitt, Peel, and Spencer Perceval (the only prime minister to have been assassinated) – their glazed white eyes were unamused. But the fall did not hurt her and at the foot of the staircase she shook out her fur and twitched her small nose. She could smell food, unmistakably. Her flight from the upper regions had brought her near the kitchens . . .

She passed a dining room so vast that she thought she was outside again – the ornate gilt ceiling could have been sun-speckled sky, and the massive portraits in oils on the green-papered walls a landscape of giants.

But there were crumbs under the tables and on an uncleared tray on a side wagon was a small jug of cream. The kitten drank from the Rosenthal bone china and the first small purr of her life throbbed from her throat.

She wandered through the rambling white and chromium kitchens, from one area to another, intoxicated by all the different smells. She would live here in this strange place, she decided, now that she knew where she could always find food. It meant sleeping during the daylight hours when the place was invaded by all those noisy people, and hiding late into the night. But in the small hours until dawn it would be all hers. Long empty corridors to play in, acres of carpets, hundreds of new warm places to curl up in, the creaking of the heating system for company, whispers to chase, ghosts to stalk . . . and as she grew older she discovered that there were mice to catch.

And she had a garden of her own to play in. It was once called the Privy Garden but was now Black Rod's garden, with a small lawn and flowerbeds full of roses. It was easy for her to squeeze through the gaps in the tall iron gates to get there.

Sometimes she wandered along Dirty Lane, an old thoroughfare that now had a more respectable name, and into the Victoria Tower Gardens where Rodin's *Burghers of Calais* stared at her with expressions of grim pity.

There were strange vibrations about the building that puzzled the cat, though she did not know why. The same twelve acres had once been a township and housed many thousands of people – craftsmen, artisans, men-at-arms, cooks and courtiers as well as a royal family. She sensed burning, although she did not know there had been two Great Fires and an air raid on that spot.

She also sensed death and this made her fur prickle. There were echoes of agony in the cobbled courtyard where men had been hung, drawn and quartered and now trees were dying in their concrete beds. More recently there had been the sharp explosion of a bomb near the cloisters, and the acrid fumes clung to the stone.

She loved to stroll in other parts. . . a beautiful red and gilt robing room with priceless furniture and a single high chair that was out of the draughts . . . a long gallery with full-length portraits of quiet, gracious people with dignified faces. But it was the White Hall, or Court of Requests as it had once been called, that she liked best – another lofty room so ornate that it all quite dazzled her. There were three great chairs on a platform with deep red carpeting on the steps – the room was palatial when the moonlight was streaming through the stained glass windows.

Below the three chairs was a wide, rectangular red seat, the cushion of which was stuffed with a blend of commonwealth wool, and the cat found this a very comfortable perch from which to view the magnificence of her surroundings.

She began to learn every corridor, staircase, turret and room. She knew her way over the many different levels of roof, picking a route carefully among gothic spires and unnerving cat-walks to an unexpected small roof garden with abandoned sun-chairs, gay umbrellas and troughs of spilling flowers. She became used to the great clock that periodically erupted into fearsome clanging booms.

As the months passed she grew into a beautiful fluffy burnt-marmalade cat, shading to pale honey, with distinctive white markings on her delicate face. No one ever saw her. Not even the correspondents who worked long after the politicians had gone home, nor the custodians who patrolled the precincts at night, nor the cleaning ladies who came in droves at dawn to vacuum and clear away the litter of discarded paper.

One evening there was a banquet in the vast dining room with the green and white gilded ceiling. A woman came in a long swishing satin dress, rustling and shining with silk embroidery and there were sparkling stones balanced on her head among her hair. Another woman who stayed near her had a halo of fine golden hair and was wearing a long shimmering dress. There were a great many men too, all in black and white, some with sashes and medals, and the room was awash with swishing skirts and small feet in narrow, strappy slippers.

The cat hid under the long table that ran the length of the room by the windows, enclosed by curtains of starched white table linen. She could see all the feet, the gold and silver sandals, the shiny black shoes. Toes twitched, and some people eased their feet out of their shoes as the meal went on; sometimes a hand slipped down to scratch an ankle or pull up a black silk sock.

Crumbs came her way but she was not interested in crumbs these days. The smoked salmon people were eating was rarely dropped, but they were not very hungry, and she knew that there would be the usual mountains of delicious scraps shovelled into the waste bins for her to turn over at her leisure.

The evening dragged on, and the clattering dishes and cutlery mingled with the drone of voices in conversation eventually drove her to sleep. She woke up with a start when simultaneously all the chairs were scraped back and everyone stood up, some searching surreptitiously for their shoes. A great shout went up: 'The Queen! The Queen! God bless her.'

The cat ate too well after the banquet and fell asleep at once in her favourite hiding place. It was on a foot-shelf at the back of a huge, heavy square table with claw legs and drawers, standing in front of a baronial fireplace in the Upper Waiting Hall. Someone else had once liked this foot-shelf for it was deeply scored with spur marks from a man's boots.

She always sensed burning here too. Perhaps the great table had been saved from some horrendous fire, or perhaps it was just the smell of soot that still clung to the crooked chimney above the now unused fireplace.

She slept too long and too deeply. It was quite the wrong place to be caught in daylight. When she heard the cleaning ladies arriving with their pails and mops, she fled down into the central lobby, caught again by the barrenness of the high vaulted octagonal hall with nowhere secret to hide. The statues of medieval kings and queens stood impassively in their niches in the walls, as she crept under a long dark green leather seat, curling her tail tightly round her, freezing into immobility.

''Ere, Ethel, I thought I saw a cat.'

'Don't be silly. You're dreaming. There's no cat here. Ought to be though . . . there's enough mice about.'

The floor was cold stone though not far away was an iron grill through which wafted warm air. A statue of Queen Charlotte, sad and beautiful, loomed above; a squat red fire extinguisher sat below.

She had chosen quite the wrong place to hide, because it became very busy indeed. A queue of people constantly formed and reformed at a window, saying things like 'Four first-class and eleven second-class please,' and 'How much is a postcard to the States?' She could not get any sleep at all because of the comings and goings. People sat on her seat, waiting for their name to be called, and her tail was in constant danger of being trodden on.

Crowds surged through the lobby – tourists, delegations, policemen, parties of schoolchildren. She had never seen so many people at once. Then a policeman began to clear back the sightseers, and in solemn silence a procession marched through the lobby with men in black gowns, black breeches, one in silver-buckled shoes, another who seemed to have some sort of authority was carrying a heavy golden club. They walked through the people, along a picture-lined corridor towards the other chamber with the green hide seats and high oak galleries.

She followed curiously, unnoticed for once in all the commotion, sliding along the walls in the wake of the procession.

Never before had she seen this man with the silver buckles on his shoes and the long woolly grey hair. He looked nice, she thought, friendly and approachable. She had never approached a human being.

The procession went into the green chamber and the golden club was deposited on a pair of brackets on the table. The man with the buckles climbed into a high, canopied chair at the north end of the chamber beyond the table and put his feet on a green leather footstool. On the table were two brass-bound despatch boxes, and several heavy books, pens and stationery.

She crept under a bench at the back and made herself as small as possible. A pair of brown suede shoes shuffled a twitch away from her whiskers. There was a great deal of standing up and sitting down again. She could not understand this unusual form of exercise.

What began as a reasonable sort of exchange of views began to get noisy. Voices got louder. No one seemed to be listening to anyone else. There was shouting and interjections, unruly jeering and bursts of raucous laughter.

'If these figures are true and I do not doubt for one moment that they are, then why does not the right honourable lady admit that her policy is a ghastly failure?' a voice boomed across the floor, the microphone picking up the righteous indignation of his tone.

A wave of objections and counter-cheering almost drowned the lady's reply.

'It is not for politicians to try to take over the management of public sector industries,' insisted a cool voice.

Members sprang to their feet, waving order papers. The uproar grew. No one could hear a word.

'What price the election now?' someone shouted above the clamour.

'Point of Order, Mr Speaker. Point of Order!'

'Order! Order!' thundered the man in the tall, canopied chair, trying to make himself heard over the din. But the pandemonium grew as more Members rose to their feet, insisting on being heard, arguing across the floor of the House, encouraged by their jeering colleagues.

'Order! Order!'

The cat was terrified, deafened by the noise, her fur standing on end. Some unspeakable calamity was obviously imminent. A third Great Fire? An explosion? Were the massive stone walls about to descend on their heads, crushing them all to death?

In sheer panic, she shot across the floor of the House. But there was no immediate way out. She leaped on to the table, scattering papers in all directions; knocking over a jug of water. Her claws sank into the oak of the canopied chair and she streaked upwards, almost reaching the dusty top. The parliamentary correspondents leaned over from the Press Gallery, refreshed by the diversion.

'My goodness,' said Mr Speaker. 'Catch that cat!'

But no one could catch her. Not the Members, nor the Clerks, nor the official doorkeepers with their silver chains of office, nor the dignified Sergeant-at-Arms who was supposed to apprehend all unwanted strangers and escort them to the Carriage Gates or to the first floor detention room in the clock tower.

Then someone had the sense to open wide the heavy brass-studded carved oak doors behind the Speaker's Chair, and catching sight of an exit, the cat slithered down and fled to freedom.

News of the marmalade cat spread faster round the Palace of Westminster than an election rumour. Everyone quite liked the idea. It made the gothic mound more human.

She found that she no longer had to hide during the day and only surface in the lonely hours of the night. As she wandered around, people stopped to say hello, to give her a stroke or scratch her ears. There were several secretaries who encouraged her to visit them and to watch them typing on top quality cream-coloured paper then share their coffee breaks; the librarians were pleased that she kept the mice away from their precious old volumes and records of Hansard; more than one waitress would save an odd slice of chicken or a few prawns in case they saw her.

And you might see her too. Perhaps one day when you are sitting in the Public Gallery listening to a debate, you might catch a glimpse of a fluffy ginger and white tail under the Speaker's Chair. On the other hand, it might just be a trick of the light.

# Chimneys

It was a blustery November day when we drove down to Surrey – the wild wet leaves hurled themselves against the windscreen and fouled up the wipers. Jenny and I were going to Chimneys, outside the village of Lambhurst, to look after Aunt Polly's house while she was away in Florida for a month.

It was an arrangement which was convenient to us all. Our North London flat was being pulled apart while workmen put in a new central heating system, and I was only too happy to leave my landlord to sort out all the problems and clear up the mess.

Aunt Polly, like many house owners these days, had a fear of squatters, and was loath to leave her house empty for so long. Jenny was recovering from a bad bout of measles and the doctor agreed that a few weeks running free in Surrey would probably do her more good than a hasty return to school.

'Besides, one of those weeks is half term,' Jenny told Dr Stuart, sitting up in bed, her long fringe spiking her lashes. 'So I really shan't be missing that much.'

'Don't worry,' I said firmly. 'I shall be taking your school books with us to Chimneys so that you can start catching up, young lady.'

Jenny pulled a sweet, pert face. She was tall for her age, with Stephen's candid brown eyes and my silky dark hair, still pallid from her illness but already restless and fidgety with sudden surges of new energy.

'Aunt Polly's new house is lovely,' said Jenny, turning to Dr Stuart with enthusiasm. 'You must come and see it. We went there once last summer for tea and had raspberries picked from the garden.'

'Perhaps your mother won't want to be bothered with visitors,' said Andrew Stuart, packing his stethoscope away in his slim, executive version of a doctor's black bag. 'She could do with a rest as well. You are both too pale and skinny for my liking.'

'Oh, Mummy, did you hear that?' said Jenny cheekily. 'Dr Stuart thinks that all women should be pink and fat.'

Dr Stuart was new to the group practice and certainly Jenny had become very friendly with him during her illness. Perhaps it was not surprising, because there was no man in our life. Ours was a one-parent family.

I went cold, even now, six years later, whenever I thought of my handsome Stephen's death in a mid-air aeroplane collision over Tokyo. What could have gone through his mind in that moment, that split second of knowledge before the disaster? I could only hope that there had been no moment, that he had been engrossed in the paperback thriller I had bought him at the airport bookstall; or perhaps he had been dozing on the long flight and the whole event had been no more than a slipping into a deeper, lasting sleep.

Dr Stuart had come into our lives along with Jenny's spots and he had been a reliable guide through the worst days of her fever. He was in his early thirties, often bone weary, but with disarming laughter crinkles round his deep set eyes which could chase away the weariness. He looked as if he could do with a month at Chimneys.

'Of course we should be pleased to see you,' I said. 'Anytime.'

'Thank you,' he said. 'That's very kind.'

Chimneys stood behind a high stone wall outside the village near woods, draped in trees like a house in a fairy tale. As we drove along the lane that skirted the wall we could see the top half of the long, rambling, mellow red-brick building with its odd, disjointed roof slopes and small, square, lattice-paned windows that glinted in the watery late afternoon sunlight.

'Oh, Mummy,' said Jenny, clutching my arm with sudden excitement. 'It's going to be lovely here, I know it is.'

Aunt Polly had found the house on one of her erratic car-wandering Sundays, and fortunately she could afford to buy it. In her youth Aunt Polly had wandered a lot further afield than Surrey, sometimes dressed as a man, sometimes only with an Arab guide, and her travel books had brought her a steady income ever since.

'Mind you, they're old hat these days,' she was fond of saying. 'It's package tours everywhere. There's nowhere left to explore. It's such a shame.'

We drove past a small, narrow door set in the stone wall, its wood warped and weatherbeaten, the brick supports and overhead archway listing dangerously. I smiled to myself. I liked to think of all the slippings-in and out that might have occurred through that convenient little exit.

'Here we are,' I said, driving into the courtyard.

The beginnings of Chimneys went back to Elizabethan times when a wealthy and perhaps titled family decided to have a small hunting lodge in which to eat and rest after a tiring day's hunting over the North Downs, or in which to spend a month in the country away from London's pollution or plague.

Instead of the usual timbered Tudor style, they built a cosy tile-hung, double fronted lodge with four angular bay windows and a great central chimney.

The rooms were of unusually pleasant proportions; the ceilings ranged from low, black beams to delicate, high, scrolled plasterwork; every room had a wealth of oak joinery and panelling; a wide oak staircase was lightened by an eight-foot, coloured glass window with a golden winged horse and the inscription *confido conquiesco*; then the staircase narrowed, twisting and turning its way up into a warren of little rooms in the roof.

The gem of the lodge was an original hand-painted stained glass window set into an internal wall. It did not belong to any room so one could only guess where it might

114

have been in the original structure. Now it was part of the hall and the centre panel opened out on to the modern kitchen with washing machine and working tops, a far different view from the rolling Surrey hills it must once have overlooked.

The window was nearly four feet square, the upper three panels half the size of the lower three. Each had an exquisitely hand-painted scene – an Elizabethan huntsman, in velvet coat and plumed hat, seated on a heavy-chested, pawing horse; a demurely-dressed woman offered a jug of refreshment to a seated rider; another woman waited alone with a small spaniel at her feet – the painting was delicate and fine, the colours still as fresh as if they had been painted yesterday.

Each scene was set into small rectangular amber panes, each glowing with captured sunlight; then round the outside of each of the six panes was a row of clear bottle-top shaped glass, the blunt broken-off stalk of each round piece of glass now worn smooth and harmless by time. I could pass my hand over the entire structure without fear of a scratch or a nick.

'Oh, Mummy, it all looks like necklaces,' Jenny had said, the first time she had seen the window. 'So pretty, like big glass necklaces for horses or cows.'

She ran straight to the window as we let ourselves into the oak-beamed hall.

'It's still here,' she cried, laying her cheek momentarily against the cold glass. 'Oh, Mummy, I love it . . .'

'Of course it's still here,' I said, carrying in our cases and a basket of shopping. Aunt Polly would probably have left a full refrigerator but then she might have turned it off in the flurry of her departure to the States.

At some point in time the original kitchen and outhouses had been pulled down to make way for an elegant high-ceilinged Regency extension to the south of the lodge. The thirty-foot-long drawing-room had a high, wood-panelled ceiling, square lattice-paned windows with cosy window-seats and a massive fireplace to take huge Surrey logs. The long bedroom above had another such fireplace to take off the chill. Other additions were three chimneys and a timbered bell tower with a sweet sounding brass bell to summon wanderers to their meals or remind them that dusk was imminent and it was no longer safe to roam the Surrey lanes.

Much later a Victorian family took over the house, seeking the unsullied country air for their growing family of children. On the other side of the hunting lodge they built another extension in mock Gothic, adding the necessary enormous kitchen, a large, square, tiled dining hall with the five angels of war represented on one set of stained glass windows and the five angels of peace on another. The doors had gothic arches and carved over the stone fireplace was the motto *Virtute et fide vinco* – 'By virtue and faith I win'. With all those angels, such an awesome inscription and a bell to summon them to church, I felt the Victorian family must have been models of propriety. And they added two more chimneys.

When Aunt Polly found the house it had been owned by two sisters for years. They had lived in a couple of rooms and the rest were shut up and neglected. A builder wanted to pull it down, already having parcelled off most of the extensive grounds for a modern housing estate.

However, he had reckoned without Aunt Polly. She had lovingly restored the place, modernised the kitchen and bathrooms, put in central heating, and removed various monstrous 'improvements' so that each part of the house was as near to the original as possible.

'Don't tell me it's too big for me,' Aunt Polly said defiantly whenever she caught that look in someone's eye. 'They won't get me to move. So they needn't even try. I like space. I couldn't live in a pokey place.'

Our North London flat was certainly a pokey place by comparison and another reason why Aunt Polly's invitation had been so welcome.

'I want you to look after all my plants while I'm away,' she said over the telephone. 'I could get someone from the village to come in, but they might forget. And I've one or two rather delicate specimens.'

I guessed that might be an understatement. It was. The conservatory was a semi-jungle. I could see I was going to spend half my time indoor gardening.

Jenny immediately threw off all lingering effects of measles and took to the woods. From the kitchen window I could keep track of her bright red anorak as she ran and skipped, exploring the walled garden and the wild land beyond.

'Aunt Polly's got the sweetest little cat,' said Jenny, bursting into the kitchen, her cheeks rosy from running.

'I didn't know Aunt Polly had a cat,' I said. 'She didn't mention it to me. Only her plants . . . '

'I expect she forgot because she's getting old,' said Jenny, well aware of my poor memory. 'But we will look after her, won't we, Mummy?'

'Of course we will. I'll buy some cat food when we go into the village.'

'Can I go and play with Mopsie until tea is ready?'

'Mopsie? Is that what you are going to call her? What a funny name!'

But Jenny was quite firm about it. 'Oh no, she likes the name. When I told her, she looked pleased. She looks just like she's made of tinsel, Mummy. All Christmassy.'

I had to laugh. 'A tinsel cat?'

'She's so pretty, almost white but sort of tipped with red, like tinsel. And she had lovely turquoise eyes.'

Jenny did not play outside for long as the November evening darkened suddenly, and she came scurrying indoors for hot crumpets toasted in front of the fire, smothered with butter that dripped between her fingers. She sat in front of the log fire, licking her fingers, mesmerised by the flickering shadows cast by the flames. She looked better already. I felt some of the tension ease out of my neck and shoulders – I was always so frightened when she was ill. I could not bear to lose her as well.

It seemed a bit ridiculous standing outside calling 'Mopsie' so I compromised with the universally-understood 'Puss . . . puss,' wondering if the cat missed the warmth of Aunt Polly's fireside and the old lady's flow of chatter. The cat did not come. Perhaps she had a hideaway in the unused stables or the garages.

But obviously the cat knew some secret way in and out of the house because most nights she slept on Jenny's bed.

'She's lovely and warm,' said Jenny. 'I can feel her weight. Then if I wake up, I can hear her purring.'

The wind seemed to drive Mopsie wild. I could hear Jenny laughing as she chased after the cat all over the house.

'Mopsie? Where are you now?' Jenny scampered up the narrow staircase to the attic bedrooms. 'Are you polishing the floor with your tail, Mopsie? Whoops! Off we go again . . .'

Jenny came flying into the kitchen and went straight to the tap for a drink of water. 'Oh, Mopsie's been so funny this morning! I think she was chasing the wind! Sliding and leaping all over the place. Eventually she jumped on to a window seat and I had to let her out. She danced away across the lawn, playing with the leaves, her fur all sparkling.'

'I know,' I nodded. 'The wind does something to some cats. Perhaps it affects their acute hearing.'

Mopsie never came into the kitchen for anything to eat. The catfood in the dish went stale and I had to throw it away. Nor did she touch any of the milk I put down.

'She hunts,' explained Jenny. 'She catches all her own food. And she drinks water. I've seen her lapping at a little puddle.'

So I gave up worrying about feeding her. Cats can always look after themselves and this one seemed to have adopted a more nomadic life while her mistress was away.

'Mummy, she's sitting on the stairs looking just like one of those big china cats. Come on, Mopsie, let's go and explore . . .'

I heard the back door close as the pair of them went out. Mopsie kept out of my way. Perhaps she did not trust strange adults. Perhaps she only liked children and mildly eccentric old ladies.

I spoke to Dr Stuart on the telephone and he agreed that Jenny did not need her prescription renewed. Her appetite had returned and she was once again the energetic little girl she had been before the measles. In fact I wished she would spend more time with her books, but she seemed so happy chasing about the garden and woods that I let her be.

'Don't worry,' said Dr Stuart. 'She's an intelligent child. She'll soon catch up.'

'I wish I shared your confidence,' I said. 'It's these eleven-plus exams. It's not right that children so young should be put under such pressure.'

'Then don't put on the pressure,' he said. 'Jenny will find her own level.'

But every evening I made sure that Jenny did spend some time reading her school books and writing some of the exercises which her teacher had set. While she worked quietly in front of the fire, I sewed or knitted, making new clothes for Jenny's return to school. We always sat in the Elizabethan room for it was smaller to heat, and we both loved the pretty, ornate ceiling. When my eyes were tired from sewing it was so restful to gaze at the delicate roses and sprays of wild blackberries with which those craftsmen had decorated the ceiling so long ago.

Jenny let out a long, exaggerated sigh as she chewed the end of her pencil.

'I'm not surprised you're finding it difficult,' I said a little primly. 'You spend all day playing when you should be working.'

Jenny snuggled back against my knees. I pushed my finger through her silky hair. How lucky I was to have this precious child.

'But we've had such a lovely day,' she yawned. 'Mopsie and I found a frog. It really made me jump, but Mopsie wasn't frightened at all. She's not frightened of anything.'

I smiled and gave her a little push. 'You obviously don't intend to do any more work, young monkey. You'd better go and have your bath.'

I opened the heavy velvet curtains and sat in a deep leather armchair by the window, watching the ferocious wind whipping the last of the garden leaves in the semi-darkness. The withered leaves flattened themselves against the little panes of glass, only to be whisked away by the next gust. I switched off the table lamp, enjoying the leaping shadows from the fireplace.

Something brushed my leg and I looked down. A beautiful pale cream, almost white cat was padding silently across the carpet. The fur on her head, back and tail was delicately tipped with red, the colour of a cameo. As she moved the fur rippled and sparkled in the firelight, catching the glow, yet the light shone through the fine furry coat making her beauty almost ethereal. The cat turned and looked at me. She had the strangest eyes, almost emerald or blue-green, a kind of luminous turquoise. She had an air of quiet dignity, an expression of sweet repose. I could understand why Jenny loved her.

'Why, hello Mopsie,' I said, for it could only be her. 'So we meet at last. Will you come and say hello to me?'

I held out my hand and moved forward to stroke the cat or perhaps just to see if she would let me touch her. At the very instant I moved there was a fearful crash and the window in front of which I had been sitting shattered into a thousand pieces. Long slivers of glass pierced the chair, the arrow-like shafts slicing through the leather.

A huge branch swayed against the window, brittle grey branches poking through the lattice. The wind had torn a limb from the dead elm at the far wall and hurled it against the window.

I knelt on the floor, shaking, as the glass settled with twinkling fairy-like sounds. I broke out into a clammy sweat. I could have been cut to ribbons. If I had not moved towards the cat, the glass would have torn through my flesh as swiftly as it had ripped the leather of the chair.

Mopsie had vanished, frightened probably by the noise of the falling glass.

When I collected my senses, I put on some kitchen gloves, fetched a dustpan and brush and began clearing up the glass. It took a long time. I searched the carpet thoroughly for fragments which might injure the cat's paws. Aunt Polly had mentioned the dead elm; some tree-loppers were due to come and take it down. It had stood like a stark grey skeleton for over a year. I dragged the chair back into an alcove; it would have to be re-covered.

Jenny came down in her dressing-gown, her face pink from her bath. 'Whatever happened?' she asked, her eyes round. 'I heard the most awful crash.'

'A branch of the dead elm crashed against the window. Don't come in here without any slippers on. I have cleared it up but it's so easy to miss a little piece of glass. It gets everywhere, so be careful, won't you? By the way, I saw Mopsie.'

'Gosh, what a mess.' Jenny seemed more interested in the broken window. 'Oh, did you?'

'She's a very pretty cat.'

'I told you she was. Can I have some milk and biscuits? I've had my bath and I've washed and dried my hair.'

'All right, but have it in bed. I think it would be better if we did not use this room until I've had a chance to clear up again in daylight.' I drew the curtains across the broken window and dampened down the fire.

Before I went to bed I searched the house for Mopsie, but she had gone out her own secret way, and as I closed the front door I thought I saw a shadow streak through the distant trees.

Andrew Stuart came down the following weekend and we all went on a long, muddy trudge along the ridge of the hills. He seemed quite different in old corduroys, a thick jersey under his anorak and a tweed cap pulled down against the stinging rain. He was delighted by Jenny's recovery. She had more energy than either of us and covered twice the ground, dashing off at tangents to explore. We walked more steadily, discovering things that we liked talking about.

'I thought you would be bringing a wife and a car full of kids,' I said, as we turned for home. 'I've made a mountain of rock cakes.'

We laughed at my silly joke and he said; 'I've never had time to meet anyone. A GP's social round is somewhat limited, unless you happen to fall for a nurse. And I didn't.'

He was standing in the hallway taking off his muddy boots when he noticed the tall stained glass window, the coloured glass lighting up the opposite wall with a kaleidoscope of pastel pinks and greens.

'*Confido conquiesco,*' he said, reading the inscription

under the winged horse. 'My Latin is a bit rusty but I think that means "I believe in being still . . . in taking rest, in repose, in quiet. I believe firmly . . ." ' he went on, almost to himself.

His words found a response in myself. I had seemed so much more contented these past few days, more relaxed, as if the long, heavy burden of grief I had put upon myself was beginning to ease. Perhaps my own miraculous escape from injury and disfigurement had something to do with it.

'Take care of yourself,' said Andrew, touching my hand. The touch was half professional, and half something quite different.

Aunt Polly returned from America with a Florida tan and armfuls of gift-wrapped surprises for us. Everything over there was 'wonderful' and she was full of plans for returning next autumn.

'And sometime I'll take you with me, young lady,' she said, pulling Jenny to her. 'If you are a good girl with your school work and pass all your O-levels and B-levels, or whatever they call them these days.'

'She won't do that here,' I said drily. 'Her concentration has only been a few degrees above nil. She has spent all her time playing with your cat.'

Aunt Polly was taking off her hat and fluffing out her tinted hair. She paused before she answered. 'Oh?'

'I'm afraid we didn't know her real name, so we've been calling her Mopsie,' I went on.

'One name's as good as another,' said Aunt Polly enigmatically.

When it was time for us to go and the car was packed up with our luggage and a bunch of late chrysanthemums from the garden Jenny detached herself from us and wandered away. For a moment she stood by the little door in the wall as if she were listening.

'I'm just going to say goodbye to Mopsie,' she said. There was a little quiver in her voice and I ached for her. She was too young to begin sad partings.

She ran off and we saw her disappear into the trees.

'My dear, before you go, I must tell you something.' Aunt Polly's tone was troubled. 'I don't have a cat.'

I didn't understand. 'Oh yes, you have,' I said.

'The only cat in this house is the one in the hall,' she said strangely. I followed her back into the house. We were in the Elizabethan hunting lodge, the oldest part, where the unusual stained glass window now opened out on to the modern kitchen area. I had passed it a hundred times a day, always with a glance of admiration for its glowing brilliance.

'Look carefully at the hunting scene,' said Aunt Polly. It was the largest of the painted scenes, showing the hunt in full flight, a leaping deer followed by sturdy horses and lean hounds caught in mid-bark.

Aunt Polly drew my gaze to the lower left-hand corner of the scene where a small crack had been repaired with leading. Watching the huntsmen from a safe and secret hiding-place was a creamy, almost white cat painted with the finest streaks of red tipping its fur; a cat with eyes the colour of bright turquoise. She glowed in the painting, like a cameo.

I said nothing. What could I say? I remembered the way Jenny had embraced the glass on our arrival. I touched the cold painting lightly with the tips of my fingers. I was trying to say thank you to Mopsie.

Some weeks later Andrew brought Jenny a kitten. She had been abandoned in a dustbin by some youths. She was a daft little thing – a tabby with pretty silver streaks. Jenny called her Moppety.

When the wind blew Moppety went wild. She would dash all over the flat, her small paws skating on the polished floors sending mats a-flying, curtains flapping. I could hear Jenny laughing as she scrambled after her kitten.

Moppety would eventually scratch at a window to be let out on to the balcony. Then, with one carefree glance back, she would dance away, chasing the scurrying dust, knocking over flower pots, her feathery tail held high like a sparkling plume.

# A Family Affair

It was a confusing family at first sight. There was the father, the mother and their son, and the mother's sister. The two sisters originally lived together; the father and son had at one time lived together. But now, through force of circumstances, the whole family was under one roof.

The two sisters were inseparable. They sat close together at the top of the stairs like book-ends, or curled up under a table, lovingly entwined so that it was hard to tell who was who. If one were ill, they both had to be taken to the vet. If one wanted to go out into the garden, they both went out. It was the same with coming in.

They were a family of Colourpoints. Beautiful, exotic creatures of extravagant Persian fluff, with the delicate colouring of a Siamese, intelligent minds and gentle ways.

Cy, the father, was a massive Blue Colourpoint. But he was not a blue cat, he was a grey cat. He had an unmistakably masculine, butch face and a withdrawn nature. He did not make friends easily, but preferred to watch and contemplate. No one ventured to cuddle him. Any such familiarity would have been an offence to his patriarchal dignity. And he was huge, an enormous platter of a cat who could overwhelm any rash admiration by slow suffocation.

His mate, Chien, a Seal Colourpoint, was a pale brown beauty; she was the Vivien Leigh of the family. Delicate, well-bred, utterly enchanting . . . and yet, beneath all that beauty lurked an anatomical abnormality: her birth canal was too narrow, and her kittens did not survive. She bore one dead one after another, so Eleanor had her spayed. Chien wore her newly enforced sterility with a gentle sadness.

Fu, the only one of her kittens to survive, was a rich Chocolate Colourpoint – a male cat of outstanding handsomeness, loving and curious, an open generous nature and an air of courage. He was like a young knight, fearless and ready for life, knowing that one day he would sire a great strain of champions. But meanwhile there was the world to enjoy and explore . . .

The odd one out was Cheynne (pronounced Shay-knee), the sister-in-law of Cy, sister of Chien, aunt of Fu. She was the odd one out in every way, but most particularly in her colouring. She was that rare creature, a Tortie Colourpoint. Nature had got her brushes in a twist when dabbing the paint on Cheynne. Her face was unbelievable. At first the blotches of colour seemed to obscure all features. But gradually the patches of black, brown, red, tan and white took on shape and meaning, and a sweet, enigmatic face emerged from the blobs.

She behaved somewhat like a maiden aunt, too. She rarely approached her brother-in-law, thinking that such fraternisation might be unseemly. She occasionally crossed the path of her adventurous nephew, remembering that the family tie needed to be knotted at times. But she preferred to spend her days clinging to her sister's side like a mottled shadow, as if waiting for some of her sister's beauty to transfer itself to her.

Now that all four cats were living together it was perfect for them, confusing for visitors and expensive for Eleanor. When Cy and Fu's original owner had to go abroad, it had seemed a practical solution of what to do with the cats. Also, Eleanor hoped that the presence of Chien's husband and son would bring the young mother out of her post-operation blues.

But Cy made no move towards his wife or anyone else. He sat remotely, usually on a high point, watching the world, like some vast grey bolster. He did not even come for his food when Eleanor put it down, but waited until she had retired from the kitchen before heaving himself from aloft and stalking across the floor.

Fu was the perfect guest, amusing and friendly, making himself at home, being deferential to his mother and his aunt. Eleanor's large garden was a delight and when it snowed he leaped out, playing with the snowflakes and tumbling about in drifts like a child.

The cats were, in many ways, like her children. Eleanor had long passed the age when most of her friends had married. She thought quite calmly that it was unlikely she would ever marry now, and it did not worry her. Her parents had left her a house to live in, and in fact her life held many compensations. She could please herself, whatever she wanted to do. She could cook, or not cook. She never had to wash dirty socks, pants or shirts. She never had to clean up after muddy manly feet. And apart from her responsibility towards the cats, she could come and go as she pleased. It was a freedom she would not give up lightly . . . .

And it was just as well she did not have a husband to look after when it took over half an hour every day to groom the cats. Cy stood, as rigid as a sentry on duty, enduring her administrations stoically. Fu thought it was an extension of playtime and the brush was the prize. Chien and Cheynne behaved exquisitely as if esconced in an expensive beauty salon.

When it was time for Chien's stitches to come out, Eleanor put the two sisters in their cat box on to the front passenger seat in the car. The box was not really big enough for two cats but they were used to this mode of travel and curled round each other, noses poking through the fluff for air.

Eleanor thought Chien was still off-colour so she drove extra carefully to cause the least distress to her passengers. It worried her that Chien was unwell. She remembered how Chien's eyes had tried to tell her something during the long, difficult birth of her last dead kittens. Eleanor had felt so helpless. Now, at least, the cat would not have to go through that agony again.

There were so many ruts in the road – the council seemed

to be forever digging it up for one reason or another. Eleanor slowed down as she saw new roadworks ahead and a red light halting her lane of traffic.

When the light turned to green, everything else moved except Eleanor. Her car stalled. Again and again she tried to bring the engine to life, but it only turned over with a dull whine.

'Hell,' she said, and got out of the car to see what was the trouble.

'I sympathise profoundly. An embarrasing situation for the liberated female drivers of today, unless, of course, you really do know what goes on inside that car bonnet?'

Eleanor turned to the speaker. She met the granite-grey eyes of the most attractive man she had seen for years. He was sitting at the wheel of a dark E-type Jaguar, regarding her with amusement, an aura of success on his well-built shoulders as surely as if he had his bank balance clocking up on the veneered dashboard.

'I must confess, I don't. I was hopefully going through the motions. There might be a loose wire or something . . .'

'What innocence! Let me have a look,' he said. He swung his car off the road and climbed out without opening the door. He poked around the innards of Eleanor's old Hillman, tried the ignition again, then got out of the driver's seat, wiping his hands on a spotless silk hand-kerchief.

'You've run out of petrol,' he said.

'Hell,' said Eleanor again.

'Can I telephone your husband for you? Perhaps he could come and collect you?'

'No husband,' said Eleanor. 'Don't worry, I can manage.' She lifted the cat box out of the car and locked the doors.

'What are you going to do?' he asked.

'Walk,' she said. 'I'll come back later with a can of petrol. Thank you for your help.'

'Have you got far to go?'

'It's about a mile and a half.'

'Hop in. I'll take you. It's no trouble. Let me put your

box in the boot.'

'How kind, thank you. But I'll keep this on my knee – it's a cat box.'

She felt the man beside her almost stifle a shudder. There was a slight pause as he concentrated on moving the low car out into the traffic.

'You'll forgive me if I don't go into raptures and say nice pussy,' said the man with some apprehension. 'But I suffer from ailurophobia – a fear of cats – like the great Napoleon.'

'Perhaps I'd better get out,' said Eleanor. 'I have two cats with me.'

'I shall be all right,' he said, looking straight ahead, 'as long as I don't hear them, see them or smell 'em.'

'They don't smell,' said Eleanor quickly.

'Right, then let's talk about something else.' He started telling Eleanor about himself, and she wondered how anyone could be afraid of cats. Was it their fur that set teeth on edge? Or the stealthy way they walked, or the unfathomable inscrutability of their eyes? She could not ask him.

His name was Bruce Levant. He worked with a record publishing company and travelled extensively promoting new groups. It all sounded very glamorous, moving in a circle of pop stars, flying to New York and Las Vegas, golden and platinum discs, million dollar sales . . . a far cry from teaching in a girls' private school and living in the same house all her life with four Colourpoint cats.

A week later Eleanor was shooing the four cats into her bedroom. Cy was reluctant to leave his perch on the dresser and she had to carry him, heavyweight that he was, upstairs.

'I'm very sorry,' she said, slightly out of breath. 'I know you think this is undignified but I've got a visitor coming. And although he's very nice in every way, he just doesn't take to cats.' They regarded her with offended eyes. Chien, who had still not fully recovered her spirits, looked both pained and hurt. Fu decided to make the best of a poor show and jumped on Eleanor's bed with a look of defiance.

'Okay,' said Eleanor, giving in. 'You can go on my bed, just this once. But don't make a habit of it.'

They would not have done, except that Bruce began to make a habit of visiting Eleanor. She simply could not understand it. She was six years older than him. He was devastatingly attractive, whereas she . . . well, she had always thought of herself as very ordinary, although now she noticed a glow in her cheeks, a sparkle in her eyes. She lightened the shade of her hair with a minky-coloured tint, darkened her long pale lashes with mascara. And she bought some new clothes, willowy and thin, all quite useless for school.

'Because you are different,' said Bruce, when she asked him why he wanted to see her again. 'You are so refreshing. All these pop singers, punk stars, groupies . . . my dear, if only you could see yourself beside them. Then you would know why I am falling in love with you.'

Eleanor's heart lurched. She could hear her own heartbeats. It was all too soon . . . and wonderful. She was afraid to let herself fall in love. After all these years? How could she really believe that this was happening, and with someone like Bruce?

'Stop pretending you're a little mouse,' he teased. 'Have a look in the mirror. Has no one ever told you that your eyes are the colour of pansies? So blue and velvety, and so shy and demure.'

'I'd better go and make some coffee,' said Eleanor briskly, 'before you make any more silly remarks.'

'Fine, I'm all for some coffee,' he chuckled. He turned the lights down and leafed through her records for some soft music. 'But I warn you, I'm about to make a lot of silly remarks . . .'

Later that evening, much later, as she heard the low throb of Bruce's car driving away, Eleanor drifted up to her bedroom and found all four cats curled up on her bed in a great heap. They blinked at the sudden light and Chien sneezed.

She sat on the edge of the bed, stroking them absent-mindedly in a circular movement that encompassed all four.

'What on earth am I going to do?' she asked them. 'He can't live with you, and I think I can't live without him.'

But it was a problem she happily shelved. The girls at school whispered among themselves, 'Miss is in love!' giggling when she came into the classroom. Bruce collected her from school the Friday afternoon before half-term, and she could sense the ripple of admiration and amazement as the girls took in his good looks and expensive car.

'Hello darling,' said Bruce, kissing her lightly as she got into the car. 'You look pretty. I've missed you so much.'

'Since yesterday?' she laughed softly to herself.

'It's seemed like an eternity, sweetheart.'

They planned to drive down by the river and eat in a small restaurant whose grounds sloped to the willowy water's edge. It was a picturesque setting and Eleanor was looking forward to some peace after her hectic day, and a romantic meal with Bruce.

He started the car and drove slowly out of the school grounds. 'Darling, I've some good news and some bad news. Which do you want first?'

'The bad news.'

'I'm sorry, but I have to break this date. Something really important has come up. There's a new Brazilian group who are going to be worth millions this time next year, and a certain American company are all set to sign them up. Well, I'm going to get to them first with an offer they can't refuse. I'm booked to fly to Rio tonight.'

'That's not such bad news,' said Eleanor, quickly hiding her disappointment. 'It's your job. I understand. Just take me home and I'll have a peaceful evening watching television and thinking of you flying to the sun. I'm quite envious . . .'

'Then you'll like the good news,' he said, quietly serious. 'When I return, we're going to get married. No more single trips. Next time I go abroad, you're coming with me.'

Eleanor's breath almost stopped at the suddenness of his proposal. He grinned and caught her hand.

'We can live in my flat or your house. Either would suit me – it's your choice. I travel about such a lot, I just need a base. And wherever you are is going to be my base.'

'Oh Bruce . . . ' Eleanor was lost for words. She tried not to think of her cats at that moment; she wanted to savour the joy and delight of knowing that Bruce wanted to marry her. And she need not move from her home. He was being so kind, not asking her to completely change her life-style. But if she married him, the cats would have to go . . . all four of them.

As he kissed her goodbye, she felt the stirring passion in his powerful arms. 'Not long, darling . . . ' he murmured.

Then he pulled away from her and slapped his hand against his breast-pocket. 'Oh God, I've forgotten my wallet!' He made a frantic search through his pockets. 'I went home and changed into this lightweight suit. Hell, I've left everything in my other suit . . . air ticket, travellers cheques, credit cards, currency. How much time have I got? I'll just make it back to my flat if I put my foot down. Sorry, darling, I must hurry if I'm going to catch that flight.'

He kissed her hastily. In that split second Eleanor saw his car, a crumpled, tangled wreckage on the hard shoulder of the motorway, its wheels spinning madly in the air. She saw rivulets of blood escaping through the shattered glass.

'For goodness sake, don't panic,' she said quietly. 'Come inside and I'll lend you the money.'

She herded the surprised cats into the kitchen, and Bruce followed her to the sitting room.

'Are you sure?' he asked. 'It's a lot of money. But it would be a great help. I hate cutting it fine, and I must get that flight. Tomorrow would be too late and the contract really is worth a fortune.'

'Of course you are going to make the flight,' said Eleanor. 'All in one piece.' She got her chequebook out of her desk. 'Now, how much will you need?'

'The plane ticket to Rio is £2,013. I'll be able to get a refund on the other one when I get back.'

'£2,013?'

'First class return, darling. I always travel first class. I need the leg room.'

'And your other expenses?'

'A couple of nights in a hotel, taxis, entertaining . . . say, another eight or nine hundred if you can manage it. The bank at the airport is open twenty-four hours a day. With your cheque to pay in, they'll let me have travellers cheques to the same amount and I'll use them to buy a new ticket. It's simple.'

'Are you sure?' Eleanor asked, writing the figures with a steady hand. 'I'll make it a round £3,000. A little extra for emergencies . . .'

'Darling, you're marvellous. You don't know how much I appreciate this.' His smile was warm and reassuring.

Eleanor felt almost married already as she handed him the cheque. There was no need for him to know that it would take all her savings. Anyway, it was only for a short time. He would pay her back as soon as he returned. She clung to him as he made to go.

When he had gone the house was very quiet. The four cats sat in the kitchen, not resentful but looking at her with resignation. Fu rubbed round her ankles, being the most forgiving of the four. She fondled his neck, feeling a lump of matted fur that reminded her that she had forgotten to groom them again. At least she could do that this evening. Cheynne jumped on the draining board, perking her head to one side, asking for a drink.

'My dear pussycats,' said Eleanor uncertainly as she fetched clean bowls and filled them with milk and water. 'What am I going to do about you? You are all so helpless. You depend on me, don't you? And you trust me . . .'

Eleanor could not sleep that night. She twisted and turned, thinking of Bruce flying high in the clouds, vulnerable in that tiny metal capsule. She heard one of the cats sneezing downstairs, and eventually, near dawn, she gave up trying to sleep and went down into the kitchen to heat some milk.

It was Chien. She was crouching in a dark corner, away from the other cats, sneezing, her eyes and nose running, an air of wearied despair in her trembling body. Eleanor was appalled by the change in her beautiful cat. She knew she had to act fast – cat flu could kill in a few hours. She would have to call the vet for some immediate treatment with antibiotics.

Quickly and gently she moved the sick cat into a box with clean blankets and placed it by the sitting-room fire. She tried to tempt the cat to drink, but Chien only hung her head over the bowl, uninterested.

'I'm sorry to call you out so early, but it's Chien,' said Eleanor on the telephone. 'I think she has flu.'

'I'll come right away,' said Arthur Dawes, the vet. He knew her cats well, and was a kindly man.

'You were right to call me,' he said later, washing his hands in the kitchen sink. 'Pneumonitis does respond to early treatment. But the recovery can be long and slow. I hope you feel up to nursing a sick cat – it's a time-consuming job if you are going to save her.'

'I don't mind that . . . but, well, I was going to have to think about finding new homes for all my cats,' said Eleanor in a small voice. 'For personal reasons.' She hid her face and bent to stroke Chien very lightly on the fore-head. The cat was still very feverish.

'Completely out of the question at the moment, of course,' said the vet, packing away his equipment. 'And pretty dubious in the future, I should think. These cats are a family. You can't break them up. Chien would certainly die if you separated her from her sister. She would just give up. Cheynne too. By the way, have you ever thought of breeding from the Tortie? She's so unusual . . . ?'

As he was leaving, he gave her instructions for the next few hours. 'I want you to keep giving Chien a small quantity of glucose dissolved in warm water – it'll help to keep her going till the antibiotics take effect. I'll leave this medicine dropper with you, and I'll call round again later this morning after surgery.'

'You're very kind,' said Eleanor unsteadily.

'She's worth it. She's a lovely cat.'

By evening the fever was abating, but Chien was still very sick. Eleanor had her work cut out keeping her isolated from the other cats, who tried every means of slipping into the sitting room. Cheynne was desolate without her sister, searching restlessly through the house for her.

133

Eleanor lay back in a chair, exhausted by the long day, listening to Chien's laboured breathing. Her thoughts were in a turmoil. She could not decide what to do. As the light crept away, she switched on a low table lamp so as not to disturb Chien, and took a writing pad from the desk.

'My dear Bruce,' she wrote. 'This is the hardest letter I have ever had to write. Please try to understand how I feel, and that I have a responsibility which I took on and cannot give away just like an unwanted parcel. I know I am putting this badly . . .'

When the letter was finished, she put it in an envelope and left it in the hall. She did not have his full address. She knew he lived in a flat in the Barbican, but she did not have the number. She wanted to post it so that it would be there on his return from Brazil.

She refilled the medicine dropper with glucose water and fed it to Chien through the side of the cat's mouth. Drop by drop the liquid went in. Chien's eyes followed Eleanor's movements. She knew that Eleanor was saving her life. She lay on her side on the bed of blankets, wheezing, too weak to lift her head.

Later, as Chien's breathing got easier, Eleanor fell asleep curled up in a chair. Several times she woke to wipe away the mucus from the cat's nose and to feed her more sugary water.

Cheynne was awake too, padding around the kitchen. Eleanor was terrified that the other cats might develop the flu even though the vet had inoculated them – there were so many forms of the virus that it was difficult to give the correct vaccine.

Eleanor changed her shoes yet again, washed her hands, and went through to comfort the distressed Tortie. 'She's getting better,' she murmured, stroking the worried little face. 'You'll be able to see her soon.'

By Monday morning, Chien was definitely improving – her high temperature was coming down and she lapped a drop of milk. Eleanor was stiff and tired. She eased her neck and promised herself a hot bath after she had posted the letter.

She telephoned the renting office at the Barbican and

asked them to look up the number of Bruce's flat. The girl returned to the telephone some minutes later.

'I'm sorry but we don't have a tenant of that name. Perhaps it's some other block of flats.'

'I felt sure he said the Barbican,' said Eleanor, puzzled.

'Maybe he shares, and the flat is in another name.'

'That's probably the answer. Thank you. I'll contact his firm and get the number from them.'

Eleanor looked up the number of the record company and dialled it. The switchboard operator misunderstood her at first.

'Mr Leander? One moment please and I'll put you through to Mr Leander.'

'No, no. You've got the wrong name. Mr Lefant. Mr Bruce Lefant. I want to speak to someone who can give me Mr Lefant's home address.'

'I'll put you through to Personnel. One moment please.'

Personnel were mystified. There was no Bruce Lefant on their staff. Never had been. If she insisted they would check with Contracts. Rio? No, no one was representing them in Rio. Sorry, but they did not know of any Brazilian group which had a chance of making the British charts, let alone the American. . . someone must be pulling her leg.

Eleanor put down the telephone. Her hand was shaking. It was no joke. No joke at all. She picked up her letter and tore it into confetti. She knew that there was no need to send any letter. She would not be seeing Bruce again.

She felt physically sick. She wanted to crawl away and hide somewhere. The hurt was a stunning pain that made her want to die, to feel nothing any more.

She went through to the kitchen in a daze, not really knowing where she was or what she was doing. Mechanically she went through the motions of filling the kettle and putting it on the gas stove. Then she slid down on to the floor and wept.

Cy had been watching her from the top dresser shelf. Cy, the father cat, the big Blue Colourpoint who was really grey, who gave no concessions to anyone, who kept himself to himself.

Cheynne sat close by the sitting room door, her pretty

135

patched face still pleading for one glimpse of her sister. Fu was on the windowsill, watching a bee buzzing among the creeper outside. He longed to be let out to play, but he knew this was not the moment to ask.

Eleanor cried until she thought there could be no more tears left inside her. She searched her pockets for a handkerchief.

Silently the big Cy leaped down from the dresser and padded over to where Eleanor sat on the floor. She looked at him in surprise through blurred eyes. He had never come to her before.

Quite slowly, as if not totally sure of his welcome, he climbed on to her lap, a huge, heavy, warm, wonderful creature offering the only comfort he knew.

It was then that Eleanor realised she still had time to telephone her bank and stop the cheque. As the handsome Bruce had not been on his way to Rio, he would not have gone to the airport. He would be paying that cheque into his account this morning.

Eleanor sighed. He had made a mistake in underestimating her devotion to her family. Devotion which had made her write a letter.

But she did not rush to the telephone. She had to talk to big Cy for a few moments, to get to know him, to make the first overtures of friendship.

# Felis Domesticus Surrentum

From the age of five Elisabeth Fiorentino had been singing.
The daugher of an English schoolteacher and an Italian
cellist, singing came as naturally to her as breathing and she
was given every encouragement. As the years went by she
progressed from 'Ding, dong, pussy's in the well' to 'The
Sound of Music', till eventually she was studying Mozart at
the Guildhall School of Music and famous arias floated
from the open windows of her bedroom, soaring to the
treetops like birdsong.

The world of music recognised her talent as her voice
grew more beautiful, and she travelled extensively on singing engagements. But Elisabeth found that the dedicated
life of an opera singer was a lonely one. She desperately
needed company other than that of other professional
singers or her business manager. Men seemed almost afraid
of her – or of the effortless sounds that came from her
throat, as if she were not quite human.

The few men who did enter her life did not stay long once
they discovered how many hours went into the perfecting
of each note and phrase. They could not compete with her
discipline, nor did they care to take second place to a voice.

So cats became Elisabeth's friends and travelling companions. The first was called simply Fluffy, then, at intervals arrived Fluffy-Two, Fluffy-Three and Fluffy-Four.
They were acquired and christened because of the strict
quarantine laws of great Britain. When Elisabeth first flew

abroad to sing *Tosca* at the Metropolitan Opera House in New York's Lincoln Centre, she took with her a pretty grey and white Persian kitten in a quilted travelling cat box. It was cold in New York with dirty snow piled high on the corners of the streets. But Elisabeth loved the towering skyscrapers and walked the full length of Fifth Avenue with her small friend, learning many things about that brash and bustling city.

But on Elisabeth's eventual return to England, Fluffy had to go into cat kennels at Tunbridge Wells for six months. Lonely and depressed, Elisabeth bought Fluffy-Two, a similarly enchanting kitten. The exercise repeated itself when Elisabeth was booked to sing in Zurich, and again when she went halfway across the world to sing in the butterfly-shaped Sydney Opera House.

She was now accompanied by Fluffy-Four and re-cuperating from an exhausting series of recitals in Italy culminating in a gala performance at La Scala. A doctor warned her not to sing for at least two weeks and she decided to stay at the Hotel Excelsior Vittoria in Sorrento, hoping that the gloriously rugged scenery of the peninsula and the heavenly blue of the sea would restore her jagged nerves and overtired vocal chords.

The fertile plain of Sorrento was a vast terrace above the sheer cliffs that fell into the Bay of Naples, acres of orange and lemon groves, walnut, fig, cherry and pomegranate trees. The villas intruded through the flowering greenery, red-washed, faded pink or white, civilisation encroaching on what nature had intended to be simply a huge garden. There were no beaches – sunbathing platforms stretched out to the sea for the tourists to invade.

Fluffy-Four, or Four, as he was more familiarly called, resented the jolting ride down the long, paved drive from the Piazza Tasso to the entrance of the hotel. It was ignominious to be perched on top of Elisabeth's matching hide luggage and wheeled in on a trolley by a porter. He protested loudly but no one took any notice.

Four could smell aromatic orange and lemon trees and he wanted to be out and exploring. Milan had been so boring. He yawned. Through the slits of his tartan-lined wicker travelling basket (Four detested tartan) he caught tantalising glimpses of trees dripping with orange and yellow globes, of Elisabeth's pastel mink coat swinging from her slender shoulders, of her mane of honey-coloured hair tied back with a silk scarf from Yves St Laurent. He miaowed again to attract her attention to his plight.

Elisabeth turned and took Four's basket off the trolley before her luggage disappeared into the lower depths of the rambling cliff-side hotel. It had once been three imposing villas built a century earlier, relics of another era, each clinging with fortress-like buttresses on impossible sites. Two were painted red, the third was a white palace. Now all three were married into one by somewhat haphazard additions of a Swiss-style chalet and a high, glass foyer and entrance. The foyer looked like a gilded bird cage with enough magnificent potted palms to house a whole aviary of exotic birds.

'I am Elisabeth Fiorentino,' said Elisabeth. 'You have my reservation. And I trust there is no objection to my cat.'

'None at all, Signorina Fiorentino. We are delighted to welcome such a famous singer to our hotel. We have reserved the Caruso room, or you may care to see the Princess Margaret suite? Her Royal Highness stayed here in May 1949.'

'And what about Four?'

'You want to see four rooms?'

'Four is my cat.'

'You have four cats?'

'Four is the name of my cat. He is one cat,' said Elisabeth patiently, knowing she must not raise her voice.

The manager had been trained not to show bewilderment. 'Pets are not allowed in the public rooms or in the restaurant,' he said. 'There will be a charge depending on size.'

'You mean you are going to measure him? From nose to tail, or side to side?'

'Is this a small cat or a large cat?' the manager queried.

'I should say he is a large small cat,' said Elisabeth, suddenly tiring. 'He is a small cat inside a lot of thick fur.'

Each of the villas was a period piece. Marble staircases

with pastel murals, grand master bedrooms, extensive balconies that took in panoramic views of the Bay of Naples, the majestic snow-tipped Vesuvius and the range of Lattari mountains.

The Caruso bedroom was a high-ceilinged confection of ornate gold and white marble, a vast gilt bed, full length brocade curtains billowing in the sea breezes, priceless pieces of furniture. Elisabeth imagined the bill if Four sharpened his claws on the legs of the antique desk and shook her head.

The Princess Margaret room was a corner sun-trap with three big windows opening on to balconies. It was large enough to hold a party in. Elisabeth and Four would be lost among the beautiful furniture, overpowered by the magnificent chandelier, awed by the palatial marble bathroom. Across a hallway that could be shut off was a private sitting room, again furnished with antiques. Elisabeth shook her head. Four yawned. He was used to this. Elisabeth was very particular about rooms.

'Perhaps one of our de luxe suites would be more suitable?' He thought . . . the Fiorentino suite would sound good.

The top floor suite in the white villa was far less overpowering – airy, more modern, with rugs on highly polished floors, a built-in wardrobe with painted flowers on the doors, a vast double bed, a luxurious bathroom across a small hallway, and, best of all, a completely private, walled, corner balcony overflowing with urns of flowers.

Quite nice, thought Four, jumping out of his detested basket and having a delicious stretch. He could smell the sea, fish, flowers and unknown herbs, and a shiver of excitement rippled along his fur.

Elisabeth laid her cheek on his velvety coat. 'I shall get better here,' she told him. 'We will sit in the sun and wander around and be just like other ordinary tourists.'

It sounded perfect to Four, especially sitting in the sun. He began to purr and nudge her chin. He wanted to get going.

But Elisabeth had to unpack first. Four helped. He attacked her fluffy swansdown slippers, hid under a pile of cashmere sweaters, had to fight to the death with a box of tissues. Finally he dragged a cobwebby shawl under a chair and trampled it into a new bed.

Elisabeth went on her knees and tugged at the shawl but his claws were firmly enmeshed in the wool. His eyes glinted with glee. He loved a tussle.

'Now you're being very naughty,' said Elisabeth sternly. It was a clash of wills that was resolved when there was a discreet knock on the door. A waiter had arrived with Four's supper served in special cat dishes, on a tray, and Elisabeth took the opportunity to disappear for her own. Four settled down to demolish flaked fish, freshly caught that morning in the Bay, artistically topped with curls of butter, unaware of the stir his beautiful mistress was making on her arrival in the elegantly-pillared dining room.

Waiters straightened their white jackets; the maître d'hotel immediately gave her the best window seat; diners stopped eating, forks in mid-air; heads swivelled to catch a glimpse. She was wearing a cream silk suit, pale and shimmering, her hair caught up in a loose knot with escaping tendrils, and dangling gold earrings.

Chester Ridgway had no inhibitions. As soon as Elisabeth had eaten and moved into the many-mirrored lounge to order coffee, he strolled over, one hand casually in the pocket of his dark blue velvet jacket. He was a handsome young man, not very tall, with curling brown hair touching his well-shaped ears; his half-closed blue eyes regarding Elisabeth with admiration.

'May I join you for coffee?' he asked, confident of his acceptability.

Elisabeth shook her head.

'But you should not be alone,' he said persuasively. 'A beautiful woman should always be complemented by the rugged contrast of male company.'

Elisabeth sighed faintly. She pointed to the small cigar smoking in his fingers and then to her throat. He apologised immediately.

'Of course, Miss Fiorentino, I should have been more thoughtful. I do apologise.'

Her heart fell. He had recognised her. Now she would

never get rid of him. She smiled distantly and again pointed to her throat, shaking her head in pantomime.

'Ah, I understand. You're resting that exquisite voice of yours. Then you are certainly in dire need of entertaining company,' said Chester, settling himself in the other deep armchair, and signalling to a steward. 'Two more coffees, a Drambuie and a Brandy Alexander. Ladies always like a Brandy Alexander,' he told Elisabeth, a hand sliding automatically into a pocket for his cigar case. 'My name's Chester Ridgway. I daresay you've heard of Ridgway Tiles? My father started the business just after the war. I'm a director, of course. I do a lot of travelling for the firm.'

So it seemed. There was hardly anywhere he had not been. He also knew all the local excursions from Sorrento, and seemed to think it was his mission in life to arrange her stay for her.

Elisabeth listened and sipped her frothy cream drink, wondering how she could politely take herself from this well-meaning but boring young man.

'And, of course, you mustn't miss the magnificent coastal drive to Positano and Amalfi. The views are quite splendid. Perhaps you would allow me to escort you?' he offered, his feeling of confidence growing as he marvelled at her flawless skin and tumbling tawny hair. She was a real catch.

Elisabeth shook her head and smiled politely. 'You are very kind but my husband is arriving tomorrow,' she whispered. She stood up. 'Thank you for the drink. Now I must take my cat for a walk. Good night.'

As an exit line, it was effective, whether it was the husband or the cat that did the trick, but she left Chester staring after her blankly.

The next day Elisabeth and Four set out to explore Sorrento at their leisure. They caused quite a stir. At first the Sorrentine shop-keepers were astonished and amused by the sight of the slight young woman leading a blue-grey cat on a lead. But then Elisabeth's sad brown eyes, almost hidden by her long fringe of honey hair, made each man sigh and long to bring a smile to her face. Four was universally admired by the women and petted by the children. And rightly so. He was a fine and proud Short-hair Blue-Cream Burmese, whose delicately shaded coat was like thick grey velvet. Four looked back at his admirers with large fierce eyes that reflected the elusive golden light of the Sorrentine sky.

Four strained at his lead. He was ecstatic with curiosity. Sorrento was definitely a cat place, and he could hardly contain his high spirits.

Leading from the Piazzo Tasso was the Via S. Cesareo, a narrow alley crowded with open-fronted shops. Glistening fresh fish lay on wet slabs within sniffing distance; goat cheeses swung from doorways; fruit was piled high in casual confusion still twigged with dark green leaves from the local groves.

A tortuous, twisting stone-stepped path led steeply through narrow old houses dating back to the fifteenth and sixteenth centuries, now festooned with twentieth-century washing, jeans, printed vests and drip-dry sheets.

Four's nose told him when they were nearing the Marina Grande, the original fishing harbour still cluttered with brightly painted fishing boats, yards of orange nets being repaired, and ragged children playing on the dark volcanic sand among dead fish, straggling seaweed and washed-up flotsam. Cats roamed in packs. Dozens of them. They glared at Four from under upturned rowing boats. He glared back, unafraid, a low hiss coming from his throat, thoroughly enjoying the sensation. It was a long time since he'd had a good hiss.

The little shore was bustling and noisy, cluttered with vehicles and boats, fishermen smoking and yarning and mending nets, women carrying their shopping and washing on their heads, children squabbling and chasing each other, barefooted and dirty. The closely built, red-roofed houses clung to the hillside, almost crowding out the fishermen's church on the front, cheek by jowl with dim taverns and bars, with hardly a postcard or souvenir in sight.

'The real Sorrento,' said Elisabeth, stepping carefully over the rubbish washed up on the cobbles by the night's rough seas. Four tugged hopefully in the direction of some fish-heads, but Elisabeth had glanced back and caught sight of Chester Ridgway descending down the same stone-stepped path, a suede jacket slung casually over his shoulders. It was no coincidence.

For a moment Elisabeth panicked. She darted along a lane and up some steps, only to find herself in someone's backyard among washing and crates. Another alley led to the landing of a house. Next she found herself facing a blank, sheer cliff face. Marina Grande seemed to be a labyrinth of alleyways leading nowhere. She did not want to go back the way she had come and meet Chester. The one road at the far end was a nightmare of revving mopeds, cars trying to turn, hooters blaring and no pavement. Four would be terrified out of his wits.

They were trapped, and Chester Ridgway was catching them up. He knew she could not escape. Any moment now he would stroll over, ready to pin her down with an invitation, arranging her day, planning her evening for her. At least he could see now that she really did have a cat.

A hefty fisherman's jersey suddenly blocked her way. Its owner side-stepped and started to stride away with purpose, as if he knew where he was going. His face was darkened by the sun, his grey hair roughened up by the wind, longish but well cut. Elisabeth spoke without thinking.

'Please can you help me?' She said it in English.

The man half turned and stopped. He did not look surprised, as if beautiful women were always asking him for help.

'But, of course. . . ' he said, a trace of accent in his voice.

'I'm lost. There are so many blind alleys. It's very confusing and I must get out quickly. Can you show me a back way up to the town?'

'There is the road. . . '

'My cat would be terrified and there's no pavement. Besides, I would be seen.'

Chester Ridgway had seen her. He raised an arm in salute and was rapidly negotiating a route between the drawn up fishing boats, trying not to step on unmentionable debris.

The colour drained from Elisabeth's face. She turned to the stranger, trying to glean his character from his face.

'Please. . . could you pretend to be my husband. . . just for a few moments?' she asked urgently, in a low voice. 'It's very important to me. . .'

It must have been the look of desperation in her eyes, for the stranger calmly took her arm and began to guide her from the harbour front. Chester was only a few yards away.

'Did you enjoy your walk?' the stranger said casually but loud enough for Chester to hear. 'The air is very refreshing. I thought you looked a little pale last night.'

'I was awfully tired,' said Elisabeth, racking her brains for some long-married conversational phrases. 'And I had a headache. But it's gone now. Did you get the shopping you wanted?'

'No. You know I don't enjoy shopping without you to help me choose.'

Elisabeth had a sudden feeling that the man was laughing at her, but his expression was quite serious.

'Hello there,' called Chester, beaming.

'Good morning,' said Elisabeth, then turned to her newly acquired husband. 'You're a little late, you know. I thought that any moment I was going to be shouted at in Italian for trespassing on private property.'

'Forgive me for keeping you waiting. . .' He began to lead her through an archway then along a dank subterranean tunnel. It came out at some steep stone steps cut in the hillside, the back walls of houses shutting out the light. Four leaped up the steps agilely at the full length of his lead, easily keeping up with the man's long strides. By the time they reached the main road, Elisabeth was out of breath. But they had lost Chester on the way.

'Don't attempt that way on your own. Particularly at night.'

Elisabeth leaned against a wall, keenly aware that he was watching her. 'I couldn't even remember it, if I tried,' she said.

'Why do you keep your cat on a lead?' he went on.

'Because I'm afraid of losing him,' said Elisabeth. 'He is all I've got in the world.'

Four sat down and began to rearrange his fur with his pink tongue. He always felt slightly embarrassed when people began to talk about him. But he had enjoyed the chase up the hillside. He had not been quite sure what they were chasing, but it had been fun. He was not at all puffed. He hoped the man would take them somewhere else. . . .

The man paused, taking in her expensive white trousers, cashmere sweater, the gold bangles jangling round her thin wrists. He seemed rough and shabby by contrast, but if Elisabeth had looked closely she would have seen that his hands were strong but not coarsened by hard manual labour. Nor was he as old as his greying hair might indicate. His accent was clipped, faintly Germanic.

'You look as if you have got everything,' he said shrewdly.

Elisabeth recognised that they were at the other end of Corso Italia, the main street. She now knew her way back to the hotel.

'Thank you for helping me.'

He nodded briefly. 'My pleasure. Anytime you have need of a husband. Bar Genny makes good coffee. Ciao.'

The man walked away without a further look. The idea of some coffee was tempting so she crossed the road to the unpretentious little café. It was crowded with locals leaning against the bar in the pleasant steamy atmosphere, talking or watching the portable television behind the bar. Thick white cups stood in a deep tray of hot water. The customers looked at her curiously, but after a first admiring glance, returned to their gossip.

The man was right. The cup of cappuccino arrived piping hot, delicious tasting with powdered chocolate sprinkled on the frothy top.

Four had seen something interesting: two lads were playing a machine which had white spots of light bouncing around and was making bleeping sounds. It was fascinating. He was mesmerised by the bobbing lights. Someone found him a stool and he jumped up on it to be nearer the game. The youths were amused by the cat's interest and put in more 100-lire coins so that they could play another match for him to watch.

Four was mesmerised, tense and excited, his eyes gleaming. Eventually he could resist the balls no longer. His paw shot out, making wild swipes at the bleeping lights. He sat back on his haunches, frantic paws windmilling like a drunken boxer. Elisabeth began to laugh at the cat's antics – it was the first time she had laughed for months.

That evening Elisabeth sat alone at her table in the dining-room, listening to the uncanny boom of the waves lashing at the rockface below, but without being able to see anything out of the darkened windows. The weather was changing. She briefly acknowledged Chester's wave, then pretended to be absorbed in admiring the vaulted ceiling painted blue with pastoral scenes of cherubs and angels. Very Florentine. Rain spattered the paved terrace outside the windows. The night was black and chilly with only the string of flickering lights across the Bay to show that at least Naples was alive.

A howling wind tore at the cliffside. No wonder the lemon and orange groves were protected from the lashing winds and winter frosts by acres of untidy bamboo mats and cages.

Elisabeth did not linger but quickly took Four for a walk along the paths that crossed the groves of the hotel's garden. Four did not like rain, and trod fastidiously over the puddles with delicate steps.

Elisabeth stood in the midst of the gale, the scarf round her precious throat being whipped away, streaming behind her. She wondered what she was doing there. Totally alone. She was famous and successful, but no one cared about her. She could disappear tomorrow and in days she would be forgotten. When she returned to the glass foyer, the kindly hall porter who opened the door did not know whether they were tears or raindrops on her cheeks.

The next morning the sky had miraculously cleared and from her breakfast table Elisabeth saw the white steamer coming from Capri. Her spirits lifted. Already a small crowd had gathered on the landing stage at the promise of a fine day and a good crossing. Elisabeth hastily swallowed her sweet roll and coffee, then hurried to fetch Four. He looked at her inquiringly as she bundled him into his travelling basket. No brush and comb this morning?

'We're going to Capri,' she whispered. 'Let's get the lift. We've just got time.'

Four did not care for the motion of the steamer, but he bore it with fortitude, sitting at Elisabeth's feet on the top deck. She found the forty-five-minute trip bracing and exciting, and her cheeks were flushed as the *Epomeo Napoli* reversed between the towering cliffs into the quay at the Marina Grande. No wonder people fell in love with Capri and returned time after time. The harbour was still small enough to be picturesque. Houses straggling up the verdant hillside in colourful profusion, the curves and soft corners of their beaten plaster walls merging with the flowers.

The steep funicular railway was a new sensation for Four, accustomed as he was to air and car travel. He was quite surprised to find how high up he was when Elisabeth took him out of his basket on the paved terrace of the hilltop town of Capri, overlooking the Marine Grande. The sea was a long way down, beyond the carpet of faded roofs and gnarled olive trees, the waves sparkling with a special luminosity.

The small, oddly-shaped Piazza Umberto I was bustling with warmly-dressed locals and cosmopolitan visitors, even though it was not the summer season. The rash of mink coats was quite startling in such a quaintly old-fashioned square, for despite the expensive dress shops and trendy boutiques in the sprouting alleyways, much of the town's eighteenth-century character was untouched. Remains of a megalithic wall were visible by the funicular railway, going mostly unnoticed and unrecognised, built into existing houses.

Elisabeth wandered into a narrow passage. She should have known it. There was Chester. He was obviously on the tourist trek to Anacapri and the famous Villa S. Michele. Elisabeth immediately chose the opposite direction, following the Via Fuerlovado to Caesar Tiberius's ruined villa on the top of Mount Tiberio. The Roman *stradetta* was only wide enough for two people to pass, covered part of the way, occasionally broadening at crossroads. The route was clearly marked with coloured ceramic tiles or the inscription 'Villa Jovis' on marble.

She climbed higher, Four leaping ahead. A twisting path took them between villas and gardens, steep enough to become steps on the bends, glorious views of the island behind and in front of them as the extensive ruins came into sight.

The last few hundred yards were all steps. She sat on a tiled base of the Imperial loggia, getting her breath, leaning her back against the cold white stone. Four lay stretched out in the sun like an emperor himself. It was still and peaceful, the sweet silence broken only by an occasional firecracker being let off by late New Year revellers. Some German students clustered beneath the greened bronze statue of a saintly Maria del Soccorso, their clear young voices not disturbing the stillness, but reassuring her that ghosts of Roman senators, togas flapping, would not stride out of the baths below, demanding that she serve wine and figs immediately.

Elisabeth understood the ageless magic of Capri. The island seemed so light, as if it were a ship moving on the oceans. Cliffs fell dramatically to the sea on both sides and, beyond the slopes, rose again dotted with tiny villas, their dark windows like cubic eyes.

The ruins of the Villa Jovis sprawled across the whole hilltop, once a dominating fortress, but now the towering stone walls were hardly recognisable as the great hall, the baths – hot, cold and tepid. A mass of stairways, terraces and promenades linked the roofless rooms, descending to the more prosaic living quarters, kitchens and sewers.

A dog had followed the workmen as they cemented the present path and 162 steps for tourists, writers and lonely singers. Its paw-marks were imprinted in the cement, more real to Elisabeth than the great Caesar Tiberius who had once strode on this same loggia, contemplating his retirement from the complicated politics of his office.

'And how is your marital situation today?' the man asked, coming into sight as he climbed the crumbling steps to the loggia.

'Safe and single at the moment,' said Elisabeth. 'But I have a feeling I may need a husband on the return ferry.'

'Then perhaps I should get in a little practice,' he said, and again she did not know if he were serious or teasing her. 'How do you explain why we are not staying at the same hotel?'

'I don't know,' she faltered. 'I had not thought it out that far.'

'We could pretend that I am allergic to your cat.' Elisabeth shot a quick glance at him, but he was calmly taking in the magnificent view. 'Nasal or skin?'

'I beg your pardon?'

'Sneezing or lumps? The allergy. . . '

Elisabeth bent down to hide her amusement by touching Four's soft, velvety head. 'Four wouldn't give anyone lumps!'

'I think perhaps you should tell me your name. I cannot call you darling all the time, however delightful that is.'

'Elisabeth. Elisabeth Fiorentino.'

'Mixed parentage? That explains the Italian eyes and the Anglo-Saxon colouring. But not your cat on a lead. Poor cat.'

'He's not a poor cat,' she said defensively. 'I can do what I like with Four. It's a free world.'

'But not for your cat. Your cat is a prisoner.' He lifted the slack of the lead with the toe of his sandal. Four stirred and stretched, and rolling over to warm his other side, claws retracting. He liked this man's voice. He knew who it was without opening his eyes. He hoped there would be another exciting chase. . .

'I don't agree,' said Elisabeth, but guilt had crept into her voice. She knew playful, amusing Four was soon destined for six-months' captivity in a kennels where her other cats still languished. Fluffy-One's quarantine had expired and Elisabeth would fetch her as soon as she arrived back in England. But her agent had already signed up another overseas engagement – Elisabeth had no choice but to start the cat on the same merry-go-round. 'No, I don't agree,' Elisabeth repeated very firmly.

'The cat is a symbol of liberty,' said the man, still gazing into the far shimmering hills. 'The Roman goddess of liberty always has a cup in one hand, a broken sceptre in the other and a cat lying at her feet. You don't know freedom, eh, puss?'

'You're talking about statues. Carved pieces of marble. What nonsense! They mean nothing.' Elisabeth was not used to being lectured.

'You can't say that, in Italy of all places. Tomorrow you should go to see Pompeii. I will take you.'

'You sound like Chester.'

'Then you are making yourself a prisoner also.'

'But I am already. A prisoner of my career.'

He walked over to the edge of the loggia. The ruins scattered down the hillside, overgrown with weeds and flowers, almost unreconisable as the luxurious Roman villa.

'We only come to this earth once,' he said, almost to himself. 'My name is Hans Johanson. I am Swiss. This much you should know about your husband. Shall we walk now?'

They walked back down the 162 steps, strolling through orchards and olive groves, flowering oleanders spilling on to the path. Hans told her about the famous people who had villas on Capri. Everyone knew about Gracie Fields and her swimming pool restaurant at Marina Piccola, but Elisabeth was surprised that Ginger Rogers also had a villa. . . bright haired, ageless, still dancing. Others who had lived there included the Marquis de Sade, Gorky, Chaliapin, Tchaikovsky, Alex Munthe, D.H. Lawrence, and now modern industrialists who made their fortunes from household products had moved in.

A terraced bar overlooked a steep downward path. Plain wooden tables were laid out in the open. The cooking was done in a cave, rock walled; a woman and her daughters were chopping food on boards. Aromatic smells wafted from their cooking pots.

Elisabeth and Hans ordered a simple spaghetti Neapolitan with a bottle of local red wine. The elderly man who served them brought a dish of fish pieces for Four, and a bowl of water, without being asked. 'We have no milk,' he apologised.

Later they walked down the twisting steps, every turn presenting an even more magnificent view. They came to the Arco Naturale, a soaring archway formed in the limestone rock by slow erosion. The arch rose into the sky, but by moving to different angles, Elisabeth could look through the eye of the arch and see a vista of receding pools, each bluer than the other, unbelievably still. Four leaped on to the low wall of the viewing point, the wind ruffling his velvet coat into wavelets.

Hans was standing close behind Elisabeth. He bent unexpectedly and kissed her. It was a kiss without passion, but with a gentleness that stirred a quiver of emotion in Elisabeth's heart.

They were quite alone. They had the island to themselves. The crystal moment was handed them by the Gods.

'Just practising. . . for the return trip,' said Hans lightly, but the intensity of his expression did not match the lightness of his voice. He was searching for something he could not find. His dark eyes were unfathomable. Elisabeth found she was shaken to her very roots.

An American family joined them on the return ferry. They had two miniature-adult, crew-cut small sons and had saved for a long time for this trip to Europe.

The father was resigned to their tour operator's lightning itinerary, but still American enough to make fun of it.

'We had ten minutes of Capri,' he said. 'Or was it twelve? My wife dashed into one shop, I went into another. We threw our money on the floor and shouted "Give us something!" '

Hans and Elisabeth laughed. 'If only you had come with us,' said Hans. 'My wife and I had a most enjoyable walk up to the Roman villa on the top of the hill.'

It was almost like a stab. Elisabeth had to steady herself against the rail. He had said it so naturally, words that she had never expected to hear. Even though it was a pretence, they kindled a tiny glow within her.

Capri was slipping away from them in the distance. It had been a wonderful day, and she did not want it to end. It was cooling fast and the passengers began to crowd into the steamy cabin. She did not know which would be the most harmful, the chill wind or the incubating germs in the cabin. It had seemed pretentious to go to Capri in a mink coat, but she was shivering now. Always her voice. She must not do this, or that. . . she must cosset it, care for it. The voice was more real than she was. Elisabeth Fiorentino was simply a shell that housed the precious chords. . .

'You are cold, darling,' said Hans, draping his anorak on her shoulders and zipping it up high under her chin. She immediately felt the warmth it still held from his body.

'How about you?' She was lost inside its size.

'I am like Four. I have an in-built wind resistance. Remember, I am used to mountains and snow.'

'You must be a skiing instructor,' said Elisabeth, reminding herself of everything she had heard about skiing instructors.

'Wrong. But be careful. Your admirer approaches.'

Chester was bearing down on them, two brandies in his hand. He looked momentarily disconcerted to find Hans with Elisabeth, the wind spraying her hair across his chest in tangled locks.

'Oh. So you're the husband. You do exist then,' said Chester. 'I was beginning to wonder.'

'Most certainly,' said Hans, shifting slightly so that he shielded her from the wind. 'I exist.'

'I thought you might like a brandy,' Chester turned to Elisabeth. 'It could get rough. I'm feeling a bit queasy myself.'

'What a kind thought,' said Elisabeth, feeling safe now that Hans was with her. 'I'm sorry you don't feel well. You must stay in the fresh air.'

'Not staying at the Excelsior, are you?' Chester probed.

'No. Unfortunately I am allergic to my wife's cat.'

'Sneezes,' said Elisabeth.

'Lumps,' said Hans.

They both spoke at the same time and Chester could not understand why they started to laugh. It did not seem at all funny to him.

'What happens when you are at home?' he went on. 'You

don't live in separate houses, do you? All for a cat?'

Elisabeth smiled sweetly at Hans. He could deal with that one. But he was not lost for an answer.

'No, at home, it is the cats who have a separate house. Not me. Just like some people have a granny-flat, we have a cats-flat. Is it four cats we have, darling?' Hans sounded suitably confused.

'Four,' Elisabeth confirmed.

Hearing his name, Four called out from his basket. His fierce amber eyes were watching everything. Elisabeth stroked his chin. He was a beautiful cat. He deserved more than the kind of life she was committing him to, but what else could she do?

It was dark when the ferry reached the quay below the hotel, its windows bright with lights like a many-layered birthday cake. Hans took her arm and guided her across the swinging gangway. The waves were washing over the landing stage and they ran to higher, dryer land. They walked back to the hotel along the winding Via de Maio that climbed the narrow ravine. They were strangely silent. The Piazzo Tasso was bustling with café customers sipping drinks, and Neapolitan music floated into the evening air.

'Will you be all right?' he hesitated at the drive.

'I think I can handle Chester now that he knows you really exist,' said Elisabeth, the words almost choking her. They were not what she wanted to say at all.

'I'm planning to catch the 9.55 train to Pompeii tomorrow, if you need me.' He touched her hand lightly, briefly.

Chester wanted to take her up to the crater of Vesuvius, and spent most of the evening trying to persuade her to go with him. 'Craters are just not my scene,' she kept refusing.

He followed her from the dining-room into the lounge. They made a handsome couple, reflected in the gilt mirrors on the walls. The romping, round-cheeked cherubs were still absorbed in their everlasting game of draping garlands of rosebuds from mirror to mirror. How solid everything was. . . cast iron free-standing radiators decorated with scrolls, almost museum pieces; even the blanking nut was faced with petals of a flower. The handles of the tall glass doors opening on to the terrace were the two halves of an oyster shell. Everywhere were signs of long lost workmanship. . . .

'You can't come to Sorrento and not see Vesuvius,' Chester insisted. He waved over the steward to give his order.

'I can see Vesuvius from my balcony,' said Elisabeth. 'Besides, I am going to Pompeii with my husband tomorrow.'

'I don't understand this marriage of yours,' said Chester.

'Hans is allergic to Four. It's quite simple.'

'It's a ridiculous arrangement,' he said laconically. 'Get rid of your cats. Or get rid of your husband – I daresay you would soon find a replacement who even liked cats.'

'I find that remark offensive,' said Elisabeth rising. 'Goodnight, Mr Ridgway.'

Elisabeth locked the door of her room and took Four up into her arms. It was so silly to be upset by Chester, when she did not even have a husband. She had even started to think that Hans. . . 'Oh Four, I wish you were a big fierce Alsatian dog to guard me,' she said vehemently. Four felt a tremor of alarm. He didn't like the idea of dogs at all.

He was even more alarmed when Elisabeth hurried to the Circumvesuviana station the next morning. He was jolted about in his basket and had to protest loudly before she slowed down.

'Oh, I thought I might miss you,' she said as a tall figure, reassuringly familiar, came from the booking office.

'I came early,' said Hans. 'I have bought two tickets. It's quite a short journey really. Ah, I forgot my duty. . . good morning, darling. Did you sleep well?'

He took her hand quite naturally. It felt warm, firm and comforting. Elisabeth had a heady feeling, as if she were suddenly sixteen again, and singing was no more than a girlish daydream.

Pompeii was a humbling experience. The splendid Roman city still lived on in all its pomp of long ago – when senators strode among the columns of the great Forum, the Roman ladies took the baths, servants tended the lordly villas, townsfolk sold wine and baked bread, the priests prayed, the gladiators fought their bloodied battles in the vast amphitheatre.

Elisabeth found it affected her deeply, especially the small things – the worn stepping-stones across the cobbled streets, the deep ruts made by the chariot wheels, the ancient graffiti scrawled in red dye on the walls, small household articles found intact in the ashes. . . bottles, pots, combs, tear phials. . .

A guide took them round the better preserved villas which were protected from the general public.

'Oh, it is locked,' he exclaimed theatrically outside an ornamental portico. 'I have forgotten the key. The key is with my brother who is visiting a sick aunt in Padua. . .' His face was as wrinkled as an old walnut.

Hans put his hand casually in his wallet and pulled out some torn lire notes. The guide's expression lightened.

'Ah . . .' he sighed with elaborate relief. 'Of course, I have, after all, another key in this pocket. Come . . .'

Four followed curiously. He loved exploring but he knew something was desperately wrong here in this strange hollow place of broken walls and crumbling marble columns. The volcanic ash still lingered in cracks and crevices, with all its sense of imminent death and disaster. He kept close to Elisabeth, getting right under her feet, to feel safer.

Hans caught her from stumbling. She picked Four up and he dug his claws sharply into her skin. 'You are in a funny mood,' she chided.

Suddenly a Roman deluge began. Vesuvius was lost in cloud. They ran for shelter to the cloisters of the gymnasium, which at least had a roof. The Grand Palestra had housed the crowds watching athletic feats held round the now empty marble-walled pool. Rain poured through gaps in the roof. Elisabeth wandered away from Hans, trying to bring her thoughts under control. Her heart was aching. This quiet man was stirring emotions in her that had lain hidden for years. It seemed she knew every line of his face, every curve of his shoulders, every inflection of his accent.

Through the grill of a wooden side-door, a small figure lay on its back in the grey dust, its skull broken open. It looked very small. A femur lay on the ground alongside. Other bones were piled in the dust. As Elisabeth's eyes grew accustomed to the gloom of the storeroom, she saw with horror that the yellow plastic trays were stacked with bones. Excavations were still being carried out. She shivered and hurried back to Hans.

'Your boyfriend is following us,' said Hans.

'I thought he'd gone to Vesuvius.'

Chester appeared at the far end of the cloisters, waving a large, coloured golf umbrella. The rain dripped off his brown curls, making him look like a Greek god in modern dress.

'Are you sure you still want me to act the husband?' Hans asked dubiously. 'He really is a most attentive young man, and he does have a very capacious umbrella.'

'I'd rather get wet,' said Elisabeth, tucking Four inside her jacket and pulling up the zip so that only his furry face was showing. He flattened his ears in disapproval of this whole rain business. He did not mind being carried about like an Eskimo baby, but he had a feeling he was still going to get very wet. He eyed the bright umbrella weaving its way towards them. It seemed a sensible solution. As Chester neared, Four did an elaborate gyration and slithered out from the bottom of Elisabeth's jacket. With one bound he cleared the nearest puddle, scrambled up Chester's suede coat and clung on to his shoulders.

'Ouch! Get off! Drat the creature!' Chester felt Four's claws dig into his neck. He tried to shake the cat off its perch, but Four was not going and hung on to Chester, his back arched, his wet fur spiked like a porcupine.

'Four, come down at once,' said Elisabeth sharply, but inwardly she was laughing at Chester's predicament. The umbrella rolled wildly, sailed out of Chester's hands and landed wrong-way up in a rushing stream of water. Hans waded after it as it drifted away like a gaudy boat.

Chester was nearly doubled over, trying to dislodge Four, almost blinded by the rain, staggering from one slippery ridge to the next. Four felt decidedly unsafe and with his usual quick thinking leaped back into the shelter of the cloisters, picking up his paws and shaking them delicately.

'You are in disgrace,' said Elisabeth, catching him up into her arms. 'I'm ashamed of you.' Four was not at all taken in by the tone of her voice. It had all been great fun, and he felt better for it. Now Hans had the umbrella and that meant it would soon be sheltering Elisabeth. He poked a wet nose into Elisabeth's ear, asking forgiveness.

'You'd better have the umbrella,' said Chester, wet and practically choking. 'Because of your precious voice. . . '

'Thank you, how kind. Perhaps we had all better get back to Sorrento,' she said hurriedly. 'This rain looks permanent.' Hans was looking at her strangely. 'What does he mean about your voice. . . ?' his eyes were saying. The journey back to Sorrento was strained. A chill settled on the group and they were silent. Elisabeth looked out of the train window at the grey suburban flats and houses and wondered where the colour of Italy had gone.


On her last evening in Sorrento Elisabeth sang in the cathedral. Three professors from Naples were to give a recital in the warm toned, pink and brown marble church, and when they heard that Elisabeth Fiorentino was staying at the Excelsior, they asked her to sing just one aria.

She sang the Easter Hymn, her voice soaring to the vaulted ceiling like a bird's, while the chandeliers shone and twinkled like stars in the heavens. Hans sat unseen in a pew at the back, Four curled up beside him. Hans did not know how he would be able to live without her. Each flawless note took her further and further away from him, underlining the difference in their lives.

Afterwards, as they walked slowly back to the hotel, she told him about her singing, about her career, her loneliness and her many cats. Tomorrow she would be flying back to England.

'Now is the time for our divorce then,' said Hans. 'Tomorrow you return to being the big star, Four will begin his six-months' quarantine, and I suppose next week you will go shopping to Harrods for number five.'

'Oh Hans,' said Elisabeth, shocked and hurt. 'What a cruel thing to say.'

'But it is true. You are using your cats as you would not dare to use a human. Or do you also cast off human relationships as quickly when they have finished their usefulness?'

'Why are you talking to me like this?' Elisabeth cried. 'Why are you being so unkind?'

'Because you have finished with me too. I am cast off like Four. I am fallen in love with you, Elisabeth, but I know it is no use. Our lives take different paths. You know nothing about me . . . I am a farmer. I have a small farm in the mountains. I work in the open air. We make good cheese. My house is of logs and when the snow comes there is no way down to the village. Sometimes I do not see another person for weeks. It is not your world at all. . . '

She was crying silently. Of course, it was true. How could she have thought, even for a moment, that Hans could fit into her life as a singer? But that kiss on Capri had been a miracle, when she had despaired of ever feeling love stirring within her.

'I'm not really like that,' she whispered. 'I don't want to leave you. Hans. . . please help me.'

Her eyes swam with tears as she fumbled with the collar round Four's neck. She picked the cat up and hugged him ferociously, kissing his soft grey forehead, stroking his ears with trembling fingers. It was a long moment when time seemed to stop.

Then she put him down on the paved path between the orange and lemon trees whose sharp fragrance drifted in the wind. 'There you are, Four. You're free. No nasty cage for my beautiful puss.'

Four shook himself. It felt strange without his collar. He had never been without that narrow leather strap before. The air lifted his fur and ruffled his neck. He turned himself round Elisabeth's ankles lovingly, and licked her hand with his rough moist tongue.

Then with one bound he was away. He knew where he was going. He streaked out of the hotel drive and down the Via S. Cesareo. His nose led the way. A right turning took him past the fourteenth century cloisters of Saint Francisco, down the cobbled steps to the Marina Grande. All the grand, tantalising smells of the harbour wafted up to meet him.

A quiver of excitement rose in his throat. This was to be his life now! He was free. . .

These days Four lives with a pack of half-wild cats that roam the harbour, well established as their leader. Often he can be seen sunning himself on the keel of an upturned boat, a beautiful Short-Haired Blue-Cream, a little out of place among the mixed breeds but obviously well-fed and content with life as a Neapolitan gipsy. And there are quite a few younger cats playing around him with a definite look of Blue about them.

Elisabeth and Hans come back to Sorrento regularly. It is their special place for holidays and the odd weekend break from her singing engagements. It took Elisabeth over a year to decide to marry Hans, but she found it was not so difficult after all to combine her career with being a farmer's wife. She can commute from Zurich easily. She loves Hans' log-built farmhouse in the mountains and the clear, sweet summer air is marvellous for her voice. But the time she likes best is when the snows come and there is no way down to the village. The fir-clad slopes stand white and silent, and she and Hans are together.

Chester returned to the Rome headquarters of the Italian police to whom he was on temporary loan. His next assignment was less glamorous – a wealthy Brazilian industrialist and his wife who were visiting Rome. The Italian Government, concerned by the number of kidnappings and ransoms that plagued their country, took what steps they could to protect potential victims.

Four always seems to know when Elisabeth and Hans are returning to Sorrento for a visit. His special sixth sense wakes him from his sun-baked slumbers, and, leaving his large family to tumble on the sands, he bounds through the back alleys up to the Piazzo Tasso. Then as their car turns into the drive of the Excelsior Vittoria, he emerges nonchalantly from the flowering bushes as if he has been there all the time.

Then, of course, Elisabeth rushes from the car, gathering him into her arms and covering him with joyous kisses and tears.

Four always stays at the hotel with them. He enjoys the occasional taste of luxury, but he knows that it is like all holidays. It is not real life. And for every cat, life is liberty.

BOOK TWO

# More Cat Stories

*To Nancy Webber,
my editor and friend*

# The Clown

The cat knew that his name was Cecil but he could not understand why that made everyone laugh. He said the sound over and over again in his mind: 'Ses-sil, Ses-sil . . .' but he did not find anything funny about it.

Every time there were visitors to the house, Mrs Billington would scoop him up into her arms, his four paws waving frantically and helplessly in the air like erratic windmills.

'This is Cecil,' she would say with a merry trill. 'He's such a clown.'

The visitor would tickle Cecil's tummy (which he loathed) and then laugh uproariously. He could not see what was so funny. He did not understand it at all.

They did not laugh at people called Cecil. There was an Uncle Cecil who dropped ash all over Cecil's fur; and the postman's name was Cecil, and no one had hysterics when he dropped those flat white things through the letter-box.

And clown. What did clown mean? Cecil thought he was a cat, a cat with black paws, which were mostly what he saw of himself. He was positive he was a cat. But apparently he was also a clown. Everyone said so. But it was something mysterious and beyond his comprehension.

He skidded across the hall floor and landed in a heap against the front door. Then he sat up and rearranged his ruffled fur. He resolved to spend at least the next seven, eleven or ninety-four minutes on finding out what a clown was. He owed it to himself for his own peace of mind.

Cecil looked at the kitchen clock. He knew it was the right thing to do. People were always looking at the clock. It was ninety-three minutes past half-past one. He had plenty of time. He knew how to tell the time now.

He climbed into Mrs Billington's shopping basket and closed his eyes to think. He always thought better with his eyes closed. Mrs Billington spotted him and hooted with laughter.

'Look at Cecil! He thinks he's coming shopping with me. Isn't he a scream?'

She tipped him out and he fell head first, somersaulting with a neat twist of his body. It was a normal feline four-point landing after an awkward take-off.

'Cecil's standing on his head!' she shrieked.

Cecil walked away with some dignity. He was not standing on his head and never had been. He began to wonder, not for the first time, if he and the Billingtons were really compatible.

Late that night Cecil went down to see the brown owl that lived in the copse at the end of the garden. He had heard that an owl was supposed to be a wise old bird, but Cecil doubted it, with all that pointless twit-twooing and demented staring.

The owl blinked down at the cat from the hollow in his tree. Cecil asked him if he happened to know what a clown was.

'A clown?' the owl crooned wisely. 'A clown is a clown.'

'Is that ye-ow-all?'

'Twit-twoo,' agreed the owl, spotting a field-mouse that was trying to hide under a discarded chocolate wrapper. He took off silently, his great wings casting a shadow over Cecil.

Fat lot of use, thought Cecil, wandering back to the house with a couple of jaunty side-steps. He jumped over imaginary obstacles, punching the air like a goal-scoring football player. Perhaps a clown was something anti-social. After all, none of the birds would talk to him, the dog next door was positively rude, and those foxes down by the stream had a mean look.

Cecil sat on the top of the yellow monster with four round legs in the drive and waited for morning to come. The monster was asleep, so it was safe to sit on it. The frost tipped Cecil's fur with spears of ice. He tucked his nose into the warmth of his tail and prayed not to be a social outcast.

He knew that something was happening the next day by the frantic activity. Bags, boxes and cases began to pile up in the hallway like a hastily erected flood barricade.

Cecil sat on top of the luggage, an oversized cherry on an ice-cream sundae. His rule was never sit on the floor if there was a chair, never on a chair if there was a window-sill, never on a windowsill if there was room on the bookcase, and so on up to the hat shelf, curtain pelmet and the top of the wardrobe. An unsteady pile of luggage rated about grade three.

'Exterminate . . . exterminate,' droned one of the junior Billingtons who conducted an endless war with Cecil. Cecil scrambled over the luggage in retreat, tail waving surrender, and hid inside a bag of beach gear with only his head showing.

'Eliminate . . . eliminate,' the drone went on.

Mrs Billington swooped in, putting a faded straw hat on top of Cecil's ears. She stood back, shaking with laughter. 'That cat's a real clown. Going on your holidays, are you?'

Cecil leaped out of the bag, hat askew, knocking everything over. He fled. They were going to Majorca for Christmas, they said. He was suddenly afraid. What did it mean? What was going to happen to him? For Christmas? Could they eat it?

It was peaceful when they had all gone away in the yellow monster. He sat in the garden, slowly getting cold, then hungry. It started to get dark. Perhaps he ought to go and ask the owl. He decided that at half-past twenty to eleven he would go and see the old bird.

But light footsteps came hurrying down the empty drive with a voice on top.

'Puss? Puss? I'm so sorry. I know I'm terribly late. That damned train was held up again. You must be starving – and frozen. I'm afraid I've got to feed you outside even though it's no weather for a picnic. They didn't leave me a key.'

It was a girl, a pretty dark-haired girl with rosy cheeks and smiling eyes. She pulled off her woolly gloves and started to unpack a bag. She had brought warm milk in a thermos and chicken in aspic on a bone china plate.

'I hope you don't mind party food,' she said, chatting away as she poured milk into a floral-patterned soup bowl. 'So much nicer than that tinned stuff. And this is skimmed milk. Low fat, you know. But if you don't like it, just say so, and I'll get your favourite tipple.'

Cecil was amazed. She was actually talking to him as if he was real. And party food! He forgot all about visiting the owl. He looked at the young woman closely to see if she was laughing at him. But she wasn't. She was smiling and that was quite a different sensation.

'I promise I'll be on time tomorrow,' she went on, as he ate his supper. 'It's Christmas Eve and I'll be home from work early, thank goodness. Then, of course, life is one long holiday.'

Cecil felt almost dizzy with happiness. The young woman was discussing plans with him quite seriously.

'I hate leaving you out all night. Are you sure you'll be all right? There are those awful foxes around, but I suppose you're used to it. By the way, I'm Jane. Good night, puss.' She dropped a kiss onto the top of his head

168

and hurried away.

Cecil staggered around the garden as if he were drunk. She had not laughed at him once, not a single once, and she was coming again tomorrow and the next tomorrow. It was all too marvellous.

She kept her word. She was right on time the next day. She stomped about the garden, swinging her arms, as Cecil ate his fish canapés.

'This is silly,' she said, her breath coming like a white mist. 'We're both getting frozen. You might just as well come home with me. Would you like that? I only live two doors away.'

The number of doors presented no problem. Cecil simply followed her along the pavement to the big house on the corner. It seemed Jane lived in the downstairs, someone else lived in the middle and quite another person lived at the top. Weird, but no different to trees.

Cecil explored her flat, fascinated by the pot plants, the books, the cushions, her collection of records and tapes. It was quite different to the Billingtons'. She sat down on the floor beside him with a mug of coffee.

'Make yourself at home,' she said.

Cecil needed no further invitation. He crawled onto her lap and went to sleep.

On Christmas Day he shared roast turkey and chestnut stuffing with Jane and Philip, a tall young man from upstairs, whom Jane was also feeding. They were pulling crackers and reading terrible jokes which made them laugh. But they weren't laughing at him, even when Jane put a little paper clown's hat on Cecil's head and the elastic strap under his chin.

'You look very sweet,' said Jane with a hesitant smile. She quickly took it off him and tied the hat to the back of a chair. 'But it's much more fun to play with it.'

It was too good to be true, and too good to last. It didn't last. Cecil knew it wouldn't.

'You'll miss Cecil, won't you?' said Philip, as he helped her with the washing-up one evening. For a teacher of ancient languages he was remarkably handy with a tea-cloth.

'I will indeed. He's good company, and a nice, friendly cat. I've grown very fond of him. But the Billingtons are due back tomorrow. Their plane lands at Gatwick at five.'

Five, eleven or ninety-four . . . it all meant the same to Cecil. How could he measure his happiness when it was running away like sand through his paws? He followed her reluctantly along the pavement, trailing his tail. Every few steps Jane bent and stroked him, murmuring words of encouragement.

'We'll see each other,' she said. 'Ever such a lot.'

The Billingtons were already home, all of them. Cecil had never really counted how many of them there were; they were just the Billingtons *en masse*. They had brought Jane a bottle of Spanish wine and a two-foot-high grey donkey for Cecil.

They sat the donkey on the floor facing him. It had button glass eyes and a leering grin. Cecil backed off, hissing, his tail twitching. Then he fell over his tail and they all began to laugh, pushing the donkey at him. He tried to close his ears to the sound of their laughter, but there was nothing he could really do. Everything was all horribly the same again.

But something *was* different. Cecil sensed it. They were preoccupied with a new activity. It seemed that Mr Billington had met someone in Majorca who had offered him a job 'up north'. They talked endlessly about 'up north', and quite soon the house was full of more boxes, and everything was being put into these boxes. Even the despised donkey went into a box.

'Of course we're taking Cecil with us,' said Mrs Billington. 'I've bought him a lovely travelling-basket. He'll make everybody laugh up north. He's such a clown!'

She kept putting Cecil in the basket. He kept jumping out. Life became a perpetual yo-yo, in and out of the basket. Mrs Billington lost a little of her usual good humour.

'We shall have to make sure the strap is fastened on moving day,' she said, slamming the lid on Cecil.

Cecil observed the preparations with apprehension. The small boxes went into big boxes, and were then carried into a bigger box that stood on round legs and which had arrived outside the house and promptly gone to sleep. Cecil watched the procession of boxes disappearing into its inside. They had even packed his food dish and he had had to eat his breakfast out of the tin.

Cecil glanced at the clock. It was three-quarters to fifteen o'clock. He had plenty of time to think.

He was wrong. Mrs Billington produced the travelling-basket and put it on the floor. He could tell from her expression that there was no jumping out this time.

Cecil did not know what to do. For a moment, he panicked. He wanted to create some kind of diversion – anything – but his wits had deserted him. He could think of nothing. He began moving – anywhere – faster. He slid along the bare boards, his paws spread to the four winds; then he danced sideways along to the front doorstep, tumbling and somersaulting down the steps; he chased his tail, rolling over and over, shadow-boxing the air. It was all pretty normal stuff.

'Look, Cecil's standing on his head again!'

They leaned against the walls, laughing.

'My word, that cat's a clown,' said Mrs Billington, wiping the tears from her eyes. 'He's too funny for words.'

By the time they had stopped laughing, Cecil had disappeared. They searched the house and the garden, calling for him everywhere.

'Ses-sil. Ses-sil . . . Ses-sil.'

But there was no answer.

Cecil watched them go. He watched the big box monster and the yellow monster waking up and driving off. He was up the tree, watching from the hollow where the owl slept. He waited there a long time, perhaps six, eleven or ninety-four minutes before he judged it safe to climb down.

He went straight along the pavement to Jane's downstairs house and miaowed outside her door. She heard him and came to let him in.

'Hello, puss,' she said, as if she had been expecting him. 'Didn't you want to go up north?'

Cecil walked in with some hesitation, a little unsure of his reception. After all, he was uninvited. He fell over the newspaper, scattering pages all over the floor, landing on his back with the front page of the *Daily Mail* like a wigwam on his head.

He waited for Jane to burst out laughing. And she almost did. But it was a sweet, gentle sound and it did not hurt him at all.

'Philip said you were a funny cat, and you are,' she said, removing the newspaper from Cecil's head. 'What do you think you are? A clown? Everybody loves a clown, you know . . .'

Cecil closed his eyes to capture the moment. He had found out at last. At last he had found out what a clown was. He should have known that Jane would tell him. A clown was a cat that everybody loves.

# The One-Eyed Angel

There had been a very heavy frost the morning they found Rags, and a bitter wind with a piercing drive came from the east. The windows were thick white with frost rime and Lynne could hardly see out of them. Philip pulled on a sheepskin coat, intending to de-ice the car windows, but on stepping outside almost fell over a small huddled mound.

'Found this on the path,' said Philip, carrying the inert bundle into the kitchen. 'It's half frozen to death.'

Lynne came over with Philip's breakfast mug of coffee. She was only half awake. 'Good heavens,' she said. 'What is it?'

It was, in fact, the ugliest cat they had ever seen, with a face that was a cross between a bear and a seal, and short stubbly fur that resembled a freckled doormat. The cat looked even worse at that moment because he was covered in mud and one eye was closed with blood.

'Probably a hit-and-run casualty,' said Philip. 'The roads were pretty treacherous last night.'

'He must have dragged himself into our garden. He's badly hurt. I'd better take him to the vet's.' She began to bathe the damaged eye with plain warm water. 'He does look a rag-bag. I think I'll call him Rags. Whatever happened to you, poor Rags?'

173

Rags growled. He didn't know. He couldn't remember a damned thing. His bones ached, his head ached, his eye hurt, he was tired and hungry and he hadn't the slightest idea how he came to be in this rather small kitchen being tended by a slip of a girl with gentle hands and shy face.

He staggered about in a dazed fashion, then took off roughly in the direction of a saucer of warm milk. Lynne watched him closely. The cat did not seem at all right.

'I think he's got concussion,' she said.

Rags drank the warm milk, hardly stopping to breathe. Then, stumbling over his long rope-like tail, he suddenly went to sleep in a heap on the kitchen floor.

'Definitely concussion,' said Lynne, seeing her brother off to work at the door. Shivering as the chill air struck through her thin dressing-gown, she waved goodbye but Philip was not watching. She turned back indoors and viewed the day's routine chores with resignation.

Lynne kept house for her bachelor brother, a kind, vague man who was fifteen years her senior. She had been studying textile design at art school in London when their mother died quite suddenly from a heart attack. Philip had been hopelessly lost and quite unable to cope, muddling along on cold baked beans and putting on damp shirts. So Lynne had come home to look after her big brother. At first it had only been a temporary measure – until he got a suitable housekeeper, Philip reassured her. But two years had gone by and a 'nice, capable woman' had not materialised. And Philip had stopped advertising.

'Now I suppose I've got another lame duck to look after,' said Lynne, stroking the ugly cat behind his ear. He made a low, growling sound. It might have been a purr. Whatever it was, the sound made Lynne feel less alone. 'That's better,' she said.

She took the injured cat regularly to the vet's. The bruises and stiff joints soon healed, but the eye was permanently damaged and never opened properly again.

Rags had a very rakish air.

'Can a cat have concussion?' Lynne asked the vet.

'Quite possibly,' said Mr Browning, who was very hygienic and efficient in a white coat. 'If they get hit on the head, the injury is the same as in humans.'

'Sometimes I think Rags has got amnesia,' said Lynne. 'His behaviour seems positively uncatlike. He doesn't seem to remember that he's a cat.'

'Of course he's a cat!' laughed Mr Browning, rubbing the stubbly fur with brisk affection. He hadn't time to go into anything as fanciful as feline amnesia. 'I don't think you need bring Rags again unless you're worried about anything.'

'I'm worried about his amnesia,' said Lynne with a determined thrust of her small chin.

'It'll just take time,' he said, showing them out of the door. 'Next please.'

'I'm sure you don't know you're a cat,' said Lynne to Rags through the wickerwork of the cat basket as she carried him home. 'I've been watching you, and you don't behave like one at all.'

Rags arr–owed his strange miaow. He didn't have a clue what he was. It was very disturbing and puzzled him a lot. Now that he had almost recovered from the accident, he was reasonably sure he was not a lame duck. He often wandered about the garden, jumping off the rockery with his paws splayed out straight in case he was a bird. But the squabbling black crows told him where to get off. It was quite unpleasant.

On either side of Philip's house lived a dog. One was a fat white woolly dog with hair all over its face, who lay on the front doorstep in perpetual exhaustion, his tongue hanging out and panting. On the other side lived a mad mongrel puppy forever chasing its own tail and grinning mischievously.

Rags spent one entire week being the woolly dog, flat out and panting with exhaustion; then the next week being the puppy, chasing his own tail in ever increasing giddy circles.

'Don't be so stupid, Rags,' Lynne scolded him. 'You're not a silly dog so stop acting like one. Come and have some supper. I've done you some lovely minced rabbit.'

'I suppose I've got minced rabbit as well,' said Philip. 'You make more fuss of that cat than you do me.'

'You've got rabbit pie,' said Lynne, hiding a smile. 'Rags only got the scraps.'

'Perhaps he'd like to come and sit at the table,' Philip suggested with a hint of sarcasm.

Rags sat quietly on the windowsill, looking out into the garden with his one eye. If he wasn't a bird, or a dog, or a lame duck, then what was he? He watched the rivulets of rain running down the windowpane and knew instinctively they weren't worth chasing.

'You used to like drawing,' said Philip over supper. 'Why don't you enrol at an evening class? You ought to get out more. Or you could do cooking or needle-work . . . There's lots to choose from. You've been looking a bit peaky lately.'

Lynne grasped at Philip's suggestion like a drowning sailor for a straw. 'Yes, I'd like that,' she breathed. 'But not cooking.' She spent the evening hunting out her old brushes and paints. The tubes of oil paint had hardened and were useless. She would have to buy some more. She found some broken charcoal and pastels, and a pad of art paper. She touched the texture of the paper with loving fingertips . . . She could almost feel a picture growing.

How the wind howled for her and the rain cried the first evening Lynne went to her class. The group of aspiring artists gathered round a cage in which there was a gorgeously plumed parrot. He side-stepped on his bar, regarding them doubtfully as they took up their brushes. 'Gertcher,' he remarked gloomily.

Lynne caught his beady look as he peered over his shoulder. It was not textile designing but it was good to feel a brush in her hands again, and to experience that single-minded concentration. Thoughts of food and cleaning vanished.

'Oh, I have enjoyed this evening,' said Lynne, arriving home windswept and wet. She carefully unwrapped the rain-spattered polythene sheeting from her picture. 'There you are . . . What do you think of it?'

'Not exactly a Rembrandt,' said Philip, glancing up from his paper. 'Perhaps a touch of the Dali's. Couldn't they afford a real model?'

'It wasn't stuffed!' Lynne protested. 'Look, even Rags can see it's not a stuffed parrot.'

She propped the picture against the wall, and hearing his name mentioned, Rags ambled over to look at it. Perhaps they were telling him what he was – a stuffed parrot. He certainly had a long tail like the parrot and he could look over his shoulder with a beady eye . . . But this creature seemed to be inside a cage thing. Rags scratched his ear and stretched. He began to wander round the house looking for a possible cage thing.

'I don't know what's got into Rags,' said Lynne with some exasperation when Philip came home from work the next day. 'He spent the entire day sitting in my wire vegetable rack with his head crooked over his shoulder.'

'Positively unhygienic,' said Philip.

'Do you think he's paralysed?' Lynne asked anxiously.

'Probably peckish for an odd carrot to help him see in the dark,' said Philip, tipping the cat into the garden. Rags fled. He was fed up being a parrot. His neck felt permanently out of joint.

Rags strolled through the grass, his long tail thrashing the slender blades. The sky was dark and rolling murkily. Something was going to happen, he knew, his whiskers twitching. Minutes later flakes of white landed coldly on his fur and melted. Rags shook himself free of them and growled. He trod gingerly on the falling snow and hurried towards the lights of the house, but they had closed the curtains and switched on the television and did not hear his howls of indignation.

When Lynne eventually found him, huddled up on the doorstep, Rags was covered in snow. His one eye glared at her . . .

'Oh my goodness,' she laughed. 'What have we got here? A polar bear, to be sure.'

Rags growled at the white flakes on his nose.

'Poor bear,' she said, bundling him up in a warm, sweet-smelling towel. 'I'll give you a lovely rub-down.'

Rags liked the rub-down. Perhaps being a bear would not be so bad. And it was quite fun leaping about in the snow when you got used to wet paws. But he knew nothing about the snow thawing and one morning when he was being a flying bear, he went right through the thin ice on the fish-pond and landed up to his neck in algae. He came indoors and sat on the kitchen floor, eyeing Lynne defiantly and dripping green everywhere.

'I don't care what you think,' said Lynne, tying a plastic apron round her waist. 'But you will have to have a bath.' She tested the water with her elbow and grasped the cat firmly with gloved hands.

Rags thrashed and spat. He did not exactly bite her, but he put up a hell of a good fight. She got soaked. The walls were streaming, the floor became a skating rink. As fast as Rags scrambled out of the sink, so Lynne put him back in. His wet fur clung to his skinny body and he looked worse than a drowned rat . . .

'Okay, time's up,' said Lynne, drying him briskly on her lap. She flicked strands of wet hair out of her eyes. 'At least you smell better now.'

While Lynne was mopping up the kitchen floor, Rags stalked into the sitting-room to lick down his dis-arranged fur. He sat in front of the flickering television, seething with rage and not talking to anyone.

The matinee film was starting. On the small screen appeared the head of a magnificent animal, a wonderful mane of golden hair falling to its shoulders, its powerful jaws yawning . . .

It roared, and Rags jumped back. The lion roared

again, and Rags was transfixed with adoration. He had never seen anything so superior and awe-inspiring. A small growl began in his own throat, growing, gathering volume until it became a miniature roar.

'Oh dear, I have upset him,' said Lynne, still on her knees in the kitchen. She had planned to have the film on while she did the ironing. It made the task less boring.

Rags practised his roar for several days, then he took to sitting on top of the television set, roaring in all directions. He looked happier than he'd ever looked before.

'Can't you shut that cat up?' said Philip. 'I want to watch Panorama, and I can't hear a damned word with that cat bellowing all the time.'

'He thinks he's the MGM lion,' said Lynne, who was quite quick on the uptake. 'Don't disillusion him . . .'

Rags eventually settled down into being a kind of parroty bear with lion overtones. Occasionally he lapsed into chasing his own tail or leaping off the rockery. He decided not to worry about his identity any more.

There came overnight a blessed change in the weather, and a south-west wind warmed the rain-clouds. Before you could say cuckoo, the birds were all madly building nests and gardeners got their annual dose of planting fever. In no time at all it was the summer flower show, and the organiser, Mrs Weston, was charming everyone into taking part.

'You will enter something, won't you?' she said, stopping Lynne outside the shops. Mrs Weston was a bustling and energetic widow, with a sweet, winsome smile that made it difficult to refuse.

'Well, all right,' said Lynne reluctantly. 'But I don't grow anything special, and my jams never set.'

'I'm sure you'll find something,' Mrs Weston smiled. 'It's taking part that's important, not whether you'll win a prize. Here's an entrance form. I look forward to seeing you on Saturday, my dear.'

Lynne read down the list of classes: roses, sweet peas, dahlias, preserves, vegetables, dried flowers, miniature arrangements, handicrafts . . . There was nothing she could really enter. Then she saw the last class in the children's section: the best-loved family pet. There was no alternative. She would have to enter Rags.

Rags did not take kindly to being put into his wicker basket on a hot Saturday afternoon and carried to a fenced-off area of the crowded park. Lynne stood in a line with the small owners of the white woolly dog, and the parrot, and various rabbits and hamsters.

'You're a bit old,' said the organiser dubiously. It was Mr Browning, the vet, who did not quite recognise her.

'It's my little brother's,' said Lynne. 'He's too shy to come.' Rags roared noisily in agreement.

'Well, I dunno . . .' said Mr Browning. 'I'll have to ask Mrs Weston.'

Mrs Weston did not mind bending the rules a little bit, just so long as everyone came. And of course, Rags won first prize. After all, who could resist a one-eyed cat with fur like a doormat who thought he was the MGM lion? There was much youthful waving and cheering, and Rags was presented with a yellow rosette.

Lynne hurried home to get Philip's tea. There would be time to make some scones and some rock cakes. She was washing lettuce and radishes when someone stepped lightly down the garden path and rang the doorbell.

'I'll answer it,' said Philip, coming in from the garden.

'You forgot your cat's rosette,' said Mrs Weston. 'For the best-loved family pet.' She held out the ribbon.

'Oh?' said Philip.

'And are you Lynne's little brother? The one that is so shy?' asked Mrs Weston, with the suspicion of a twinkle in her very pretty blue eyes. Philip stared down at her.

'I beg your pardon?' he said.

Rags finished his celebration supper of chopped liver and then chewed thoughtfully on his yellow rosette. The best-loved family pet. Was that what he really was? What a mouthful . . .

Rags had almost got used to the idea, when one

180

rustling and fragrant autumnal day Philip came home and took Lynne gently aside. 'I've got something serious to tell you,' he said, his kind face looking troubled. Lynne stopped laying the supper table.

A little while later, without even having his supper, Philip went out, and whatever it was he had told his sister, Lynne looked far from troubled. She came dancing into the kitchen and scooped Rags joyfully up into her arms.

'He's going to marry Angela Weston,' she sang happily, her eyes bright and sparkling. 'She's only two years older than him and they've fallen in love! Oh Rags, isn't that marvellous. Now I can go back to art school and start living my life again . . .'

She gave the cat a big, contented hug. 'And it's all thanks to you,' she smiled. 'Rags, you're an angel!'

Rags licked her chin and began to purr. An angel . . . Yes, he'd settle for that. It suited him.

# The Window-Dresser

She was almost at the end of her tether when a helper
from the Cats' Protection League found her, cold and
hungry, huddled on derelict ground, and took her to the
local branch. Her fur was matted and full of fleas; her eyes
were stuck together, and her ears torn and bloodied
where the irritation from mites had nearly sent her mad
with scratching.

'Well, you're a sorry sight,' someone said, trying to
put a comb through her coat. 'I wonder where you've
come from.'

The cat could not say. The weeks of starvation had
robbed her memory of details, but she remembered a
special diet of minced chicken, vitamin pills and loving,
although almost clinical, care.

They fed her from an enamel dish, and although she
could not see properly through her stuck-up eyes, her
smell was as keen as ever and she did not turn up her pert
little nose at a single morsel. She finished the lot,
including a large saucer of milk.

'Poor thing, starving as usual,' said the vet. 'And yet
this one looks as though it could have been shown. It's
probably got a pedigree.' She sat obediently still while he
cleaned out the eyes with swabs of cotton wool. 'She's
got beautiful eye colour,' he went on. 'A long-haired

cream under all that flea-ridden matt. Sorry, puss, but this is going to be a scissor-job.'

It was some days later that a business-like young woman in sharp knee-breeches and a leather jacket came striding into the CPL, swinging her skid-lid against her long black boots. 'I want a working cat,' she said. 'My shop's got mice.'

Kate Windsor was not a cat person. She had not been brought up with pets, and the nearest she had ever got to owning one was winning a goldfish at a fair, which had expired on the way home. She knew nothing at all about cats except that they caught mice. And her second-hand shop, in which she had invested £250 borrowed from her bank manager, was overrun with mice. She could not afford to have her stock nibbled or eaten, and when she found a 1930s beaded evening dress ruined by little teeth-marks, Kate decided it was time for a cat.

'Any cat will do,' said Kate. 'I don't care which one. It's an emergency. I'm under attack.'

At that moment she caught sight of the long-haired cream – or what was left of the pale fur. It had been quite a drastic scissor-job and the cat looked more like a skinned rabbit.

'Is that a proper cat?' Kate asked. 'She looks a bit like Snoopy. What happened to her?'

'The poor creature was in a dreadful state when we found her, but the coat will grow again. She's actually a very beautiful cat, as you can see by the eyes.'

Two wide eyes looked up at Kate with a touching dignity, without a trace of pleading. They were haunting eyes, a pale amber with a hint of green depths, like clear meadow-stream water with freckled sunlight playing on it. The woman and the cat looked at each other and it was something at first sight; something that neither could define. Kate only wanted a cat to catch mice. The cat stretched out a paw against the wire of the cage in un-spoken appeal.

'I suppose that one would do,' said Kate dubiously.

'Are you sure its fur will grow? It looks awful. My friends will laugh.'

'She's very intelligent and sensible.'

'That would help,' said Kate, convincing herself. 'I need an intelligent, sensible working cat. Have you got a box I can put on the back of my moped? Come along home, Snoopy, you've got yourself a job. You'd better wear my scarf or you'll catch cold.'

Snoopy had never been on the back of anything before. It was not unpleasant; in fact the ride was exhilarating. She had complete confidence in the young woman, and the fresh air blowing through her whiskers was like angel's breath.

Home was a tiny flat above Kate's shop. It was up to its ceiling with unsold stock, boxes and crates of memorabilia from the 1920s to the 1950s.

'It's not actually a second-hand shop,' Kate explained as she unlocked the door and carried Snoopy inside. 'But the period's not old enough to be antique. It's in between. That's why I call it the Between Shop.'

Snoopy jumped out of the cardboard box, the scarf still wrapped around her. It looked interesting and she sniffed politely, not terribly sure what was expected of her in this new place. The young woman was not used to cats, anyone could tell that, but Snoopy trusted her to do the right thing.

'How about a cup of tea?' Kate said as she put the kettle on. Snoopy was game for anything. Her supper of fruit cake and salt and vinegar crisps was an entirely new experience, and one to which she felt she could become quite accustomed. She went to sleep in a large paper bag, dreaming of glorious rides, of catching her claws in the young woman's long windblown hair, of that warm laugh that echoed sweetly in her clean and nearly healed ears.

The next morning Kate shared her bran flakes and milk with the cat. Snoopy was a neat eater, not a drop spilled onto the floor. She wondered if Kate had heard about minced chicken.

'Now sit still and be good,' said Kate, lifting Snoopy awkwardly onto her lap. 'I'm supposed to brush you every day. As if I haven't got enough to do.'

Snoopy felt a little growl grow in her throat as the brush gently went through her new fur, massaging the skin. She shut her eyes in bliss as Kate grew more confident with the grooming.

'I wish someone would brush my hair for me,' said Kate, shaking back her heavy plait. 'You're just spoiled. I hope you'll show your gratitude by getting rid of those mice. That's your department, Snoopy. I'm relying on you.'

Snoopy went downstairs with Kate into the shop, ready to start work. Kate began to unpack a parcel of hand-stitched, parlour-maids' aprons which she had bought at a house clearance. The workmanship was exquisite. It gave Kate a feeling of satisfaction to have saved them from the recycling mill.

'Right, Snoopy,' she said cheerfully, giving the cat an encouraging shove. 'Now it's up to you. Go catch a mouse.'

Which was easier said than done. Snoopy had lived a mouseless existence before: without mice, without fleas, without dust, boxes or crates, and totally without anything second-hand. It had been a scrupulously hygienic life, and the only mouse in sight had been the little pink rubber shape they had given her to play with in her pen.

Still, Snoopy was eager to help. She padded around, sniffing, made a mild attack on an Alpine walking-stick, practised a few growls at a feathered cloche hat and, after exploring the shop from wall to wall, fell asleep exhausted in the drum of an ancient spin-drier which Kate was selling for a friend.

Strangely enough, Kate sold the machine that morning. The lady who bought it wanted to know if the cat went with it. Kate pocketed the notes with a quick smile.

'Sorry,' she said. 'But that's my assistant. Mouser in chief. Although she hasn't caught anything yet.'

'Sometimes just the smell of a cat around is enough to get rid of mice,' said the woman. 'Anyway, she's got beautiful eyes.'

Snoopy gazed at them, clear-eyed and trusting, the little tufts of fur in her ears sprouting like feathers, her white whiskers twitching like fairy aerials. Kate bent to touch the short cream fur on the top of Snoopy's head. It was the first time she had ever stroked a cat. The softness was unbelievable, swansdown. Snoopy arched her neck so that the fingers continued down her back. The purr began again, low and throaty, threatening to break out.

'I'll go and buy us a quick lunch,' said Kate, straightening up in a matter of fact way. 'Would a cheese omelet suit you?'

Snoopy curled up in a cracked flower-patterned china wash-bowl and kept an eye on the shop while Kate was out.

That afternoon a schoolgirl rushed in to buy the bowl. It would be perfect for her plant garden, she said.

It was quite late that evening before they could share a supper of fish fingers and chips, then sit together and count the takings. It had been a very good day.

'Didn't notice you catching many mice,' said Kate, peering over her book-keeping. 'That's what you're here for, you know.'

Snoopy looked faintly apologetic. She hated letting Kate down. She would try harder tomorrow. She must catch something.

The next morning she roamed the shop, playing and pouncing, getting into training. She chased motes in the air, boxed a few rounds with silk tassels, leaped to catch at price-tags. Then she was wholly successful. She dragged a dead pair of evening gloves to Kate's feet and sat there growling with pride.

'Oh, Snoopy, you horror. They cost me a pound!'

But Snoopy's sharp eye-teeth had not damaged them.

She had a very gentle mouth. Minutes later she returned with a suffocated bundle of lace curtains, closely followed by a throttled Chinese fan. She couldn't understand why Kate was not pleased.

'I think I'd better go to that auction before you assault all my stock,' said Kate, tucking her long hair inside her helmet. 'And you can come with me. You're not safe to leave anywhere.'

Snoopy leaped into her cardboard box and stood obediently while Kate wrapped the scarf round her. The scarf had become obligatory. Snoopy wouldn't go anywhere without it. And she had no fear of travelling. She would have followed Kate to the moon.

The auction was being held in an old country barn, and people brought goods to sell from miles around. Kate was a regular buyer of the periods she specialised in, but there were lots of large household goods which were of no interest. There was one item she really wanted. It was a miscellaneous collection of pre-Second World War children's games – lotto, dominoes, snakes and ladders, happy families, ludo, tiddly-winks – all old but so well made, despite being worn with use. They were all jumbled together in a large oval-shaped wicker basket with lid, the sides patterned with close and open weaves. Kate bid for the collection and it was knocked down to her. 'Does the basket go with them?' she asked the auctioneer afterwards.

'All yours, miss,' he nodded.

'Good,' said Kate in a stage whisper to Snoopy. 'You can have the basket instead of the cardboard box before it falls to pieces. Good idea, eh? Brainwave, in fact.'

Kate spent the evening making the basket wind-proof and cosy for Snoopy to travel in, and a foam cushion for her to curl up on. Snoopy inspected the transformation and decided it was not bad, not bad at all. A test trample passed A1.

Kate remembered the vet's instructions and got out the ointment for Snoopy's eyes, the drops for her ears and the spray for her skin. 'I am beginning to wonder,' she said, unscrewing the silver tube, 'just who is working for who. I haven't stopped doing things for you since you arrived.'

Snoopy licked up the last crumb of crisp. A few crisps were her reward for keeping still while Kate did her treatment. Her eyes and ears were almost better, and her coat was growing again with the help of the daily brushing. It was a delicate cream colour, pure white in places, touched with the palest fawn in others. It was growing long and soft, floating round her like a halo of light.

She spent all day in her playground: the shop. There were so many delightful things to amuse her . . . velvet pincushions, fringes and beads, china dolls and ancient teddies, wooden ornaments, macramé and wool, knitting-needles, and glass marbles that scattered beneath her paws.

As she played, dancing and prancing, light as thistle-down, people gathered at the shop window, drawn by her unconscious innocence and artless grace. They came to watch, lingered, and often stayed to buy. Kate's business flourished. It seemed that whatever Snoopy touched, Kate sold. Soon she was able to pay back her overdraft at the bank.

It was at an antique fair that Kate met Peter Madoc. He was one of the sons of Madoc & Sons, a well-known firm of London antique dealers. He noticed Kate the moment she got off her moped in the driveway of the old mansion; she shook free her long hair from the confines of a helmet and then took a cat out of the basket on the back of her bike.

She held the cat high and close to her face, and he was struck by the look of understanding and love that the cat and the woman exchanged. There was a magical rapport between them that he knew he would not easily forget.

She took a bag from her pocket, and the cat was eating from the palm of her hand.

'Hello,' he said, strolling over. 'I've never seen a cat eating crisps before.'

'She's addicted to them,' said Kate, turning away. He was a very attractive man with a thatch of prematurely grey hair above a young face. He wore rimless glasses that were held together by a double bar of gold across the bridge. 'They're a treat, a reward, but I can't think what she's done to deserve them. She is supposed to catch mice in my shop but so far she hasn't caught one.'

'Have you still got mice?' he asked, following her.

'I don't really know. I think they've gone. Perhaps Snoopy's scared them off.'

'She's a lovely cat.'

'Do you know anything about cats?'

'A little,' said Peter Madoc. 'I've an aunt who breeds cats. Cats like yours, actually. Long-haired creams. She shows them at shows and gets lots of prizes. Has your cat got a pedigree?'

'I haven't a clue,' said Kate. 'I got her from the CPL. She's a stray. She was in a terrible mess and they had to cut off her fur. That's why she's called Snoopy.'

Peter Madoc tilted Snoopy's chin, looking at the shape of her head and staring into her fearless eyes. Snoopy recognised the hands of an expert. She had been handled like this before. She wondered what was going to happen next.

Peter Madoc was also wondering. He was in a quandary. He knew what he should say next if he was to be honest, but he was also remembering the moment when the woman had held the cat against her face. And then there was Kate herself. He found himself more disturbed by her than he cared to admit.

'A few months ago my aunt lost one of her queens, a beautiful female cat called Honeymist Sherrypuff. She was being taken to a cattery to a stud cat when somehow she escaped. I hate to tell you this.' He was still hesitating. 'But I know my aunt's long-haired creams. I think this is her lost cat. I think this is Honeymist Sherrypuff.'

Snoopy maintained a perfectly blank expression, while Kate's arms tightened round her. 'What nonsense,' said Kate. 'Of course this isn't your aunt's cat. You must be mistaken. There must be thousands of cats that could look like this Honeymist cat. This is my cat and no one is going to take her away from me.' She marched off, head held high, Snoopy peering over her shoulder with a look of complete satisfaction.

'Stop spitting at me,' Peter Madoc called out. He came after her with long strides. 'I wasn't going to take your cat away from you. I can see with my own eyes what you mean to each other, and my aunt has half a dozen other cats. But I'll make a bargain with you.'

'A bargain? I don't understand,' said Kate.

'My silence for that hat-box.'

'Hat-box? What hat-box?'

'The hat-box you're trundling around on the back of your moped. I just hope Snoopy hasn't chewed the edges.'

'Snoopy never damages anything,' said Kate haughtily. 'She's very well-behaved.' Suddenly she was all business woman. 'Is it valuable?'

'My dear young lady, that box is an eighteenth-century travelling hat-box. They were mostly used on the Continent by middle-class folk: country doctors, farmers. Because they were not durable, they are very hard to find.'

'What a nerve,' Kate stormed. 'In the first place, they're my hat-box and my cat. You can't have either. I could complain to someone about this. You're being very unethical.'

'No, I'm not. I believe that to be my aunt's cat, a valuable breeding queen. But the situation is negotiable. Will you start by having lunch with me?'

'I don't blame your aunt's cat for escaping,' said Kate fiercely.

They stopped arguing and began to laugh and Snoopy did not understand why. The negotiations seemed to take quite a long time. Peter organised many visits to the shop, drives to the coast, candle-lit suppers, riverside walks and picnics in the hills. They came to a very amicable arrangement. Peter would sell the hat-box for her, and buy Snoopy a new ultra-modern, super-hygienic, wind-proof, scenic-sided carrier out of his percentage. And not a word to his aunt.

'He must love me,' she confided happily to Snoopy one day. 'Now if only you would catch a mouse, life would be perfect.'

Down the high street was a big silver tabby tom who was keen on Snoopy. He thought she was the cat's whiskers. He was also an excellent mouser, but thick with it. It was child's play for Snoopy to take his latest catch off him. She patted the revolting thing up the back lane to the shop, through the rear entrance and pushed it in a casual, off-hand manner towards Kate's feet. She then sat back to clean the labour off her paws.

'You've caught a mouse!' Kate shrieked, before picking it up with tongs and putting it in the dustbin. 'You clever puss,' she said, giving Snoopy a crisp. 'Your very first mouse.'

And my last, thought Snoopy. Thank goodness that was over; she need never think about mice again.

She jumped up onto a fretwork table in the centre of the shop window and began washing the salt off her whiskers. She did not know she was reflected in the shell-edged mirror on the side shelf, nor that people were gathering to watch. Snoopy had found her true vocation. No one had told her that window-dressing would be such fun.

# Independence Brown

Independence Brown was her name right from the very beginning. The name sounded like the heroine of an early American pioneer film and it suited her. They could almost imagine her trekking across the plains of Arizona in a covered wagon, repelling Indians and enduring great hardships.

The Browns called her Independence in the first place because they got her on July 4 and were sorry about the American Revolution and the Boston Tea Party. But it soon became obvious that the tiny scruff of mottled fur was a fiercely independent and ornery cuss from the word go, determined to stand forever on her own wobbly four paws.

She did everything in her own time. Lifted onto a lap, the kitten fought furiously for release, only to return minutes later, acquiescent and docile. Put on a litter tray, she scrambled out, granules flying over the floor, only to sit politely by the door asking to be let out. Food and drink were ignored: she ate when she wanted to, be it dawn or midnight.

It took the family a long time to get to know her; if they met outside, Inde merely glanced at them as if they were strangers.

'I sometimes wonder if that cat belongs to us at all,'

said Mrs Ellen Brown. 'She gives us all the cold shoulder.'

Inde grew into a striking British silver tabby. The dark symmetrical markings on her grey fur were like blotting-paper images, and the lines and splodges on her small face gave her a curiously clown-like look. It was perhaps this frivolous appearance that she was determined to live down.

The only person Inde acknowledged was Corrine Brown – if acknowledge was the right word. They had something strongly in common and recognised in each other a kindred spirit. At sixteen, Corrine was going through a fight for her independence, and she often envied Inde's ruthless demolition of any Brown plans for her life.

Several times they made an appointment for a very necessary visit to the vet's. Inde refused point-blank to go. She was up and over the garden wall and into the woods, and was not seen again for thirty-six hours. Then one day she climbed into her travelling basket and sat there waiting for Mr Brown to get the car out. When she was brought home, she sat groggily licking the sore place with an air of comical sadness, as if she knew all about denied kittens and the lost joys of motherhood.

That evening she curled up on Corrine's lap all through a James Bond film. They thought that at last Inde had mellowed. But they were wrong. The next day she had recovered, and spat at anything that moved.

The neighbouring woods were her delight. She played and explored and scavenged. Every square inch was known territory. As the woods changed with the seasons, so Inde found further joys and excitements. She flew down the garden with the long rippling strides of a tiger, took the wall with the graceful leap of a front runner at the Grand National, sped across the stepping-stones of the brook with the sure-footedness of a gazelle. Corrine never failed to feel a surge of admiration watching this co-ordination of movement; it was beautiful. She would look up from her studies and watch from the window as Inde took her path to freedom. Corrine sometimes fancied she could share the joy of the cat as Inde headed for the woods. Corrine wished she knew where she herself was going, and what lay beyond school examinations and perhaps university.

Inde deliberately strengthened her independence. During her periodic disappearances, they did not look for her. Her return to bed and board was heralded by a sharp *yeowell* at the back door. She did not apologise for the wisps of dry fern and moss clinging to her fur; she had been roaming her beloved woods.

'I can't think what's got into Inde these days,' said Ellen Brown with some exasperation as she threw away an untouched dish of cat-food. 'She's always had eccentric eating habits, but she's never ignored food altogether.'

Corrine went on her knees to stroke the cat. There was something odd about Inde. She was creeping around as if half-expecting to be set upon, front paws held out in a curiously stiff manner. Inde licked the salt off Corrine's fingers with her rough sandpaper tongue. It was the first sign of affection she had ever shown.

Corrine put some morsels of chicken in the palm of her hand and held them under Inde's nose. The small tongue shot out and the chicken was gone in a flash. The cat was starving.

'Well, I never,' said Ellen from the pastry board. 'She ignored it all yesterday.'

Corrine filled a dish and put it at Inde's toes. The cat crouched down on her haunches and polished off the lot. It was the same with some milk.

'How strange,' said Corrine, worried. It was so unlike Inde, to have to be waited on. Her spirit was fiercely valiant, but something was defeating her now. 'Perhaps we ought to take her to the vet.'

'Give it a day or two and see if she gets over it,' said Ellen. 'I've a heavy week. Two committee meetings and a flag day.'

And Corrine was busy packing. She had collected the right number of grades and was to read history for three years. Her parents had hoped she would accept a place in London so that she could still live at home, but Corrine had opted for a university in the industrial north. She was apprehensive about the move. What would she find there? What would the people be like? She knew she must take her courage into her two hands and run at it, in the same way that Inde ran to her beloved woods.

Corrine took Inde upstairs with her. She felt in the need of uncritical company. She was on the defensive, with her mother still trying to organise everything for her. She started to sort out her books so that she knew which ones to leave at home, making a list of their titles.

It was an absorbing task and the two piles of books grew, hiding Inde from view. Suddenly the piles fell over and Inde shot across the room; she crashed headlong into a record case, fur flying and paws askew. Inde stepped back and crouched on the carpet, trembling, her long ringed tail swished from side to side. But it was not in anger. It was more like the sweeping of a radar beam.

Corrine walked on her knees to the stricken cat and tried to calm her.

'Easy, girl,' she soothed. 'Did the silly old books frighten you? There . . . there . . .'

She looked carefully at the cat from all angles, ran her hands down each limb. Then she put a cushion on the floor and moved away to the other side of the room. A kind of chill settled on her actions. She tapped the leg of her bed with a pencil and called out: 'Inde . . . Inde . . .'

Inde got up, ears perked forward, whiskers twitching. She did not leap over the cushion or step across it. She did not side-track either. She walked straight into it.

Corrine picked up Inde gently and sat on the floor, cradling her in her arms. Silently tears fell down her cheeks. She had never felt so sad in all her life. A light had gone out, Inde's light. The light of Independence Brown.

The cat was blind.

The vet thought Inde must have been in an accident during one of her disappearances. Perhaps a car wing had caught her a sharp blow to the side of the head; perhaps she had fallen from a high tree and detached the retina. They would never know. The vet suggested that the kindest thing would be to have her put down.

Inde was carefully exploring the vet's examination table, sniffing the edges, alert and curious. The afternoon sunlight streamed through the windows, catching all the silver in her coat. Her fur was alive and sparkling. No one could destroy anything so beautiful.

'Oh no, I think we'll give her a chance,' said Ellen Brown slowly. 'She's got such an independent nature.'

At first they moved every awkward object in the house out of the way – the umbrella stand, the log basket, waste bins. Then they realised that this was not really doing the cat a favour. It was better that Inde learned where everything was and tracked round them. Everyone became consciously tidier, no longer leaving shopping, briefcases, shoes on the floor.

Inde responded to noise; she recognised the sound of the tin-opener, the refrigerator door being opened, milk poured. She kept out of the way when the telephone rang or there was a knock on the door. She became far more vocal. If she was quite lost, she stood still in that foreign place, miaowing for someone to put her somewhere more familiar.

By the time Corrine came home from her first term at university, Inde had come to terms with her blindness. She still walked with a strange gait as if she was not completely relaxed, but her independence had reasserted itself and she did not want to be helped. She knew the lay-out of the house and garden intimately, only thrown occasionally by someone's carelessness. She still ruled her own life. She had no intention of being an invalid.

One day Corrine found Inde sitting by the foot of the garden wall. She looked melancholy, as far as a clown-faced cat can look melancholy. She let out a single, sad wail.

'Why, I believe you are missing your woods,' said Corrine. 'You know they are over there, don't you, the other side of the wall? Poor Inde, you can smell them and hear them but you can't cope with that wall. You need a helping hand.'

She lifted Inde up to put her over the wall, but the cat struggled and flopped out of her grasp, falling onto the waste ground the other side. Inde streaked off into the undergrowth, careering headlong through grass and fern like a demented creature. Even when she was out of sight Corrine could still hear the small sounds of her crashing progress through the woods.

Corrine hung about, but Inde did not come back. Eventually she gave up and went indoors. Late that evening they heard a piercing *yeowell*. It was Inde waiting to be returned over the wall. She was wet. She had obviously tried to cross the stepping-stones and fallen in the brook.

'Well, I'm much too busy to ferry her backwards and forwards over the wall,' said Ellen. 'I can't be around to do wall duty every day. What's going to happen when you go back to university?'

'I'll think of something.'

It did not seem feasible to knock a hole in the wall, so Corrine devised two planks leaning against the wall, one either side, so that Inde could get back. She wedged the foot of each plank with a stone and introduced Inde to her walk-over. Inde sniffed, then after a few hesitant, tentative steps, she understood. When she got to the top of the wall, she sniffed the air, not sure what was expected of her. She was about to leap off when Corrine restrained her.

'Oh, no, you don't. You've got to learn the way down too. Then you'll be able to get back.' Corrine guided the cat to the edge of the plank that led down to the ground. Inde stepped forward with perfect trust. She caught on

197

immediately and sped down the plank. Without a murmur of thanks she darted off into the woods with rather more care for the undergrowth.

Corrine stood there, laughing. She had given Inde a bridge to freedom. She wondered if someone would give her a bridge into this new adult world she had so recently entered.

Inde never hesitated again. She flew down the garden, unerringly straight for the plank, up and over and into the woods. No one would have known that she was blind. It was a joy to watch the animal flying through the air.

One night there was a gale and the wind and heavy rain dislodged the planks. Inde shot out of the back door, straight down the garden but pulled up short of the wall. She sniffed around and found the fallen plank and sat on it, waiting for someone to do something about it.

A young Canadian student, Bruce, was staying overnight. After breakfast he went down the garden with Corrine to look at the damage.

'Well, if I'm going to be an architect, I might as well start my career with a cat bridge,' he grinned. He put stakes in the ground at intervals and lashed the planks to the stakes. It was firm but amateurish.

'If I had more time I'd build a brick–supported ramp,' he said, wielding a mallet on the stakes. Inde sat at a safe distance, listening to the noise with concealed curiosity. 'Though it seems a lot of work just to get one cat over one wall.'

'It's all in the name of independence,' said Corrine mysteriously. 'You could always come again in the spring holiday,' she added.

'So I could,' he said.

The bridge was Inde's lifeline to freedom. Over the years Bruce made adaptations and improvements to its design. Inde took to each change with trust and confidence. She now knew every inch of the woods. It was still difficult to believe that she could not see. She did not let her blindness stop her doing anything she wanted to do. She even climbed trees, moving carefully along swaying branches. Sometimes Corrine watched with her heart in her mouth as Inde took a calculated leap into the air to reach another branch. Sometimes the cat missed.

She learned the size and position of each of the stepping-stones and could walk across them with scarcely a hestitation. Her mind was a complicated file of maps and routes and angles, all painstakingly learned by trial and error, committed to memory, and once there, acted upon with total confidence.

In her first year of teaching Corrine came home regularly, but gradually there were other countries with sites of historical interest to see, new friends to visit, holidays with Bruce. Inde accepted that her dearest friend should be finding new worlds and had less time for her. She turned to Ellen and grew closer to her.

Ellen was slowing down her good work for the community as younger and more enthusiastic women moved into the neighbourhood. She sat more often in the garden with her sewing or writing letters, Inde stretched out on the grass beside her, the sun warming her body.

'I'm quite glad I've given up all those committees,' said Ellen. 'I can enjoy my own garden now without having to get up and rush off somewhere.'

Absent-mindedly she put her hand down to stroke the cat's head. Inde put out her tongue and licked at Ellen's fingers. It was the first time that Inde had ever shown any sign of affection towards Ellen and she was unaccountably touched. All those years of tapping saucers and leading the cat with her voice; all those years of watching and caring for the independent creature had not gone completely unnoticed.

She stroked the cat's chin. There was the faintest vibration in Inde's throat. It was the birth of a purr. Ellen felt rewarded beyond measure.

'Both of us getting old,' she teased. 'Soft thing . . .'

Inde had an annual check-up at the vet's. He thought

she was remarkably fit despite her disability and her age. 'A touch of arthritis,' he said. 'But that's to be expected at her age. Keep an eye on her if we have a very cold snap this winter.'

Corrine came home for the whole of the summer vacation. She was packing again. This time she was off to Australia on a teacher-exchange scheme. It was an exciting prospect. They were even going to exchange flats, and Corrine would be living in Sydney not far from the sea.

As Corrine's world grew, so Inde's shrank. She did not wander so far now. She had got thinner and the bright silver in her coat had dulled. She stood on the doorstep facing the garden, her face lifted towards the sun and towards the life that used to exist beyond.

'I think she wants to go to the woods,' said Corrine. 'Shall I take her? She used to love them so.' Corrine began to stroll down the garden. 'Inde . . . Come on, Inde . . .'

Inde followed stiffly. The bottom of the garden seemed a long way. Corrine bent to carry her over the wall, but the cat struggled out of her arms and insisted on crossing the bridge by herself, slowly and a little unsteadily.

'All right, have it your own way,' said Corrine.

They wandered through the woods together, the cat sniffing old haunts and new growth, remembering all the joys that had once been hers: oak moss, leaf mould, wild violets; Corrine thinking of the new paths that were opening up for her, if she had the courage to take them.

When they came to the brook, Inde hesitated. She had forgotten the exact sequence of the stepping-stones. Corrine went ahead, tapping each stone and calling. Inde followed. Once she almost slipped, but Corrine was there to catch her and set her back on the stone. Inde took a great leap from the last stone onto the opposite bank. That much she remembered.

It was a lovely afternoon for both of them, golden and

warm; the silver cat's splodges and stripes merging with the dappled shadows until she was almost part of the woods themselves.

Inde was very tired by the time they got home. She drank some milk and stretched herself out before the newly lit fire and went to sleep, her paws still twitching with memories of her old exciting life.

'I suppose I may not see Inde again,' said Corrine, her hand faltering on the soft fur, feeling the gentle rise and fall of that stubborn heart. How quickly the years had gone by, and Corrine had become too busy sometimes to give any time to her cat. Every day Inde had lived in her shadowy world, day after day, refusing to give in, following the promise in the wind.

'Probably not,' said Ellen, turning her face away.

Corrine continued to stroke the silver coat, remembering the cat's endless courage and determination; her fight for everything that she had a right to have. 'You'll stay with her, won't you?' she said in a low voice.

'I'll be here,' said Ellen.

The following week Corrine left for Australia. She did not hesitate. Her plane flew unerringly straight, up and over, taking her across a bridge to freedom.

# Toby's Diary

*2.31 a.m.* Awoken by sound of stairs creaking as someone comes down. I know from the light tread that it is the woman. And she is barefooted. I do not move because she does not mind if she finds me in the shoe cupboard, curled up on his suede shoes. The only time she has ever been cross with me was when I used her new brown boots as a scratching post.

*2.32 a.m.* She has put the light on and is filling the kettle with water. That means a cup of tea. And if there's tea in the offing, that means milk, and if there's any milk about, I shall soon make a studiedly casual appearance.

*2.35 a.m.* The refrigerator door is being opened. Time to make a move.

'Hello, Toby. Can't you sleep either?' the woman asks. 'Would you like some milk? It'll be too cold straight from the fridge, so I'll pop a drop of hot water in it. There you are.'

*2.39 a.m.* Drink milk. She is sitting at the kitchen table, sipping tea and reading yesterday's newspaper. She often gets up in the middle of the night to read the paper, especially recently. She is wearing a red quilted dressing-gown which I like to get my claws into. I jump onto her lap and settle down for a snooze.

'There's a nice Toby,' she says absently, her hand

passing lightly over my head. 'You understand, don't you?'

*2.59 a.m.* Awake with jerk. Nearly fall off lap. She is crying and hunting for something in her dressing-gown pocket. I am dislodged and clamber back to my perch as she blows her nose on a handkerchief.

'I can't seem to stop crying. I shall look dreadful in the morning, eyes swollen and a red nose, I know. I'm such a fool and I do worry so about things. But this is important, Toby. I ought to ask him, I see that, but I can't . . .'

*3.05 a.m.* Am just settled down again, when hey-ho I'm tipped onto the floor. She really has got the fidgets. She is pouring herself another cup of tea. I see I'm not getting seconds. Still, she is upset . . . all that crying. It can't be healthy.

*3.10 a.m.* Sit in my wicker basket like Goody Two-shoes. I shall vacate it the instant that she leaves the room. I was given it for Christmas ( would somebody please explain Christmas?) which means I am supposed to be grateful. But I am not. It's scratchy. It's cold and smells of a damp shop and sawdust and cages. Therefore I hate it. Therefore I only sit in it for the absolute minimum.

*3.20 a.m.* She is still sitting there crying over the news-paper. It must be all bad news. I cannot stand the basket one second longer and jump out onto the floor. I begin to wash myself. My motto is: if in doubt, wash.

'One I would expect, two perhaps,' she sobbed in-coherently. 'But not THREE. Oh, Toby, not three . . .'

*3.21 a.m.* I cast a weary eye at the clock. This is no time to begin guessing games. I'm longing to get back to the shoe cupboard. The windowsill has no appeal in the middle of the night. The wood is hard and cold. But in the morning, it's quite different. I really like it there in the morning. I can see the postman arriving and perhaps the milkman (especially the milkman) and that dim dog from next door being taken for a walk on a piece of string. I can glare and smirk and thoroughly enjoy his discomfiture in complete safety. I'd like to see anyone try leading me about on a piece of string.

*3.30 a.m.* She's off upstairs at last. Whip into cupboard. Suede shoes still warm. They really are remarkable. I believe I ought to write to the makers: Dear Sir, As a satisfied customer, I feel I . . . yawn . . .

*3.31 a.m.* Asleep.

*7.20 a.m.* Rudely awoken by male elephant stampede in kitchen. Lights flash dangerously. Kettle flung on stove. Cups clatter. Cupboard doors bang. I tuck my head under. I've heard it all before.

'Hell, I've overslept again! Sally . . . Sally,' he shouts up the stair. 'I'm late. That damned alarm didn't go off.'

'It did go off. I heard it.' Sally's voice is thick with sleep.

'Then why didn't you wake me?' he accuses.

'I thought you'd heard it.'

'Well, I hadn't.'

'How was I to know?' She appears, tousled, tired, depressed already, and the day has hardly started. She begins making him a cup of instant coffee with the top of the milk. He always gets the top of the milk.

'That damned cat is on my shoes! Get off my shoes.'

*7.22 a.m.* Danger! Danger! Abandon cupboard. Flank attack. Escape to safety of dark space under sideboard. Crouch there, glowering. Twitch cobwebs off whiskers. Do not take kindly to being spoken to so roughly, particularly first thing in the morning when my nerves are delicate.

'I've told you a dozen times to keep that cupboard door shut. I will not have that cat sleeping on my shoes. Look at all the hairs . . . they're practically glued on. I can't wear them like that. I'll have to wear my new ones.'

'He likes your shoes, Pete. It's the suede. There's something about the suede.'

*7.23 a.m.* I am glad about the hairs. I wish I'd had a good scratch as well.

'Right, Sally. I'm off. I'm going to be late for work.'

'Me too,' Sally sighs.

*7.40 a.m.* Light breakfast of Kattifood, liver flavour. One brewer's yeast tablet. Saucer of milk. Tipped out into garden. Sit on garden step, washing my whiskers, although they are spotless. Eye two cheeky sparrows on lilac tree. They are wondering whether to risk a quick peck at the lawn. I thrash my tail in warning.

*8.15 a.m.* Alerted by sound of door opening. Streak indoors, doing three-minute mile, between her boots (same brown boots) in hall, up stairs, under bed.

'Oh no . . . Toby,' she howls. 'Not now. Don't start playing games, please. I'll kill you if you make me miss my train.'

*8.17 a.m.* Am dragged out from under bed. Go limp and totally unhelpful. Am bundled outside again, but she stops to give me a forgiving pat and a quick kiss.

'Now, I'm leaving you in charge, Toby. Look after everything until I get back. I do hope the postman comes. After all, we've only been married a year and surely romance ought to last longer than that?'

*8.45 a.m.* Postman comes down the path. I open one eye but do not move. I am not freaky about postmen.

'Hello, cat,' says this one, bending to stroke my ears. 'Nothing for you today.'

*8.46 a.m.* Not surprised. There never is anything for me. Still it's friendly of him to tell me. Leave trail of pale hairs round his trouser cuffs which he does not notice.

*9.25 a.m.* Action stations! Milkman is imminent. I can hear those clinking bottles half a mile off. Go to meet him. Believe in keeping in with the right people. Sally is not mean on the milk, and he is carrying our regular three pints. He puts them in the plastic carrier and takes out the rinsed empties.

'And what's your order this morning, puss? Half a pint of the best double cream and a carton of Devon clotted?' he says.

*9.26 a.m.* It's one of our jokes. Delivering milk has made our milkman a happy man and even when it's raining, or snowing, or the path is like an ice rink, he still finds time to speak to me. Sometimes he brings me a split carton of single cream or a cracked egg. He's not a man for letting anything go to waste. Perhaps he hasn't got a cat of his own. He is my knight in shining armour, even if his steed is an electrically operated float. I watch him drive away.

*9.31 a.m.* Scare off crowd of silly birds who think those old crusts are for them. They are my elevenses. Sally threw them out for me. I'm sure she did. Walk round the garden inspecting things. Seems all right. The sun has a chilly sparkle. Snowdrops are peeping shyly from between their leaves, their heads hanging like little wax bells.

*9.33 a.m.* Tread on fly.

*9.34 a.m.* Let fly go. Spring is in the earth and this is no time for killing.

*9.45 a.m.* Feeling weary; after all I've been up since half-past two. Curl round on pile of old newspapers stacked by the side of the house. The newspapers are warm but the wind is taking a short cut through the carport. I tuck my nose under my fur, flatten my ears and pull up the drawbridge, so to speak.

*4.35 p.m.* She should be home soon. Start pacing the path. Hunger is gnawing at my vitals. I want my supper.

*5.10 p.m.* She is late.

*5.15 p.m.* She's very late. She's missed her train. She's not coming home. She's gone to live somewhere else. She's completely forgotten me. Whatever will become of me?

*5.20 p.m.* Sit on top step, near pavement.

*5.25 p.m.* Hear familiar tread. I can recognise her footsteps even with boots on. I miaow loudly, protesting at long wait.

'Toby darling . . .' she calls from a distance.

*5.26 p.m.* She scoops me up into her arms. I lick her cheek, her chin, her collar, her ear. I'm pleased to see her. It's been such a long day and I get lonesome, even with the milkman and the birds and being in charge. She laughs and tries to avoid my tongue.

'Toby, please . . . I don't need a wash. Let me get my key out and we'll soon have the kettle on. And I've brought some lovely coley for you.'

*5.30 p.m.* She gives me some milk and dry crunchy cat biscuits. The kettle is on. She turns the mail over in her hands and they are shaking.

'Three bills for Pete. A circular from a book club and a letter from Aunt Sophia. But nothing for me. Nothing at all for me, not even one tiny little card. Oh Toby, those three cards . . . I wish I'd never found them in his desk. I suppose he's sent them to his old girl-friends, or perhaps he's found someone new . . .'

*5.35 p.m.* The kettle is boiling, but Sally does not seem to notice. The steam is shooting towards the ceiling like white foam. It alarms me and I call out to her, but she does not hear. I paw her skirt and tug at it, but she brushes me aside. There is nothing I can do.

*6.00 p.m.* My coley supper is ready, right on time. Very nice. She certainly knows how to cook coley.

*6.21 p.m.* Man rushes in. Also cold air.

'Please shut the door,' says Sally testily.

'Is that all the greeting I get after a hard day's work? "Shut the door"? "Hello darling" would be more inviting.'

'Hello darling and shut the door.'

'That's better. How's my baby? Give us a kiss.'

'Your baby is tired, hungry and wondering if you happen to know what day it is.'

'Tuesday? Wednesday? Does it matter?'

'Yes, I think it does matter.'

'Sally, you're talking really weird. Is there a cup of coffee going? These new shoes are killing me. Where are my old suede ones, the pair Toby likes so much?'

'In the cupboard. I'll just fetch the milk.'

*6.40 p.m.* Door opens. Cold air rushes in again. These humans must have leather skin.

*6.41 p.m.* Door bursts open. At this rate I shall get

pneumonia. She is bringing in the carrier with the three bottles of milk which my friend, the milkman, left this morning. There are envelopes attached to the bottles.

'Pete,' she cries. 'Three cards! One tied to each bottle of milk.'

'Well, well. You don't say. Aren't you going to open them?' He is grinning at her.

'There's one for each of us. "To my dearest wife", "To a hunky man" – '

'Wonder who that can be . . .'

'And one for Toby! Oh Toby, look . . . Someone has sent you a Valentine's card.'

*6.42 p.m.* I look at my card. It is a picture of a fluffy white female cat wearing false eyelashes and a pink bow in her fur. *Urgh* . . . A PINK BOW. I knock the card over with a light swipe, chew one corner thoughtfully and then sit on it. I guess I ought to show some gratitude.

'But why the milkman? That's what I can't understand,' she smiles. 'Why get the milkman to deliver the cards?'

'Because you were expecting the postman to bring them. I thought I'd be a little more original than that. I rushed out and gave them to him at the depot. He's a very obliging milkman.'

'Darling Pete . . . I should have known you wouldn't forget.'

*7.15 p.m.* Stone me, if I'm not out in the garden again. They were hugging and kissing, then suddenly it's hats on and they are off out for a Chinese at the Golden Pagoda. After keeping an eye on things all day, I'd been looking forward to a quiet evening at home on Sally's knee watching Crossroads through to News at Ten. Instead of which I'm banished to the front step and there's no knowing what time they'll be home. I don't believe that's justice.

*7.18 p.m.* Still at my post. When they return they will no doubt find me frozen solid. They will have to thaw me out in the linen cupboard.

*7.20 p.m.* There is a family of pesky dormice scuttling about among the dry leaves. The old owl has woken up in the tree and his eyes are shining like yellow beacons. The moon is smiling at me behind the dark branches. Hello, moon. Somewhere a fox is calling.

*7.21 p.m.* This has been a nice day. I shall have a lot to put in my diary. I really like keeping a diary. It gives me a purpose in life. The one drawback is that being a cat, I never know the date.

# The Terrible Three

They became known as the Terrible Three following the afternoon they dug up Mr Arkwright's prize cos lettuces and left the helpless threads of leaf strewn across the garden like the trail of a scavenger hunt.

'It's those terrible three,' Mr Arkwright stormed, as he went down on his knees to lift the chewed stems of the seedlings. But even his green fingers couldn't give them back life and he consigned them to the compost heap, wondering if he would have anything ready for the horticultural show in July.

'I know it's you,' he shouted, as he caught sight of three long tails whisking to and fro in the hedge. 'And I'll catch you at it one day. You've been warned! Dratted cats.'

The lettuces were only one incident in a long line of delinquencies. They terrorised the local goldfish; they knocked over milk bottles; any washed car immediately invited a muddy game of pawball. They jumped on unsuspecting dogs; chased the postman; and regularly pilfered anything worth taking from the bird tables along the road. They particularly liked fruit cake and canapés.

'Oh no, you must be mistaken,' said Lavinia Robbins as the neighbours queued up to complain. 'Not my three little angels . . . Look, there they are in front of the fire.

You couldn't have three more darling little cats.'

The Terrible Three looked smugly at each other. They were indeed angelic: clean, dainty, affectionate and not a whisker out of place. They washed their faces with soft paws that couldn't hurt a fly, and purred gentle songs of happiness in front of the glowing flames.

'There you are,' said Lavinia, going on – and she could go on – quite a bit. 'It must have been some other cats. Your best lace curtains? Oh no, it wasn't my pussies.'

Lavinia had acquired three cats practically by accident. When she retired from a nursing post in Penang and returned to live in England, she was quite lonely and thought a cat might be company. She read an advertisement in a shop window for a litter wanting good homes, and she thought she could indeed provide a good home.

She had an adequate pension, and with her carefully hoarded savings had bought herself a small timber-framed house and tiny garden. Everything in it was spick and span, and the idea of a spick and span cat for company was pleasing.

There were only two kittens left when Lavinia went round to see the litter. And she couldn't make up her mind which one to have. When two pairs of sapphire blue eyes gazed up in wonderment at her, Lavinia realised that the choice was not which kitten to have, but which one to reject. It was a cruel choice.

As she watched the tiny tumblers skating over the floor, attacking each other in mock combat, minute teeth gripping soft furry necks, she realised that it was impossible to separate them. So both kittens went home with her in a shopping basket.

The third cat chose her. Lavinia did not even really like Siamese. She thought them too skinny and sharp-faced for a proper cat. But one drizzly morning she opened the back door to fetch the milk, and a thin, wet Siamese cat stalked into the kitchen, calmly sat down in the middle of the floor and howled in protest.

'Shoo . . . Shoo . . .' Lavinia said ineffectively for

three days, but the Siamese was not budging. As fast as she carried him out into the garden, so he streaked back in at the first opportunity.

The three cats got together and formed a tableau, the two tabby kittens sitting either side of the stately Siamese, like bookends. Lavinia's heart contracted and she gave in. She was not to know that they had actually formed an unholy alliance.

'Well, since you all get along so well together, you may as well stay,' she said to the Siamese, who forgave her for the three wells. He leered and wound his long whip-like tail round her ankles. She rubbed his bony head and marvelled at the turquoise glint in his beautiful eyes. 'But you have got to behave,' she added, as if reading the future.

The tabby kittens were called Tiggy and Daisy. Tiggy was a well-marked silver and black tabby, with dark rings down his long tail; his sister had a lot more white on her body, with the tabby markings endearingly smudged on her little face, giving her a look of elfin charm. The Siamese was a seal-point, with rich brown fur shading into pale cream down his elegant body, and big pointed ears. For a long time Lavinia could not think what to call him. Then, remembering her days in Penang, she called him Chang. He quite liked it . . . if you can tell when a Siamese likes anything.

Chang was, of course, the leader of the Terrible Three. He assumed the position by virtue of size, age and intelligence. He led the kittens into terrible scrapes as soon as they were old enough to stagger outside. Even the sweet-faced Daisy was game for any mischief. She became the gang's moll, ready to follow her peers anywhere.

They had one unwritten law. They never did anything dreadful at home or damaged any of Lavinia's possessions. That was why she simply couldn't believe all the accusations levelled at her pets. Her neighbours must have a grudge. But what?

It took Lavinia a long time to work that one out, but

she came to the conclusion that it must be something to do with the horticultural show. There were several elderly people in the road, and retired people like to grow things to prove that life still goes on. They took the show very seriously.

Lavinia had brought with her from Penang the knack of growing orchids. They flourished on her windowsills like an exotic tropical garden, their gorgeously fragile flowers blooming one by one throughout the winter, much to the envy of her neighbours. There was no doubt in their minds that Miss Robbins would scoop many of the prizes with her orchids. They did not know that she had no intention of showing them. She grew them only for her pleasure.

This, decided Lavinia, must be the link. She had no way of knowing that the Terrible Three deserved every harsh word thrown at them.

'My very good pussies,' she said absently, putting down three equal saucers of milk. 'That Mr Arkwright doesn't know what he's talking about. What a lot of fuss about a few lettuces. There's plenty of time to sow some more if he's that keen on them.'

The three cats lapped their milk in unison. They had not thought the lettuces up to much – definitely not worth a prize. Now that custard-coloured canary over the road was worth a prize – it would make a tasty snack any day of the week.

The catalogue of crimes continued, and although it was an excellent way of becoming acquainted with one's neighbours, Lavinia had the feeling that it was not going to improve her social life. She became accustomed to opening the door and finding an irate person with ruined tights, or broken flowerpots or chewed geraniums.

'But I assure you, it's not my pussies,' she insisted, shaking her head sadly. 'They've been at home all afternoon, as good as gold.'

The fourth time Mr Arkwright came round, he was almost incensed with rage. In his hands he held the snapped necks and crushed heads of his giant shaggy dahlias. He had been nurturing them carefully, waiting for their perfection to peak exactly the week of the show. Now the whole flowerbed looked as if a herd of elephants had been playing leapfrog over them.

'Where are they?' he exploded. He had once been a major in the Marines, and he had a voice to match. The tabbies heard the angry tone and cowered nervously nearer to Chang. The Siamese merely sniffed and looked out of the window. It was so uncouth to shout.

'I'll kill them,' he bristled, shaking the ruined blooms under Lavinia's nose. 'Those damned cats of yours . . . Look what they've done. Months of work . . . absolutely ruined.'

'I'm terribly sorry, of course,' said Lavinia. 'But it wasn't my cats, really it wasn't. It was probably a fox.'

'Ever seen a striped fox? Two striped foxes playing hide and seek with a Siamese? How about that?'

'Well, I'm sure they'd never . . .' Lavinia began.

'They did. And one day I'll prove it to you,' said Mr Arkwright, marching down the path. 'Wait and see. I'll prove it.'

She watched his retreating back, thinking he must have been a fine man in his prime. She had nursed many such fine men, but there had never been anyone special.

Joss Arkwright stomped back to his garden, determined that he would nail those cats to their own whiskers. He would catch them out. He would prove to Miss Robbins that she had been giving house-room to a feline branch of the Mafia.

His chance came sooner than he expected. It was one of those luminous English afternoons when cottonwool clouds floated in the azure blue of the sky and birds flew around with dazed expressions. Bright-winged butterflies hovered with quivering excitement over pools of nectar, their brief life-span seeming like an eternity.

Gardening provided Joss with his best thinking times, as he balanced on his heels on the grass, his fingers deep in the warm brown earth. Joss thought a great deal about his days in the Marines, the cruelty of war, the dirt and squalor endured by innocent victims.

Yet in the same world were flowers . . . petals of amazing diversity and fragility; fearless robins, like the perky male watching from the handle of the spade; a tiny spotted ladybird crawling up the outside of his sleeve. Joss was watching the ladybird negotiating the chunky cable rib with fascination when he heard a clatter and a din.

Looking across the garden to his neighbour's downstairs window, he saw mayhem breaking loose on Lavinia's windowsill. Her precious orchids were flying in all directions; flowerpots crashed to the floor; earth flew up like dust caught in a whirlwind. Joss jumped to his feet, his face breaking into a grin.

'Those cats. It's those damned cats. Now perhaps she'll believe me!'

Daisy peered distantly at him from among the blooms, her blue eyes wide with fright. She clawed at the windowpane. Then she leaped from sight, her tail straight and rigid, sending another plant flying as she vanished.

Joss went to Lavinia's backdoor, relishing this moment of triumph and vindication. It was swinging open.

'Miss Robbins,' he called out. 'Miss Robbins?' But there was no answer. He went further into the house.

'Oh my God,' he said.

An hour later Lavinia was sitting in Joss Arkwright's sitting-room, drinking Marine-strength tea from a thick mug, a Marine-style bandage and dressing on the cut on her head. The police had been and gone, but she was still shaking. She had told them her story and a young sergeant had written it down.

But now she was telling it again, and Joss let her. He knew that talking would help with the shock.

'I was just returning from the village when two young

boys followed me up the path. They asked if I had anything for their jumble sale, and I couldn't remember whether I had anything or not, but I said I would go and look.'

She stopped to take a deep breath, and Joss waited.

'When I returned with a few little bits and pieces, these boys were in my kitchen, looking in my shopping basket. One of them had his hands on my purse. Well, I told them to stop that at once and go away, but they didn't. They just laughed at me and took out my pension money, which I had just collected from the post office.'

At this point Lavinia had to put down the mug, her hands were shaking so much. She was remembering the boys' eyes, shifty and insolent, their loud and callous laughter. They were so young, and yet they had frightened her. Lavinia had nursed during the war, then lived for years in a foreign country, far, far from home, and never once been afraid; now two boys from an English village had brought fear into her home.

'How about stewed cat, missus,' one of the boys had jeered swinging Chang up into the air by a leg.

'That, of course, was their mistake,' Lavinia went on. 'I rushed to save my darling Chang, and the other boy pushed me over and hit me with his clenched fist. Chang went wild. The lad was holding him by one paw, but that still left Chang with three – and he's a very strong cat.'

Joss nodded. He wouldn't argue with that.

Lavinia's voice warmed with pride. 'Chang dug his claws into the boy's legs. He was wearing those tight jeans and they weren't much protection. He yelled out, and that frightened Tiggy and Daisy. They jumped onto the windowsill and my poor plants went flying. I don't know what happened then . . .'

Joss refilled the mug of tea and handed it to her. Obediently Lavinia sipped the hot brew, trying to remember the last time a man had done anything for her. It was not something that was easy to recall.

'I found you lying in a pool of blood on the floor,' he

said. 'You'd obviously fainted. The boys had gone, but I caught sight of them running down the road. I've a good idea who they are.'

'How lucky I am that you came along,' said Lavinia. 'I might have lain there for days, or bled to death. It really was most fortunate.'

'It was your cats,' said Joss grudgingly. 'Caught my attention, so to speak.'

'My poor darlings were so frightened,' Lavinia sighed.

The Terrible Three hesitated in the doorway of Joss's sitting-room, like uninvited guests waiting to be asked in. They sat, one tabby either side of the Siamese, giving credible impersonations of meek and innocent pussies.

'Oh look,' said Lavinia, her eyes lighting up. 'There they are. They must have been wondering where I was. They've been looking for me.'

Joss looked down at his three enemies. They stared back at him unflinching; three Davids meeting their Goliath. He had to admit they had courage.

He scooped up the two tabbies, one in each big hand, and deposited them on Lavinia's lap.

'Here, take them. They'll keep you company while I go next door and clear up that mess for you. Orchids don't like being treated rough. I'll see what I can do. Replant them for you.'

'How very kind,' said Lavinia. There was something in his expression that stirred her; it ignited a small current of affection that she quickly hid. This was not the time. They were in no hurry.

As Joss went to go out of the room, he came face to face with Chang. The narrow, glinting turquoise eyes were sizing him up, orientally inscrutable.

Man and cat stared at each other. Chang stepped aside. It was a movement executed with elegance and a certain amount of dignity. Joss understood. He was being offered a negotiable truce.

# Black Tom

All my life I have known the wild weather. The wild country and the wild wind are my constant companions. We exist together in bleak, raw, uncompromising closeness.

Here I wander the brown and purple moors, following solitude, finding loneliness, skirting the chattering beck which tumbles down the slope; where into the distant horizon the hills rise, wave upon wave, like the sea I have never seen. Sometimes in summer the beck is a mere trickle seeping over moss-covered pebbles, and then the air is soft and warm and the white-bibbed mountain blackbird trills a high sweet song.

But these moments are rare. It is the wild weather which dominates the moors . . . thunderstorms and forked lightning stabbing the turf, torrential rain, and wind that tears at the root of the heather and cotton sedge, and twists the gaunt trees into grotesque shapes.

Then I crouch under some friendly bush or shrub, or in the lee of a stone dyke, blinking my eyes against the furious rain, knowing that the elements and I are at war, but knowing that I can become stronger by leaning into their fierce onslaught.

When I return to the hillside village, the rain is streaming down the cobbled streets and the horses are in danger of slipping backwards. The old stone houses look as if they will topple down the steep street and fall onto the bridge that spans the rushing beck.

I have been brought to live in a house of grey stone, heavily roofed with slabs to withstand the wind. It is built on high ground, beyond the church and the crowded churchyard where the moss-covered tombstones stand shoulder to shoulder like an army of silence.

I remember the day that the family came to the house. A canvas-covered wagon lumbered up the steep incline, followed by seven carts full of their household belongings. The villagers stared from behind their curtains, for it seemed the man was of importance to their lives. A crowd of children of all sizes spilled out of the wagon, quietly behaved but excited, running all over the garden and narrow paths through the churchyard. A woman moved aside from the mountain of luggage and looked at the bleak moorland house and the rugged hills surrounding it. Her delicate features were set into a peculiar longing. This could never be a home for her. She was from the warmer, softer south.

She tried, but quite soon her spirit fled and the sorrowing children were left to play unsupervised among the hills. There were six children, five little girls and a boy.

The eldest girl strived to be a mother, and it was then I was brought into the household to amuse the little ones, who were withdrawn and quiet. It was a very cold house. But it became too much responsibility for the girl's young shoulders, and an aunt arrived who immediately lit an immense fire in the grate in her bedroom and began to turn the house back into a home.

The house was almost part of the moor, sharing its bleakness and raw weather; the doors open to its moods, a free sanctuary for the animals. There were other cats that came and went; the dogs, of course, Keeper and Flossie and Jasper; wild geese and some tame ones; Hero the hawk. We were cared for like people, not pets. They talked to us, drew sketches of us, took us with them onto

219

the moor. It was unusual in these harsh living conditions.

'I fed Rainbow, Diamond, Snowflake and Jasper this morning,' the tall thin girl wrote gravely in a little book. It was the dogs and the moorland hawk that she loved the most. Sometimes I followed her flapping black skirts across the moor. She was like a bird herself. If the wind had taken her into its arms and borne her away, I would not have been surprised.

There was a short, plain girl called Lottie, who was too busy for much tenderness towards the animals. She drowned herself in her studies, spending hours reading and writing, then bustling about with the many house-hold chores that fell her way. But she too escaped to the moors in all weathers whenever she could, holding her stiff black bonnet to her cheek, her short-sighted eyes raised fervently to the distant hills.

'I must escape,' I heard her saying. 'We must all escape. I shall see that we all escape . . .'

The wind carried her voice away, and she stood still, as if she could see the words escaping into the air while her body was chained to the muddy earth. She shrugged her shoulders with despair, and then set off along the track at such a pace I could hardly keep up with her.

It was the youngest girl, Anne, who loved me the most. She was violet-eyed and delicate and often ill. I would curl up at her feet as she lay on the sofa in the dining-room, her cheeks flushed with fever and a cough racking her chest.

'Oh Black Tom, Black Tom,' she said tenderly. 'What will become of us all in this wild place? If only I were a cat like you, and could bury my face in my fur to keep out the cold. Will you teach me how to do it?'

She laughed, and that started her coughing and she held the pain in her side until it stopped. She wiped the tears away with a cambric handkerchief and lay back against the pillow. The delirium took her wandering in her mind and she found herself stepping lightly into a cart that was to transport her on the long journey. It was a still dark April dawn and she had a long way to travel in her troubled dream.

I followed the silently lurching cart down the steep lane to the bottom of the valley, and then as it began to climb up the other side. But I went no further and sat in the sombre light thinking of my Anne. I dreamed I was old and thin and would not see her again, and my limbs twitched.

The father of the family was a tall, proud figure with an awesome head. He taught the children, the girls as well as the son, but he could not stand their childish prattling. After his wife died, he retreated more into his study and only shared the breakfast meal with the family.

'Tabitha,' he said sternly to the maidservant, polishing his small steel-rimmed spectacles. 'I will take my supper in my study from now on.'

The summers were a lovely time, when the becks were tumbling with clear sparkling water and the children wandered for miles over the moors. They had a special waterfall that they called their own, and often I went with them over the heather, half listening as they laughed and told each other stories. In the winter, it was often too cold and wet to walk; then they gathered in the warm kitchen while Tabitha worked, and acted out plays they had written by the flickering light of the oil-lamps.

One by one the older girls were sent away to a boarding-school; but not the boy, who was being taught Greek and Latin by his father; and not my Anne, who was too delicate.

'We are to go to Cowan Bridge,' announced Lottie in a voice of doom, tinged with excitement. 'To a school for clergy's daughters. We have to go. An education is our only hope to better ourselves. Our only hope of escape.'

'But I can't live without the moors,' said Em fiercely. 'It'll be like a prison. I won't go. I won't. I'd rather stay here and work as a servant.'

But they went to school. One by one, the cart took them away, forlorn and desperately homesick children.

221

When the two eldest girls succumbed to the damp and chills and died, it was as if the storm-clouds descended on the stone grey house and wrapped it in a fine black mist. May 6 and June 15 . . . two days so close and so overlapping in grief. The children wept. Anne was like a ghost herself, wondering how long it would be before she joined her sisters and her mother in the crowded graveyard.

But Lottie was angry too. She raged at the school which had hastened her sisters' deaths. Maria and Elizabeth had only just recovered from complications of measles and whooping cough when they went to Cowan Bridge, and the smell of rancid fat and unsavoury meat pies and bingy milk robbed them of any appetite even though they were hungry.

The two-mile walk from the school along unsheltered tracks to the wind-swept church was a weekly agony. The children ate their cold dinner in the porch between services, shivering with cold, longing for home. No one seemed to notice how ill they were.

'They killed them,' Lottie insisted, under her breath, as she busied her needle with repairing a torn undergarment. 'That school . . . It was monstrous . . . My poor sisters . . .'

Now the aunt gave them lessons at home and taught them household skills and her own strong Methodist beliefs. I curled hidden on Anne's lap, and her small fingers crept into my fur. I dared not purr, for then the aunt would chase me into the garden.

The father came home from a visit to Leeds with a set of wooden soldiers for his son. A gift was a rare thing in that family.

'Look what I've got,' said the boy excitedly the next morning, running into the girls' bedroom. 'A box of soldiers. You may have one each. You can choose.'

'This will be mine. He is the tallest, the most handsome, the most perfect of men and I'll call him the Duke of Wellington,' said Lottie, taking her hero immediately

222

to her heart.

Em, gaunt and thin, took a grave-faced soldier and called him Gravey. She was always strange.

Anne took a quaint little fellow and called him Waiting Boy, though no one knew why or for whom he was waiting. But Anne smiled her gentle smile to herself as if she knew whom he was waiting to meet. Perhaps she was also waiting. I did not know.

The boy took Bonaparte.

Sometimes I could play with these soldiers, flipping them over with my paw, and that made the children laugh. They wrote and acted out lengthy plays for the soldiers, full of fighting and heroic deaths.

But life was not just plays, studies and walks across the moors. The three girls worked hard keeping the house spotless. I kept out of the way when they were scrubbing the sandstone floors. I would jump onto one of the wide windowsills and face the blue dial of the church clock. There were no curtains, because the father had a horror of fire. There was a groove in the wood where I had stretched a claw a hundred times. Lottie crouched over the mahogany table, polishing till her face was red; Anne dusted the horsehair chairs; Em wiped the bookshelves impatiently. She preferred baking and making bread.

It was a spartan household, but the moors were their personal luxury. The wind made the aunt shudder and she shut herself in her room whenever she could. But the girls ran out to the freedom of the moors, to their favourite ravines and waterfalls, their long hair blowing, eyes laughing, their voices raised in chatter. They took off their boots and stockings and waded through the streams, their voluminous black skirts getting wet. They placed stepping-stones for me, and I unhesitatingly followed them to the end of their wild and windy earth.

All nature was a lingering delight. They exclaimed over every flower and bird, every butterfly and bee, and especially the tiny mosses that clung to the rock-faces and survived despite the cruel weather. They ran like wild creatures themselves, their cloaks and skirts billowing in the four winds that joined in their games. The dogs rushed about, barking, chasing rabbits, in their simpler world of hunting.

'We will always remember this,' said Em firmly. 'We will make it remembered. It must never change.'

They were sitting at the meeting of the waters, where a space of bright lush grass was broken by small springs and flat stones. It was totally hidden. There was nothing to see but miles of hills and heather, acres of cloudless sky like a canopy of glass, warmed by an unexpected sun.

The girls sat on the stones, heads flung back to the warmth, getting their breath. I lapped water from the clear spring and I thought I had tasted nothing as pure.

'This will be my dream,' Em went on. 'Of misty moor and hill. Where every evening closes dark and chill.'

'Don't talk of death,' said Anne, combing through her curls with her fingers. 'Not now. Don't spoil this beautiful day with thoughts of the dark evening to come.'

'You're being cowardly, Anne,' said Em. 'Weak . . .'

'That's not true,' said Lottie. 'Think how brave Anne is when she is ill.'

Em rushed to hug her younger sister. 'I'm cruel, cruel,' she cried. 'Forgive me, dear Anne. Forgive me.'

Anne forgave her immediately for they were like twins, even though there was almost two years between them. They walked together, sewed together, wrote in the evenings side by side.

Lottie was the odd one out, but she had only love, no envy, for the strength they gave each other. She knew she had ambition. She did not want to stay in the stone house for ever, and yet every time she made the effort to get away, she was almost ill with homesickness. Nor could Em survive away from her beloved moors.

Laughing, they made a bracelet from strands of Anne's hair and put it round my neck like a collar. I ran through the tangled bushes and would have fled to the higher hills, but Anne caught me and pulled me into her arms.

'It was only some fun, Black Tom,' she whispered, lifting the bracelet off my neck, then stroking down the ruffled fur. 'You are still free. We were making you into a magical creature for Gondal.' She began to cough and drew a shawl round her narrow shoulders. 'I must go back . . .'

This was their only escape; their fantasies taking them on the wind into worlds of power, love and excitement. In these dream-worlds their heroines had the courage and opportunity to make their own lives; not like the three sisters, who were imprisoned by their sex.

They wrote millions of words, crouched round the dining room table in the flickering light. Their pens scratched the endless adventures of the people of their mythical countries, Angria and Gondal. I did not understand all this, but it was enough that I could curl up beneath the table where Anne would put her stockinged feet on my back for a stool.

Lottie could hardly see, even then, and peered closely, her nose almost touching the paper. Em was like a caged beast, restless even in that familiar room, wanting to be away, being called somewhere by something she did not yet recognise.

That evening there was a terrible storm and the three girls were drawn to the small glittering window. The forked lightning lit up Top Withens with jagged white flashes, silhouetting the old farmhouse roof and gaunt trees. Anne watched nervously, ready to clap her hands over her ears when the thunder broke. Em was mesmerised, hardly able to control her passion. It was as if she might throw herself out into the furious rain and run into the core of the storm with her arms open to the wildness.

Lottie stood apart, clenching and unclenching her small hands. All that power out there, and she had none. She had to do something, some work, make some place in this world. Surely her whole life was not to be given to cleaning and baking when there was so much inside her, longing to be free.

'Goodnight, my children.' The father came to the door, watch in hand. 'Don't stay up too late.'

'Goodnight, papa.'

It was nine o'clock. They heard him bar and lock the front door, then go upstairs, pausing on the landing to wind the clock.

The girls turned their faces back to the storm. Their souls were out there on the moor, succoured by the wind and rain.

'We must get away,' said Lottie. Her sisters agreed, but there was so little they could do.

The snows came hard that winter and Anne fell ill with lung congestion. She lay on the sofa, coughing and coughing, and holding the pain in her side. They brought her nourishing broths, and Tabitha brewed humble remedies. I lay at her feet, listening to her laboured breathing, unable to help, only able to offer my company.

Eventually the snows melted, leaving frozen tufts of white coarse grass among the moss. The birds had long gone to warmer climates, and only the grouse and crows flew over the moors.

As she grew stronger, Anne became more determined to find work. They could not all stay at home. She was physically the weakest and the shyest, but she was firm in her resolve. No one knew how much it cost sweet, gentle Anne. She hid her suffering. She eventually found herself a suitable post.

They were busy all week at the parsonage preparing for Anne's departure. She carried me upstairs to her room as her sisters helped her to pack. She had so few belongings: chemises, cuffs, a plain dark dress, but she also took her books, her workbasket and her Bible. I sat on the windowsill and watched. Every time she passed me, she touched my head as if to give her fingers a long remembrance of the feel of my fur . . .

She rose early the next morning and took a long last

look at the moors. They were mysterious in mist and silent. She had a hurried breakfast, for she felt too sick to eat. The family embraced and Anne kissed her aunt, her father, and her sisters.

'Goodbye Charlotte,' she said, hugging her.

'Goodbye, dear Anne. Write to us. Write to us often. If only you would let one of us journey with you . . .'

'No, it's my wish that I be allowed to go alone,' said Anne. She turned to Em. 'Goodbye, Emily.'

'Goodbye, my dearest,' said Emily fiercely. 'God go with you and keep you safe.'

She picked me up and kissed me, and my black fur was lost in the blackness of her woollen shawl. 'Oh Black Tom, Black Tom,' she cried. It was a cry of despair.

She drew a veil over her face to hide the tears and stepped up into the cart that was to take her on the long journey from Haworth to Blake Hall, Mirfield, where she had an appointment as a governess to the Ingram family. It was a cold and dark April morning, and the sun did not exist even as a faint promise behind the dark mass of cloud.

I followed the creaking, lurching cart down the steep lane to the bottom of the village street. It crossed the bridge and then began the climb to the other side of the valley. But I went no further. I sat on the stones in the sombre light thinking of my dearest. I was old now, and thin, and would not see her again.

Every four years the Brontë sisters wrote an assessment of their lives, to be opened four years later on Emily's birthday or Anne's.

30 July 1841

'This is Emily's birthday,' Anne wrote from a new post at Scarborough. 'She has now completed her twenty-third year . . . I wonder what will be our condition and how or where we shall all be on this day four years hence . . . We are

227

now all separate and not likely to meet again for many a weary week . . .

'We have got Keeper, got a sweet little cat and lost it, and also got a hawk. Got a wild goose which has flown away, and three tame ones, one of which has been killed.

'All these diversities, with many others, are things we did not expect or foresee in the July of 1837. What will the next four years bring forth? Providence only knows.'*

19 December 1848 Emily died, aged 30
28 May 1849 Anne died, aged 29
31 March 1855 Charlotte died, aged 38

*Extract from Anne Brontë's Diary Paper, from *The Shakespeare Head Brontë,* Vol. I, edited by T.J. Wise & J.A. Symington

# The Star

Blackie growled at the brush, taking up a plucky boxing stance, refusing to let Jocelyn finish the grooming.

Owning a champion was hard work, especially if that champion was a long-haired black of spectacular beauty and with a taste for theatricals. Jocelyn did not begrudge the hours she spent grooming that lustrous coat, such blue-black fur right down to the roots, quite free from any rustiness or shading.

'You are very, very beautiful,' said Jocelyn, gazing into Blackie's large, round, copper-coloured eyes; eyes that regarded the world with a superciliousness reserved for champions. 'But I wish you'd keep still.'

And Blackie was a special champion. Her registered name was Midnight Black Beauty; she was like a star on an Arabian Night. She had won so many prizes that sometimes Jocelyn took her to shows in a king-sized pen, reclining on a matching black carpet, the walls hung with rosettes of every size and colour. On these occasions, Blackie was usually bored and fretful, chewing her goldfish mobile and spitting the bits at spectators.

Being entered in a competitive show was fractionally more interesting for Blackie. It meant days of preparation and constant attention. Jocelyn began the intensive grooming at least a month beforehand, and then on the final day a polish with a piece of silk or chamois leather gave Blackie's coat the most beautiful sheen.

'I cannot believe that all this fuss is just for a cat,' said Gregory, Jocelyn's current young man. 'It's quite ridiculous.'

'Blackie is not just any cat,' said Jocelyn, sorry that Gregory did not like cats even a little. 'She's a champion.'

'Champion layabout,' Gregory scoffed.

Jocelyn wished he was not so handsome, not so attractive, and not so suitable in every way. They agreed about everything, except cats.

'I'm not asking you to come with me,' said Jocelyn. 'I can manage by myself. I always have. Shall I see you after the show?'

'If Blackie doesn't mind,' said Gregory. 'After all, she'll probably be exhausted by all the excitement.'

Blackie yawned, showing the pink cavern of her throat, and her sharp white teeth. She always ignored Gregory. It was her policy with anything or anyone she did not like.

It meant a very early start on the day of the show. Blackie travelled in a miniature portacabin with every mod con for cats. She travelled well, but was acutely aware of the air and tension that surrounded Jocelyn's preparations.

'Now, have I got our papers? My exhibitor's badge? Comb, brush, silk, cotton buds . . .' Jocelyn was always nervous. The standard was so high and the judges looked for perfection.

'Have I got everything?' Jocelyn was still checking with Blackie as the car waited at traffic lights near the outskirts of Olympia. She had to park the car; carry Blackie and her vanity case into the main hall; find their section and pen; complete the vetting-in formalities and give Blackie a final grooming before the judges started their rounds.

Jocelyn felt the excitement rising as she entered the great exhibition hall, the rows of pens, the cries of the cats, the bustle and tension of the owners. Despite her nervousness, Jocelyn was an old hand at shows, and she accomplished all that was necessary in good time. All that remained was to brush Blackie's long fine fur into a feathery glory all round that fiercely proud face.

This was the moment Blackie enjoyed, sitting on Jocelyn's knee, the eyes of the world on the thrice Best of Breed Champion.

It was time for Blackie's party piece. Her whiskers twitched. Then she went limp, totally limp, four paws outstretched, long fluffy tail hanging like a rope, eyes closed. Even her jaw went slack.

'What's the matter with your cat?' asked the neighbouring exhibitor, peering sideways at the great heap of black fur falling all over Jocelyn's lap.

'She's pretending to be dead,' said Jocelyn, grinning, giving Blackie a minute shake. Blackie let her head roll back. The timing was perfect. 'I blame television. She watches far too much.'

It was true that Blackie was kept indoors a great deal, and Jocelyn left the television on for company for the cat. Blackie reckoned she was the only cat to have seen *The Wizard of Oz* four times. She loved old films, particularly strong dramas. But why was a cat never the star? It annoyed Blackie. Plenty of squeaky mice and foolhardy dogs scampering across prairies; horses foaming at the mouth; apes scaling the Empire State Building in New York and knocking aeroplanes off like flies . . . but cats? No one ever made a film about a cat.

'Is it catching?' the neighbour enquired apprehensively. Her own cat, another long-haired black, watched curiously.

'I doubt it,' said Jocelyn. 'But Blackie enjoys it, and that's all that matters, isn't it?'

Blackie opened her eyes an orange slit and glared at her next-door rival. The more timid soul tried to climb up the woman's head, nails entangled in the coiffured hair.

The judge arrived at Blackie's pen. He was a tall young

231

man with thick red hair and a sprinkle of freckles. He wore his white coat with authority and the moment he handled Blackie, the cat knew she was with a master.

Blackie immediately went into her star routine. She fluttered her eyelashes like Scarlett O'Hara, stretched her muscles like Tarzan, blinked moistly through the final scene of *Random Harvest*, nosed the judge's palm with a little Bambi movement of the head. It was all quite enchanting.

'What a gorgeous cat,' Edward murmured to himself. He had to be impartial, but Midnight Black Beauty had the right cobby body-shape: short and thick, shoulders broad and flat, short legs, tail well plumed, and the bright intelligent face of a champion. The cat was strong and fit. Edward gave her good points with fifteen out of fifteen for those glorious copper eyes with not a hint of green.

'Excellent, excellent,' Edward added more professionally. He had caught sight of Jocelyn, watching him from a distance. He recognised the worried eyes, the tense shoulders, the handkerchief being twisted into a rag. He wanted to reassure her, before she was shredded with nerves, but of course he could not.

Blackie yawned delicately, showing her fine teeth and small pink tongue. How much more had she got to do? Ah, there was the Dietrich routine. She peered haughtily over her shoulder and Edward grinned, putting her back in the pen.

'Saucy,' he said, recognising the talent.

'Would the exhibitor of cat number 734 please return to the pen. Your cat has no water,' came the bland tones of the announcer over the tannoy above the general noise of the show.

Blackie retreated to the back of her pen. Now for hours of excruciating boredom, relieved only by the announcements. Once there had been a demonstration . . . Now that had been fun, people throwing leaflets over the gallery. She listened to the other cats, a cacophony of cat calls and human noise filling the echoing hall. But she could not see the other cats, apart from the row of long-haired whites opposite, looking down their pink noses like medieval snow queens.

Blackie looked round for something to do. She burrowed under her blanket to hide, but she could not play hide-and-seek by herself. Jocelyn had disappeared, probably to look at the other exhibitors' cats. An official came and pinned several large rosettes on the top of her pen. Blackie patted the ribbons for a while, but it was too tame for words.

It took five minutes of calculated effort to upset the litter tray and scatter the granules all over the pen and through the bars, so that they fell like rain onto the floor below. She skated about, soft-shoe shuffling à la Astaire, till she overturned the water bowl and soaked Jocelyn's vanity case.

Blackie waited for retribution, but nothing happened. She turned her attention to the white blanket and began methodically to tear it to shreds. By this time she was beginning to look less like a champion. Her plumed tail was wet and stuck with little grey granules; shreds of cotton fluff clung to her coat like frost; she began to growl and leap about, doing her Elsa the lioness in *Born Free*.

Jocelyn was admiring some beautiful blue Abyssinians when she heard the announcement over the tannoy system.

'Would the exhibitor of cat number 1104 please return to the pen. Your cat is in some distress.'

'Oh dear,' said Jocelyn. 'That's Blackie.'

But Blackie was in no distress. She was holding a one-cat demonstration against shows and showing. Even the blanket was no fun now, piled up untidily in one corner in grubby shreds.

Edward had finished his judging. This was the part he really enjoyed, strolling about, hands deep in the pockets of his white coat, relaxed and content with the world. The tension had gone, and he could admire every cat for

233

just being a cat. He found himself looking squarely at the mutinous copper eyes glinting at him from pen number 1104.

'Good heavens,' said Jocelyn, surveying the wildly dishevelled champion. 'Blackie, what have you been up to?'

'An obvious case of *catticus sour grapepuss*,' said Edward, who had learned Latin at school.

Blackie, recognising a fellow intellectual, fell instantly moribund; a dramatic heap of long black fur expiring on a mound of torn blanket. Her fur hardly quivered as she somehow controlled her breathing.

'Whatever's happened?' Edward exclaimed, aghast. 'A heart attack . . . You know, the excitement and the heat . . . These highly bred cats.' He looked carefully at Blackie. There was something a little unnatural about the position, something a trifle contrived.

'That cat's not dead,' said the woman next door, with a sniff. She was packing up her equipment with rapid movements. Her cat had not won anything. He was a mature black Persian whose tail was a little too long. He did not care that he had not won a rosette. He did not want a rosette. He wanted to go home to his coley and cushion in front of the radiator. 'It's acting,' the woman added, as if that was a sin.

Edward unfastened the door and put his hand against Blackie's chest. There was a strong heartbeat. It was quite normal.

'Perhaps the kiss of life?' Edward offered as a becoming blush rushed to Jocelyn's cheeks. 'Cat or owner, I'm easy.'

'That's not funny,' said Jocelyn, marching away, annoyed. She had noticed him before, at other shows. Who could help noticing him, with all that red hair. But one did not talk to judges. It was just not done.

'I didn't think it was,' said Edward, striding after her. 'How about a strong coffee instead?'

Blackie opened one eye a slit. She could see that the

door was not properly fastened. Now that was an adventure. In one bound she was out of the pen and sliding beneath the tables like a black shadow. She scurried through legs and between cat baskets, a Bogart hunch to her shoulders, unseen by humans. The cats watched her progress, eyes wide and unbelieving. No cat had ever escaped before. They stirred.

Blackie raced passed the stalls selling cat food, cat biscuits, cat vitamins, china cats, wooden cats, cat stationery, cat calendars, cat badges, endless catoptrics. She looked neither to the left nor to the right, but ran the whole length of the exhibition hall. No one seemed to notice her. What was one more cat? Perhaps it had come in from outside.

Suddenly she darted towards some crates, climbing them with ease, up and up further towards the girders like a stunt man. The girders supported the gallery on the second floor and she was making for the ornamental ledge under the iron railing. She curled herself up on the ledge, her plumed tail swinging in space. It was a marvellous view . . .

Jocelyn was in the refreshment area, drinking coffee with Edward, and fast getting over her unfounded objections to red hair. They had talked shop over the first cup but were now progressing to more personal topics.

'Will the exhibitor of cat number 1104 please return to the pen. Your cat . . . er . . . your cat . . .' The announcer's voice was muffled and mysterious. Jocelyn looked up, a touch of apprehension taking the laughter from her eyes.

'Your cat . . .' the announcer began again. 'Your cat has – er gone. Vamoosed, skipped it, gone for a pint.' It had been a long day.

Jocelyn hurried back to the pen, followed by Edward. She was clutching her arms, already blaming herself. The woman next door was holding forth to an audience.

'That cat was definitely demented,' she was saying. 'Definitely demented. I know a demented cat when I see

235

one.'

'Heathcliff,' said Jocelyn, wearily. 'She was merely playing Heathcliff.'

'Attention, please.' The announcer's voice broke through the noise in an authoritative tone. 'A cat is on the loose. Would you all stand still. I repeat – will you please stand still.'

The bustle of the great hall died away as everyone slow-motioned into a freeze. It was like a film. Blackie was thrilled. The talking stopped too. For a few moments there was silence then a plaintive miaow came from somewhere . . .

A ripple of movement began to spread through the hall as the search for Blackie flowed from row to row. The cats padded up and down their pens, miaowing and scratching at the wire doors. They felt disturbed, as if a wild creature were loose.

Jocelyn was nearly at her wits' end. She was terrified that Blackie might get out into the street. She wanted to telephone the police. Edward did his best to reassure her; Blackie was far too intelligent to go outside. A show cat would have more sense.

'But where is she?' Jocelyn wailed.

'I'll go and have a look round,' said Edward.

Being tall, he tended to look upwards rather than downwards. He caught sight of Blackie perched among the girders, her long black tail swinging, her bright eyes watching everything below like the Cheshire Cat.

'Hello,' Edward called up. 'Everyone's been looking for you.'

Blackie's eyes glinted with amusement. She knew everyone had been looking for her. She had been watching the performance of everyone looking for her.

'Now stay right there,' Edward went on. 'I'm coming up to fetch you.'

Great, thought Blackie, a ripple of excitement teasing along her spine. A chase! Scenes of screaming cars, runaway trains, pounding horses went through her mind in a flash. She was up and away like Batman himself, skirting the household pets section, momentarily drawn by an irresistible smell of hot dogs and jacket potatoes. She flagged a little, small pink tongue protruding, being a cross between a Chinese refugee from *The Inn of the Sixth Happiness* and a dying tribesman in *Lawrence of Arabia*. She managed a pathetic stagger of near starvation.

A more promising scent assailed her nostrils – prawn cocktail, steak and Stilton? She stalked to her final victory with the theme music of *Star Wars* in her ears, taking over the carpeted calm of the restaurant where the judges and VIPs were entertained, without firing a single laser.

'*Miaow*,' said Blackie, loudly. '*Miaow*.'

Jocelyn was so embarrassed when Edward returned Blackie to her, the champion content and purring after a high-class meal in the best of company. Everyone was very sympathetic, but Jocelyn felt she could not show Blackie again after all the trouble the cat had caused. It was a case for an early retirement.

'I've a cottage in the country,' said Edward. 'When are you and Blackie going to visit me? I think Blackie would like it. All that grass.'

'She loves grass,' said Jocelyn. 'But I'll have to tell Gregory. Or it wouldn't be fair. He doesn't quite understand about Blackie. He thinks she's just a cat.'

Edward shook his head. 'Remarkable . . . I mean, Blackie's a remarkable cat. It's obvious she's not just a cat, and Gregory has a lot to learn.'

'Definitely,' Jocelyn agreed softly.

Blackie approved of Edward's cottage. She ran out into the garden and leaped into the middle of a pile of newly mown grass-cuttings. She thrashed about, fighting off attackers from every direction, her fur stuck over with bits of grass like a porcupine.

She scampered through a pile of leaf-mould and then discovered a dust bowl, in which she rolled over in ecstasy. In no time the black beauty had transformed herself into a wild, dishevelled gypsy covered in grass and leaves and coated with dust and grime.

'Blackie is making herself at home,' said Jocelyn, watching her from a window. 'She's having a wonderful time.'

'That's what I planned,' said Edward, taking Jocelyn gently into his arms. 'Perhaps one day, you'll feel the same . . .'

Blackie stalked a dragonfly, her elation growing. She knew she looked like the Scarecrow from *The Wizard of Oz*, grass sticking out all over like straw. She growled and lashed her tail like the Lion. She froze along the path, suddenly being the Tin Man gone rusty after a rain shower.

The world was her stage, her screen. She could play the Scarecrow, the Lion and the Tin Man. All at once. Definitely and most magnificently a star part.

# The Strike-Breakers

At first sight there were swarms of them. There might have been hundreds, all shapes and sizes, a motley of breeds and colours. They roamed everywhere, sliding in and out of shadows, padding through the darkness that was their habitat, merging with solid shapes until it was difficult to be sure if they existed at all.

A security guard, bored with the long night-watch, found some amusement trying to count the number of cats by watching his bank of television screens and noting their nocturnal activity. He listed four black, seven tabbies, three ginger, a tortoiseshell and a pure white – or was it two white? He began to get confused as the cats strayed into different areas and he wondered if he was counting them twice.

There were also several nests of kittens hidden among the silent machinery. The guard could spot a mother cat going back to her offspring with an odd mouse or abandoned cheese sandwich. He reckoned that there were at least thirty cats living among the plant and premises of the giant Allied Tools Limited.

The cats had no thought of escape. They had no knowledge of what lay outside the twelve-foot brick wall topped with barbed wire and broken glass that surrounded the plant. The world for them was the thirty-acre site forested with iron and steel, grassed with concrete and asphalt.

The Victorian ironmaster who built the original plant had left a way in for rats and mice through the sewers. They led a dog's life being pounced on by the army of cats that lay in wait for them. When a big tabby had a rat against a wall, there was no way of sending back signals about the ambush.

A factory site was not ideal surroundings for a cat colony, but it beat starving in a gutter. It was always warm, and the furnace-room was a favourite night-spot. There was shelter, companionship of a kind from the 2,500 work-force, and a source of food in the ever-present mice and rats, forgotten half bottles of milk and uneaten lunches dropped around.

Some of the cats had names. There was Big Tim, the leader of the pack, a heavy, powerful tabby with shoulders like Mohammed Ali and a flattened thug's face; Kinky, the timid black cat with a bent tail; Patch, the pretty tortoiseshell female who took up a nine-to-five working day in the typing pool, where she was spoilt silly; Nellie Old Girl, who led a double life, foreman's pet by day, wild tiger-mother by night. Sometimes it was Big Tim who fathered her kittens; sometimes a dark stranger slipped into camp.

The kittens around the factory were all related and all carried a streak of wildness. They were unpredictable. The factory nurse was used to dealing with scratches and bites on both male and female hands.

'A pretty face does not a pretty nature make,' she was fond of saying as she slopped antiseptic over a wound.

One day Big Tim was sunning himself, stretched out on the roof of a car parked in the main yard. This was his territory, and the ancient Bentley was a favourite. He heard a commotion coming from the entrance to the office block and several men came out arguing fiercely.

'I tell you, they won't accept it,' said one of the men, thin, worried and gripping a briefcase.

'They've got to,' said a heavier man, whom Big Tim often saw. 'There's nowt else I can do. It's cut or close as far as I can see. I've done all the talking I can.'

He climbed into the Bentley, and Big Tim leaped off as the engine purred into life. The big tabby faced the wheeled monster, hissing and spitting, his fur raised, his tail alert. The chauffeur drove carefully round the angry creature before making for the gates.

'What are you doing, Bates?' asked the Chairman. 'Is this a circular tour?'

'Just one of those damned cats in the way, sir,' said Bates.

'Typical,' said the Chairman. 'Typical of the inefficiency of the whole outdated place. The whole plant ought to be rased to the ground, cats and all.'

'My grandfather used to work here,' said Bates, as he drove out of the main gates. 'He started as a boy of fourteen, sweeping the floors.'

'Sentiment doesn't secure profits,' grunted the Chairman, who had the same habit of inventing proverbs as the factory nurse.

'No sir,' said Bates, heading for the motorway and the towering London office of the powerful American company which had just bought Allied Tools Ltd in a deal which involved several other firms.

A third of the work-force were laid off without notice at 4.30 p.m. on Friday afternoon when they collected their buff-coloured wage envelopes. They stood about, stunned, shaking their heads, their low strained voices occasionally bursting into outrage.

A lot of people were suddenly out of work in a community that offered no alternative employment.

'I reckon it's up to us to do something about it,' said George White, the foreman with the longest number of years to his credit. 'We can't be treated as if we didn't matter.'

'We've gotta do something.'

'You're right. We won't stand for it.'

The pack of cats liked the weekends. They knew that the stoppage of the thundering, ear-shattering machinery heralded two days of peace and quiet and freedom when the plant and premises were totally theirs. Even Kinky dared to come forth to sunbathe, his slinky coat like velvet in the sunshine. Patch missed her nine-to-five pampering but took the opportunity to flirt with the younger toms and tease them with her fluffy adorability. Nellie Old Girl paraded her kittens and taught them the ways of their restricted world.

Innocently they played and hunted, ate and slept, unaware that life, as they knew it, had changed. Nellie Old Girl was the first to notice that the source of milk had dried up. She was weaning her babies, and her prime concern was bottles of milk to knock over. She roamed the factory but found only dusty bottles rimmed with stale curd. She miaowed in a worried way.

Big Tim opened one eye sleepily from his vantage point on the fire-escape and noticed that no one had come to unlock the iron gates to the yard. They were barred, padlocked, and a chain hung on the solid structure. He was not too vexed. It had happened before. They called them holidays. Everything would soon return to normal.

But it didn't. The cats began to fret, feeling vaguely hungry and thirsty. Like rats deserting a sinking ship, the mice and vermin had disappeared. It was difficult to find a rain-puddle that was not contaminated with oil. The furnace had gone out. They sat about, wet and cold and puzzled. They could not understand what had happened.

No one thought about the cats for a long time. They were all too busy holding meetings, arguing, organising marches to London and watching television to see if they could catch themselves in crowd shots on *News at Ten*.

But one morning Jenny Arthur woke up and thought about when she used to work in the typing-pool and Patch would curl up on the sunny spot on the top of her desk and share crumbs of digestive biscuits from her elevenses, and lick out the last of vanilla ice-cream from a tub.

'Heavens,' she said, shooting upright in bed. 'We've forgotten all about the cats. They must be starving.'

She dressed quickly, and swallowing a fast cup of coffee, made a pile of pilchard-and-cheese sandwiches and hurried down to the factory. The pickets had taken up sentry duty at the main gates, so she went to the little-used side gate. One man was standing there alone, wrapped up in a heavy lumber-jacket and a knitted scarf. He was holding a bottle of milk and gazing up at the twelve-foot wall.

'Hello, Jenny,' he said, morosely.

'Good morning, Mr White,' said Jenny. She was a little afraid of anyone who worked on the shop-floor and always hurried whenever she was taking messages to the production manager, whose office was the other end of the premises. The wolf-whistles and bawdy invitations brought a flush of colour to her shy young face and she always hid her embarrassment by hanging her head and letting her light brown hair curtain her eyes.

'You can't get in,' said George White.

'I know,' said Jenny. 'I don't know what to do. I've brought some food for the cats.'

His face lit up. 'So have I! Nellie Old Girl's got kittens. I don't know what she'll be doing without a drop of milk for them. If I throw the bottle over the wall, it'll smash. They won't get the milk, and then there'd be glass everywhere.'

Jenny had always kept clear of the stern-faced foreman, but seeing him standing there helplessly holding a bottle of milk and half talking to himself, he seemed quite human.

'We'll think of something,' she said, unwrapping her sandwiches. 'Will you help me throw these? Your aim is probably better than mine.'

They tossed sandwiches over the wall, and it was not long before they heard the cats passing on the good news.

Slice after slice spun through the air, landing in the yard below.

'I didn't know you liked cats,' said George, thinking that Jenny was more than just highlights and beige eye shadow.

'The tortoiseshell, Patch, is my favourite. Though I quite like the one with the crooked tail. I'm cultivating him with shrimp-flavoured crisps.'

'Kinky? Oh yes, if you can get him to let you stroke him, then you've achieved something. Now my Nellie's got four kittens this time, I reckon. Would you like to see them?'

'Oh yes,' said Jenny eagerly.

Then they remembered.

'When we get back,' she added.

'If we get back,' said George. 'This could last for weeks, and there's no knowing what the new owners will do. Now what shall we do about the milk? The cats are still there.'

They could hear the cats miaowing, and George thought he recognised Nellie Old Girl's strident call. Jenny had not been a Brownie for nothing and she remembered her camping days.

'If we let down a small bucket of milk on a rope, then the cats will topple it over and drink the spilt milk,' she suggested.

'Right, lass,' said George. 'I'll meet you back here at the same spot with rope, bucket and ladder.'

'I'll get some more milk,' said Jenny.

But when they returned with the equipment they found to their dismay that they no longer had the area by the side gate to themselves. A gleaming blue metallic Rolls-Royce was parked by the wall, and leaning against the bonnet was a tall young man in jeans casually reading a newspaper.

He looked over the top of the newspaper and eyed the rope and step-ladder. 'Breaking in?' he asked.

His bright blue eyes regarded Jenny's discomfiture

with amusement. She did not know what to do or say. She stood clutching two bottles of milk and two tins of evaporated milk, which she had scrounged from her mother's store-cupboard. Her hair was in wild disarray and she was out of breath from hurrying.

She summoned all her courage. 'Would you mind moving your car,' she said. 'You are in our way.'

'That's right,' said George, amazed at Jenny's pluck. The size of the car, the young man's transatlantic accent, and the pair of them at the side entrance all added up to the new ownership. George leaned the step-ladder against the wall and looked defiantly at the young man. 'We're feeding the cats,' he said.

'It won't reach,' said the young man.

He was right. Anyone standing on the step-ladder would be unable to reach over the wall. He eyed Jenny's trim waist and thought how nice it might be together on the top of a step-ladder.

'I'm Hal Barnett,' said the young man. 'I could shin up the ladder, then the young lady could sit on my shoulder. I'd hold her real safe, and you could hold the ladder steady. How about we give it a try?'

Jenny nodded. 'Yes. And I'm Jenny.'

George hesitated. 'Are you sure it's safe?'

'I won't let her fall,' said Hal.

They could hear the cats calling from the other side of the wall. The cats were wild and thirsty and they could smell milk. They clawed impatiently at the brickwork, stretching their necks, their twitching whiskers sensoring the air.

'Come on, George. It'll be all right,' said Jenny.

It worked, though all three of them got milk slopped over them as Jenny negotiated the tricky part of hauling up the bucket of milk and letting it down over the wall. Hal held her firmly and steadily and Jenny felt no fear, as if they had been born to a circus life.

The cats tipped the bucket over before it even settled on the ground. Two gingers got a milky shower and

Patch got a saucerful right in the face. They leaped and slithered and scuppered, and the puddles of milk turned a dirty grey. Nellie unleashed her claws, but there was none left for her drenched kittens. She looked up, her yellow eyes blazing with anger.

Jenny blinked back a tear. 'Hopeless,' she said. 'They wouldn't wait. It spilt everywhere. Most of it got wasted.' She looked carefully at Hal. 'I suppose you wouldn't know when they are coming out from this meeting?'

'When they stop talking,' he said cagily.

'Perhaps, if there is some kind of distraction, I could slip in as the gate is opened and they come out,' said Jenny, with a demure smile. 'No one would notice me.'

'How would you get out again?' asked George.

'I'd camp out in the office. There are a couple of armchairs in the rest-room. Then I'd slip out again when they have their next meeting tomorrow.'

'What if they catch you?' George was still dubious.

'I'm not breaking the law.'

'You're breaking the picket line,' said Hal.

'Fiddlesticks,' said Jenny. 'I'm going home for some more food and some warmer clothes. I'll be back in half an hour.'

Hal began to wonder how he had got involved at all as he staged the distraction. A few words in the owner's ear about the metallic blue Rolls and workers brandishing spray cans of paint, and the man was out so fast he certainly never noticed a slight, track-suited figure slip into the factory yard.

'Ah, that scared them off,' said Hal, peering into the empty distance. 'Not one in sight.'

The cats were apprehensive of Jenny at first, but when they discovered that her carrier-bag contained goodies, they leaped at her legs and clawed at the bag. She fed them quickly, but the hungry cats knocked the food out of her hands and fought among themselves. Even Patch had forgotten her usual good manners.

Jenny escaped to the office block, her scratches smarting. There was an electric kettle in the cupboard and she would boil some water for a cup of tea and to bathe the scratches. Her spirits lifted. It was strange being in the empty factory, but she would be all right once she was in her office.

Hal was watching the late-night movie on television in his father's rented flat near Regent's Park when an awful thought struck him. He hurried into his father's study. The light was still on, as working late was a family habit.

'Where are the keys to that factory plant?' asked Hal.

'Which plant?' His father looked up from the pile of computer print-outs draped over his desk.

'The one with the lock-out. And the cats.'

'Cats? I don't know what you're talking about, but Allied Tools are in a strike situation.'

'I need the keys.'

Hal Barnett senior never wasted time or his breath.

'Contact the Chairman. The address is in the file.'

At three o'clock in the morning, the ancient Bentley and the new Rolls drew up outside the side gate of the plant, and two men got out, unlocked the gate and sprinted into the yard. It was too early to be dawn, but the darkness held a strange quality of promise, as if the light was already nudging the long shadows.

They found Jenny huddled on the fire-escape, Patch curled up asleep on her lap and Big Tim keeping guard like a dark sentry. Other cats watched from a distance, and Kinky crept back into a doorway as the men's footsteps on the cobbles broke the silence of the night.

'Are you all right?' asked Hall, lifting the little frozen figure into his arms.

'I couldn't get into the office. Everywhere was locked,' said Jenny, shivering. 'It was awful. I called out but everyone had gone. Only you and George knew I was here. Patch tried to keep me warm, but she's such a little thing.'

'Here, lass. A drop of brandy'll warm you up,' said the

Chairman, producing a small flask. 'Then we'll take you home.'

'I'll take her home,' said Hal firmly. 'But thank you for coming, sir. I'm seeing things in a different light. That talk we had about the plant being like a family. I guess my father hadn't seen it like that.'

'Aye, always been like a big family,' said the Chairman. ''Night, Jenny. Next time you want to feed cats, ask for the key.'

'Your father?' Jenny asked sleepily as Hal tucked a rug round her in the front seat of the Rolls and adjusted the heating vents. 'What's your father got to do with this?'

'Quite a bit,' said Hal, who never wasted breath either.

The negotiations took a new turn the next day, and when Allied Tools returned to work with a slimmed-down work-force, the pruning had been done in a humane way. George White agreed to early retirement in six months' time, after handing over the reins to a younger man. Meanwhile, he could start looking for a bungalow near the coast knowing he would be able to afford it.

'I wonder if Nellie Old Girl would like to live near the sea,' he mused, as he watched her allow her growing kittens to tumble all over her. He had lost count of how many sets of kittens she had had. 'Perhaps you're due for an early retirement, Old Girl,' he chuckled.

When Jenny arrived for work, there was a huge bunch of pink roses on her desk, a can of cat food and a tin-opener. The other secretaries crowded round, teasing and asking questions, but Jenny kept quiet, wondering if the roses were an American-style brush-off.

It was a long day and Jenny's nimble fingers were out of practice, and the bottle of correcting fluid thickened with over-exposure to the air. She resigned herself to never seeing the young man again, but knew he would be difficult to forget.

She nearly tripped over him as she hurried out into the yard at five o'clock. He was down on one knee, stroking

Kinky, the black cat with a bent tail.

'However did you manage that?' she asked. 'Kinky never lets anyone touch him. I've been trying for months.'

Hal straightened up, tall, lanky, his eyes warm and friendly. He took her arm and walked towards the main gates, two people among the hundreds streaming out into the evening.

'I have a theory about things that you really want,' said Hal. 'That little cat had been longing for someone to take that one step more, one step nearer, just so that he could be friends. I just went that little bit further than anyone else.'

There was no metallic blue Rolls outside. Hal's father had gone to negotiate some new deal elsewhere in the country for the parent company. He led Jenny towards an old but interesting two-seater MG.

'So my first step today was to arrange that I stay in England for three months to complete the take-over arrangements for Allied Tools. Secondly, I got myself some wheels and a landlady. Thirdly, I am about to ask the prettiest girl in sight if she'll be my steady date.'

Jenny felt like running away, just like Kinky, and yet she was longing to be friends. There would never be anyone else quite like Hal. If she let him go, he would soon find another girl. That went without question.

'If you see me smile, then I'm coming one step nearer,' she said. Then she bent forward and the curtain of hair hid her face, but he knew she was smiling.

# One of the Kilkenny Cats

There was a strange legend about the Kilkenny cats. To fight like Kilkenny cats was to fight until both parties were destroyed. The legend began in the eighteenth century, but the mere mention of the name brought a shudder to villagers still.

One person who was not dismayed was Kazza Mount. She had known from the age of nine that she was a cat as well as a young girl, and that she was probably one of the Kilkenny cats. It had first dawned on her one hot June night in Ireland when she could not sleep and lay on top of the sheet, longing to be outside in the garden rather than in the house.

From her first-floor bedroom window, the ground looked a long way down, but Kazza had a good head for heights. An old catalpa tree leaned towards the upper rooms, its large leaves beckoning, its bell-shaped white flowers dangling in the breeze, their waxy perfume lifting on the night air to Kazza's delicate nose.

Kazza rolled up the legs of her pyjamas and climbed out onto the windowsill. It was nothing to step down to the nearest thick branch and crawl along its length on all fours. A jump onto the grass below, and Kazza was out.

A small furry creature curled round her bare ankles. It was Chattie, her kitten, let out for five minutes as part of

250

her training. The kitten looked at Kazza and then the height of the tree, her round blue eyes wide with admiration.

'Wow,' she miaowed.

Chattie was a five months old Birman, the ghostly golden tone of her long silky coat glowing in the moonlight, her dark face and tail becoming lost in the shadows at the base of the tree.

She was descended from the sacred pure white cats of the temple of Lao-Tsun, which the Khmer people built high in the Asian mountains. This was one reason why Kazza could almost understand what the kitten said to her. She was a perfect Birman, with startling white gloves on all four paws as if she had dipped each paw precisely into a drift of untouched snow.

'Shall we go for a walk?' asked Kazza.

Chattie purred round Kazza's bare ankles. She loved the night, the moonlight, the sound of little animals in the rustling leaves, but she was a valuable cat and not allowed to wander. But it would be different if she walked with Kazza.

'Purr-fect,' she replied.

It was a magical night. They ran across the lawn and scrambled through the hedge at the end of the garden and into a poppy-filled meadow. They chased downy floating dandelion heads and teased each other with the long couchgrass. When they came back they were both exhausted and fell asleep together in a bed of catmint, the spikes of the purple spotted flowers covering them like a mantle of tiny orchids.

As she slept among the sweet-smelling herb, Kazza dreamed of the Kilkenny cats and she knew she had been one of them, that sometimes she was again a cat, that one day she would be a cat for all time.

When dawn came, Kazza climbed the catalpa tree and got back into her bedroom, taking Chattie with her. Her mother could not understand it in the morning when she found the bed full of grass-seeds and the kitten asleep on the pillow. There were a lot of things Mrs Mount could not understand about her daughter.

For some reason Kazza always preferred to sit on the floor; her eating habits were peculiar – she loved milk and cheese and fish, but refused vegetables, fruit, chocolate and soft drinks. She would not even touch a baked bean, though she'd eat liver sausage by the yard.

'Why can't you be a normal child?' her mother asked, as Kazza pushed away a jelly-and-banana mould.

'I am normal,' said Kazza , who at twelve years old was beginning to answer back.

The family left Ireland and went to live in a quiet Sussex village. They bought a derelict farmhouse and were busy renovating the rooms and modernising the amenities. For several weeks they were without a proper bathroom, and Kazza was able to breathe a sigh of relief. She hated baths intensely, and yet she was scrupulously clean, washing three and four times a day. Her father installed a shower unit and she immediately took to the fine spray, refusing to set foot in the new contoured bath-tub.

'What's wrong with the bath?' asked her mother, spiky with frustration at her awkward daughter. 'Why won't you have a proper bath?'

'I'm clean,' said Kazza, who was developing a habit of talking in simple, direct phrases. 'See my nails.'

She spread out her fingers. Each nail was a long almond shape, glossy with clear nail varnish borrowed from her mother's dressing-table. There was something uncanny about their ivory perfection. Kazza regarded them with pride and flexed her fingers. She always washed her hair in rainwater, and her eyes were the brightest, clearest periwinkle blue.

'No, I just don't understand you,' said her mother for the two-hundredth time. But she hugged her strange daughter and put her cheek against the mane of wild black hair. 'We would not have given you such an un-usual name, if we had wanted you to be an ordinary little

252

girl. It's from a very old German language, and you are the only little girl in the world with that name . . .'

Kazza learned to cook in the farmhouse kitchen, and years later she took a specialised catering course, passing with honours and a special recommendation for her quiche lorraine and cheesecake. She was, however, reluctant to cook vegetables and fruit, which almost always became mangled and unrecognisable. So it was fortunate that she was teamed to work with an older woman, Catherine Gray, who was a sleek, sophisticated Cordon Bleu career cook, climbing her way to a rich marriage via the directors' dining-room.

Catherine Gray was quite different to Kazza. She was a honey blonde, vivacious and charming, ambitious and ruthless; as outgoing as Kazza was quiet and solitary.

But they became friends. No one could understand why. As their work expanded, Kazza moved into Catherine's elegant London flat, only returning to the Sussex village at weekends. Chattie pined at first, sitting on the windowsill, watching for a familiar car to come bumping along the lane. But she grew used to the separation, living on her memories of cat shows and championship awards, and litters of kittens that were queening it in many different parts of the world.

'I have to go back,' said Kazza, her face against Chattie's silky fur. 'London again. Au revoir, Chat.'

Chattie sang into Kazza's ear, hoping that she would not be away too long. The partings were so sad and the Birman was afraid. She had premonitions of her mistress fighting and she could smell blood. She knew that no one would win, because Kazza was one of the Kilkenny cats, but her fears were too complicated to convey – or perhaps Kazza was now too involved in the outside world to listen.

'Take carrrr-e,' said Chattie.

Kazza zipped up the neck of her black velvet catsuit and shrugged her shoulders into a fake fur jacket. She did not like cold Monday mornings, and the drive to London would be draughty in her old car. She was still shivering when she took the high-speed lift to the top of one of London's tallest skyscrapers. The directors' dining-room had panoramic views of rooftops, landmarks and parks, the River Thames threading its way through the city like a murky ribbon.

'Don't we heat the offices enough for you?' enquired a masculine voice, tinged with amusement at her pale frozen face above the fur collar. 'I assure you the heating bills are astronomical.'

'I like warmth,' said Kazza, raising her eyes. They went on up, for Louis Sloane was six foot two tall and powerfully built. She had seen him from a distance many times but had never spoken to him. He had the aura of a man destined to go far and was, at thirty-four, already head of the Accounts Department.

At that moment Kazza could not have cared if he even knew his two times table. His dark brown eyes held her gaze and she could only wonder why she suddenly felt weak and tongue-tied. She felt a warning quiver down her spine.

'What do you do here?' he asked, trying to put her at ease. 'I take it you are one of our many employees?'

'I cook lunch,' said Kazza.

'And very well too,' said Louis, in the tone of a man who appreciated his food. 'That rabbit casserole yesterday was delicious.'

'It's chicken today,' said Kazza demurely, as the lift stopped at his floor and the automatic door opened. 'In wine and garlic.'

'I look forward to it,' he smiled.

Kazza continued upwards to the penthouse floor, her mind in a daze. Men had not played much part in her life. She laughed at Catherine's procession of boy-friends. Kazza preferred to stay at home in the evenings, lazing in front of the fire, then taking a late, lonely stroll along the Embankment.

But Louis Sloane was different, and when she saw him

arrive in the dining-room at lunch-time, she felt a sweet stab of longing. She turned away so that no one could see her eyes.

Kazza and Catherine always served lunch from the hot buffet cabinets, and drinks from the bar. One so dark, and the other so blonde, they made charming hostesses and created a good impression with visiting managements and foreign customers.

'Smells appetising,' said Louis strolling over to the buffet. 'Are you warmer now?'

Kazza nodded. 'It's hot in the kitchen.'

'You're in the right place then,' he said. Kazza served him some chicken, giving him the best portions she could find without making it too obvious.

Catherine was ready to add the vegetables: tiny carrots in butter, shaped potatoes, stringless beans, cauliflower au gratin. She took time arranging the vegetables on his plate in a pleasing pattern, then she smiled at Louis, a special slow-eyed smile, and Kazza knew with a sudden pang of despair that it would be war.

It was declared sooner than she thought. Catherine stormed into the kitchen, flinging plates into the dishwasher completely disregarding that they were expensive Aynsley bone china.

'Hands off,' she spat.

'I beg your pardon?' said Kazza, still hearing his compliments about her fluffy cream soufflé.

'I saw the way you were serving him. I saw the size of those portions. Now understand this, Kazza, Louis Sloane is mine. We've been dating for two weeks and it's going like a dream. I want this man and I intend to have him.'

Catherine's green eyes were vicious. Kazza backed away. She had never seen her friend so angry, but then never before had they both smiled at the same man. Kazza wanted to slide away into a dark corner, to hide in a deep cupboard, to turn her face to the wall. But then she remembered the way Louis had smiled at her; there was a feeling that was too precious to lose. She straightened her back.

'Are you engaged?' she asked quietly.

'No . . .'

'Has he asked you to marry him?'

'Not yet. But he will.'

'How do you know that? How do you know he's serious about you?' Kazza lashed the questions at Catherine, determined that she would not let him go so easily.

'Because I know he is,' said Catherine with a superior laugh, showing her small white even teeth. 'So keep your hands off him, pussy-cat. He's not interested in little girls like you. Louis prefers real women. I don't think he'll wait for you to grow up,' she added cattily.

Kazza took a long look at her friend. People had even called them cater-cousins because they had got on so well. But not now. That was over.

'I'm a Kilkenny cat,' Kazza warned, but Catherine was not listening. She was taking through the coffee and her home-made chocolate mints. *Octopussy* was still showing in London, and she knew Louis had not seen it. She would just mention it casually.

It was not long before repercussions rippled through the tall office block. The first major disaster was a special luncheon for a team of visiting computer experts. The menu was barely discussed, and Catherine switched her marketing at the last moment, producing vegetables which were totally unsuitable for Kazza's Dover soles. The delicate flavour of the fish was ruined. Kazza was shattered. Her Dover soles were a speciality. She was so upset she left the refrigerator door ajar so that Catherine's strawberry sorbets were pink puddles by the time she served them in the dining-room.

The row in the kitchen was so loud the computer experts fled with embarrassment. Catherine had a string of excuses for the directors. Kazza said nothing, but she moved out of the flat into a small bed-sitter. One evening when she could not get her old car to start, Louis Sloane drove her home and stayed to listen to records and eat toasted cheese in front of the fire.

He stretched out his long legs and folded his arms behind his head. He seemed perfectly at home, his eyes half-closed as the warmth of the room relaxed away his weariness.

'I've been burning the candle at both ends,' he confessed. 'Too many night-clubs, too many drives to the coast. I can't keep it up and put in long hours at the office.'

'You work very hard,' said Kazza. 'I've seen the light on in your office.'

'It's a tough world, Kazza,' he yawned. 'But this is nice,' he smiled sleepily, taking her hand. 'Don't go away . . .'

In a few moments he was asleep. Kazza moved closer to him and closed her eyes. She would protect him. She would not allow anyone, especially Catherine, to hurt him, to ruin his career with her selfish desires.

They did not fight clean. Cats don't. Lunch after lunch in the dining-room revealed the frayed edges; their battle scars began to show. The personnel officer asked them both to see her in her office.

'Twice last week the Chairman had to send out for a MacDonald's,' she said with an exasperated sigh. 'You've got a week in which to improve, or you'll both be fired.'

'I just can't understand what has got into you two,' said Louis that evening, as he and Kazza strolled by the river. 'You and Catherine used to be such friends and you worked together so well. And whatever happened to that lasagne? It tasted like seaweed.'

'Catherine tripped with the salt-shaker,' said Kazza. 'I didn't know till afterwards.'

'I had hoped not to have to ask this,' said Louis, looking into the far distance at the shrouded Big Ben. 'But am I the cause?'

'Yes.'

'You're like a pair of gypsies,' he said, suddenly angry, and his face darkened.

'A pair of cats,' said Kazza.

'I am a free agent,' he said. 'I can date anyone I like. No ones owns me, nor ever will.'

'I know . . .' said Kazza softly.

He stopped seeing Catherine and she was so wild with jealousy that she put sugar into the petrol tank of his car. Louis was not pleased. Kazza was incensed by this act of treachery and ordered a wreath of funeral lilies to be sent to Catherine's flat.

Catherine retaliated by writing Kazza's phone number in shocking pink paint on the walls of telephone boxes, and Kazza's landlady had to go ex-directory in self-defence.

Kazza recklessly went through the pages of a mail-order catalogue ordering a dozen items from a lawn-mower to a loft-ladder to be delivered to Catherine's flat. Catherine nearly had hysterics at her front door.

'Now you two have got to stop it,' said Louis, taking Kazza aside. 'I can't bear to see you destroying each other like this. No one is going to win. It's all going too far. For heaven's sake, stop it now.'

'I can't . . .' Kazza whispered. 'I'm a Kilkenny cat.'

'I don't understand,' he said, running his hand through his dark hair. 'What's a Kilkenny cat?'

'Let me tell you a story,' said Kazza with a deep shudder. 'A long time ago, during the rebellion of Ireland, the soldiers made a cruel sport to amuse themselves. They tied two cats by their tails and threw them over a clothes-line to fight. The officers were appalled and resolved to put a stop to it. But one soldier, quicker than the others, saw the officer coming, and drew his sword, cut the tails and the cats escaped.

'When the officer saw the two bleeding tails, he was told that the cats had devoured each other, all but the tails.'

'What a revolting story,' said Louis. 'So?'

'And the towns of Kilkenny and Irishtown continued to fight each other until there was little of either left.'

Kazza's voice fell away. It was the longest speech she had ever made. She did not know how she had got through it.

His eyes were fixed on her face. There was a sudden constriction in her throat. She put her hand on his arm, and he gripped her fingers tightly.

'I can't begin to understand all that,' he said. 'But it's gone beyond a joke. Please, Kazza, before it's too late.'

She shook her head.

'Do you need a soldier to cut you down?'

'Perhaps.'

'Somebody tell me what to do,' said Louis despairingly. 'I can't cope with this.'

'I'm sorry,' said Kazza.

'No, you're not,' he contradicted. 'If you were, you'd forget all this nonsense about Kilkenny cats. Kazza, you mean a lot to me . . . far more than any woman I've ever known. Don't spoil it, my darling.'

It was what Kazza wanted to hear more than anything in the world, but she was trapped by her own nature. She was hardly able to think. She longed for her home, the countryside and the companionship of her lovely Birman. But if she ran away, she would lose Louis, and Catherine would waste no time consoling him.

At the end of the week, both Kazza and Catherine were given their notice. Kazza's landlady asked her to go; she had never recovered from all the telephone calls. Kazza left immediately.

Catherine sifted through the pile of bills on her desk; she would not be able to afford the flat without a regular salary. New jobs were not easy to get, particularly as their reputation had circulated around the dining-rooms of the City.

Chattie was relieved to have Kazza home. She lay on Kazza's lap and purred rapturously, kneading her claws into the softness and warmth. Chattie could no longer smell blood, although she knew from her mistress's sadness that the fighting was not over.

'Shall we walk tonight in the woods?' Kazza whispered in her ear.

'Purrrhaps,' said Chattie. It was a long time since Chattie had been to the woods. She did not like to go alone. But she would follow Kazza anywhere.

Kazza dialled Louis' number at the office. She had to speak to him, to explain her sudden departure from London. His secretary answered his extension.

'Oh, didn't you know, Miss Mount? Mr Sloane is going to New York. He's been offered a six months' exchange visit with the American parent company. It's a wonderful opportunity. He's flying out tomorrow . . .'

The secretary prattled on, but Kazza quietly put down the telephone. He had not told her. The Kilkenny cats had now completely destroyed themselves. They had lost their jobs and their reputations; they had lost their home and their friendship, and now they had both lost Louis. Without Louis there really was nothing left.

She turned away, walking blindly out of the farmhouse. The Sussex woods and hills called and she went into their cool green darkness. As she walked the weather changed and long forks of lightning shot through the sky; a drum-roll of distant thunder rumbled and died away. She did not heed the warning. Cats were not afraid of storms.

Kazza walked for miles, not caring in which direction she went. The wild brambles caught at her clothes. She could remember almost every word that Louis had ever said to her. They were locked in her heart.

She climbed the Sussex Downs and stood at the top, hardly looking at the grey view of fields and woodland. She was no longer a Kilkenny cat; that part of her nature had been destroyed forever. She was all woman now, and she was swept by the desolation of her loss.

A small movement far below caught her eye. It was a

pale, fleeting ghost, stumbling and staggering among the bracken. Kazza's sharp ears heard the faintest mew on the wind.

Suddenly she came to her senses and went flying down the hill, slithering and sliding on the wet ground, calling out to her beloved and devoted friend. Chattie was at the point of exhaustion, her beautiful coat sodden with rain and mud, the pads of her soft paws cut on the flint-like stones of the Downs.

Kazza scooped the cat up into her arms, tears running down her face. She had almost killed her cat with her blind and selfish stupidity. Chattie lay limp and bedraggled, with hardly the strength to lift her head.

An hour later Kazza walked wearily into the brightly lit saloon bar of a village pub. She was drenched, and the locals looked at her with interest as she went up to the bar and unzipped her anorak. Chattie was tucked inside, her coat flattened and matted, looking a poor creature.

'Some warm milk please,' said Kazza. 'For my cat.'

Louis rose from a corner seat away from the door. He had been sitting there for a long time, trying to decide whether to drive the last few miles to Kazza's home, or whether to go out of her life without a word. He went over to her, not touching her, but standing there, tall and gaunt with concern.

'Are you all right?' he asked.

'I'm all right,' she said, her voice very low. 'But my cat is exhausted. It was my fault; I didn't know she was following me. Look what I've done to her . . .' Kazza stroked the spiky fur with a gentle finger. 'I've been such a fool, Louis. The Kilkenny cat has gone. I'm suffering now like a woman, and it's too late. I've lost you.'

'No, you haven't, my darling,' said Louis, looking down at her with that special warm look. 'You see, I'm here. I found I couldn't go without seeing you. Everything is going to work out fine.'

The landlord came over with a glass of warm milk standing in a saucer. Kazza poured some milk into the saucer, and Chattie stretched herself after her cramped quarters and smelt the milk. She staggered a little on her stiff legs, but began to lap, warmth and strength returning to her veins.

'I love you,' said Louis, oblivious to the long ears listening, entranced, around the bar. It was better than the telly.

'And I love you,' said Kazza.

'No more Kilkenny?'

'All gone. No one wins.'

'And you'll make your peace with Catherine?'

'I will try.'

The landlord, sensing a celebration, slung a bottle of champagne into an ice-bucket. Louis was leading Kazza back to the inglenook seat, rubbing life back into her frozen hands, their heads close.

Chattie finished the milk and sat back to clean her whiskers. Then she began on the dried mud and bits of grass sticking to her tail. She had never been to a pub before. The atmosphere was warm and friendly and no one seemed to mind her painstaking grooming.

Thoughts flitted through her memories of the temple cats in the temple of Lao-Tsun high up in the mountains of Lugh, where the priests had kept many pure white cats. The miracle of their coats taking on a golden hue, and the browning of their heads, legs and tails, was an ancient legend. It was as much a legend as the Kilkenny cats.

Chattie shook out her long luxuriant coat. But, unlike the Kilkenny cats, she had four flawlessly white paws to prove her legend.

# The Cat That Could Fly

It began on a curiously still morning when not a leaf stirred and even the butterflies seemed to hover over the flowers without moving. The dead elm stretched its ashen branches skywards waiting for the chop that was a long time in coming. A mile up, a chartered TriStar ferried yawning early starters to a package holiday on Majorca, its gentle hum followed by vapour trails in the sky.

Leopold trod the dew-hung clover with delicate paws. He was a big ginger and white cat with a wide, surprised face and fluffed cheeks. His eyes were very green and brilliant, which added to his startled look. He lived an uncomplicated life: he ate and slept; he caught the occasional bird or shrew just to keep his hand in.

The family that he lived with were what Leopold called sleek. They had everything – two cars, two colour television sets, a video recorder, wall-to-wall stereos, a deep-freeze that could take a whale, every domestic appliance on the market – and yet they were as mean as a cross-eyed snake. They bought him unbranded cat food, a mish-mash of wet cereal and unmentionable animal parts; he never got a taste of fresh liver or fish. They drank the cheapest coffee, bought broken biscuits, and cut all the tenpence-off coupons out of the paper. They were sleek all right.

They were sleek on affection too. If Leopold jumped onto a vacant lap, he was hastily brushed off.

'Gerroff my suit! I don't want your hairs all over me. Shoo. Shoo,' said the sleek man impatiently.

The sleek woman was as bad. Her clothes were also uncatable. The one person who liked Leopold was the daughter, Dana, but she was preoccupied with O levels and boy-friends, and the only time Leopold saw her was when she came in late from a disco and they shared the cosy quietness of a 2 a.m. kitchen.

As Leopold took his early-morning stroll down the garden, he heard a faint chirp–chirp. The sound made his stomach contract. He was hungry. Last night's supper was best forgotten, and they would not give him breakfast until he had been outside for at least an hour. Leopold did not understand these rules. It was another of their odd ways. He noticed that they ate broken biscuits whenever they felt like it.

Leopold crept up on the sound. It was a baby thrush, softly speckled brown and white, a big fluffy helpless creature, looking straight at Leopold with bright, trusting eyes. It staggered a few inches and fell forward onto its plump breast. Leopold's surprised expression sharpened with delight. This was obviously some sort of game. He patted the soft feathers with a tentative paw. The bird chirped encouragingly and hopped another few inches. A few trees away, the mother bird heard her baby's call but was not alarmed. It had to learn to fly by itself.

Suddenly Leopold pounced. The baby's neck hung limp between his jaws. Leopold growled, a low rumbling jungle sound echoing back from his wild ancestors. He paraded his victim, the feathers stuck out round his mouth like an air force moustache. He crunched the tiny body thoughtfully, getting blood on the short white fur under his nose.

The mother bird went crazy. She flew from branch to

branch in distress. She swooped over the ginger cat and what was left of her baby, her cries loud and distraught. But it was too late. There was nothing she could do. She took one last look at the big cat and flew blindly into the empty air, not caring where she went.

There was a great oak which Leopold liked to climb. He never went very far because he knew his limits. But today the baby bird lay heavily on his stomach, and Leopold climbed higher, hoping to leave the uncomfortable feeling behind. The thick tangled branches gave no hint of how high he was climbing. He went on, up and up, leaping from one claw-hold to the next. Because there was no wind, the branches barely moved, again giving Leopold an unfounded sense of security. When a broken branch revealed a glimpse of the land below, Leopold was quite amazed. He could see the tops of other trees, padded with green like cushions beneath him. The garden of his house was a smudge of blurred colours. In the distance was the church spire, almost eye-level. A helicopter whirled into sight, coming straight towards the oak, its rotor blades clattering discordantly.

Leopold leaped back. He forgot he was on a branch, up a tree. He took off backwards, falling head between heels, somersaulting through a cascade of leaves and broken twigs, the wind rushing through his whiskers, flashes of sky and earth alternating as he hurtled towards the ground.

He spread his paws helplessly in a gesture of supplication to the great cat god in the sky. He closed his eyes tightly. He did not want to see what was coming to him.

Leopold first became aware of a change when the swift rushing wind in his ears slowed to the merest whisper. He was still falling, but no longer that shattering, pummelling plunge earthwards. He seemed to be drifting. Perhaps he had died.

He opened one eye the merest slit. He saw the Japanese maple, a beech hedge and, below him, a bed of button dahlias, prim and tight-headed. He landed right in the middle of the flowers and shook himself.

'Gerroff my dahlias!' the sleek woman yelled from a bedroom window.

Leopold extracted himself from the damaged flowers with dignity and walked away, a curled yellow petal behind one ear like a Hawaiian hula dancer. He had too much to think about to be worried by appearances.

After breakfast he sat looking at the oak tree. It did look very high. What had happened to him? How could he have fallen all that way and survived? He knew that cats could fall from the roof of a house and land unhurt on four paws, but that tree was at least three houses high, or so it seemed to Leopold. Eventually he wandered into the wood, to the far end where it was secluded and the blackened stump of a tree struck by lightning stood lonely and unloved.

He climbed the black stump, sniffing the lingering smell of sulphur. He sat in the fork and looked down on the carpet of pine-needles below. It was about eight feet high. He could either scramble down the charred bark, or he could jump.

He jumped. He expected to land on the bed of needles in about one and a half seconds flat. But strangely he seemed to float. It took four seconds to land. It was puzzling.

He thought about it for a time, then decided to climb the stump again. He jumped off from the fork. This time it took six seconds and he landed some yards away on dry bracken.

Leopold was beginning to enjoy himself. After all, what harm was there if he wanted to spend the afternoon jumping off an old tree? What the hell! He climbed again, rapidly, like a red arrow. He jumped again, quite merrily, paws spread, wondering where he would land.

Suddenly he saw a clump of nettles right below him. Despite his thick fur, he knew all about nettles. His pink nose was particularly vulnerable. He stretched wide his paws in horror and sailed over the top of the clump.

Without thinking, he lifted both his right legs and wheeled away in a shallow curve towards an open patch of ground.

When he returned that evening, the family scolded him and said he was too late for supper! They sat round the television, dunking broken biscuits into watery coffee. Leopold licked at the dried bits still stuck on his breakfast saucer. His drinking-bowl had not been changed and the water was practically growing algae. He jumped on the draining-board and stretched his neck towards a dripping tap.

'Gerroff the draining-board, you wicked cat,' the woman shouted. Leopold obligingly removed himself. For a split second, as he jumped, he almost spread his paws but an inner caution stopped him, and he landed awkwardly, unbalanced.

'Now don't do that again! I won't allow it.'

He sat on the front steps in the dark until Dana came home from her date. She was sniffing into a twisted scrap of handkerchief and her mascara had run into panda smudges. She made herself a mug of milky cocoa and poured a large saucerful for Leopold. She knew where her father kept a hidden packet of chocolate biscuits and she helped herself, spreading out the remainder so that he would not notice the difference.

'Of course, I can never tell them about Roger,' she said to the cat, stroking his ears. 'They wouldn't understand about him not having any money, or a job. They'd never understand.'

Leopold daintily mopped up the fallen crumbs. No, they would never understand. The next morning, he was at the door, waiting to be let out, and streaked through the moment there was a crack. He spent all day practising, graduating from tree to taller tree. It was exhilarating. By mid-afternoon, he acknowledged what he had been wondering about ever since his miraculous escape from the big oak.

It was not simply this new skill which filled him with

267

joy and excitement, but the fact that it held the key to something far more important – escape. He walked back to the house quite jauntily, not caring that his supper would not make up for missing breakfast.

'Caught yourself a little mouse for breakfast, did you?' asked the sleek woman, scraping the last globule of mush from the tin. 'There's a good pussy.'

Good pussy swallowed the revolting food. It was important now to keep up his strength. When he saw the family go out for the evening, he climbed onto the roof of the house, skirting the television aerial and leaping up onto the flat top of the chimney. He sat there for a long time, his tail neatly curled over his feet. It was not that he lacked courage; it was just that this was the first time he had contemplated jumping from anything other than a tree. And it might be that trees were a vital ingredient . . . However, he would never find out just by sitting.

He stepped off into space, automatically widening his paws, claws outstretched, tail stiffened, lifting his head. These movements slowed his free fall, then he leaned carefully into a wide arc, his brilliant eyes almost crossed with concentration. He glided across their garden, past the dahlias, rising over the hedge, then soaring up as he came face to face with an overgrown rhododendron bush. The evening air was cool and peaceful as he locked into a pure, straight, calculated climb, his whiskers twitching as the wind resistance began to increase. He winked as he passed two alarmed starlings flying home to roost. As he topped the climb, he closed in his paws, tucked his head down and streamlined his descent onto the flat roof of a neighbour's garage. Shaking with relief, he sat down and began to lick back his ruffled fur. He had done it. He did not need a tree.

After that, there was no stopping Leopold. He jumped off anything and everything. His greatest day was when he managed to climb into the church belfry and then up the narrow ladder that was steel-pinned to the side of the spire. There was precious little room at the top for him and the weather-vane. The dim metal cock spun round, creaking, obviously out of control, almost knocking Leopold off his perch. Leopold took off in a perfect swallow-dive, levelling out at about a hundred feet without any effort. The thermals of air took him up higher and he gloried in the feeling of space and freedom. Below, the neat rows of houses and gardens stretched for miles. Dark green patches of woodland were all that was left of the great forests which had once covered the hills. He flew over the top of the ugly grey gasometer, tracking for fun the snake-like train that swayed along the line. People were so small, wobbling along on matchstick legs, heads down, wrapped up in their worries and dreams. No one noticed a large ginger and white cat flying casually overhead.

He began to get more adventurous, exploring the countryside and neighbouring towns. He followed the River Thames to London, but did not stay long among the high-rise flats and skyscraper office-blocks. The air traffic bothered him and the pigeons were rude.

'I've just seen a cat fly by,' said a stunned window-cleaner in a cradle at the twenty-first floor of an office building.

'Fell out a winder,' said his pal morosely, wiping a dark mirrored pane of glass. 'Probably pushed.'

'It was flying. It was a ginger cat.'

'We gotta little tabby. Company for the missus.'

The window-cleaner screwed up his eyes against the sun. Whatever it was was almost out of sight, skimming over the top of St Paul's dome and the cross sparkling in the bright rays. Perhaps it was a ginger bird. He clamped his mouth shut and turned back to his work. He did not want to get his cards.

Of course, Leopold could not keep his secret forever. He began to get careless. The family gave a party with watered gin and cut-price whisky to celebrate the sleek man's latest promotion. As they cleared up, Leopold slid among the chairs looking for morsels of cocktail snacks.

If they were anything like the general standard of catering in the house, most of the guests would have dropped them. He found a pathetic shrimp on a soggy toast finger stuffed behind a pot plant. It wasn't bad. The cheese they had used had been so stale and crumbly, it had parted company from the cubes of pineapple and there were lots of bits on the floor.

The sleek woman had also lashed out on a dip made from dried chicken soup and tinned cream. Not many people had dipped, so there was a lot left. As she was scraping it all together and wondering if she could turn it back into soup, a big dollop slopped off her finger and fell onto the carpet. Leopold raced to the rescue.

'Gerrout the way! You damned cat! Look what you've made me do,' she stormed. She swiped at him with her morocco-bound visitors' book. (Someone had written: 'Unbelievable party, darling.')

The book caught Leopold hard on the side of his head. Swift as a flash he spread his paws and leaped to the safety of the pelmet. The woman was furious and did not notice anything unusual about the ascent. She lashed out at him again and he took off, flying right across the room to a shelf on the other side.

'You wicked thing,' she shrieked, wondering if she had not watered the gin enough.

'Mummy,' said Dana, opening the French doors to let out the smoke-laden air. 'I think Leopold can fly.'

Leopold soared out into the night air. He shared a gnarled oak with an old owl and contemplated the future. They knew now. Perhaps it would not matter. After all, what could it possibly mean to them? Habit was hard to break, and at breakfast-time Leopold nodded to the sleepy owl and took off for home. He flew down into the garden and sauntered up to the back door, casually twitching his tail.

'Darling,' cooed the woman, scooping him into her arms. 'Darling Leopold, you've come back to mummi-kins! Nice pussy, come and have some lovely milk.'

Leopold was thoroughly alarmed, squashed against her second-best jumper with the sequin buttons. She smelled of musk and face-cream. He struggled, but she was holding him very tightly. He heard the back door shut and it was the thud of doom.

They sold him to a circus. As he was being driven away in the back of the circus owner's Cortina estate, the sleek family were hugging each other with glee, waving the fat cheque and planning to buy more cars, more televisions and a holiday in the Bahamas.

Leopold quite liked the circus for about two days. They put him in a large cage that smelt of bear, and people came and looked at him, bringing delicious things like fish and chips, beefburgers and anchovy pizzas.

Then the circus owner put him on the scales and declared a diet. Leopold must not gain a single ounce. Aerodynamics, he called it.

Leopold did not understand the circus. It was so bright and noisy, with strange animals growling in the night. They did feed him better food than he was used to, though he suspected it was left over from the lion's share.

The trouble started when Miss Dora, the trapeze artiste, refused to carry Leopold up the ladder to her platform high in the roof of the big tent. She absolutely refused even to touch him.

'I shall come out in a rash all over,' she said, every rhinestone on her brief costume quivering with indignation.

The circus hands rigged up a basket affair in which to hoist Leopold up to the platform. Leopold hated it. He felt sick as it swayed and jerked higher and higher up into the dim black regions of the roof. He stepped out onto the narrow platform and looked round politely. It was very high up indeed. Miss Dora stood as far away from him as possible.

'Shoo, shoo,' she said, her feathered headdress nodding with each word. 'Go away.'

Someone switched on a spotlight, blinding Leopold.

He stepped sideways to avoid the brilliant white light, and disorientated, he fell off the platform. He fell, paralysed with fear, like a stone, and landed with a bounce in the safety net, all four paws and his head stuck through the mesh; it was very undignified.

'Now, Leopold,' said the circus owner, speaking slowly and deliberately. 'When you get up there on the platform I want you to fly across to the other platform.' Leopold looked back at him with puzzled green eyes. 'Fly across, like Miss Dora. Only you're a clever pussy and you don't need a trapeze bar.'

Miss Dora scowled. 'I don't like sharing my act with a cat. It's ignominious.'

Again Leopold was put into the elevator and swung up to the platform. Again he fell into the net. The sweat began to come out on the owner's brow. He had gambled a fortune.

This time Leopold rolled over and got into such a mess in the netting they had to cut it to get him out. He tried not to look smug as he was returned to his cage.

'Please, pussy,' said the circus owner the next day, wringing his hands. 'Fly for me. I gotta lotta money tied up in you. You wouldn't want to see old Joss go bankrupt, would you?'

Miss Dora had covered her body thickly with an anti-bite ointment in order to protect herself from Leopold's deadly rash. The smell was awful. He couldn't stand it for two seconds. He launched himself off the platform at speed, did two fast circuits of the arena, then spotting the exit sign, made a bee-line for the opening. He dipped stylishly over the big top before heading off towards the far country. He felt the faintest twinges in his paws as he climbed higher in the sky. He had never reached this altitude before. His tail streamed out behind him, his fur filled with air, and the loose flaps of skin under his armpits belled out like a parachute.

Leopold was looking for the sea. He had had in mind for some time to learn to fly properly. He was a bit afraid of going to the mountains to find an eagle or a condor. They were so big and unpredictable. But seagulls, now they were a different kettle of fish. And there was no doubt about it, they could fly. Leopold's role would be that of ardent observer.

He was quite surprised when he eventually found the sea. It was not at all as he had expected, just miles and miles of heaving wet blue waste. But the seagulls were there in their thousands, screeching and diving and squabbling among themselves. Leopold particularly admired their precision take-offs and landings on water.

He went down onto the pebble beach to practise a few low level take-offs, but each time he nose-dived straight into the sea. It was horrid, and he soon discovered that he could not fly very well if his fur was wet.

'Scram, scram,' shrieked the seagulls as Leopold went headlong into the waves yet again. He gathered his dignity round him like a wet bathrobe and climbed into the heather to dry off.

When he found the cliffs, he knew he had the answer. Their sheer height was impressive; the grandeur of the craggy rock-face filled Leopold with quivering pride. This was going to be his home. He was going to be a cliff catperson; he saw himself leaping about the rock-face as sure-footed as Tarzan, catching his food among the gorse on the headland, sleeping in a small cave. He could watch the seagulls all day and learn their secrets. He would practise diligently from his cliff-top, experimenting, adapting their flight to his. It was going to be wonderful.

The seagulls were a bit alarmed by this peculiar flying ginger thing. They knew cats ate birds, but what sort of cat was this? They resorted to a Mafia-style protection racket, dropping Leopold the odd freshly caught mackerel in return for paws-off. This suited Leopold admirably. He did not fancy a mouthful of wet feathers.

Leopold ate well. Fresh fish, rabbits and mice; the dew to drink from fragrant morning puddles shot with silvery sunshine. He was very happy.

His flying improved. He could stay in the air for much longer and with a lot less effort. He could glide in for touchdown with fanatical precision. He experimented with stalling in the air, letting himself fall, heart in mouth, then pulling himself out of it moments before hitting the waves. He skimmed along the surface of the sea with carefree abandon. He learned to loop the loop, to power-dive like a blazing meteor; he perfected a victory roll, coming out of it to soar up into the sky until everything was so translucently blue that he could no longer tell which was sea and which were the heavens.

He was sailing along on one such routine flight, when he discovered he could no longer see land. He circled around, his green eyes searching the horizon. He could see nothing solid or familiar. He flew slowly, wondering in which direction to make tracks. He had no idea how far this sea stuff went.

He began to get tired, flying in ever wider circles. Then he realised that the sun had gone and it was getting darker. He was not alarmed by this as he could see very well in the dark. But this was not the night. It was another kind of foreboding grey gloom; the gathering of thunder-clouds laden with rain.

Leopold looked up as he heard far-off rumbling. There was going to be one heck of a storm, and he was going to be caught in it. He knew what would happen when his fur got wet. He knew what would happen if he had to land on water. Caput. End of Leopold.

He flew on bravely, his body aching. The first big drop of rain hit him squarely between the eyes. He blinked and adjusted his speed. He had to keep his head, or this thing would beat him.

He tried to climb higher to get above the storm, but it was too late. The thunder-clouds were dark and menacing; flashes of lightning lit up the rolling masses of horror. He began to wish he had stayed with the circus, or perhaps even the sleek family.

The storm gathered into a seething black mass overhead; the rain began hitting him like sledgehammers. In minutes he was soaked, his fluffy fur plastered to his skin. He lifted his head, trying to maintain height. Fiercely Leopold fought to hold his own, relying on the months of practising to come to his aid now. But he was losing speed and losing height. The dark water below was surging in great white-frothed waves, deep gullies sucking and swallowing each other. One bedraggled ginger and white cat would soon disappear beneath that hungry sea.

Leopold could hardly see now. His lids were glued by the onslaught of rain. He began to fall. As he fell, he mewed piteously . . .

'Jumping Jehovah, if it isn't raining cats and dogs! There, my fine fellow, don't struggle. Mike Kelly's got you safe enough.'

Leopold found himself caught by strong arms that took the impact of his fall. It was a miracle. He must have fallen straight into the arms of a saint.

The saint was wearing glistening yellow oilskins and a brimmed sou'wester, off which the rain was dripping. His lined and crinkled brown face had a pair of the bluest eyes Leopold had ever seen.

'And where did you come from? I suppose you done drop out of one of them aeroplanes? My word, we'd better take you down below and dry you off before you catch your death.'

Mike Kelly carried Leopold down into the tiny cabin and began to rub his coat with a rough towel. It was the smallest room Leopold had ever seen, cat-sized in fact. He looked around with interest. The room pitched and rolled in the strangest way, but it did not seem to disturb the man so it must be all right.

'Well, you're stuck here now,' Mike Kelly went on. 'Whether you like it or not. I'm sailing round the world and I shan't make landfall for weeks. You can get off if you want to, or you can come back to Ireland with me. Please yourself. I'm easy. What do you think?'

Leopold had already made up his mind. No one had ever consulted him before, or treated him as an equal.

'I'm needing a ship's cat and a bit of company,' said Mike, opening a tin of evaporated milk. 'So you dropped in just right. You'll earn your keep and I reckon we'll get on . . .'

It was the beginning of a lifetime of devotion and mutual companionship. Leopold sailed all over the world with Mike, following him round strange foreign places and wintering sometimes in Southern Ireland in Mike's cottage while his catamaran was docked for repairs or maintenance, and the next voyage was planned.

The circus owner sued the sleek family for misrepresentation and the wrangling went on in court for years. Eventually the judge dismissed the case, saying it was useless to go on when neither party could produce the evidence (i.e. the cat) in question. The costs were enormous and the sleek family, who had spent the cheque, were rather silent as they made an appointment to see their bank manager. Dana did not go. Instead she ran off with Roger and went to live with him in a caravan.

Leopold did not entirely give up flying, though it took him some time to get his nerve back after that terrible storm. He made sure he did not fly too high, or too far away, realising that navigation was his weak point. He even perfected a new technique of a low-level approach for a deck landing.

If Mike ever noticed his cat flying round the masthead, he was too tactful to mention it. Occasionally he was heard to mutter unsaintly comments about the Blarney Stone, or wonder if it was the Irish whiskey.

One day he vowed he'd write a book about Leopold, but then, who would believe him?

# Walkabout

The first time that Simon went on a walkabout was one of acute embarrassment for Jane Foster. It was the morning of an important meeting with a new client, and since Jane was still unofficially on probation, it was necessary for her to have all her wits about her, be on the ball, keep her cool, and every other cliché invented for similar situations.

Instead she found herself sitting on the edge of a chair only half-listening to the opening remarks of Gregory Kennedy, chief advertising executive of Hill & Kennedy, as he introduced Clive Phillips to the meeting.

'Hill & Kennedy regard this new account as a challenge,' he said, thumping the table with determination. 'We are honoured to be part of a new concept in advertising. We shall be opening up entirely new fields in public relations and the media. It will be exciting and rewarding to be part of the Phillips campaign.'

Clive Phillips looked a shade uncomfortable. He did not want to be a new field or a new concept. He had built up his considerable business by old-fashioned, reliable methods, and now that he was at last going to advertise, he wanted something simple and straightforward. It was the first time he had considered expanding his market by this means and he wanted nothing trendy. Phillips baths did not depend on sensation for their sales and steady annual profit.

'No nudes please,' he said, almost inaudibly.

Gregory Kennedy did not hear, but Jane Foster did. Her ears were acutely pitched to catch any unfamiliar sound. 'No nudes' was one of them. Most of their clients wanted nudes. They thought nudes would sell anything. There was another unfamiliar sound: a peculiar scratching at the door of the boardroom.

Jane shrank back in her seat. She recognised the scratching. Somehow Simon had got out of the cupboard.

The situation had begun on the train that morning. Jane had been absorbed in sketching out some ideas on a drawing-pad on her knees, her thoughts miles away. She was an artwork designer at Hill & Kennedy, and as she preferred to live in the country, she used the long train journey to play around with ideas.

Despite her concentration, Jane eventually became aware of a ripple of interest among her fellow passengers. It was one of those long open carriages with a central gangway.

Strolling nonchalantly along the middle, stopping occasionally but keeping his balance remarkably well, was Simon, her beautiful tortie colourpoint cat. Catching sight of his mistress, he quickened his pace, did his customary victory roll on the floor, and then a flying leap onto her lap, ignoring bag, pad and pencil.

'Oh no,' said Jane, groaning with disbelief. 'Simon, whatever are you doing here? How could you? I'm going to work.'

Simon did not care where she was going. He was going with her. He curled up on her lap, a satisfied mound of pale fluff, and tucked his dark nose under his dark tail.

There was no time to take him home. The train had already passed East Croydon, the one stopping station where she could have got out and returned home. There was nothing to do but carry on to London with the cat.

'At least you won't have to pay a fare for him,' said the lady opposite, giving Jane a Harrods carrier-bag for Simon. 'You would if he was a dog.'

'Don't tell him,' said Jane. 'He'll want to be a dog. Whatever am I going to do with him?'

Jane had no doubts about Simon's feline intelligence. The half Siamese, half Persian, had a finely functioning brain up there behind those deceptively baby-blue eyes. He was bright, all right.

She had known for months that he disliked being left at home while she went to work. He was like a disobedient child as he watched her preparations for departure. He hid under the bed, at the back of the shoe cupboard, on top of the wardrobe, trying to make his three-inch fur invisible. Once he crawled into the crack of an open drawer and burrowed right underneath leg-warmers and scarves. It took Jane half an hour to find him.

Then he started following Jane to the station with a pathetic, abandoned expression. Several times she missed her train because of having to carry him back home. Her excuses for being late did not go down too well.

'I can't leave him in all day and I can't leave him out,' she explained, none too clearly.

'I suggest you get a budgie,' was Mr Kennedy's answer, as if one could just change pets at the library. 'A lot less bother. Well, don't be late on Tuesday. Clive Phillips is coming and that account is going to be worth thousands.'

Jane knew all about the account. She had been working on designs for the advertisements for weeks. Phillips bathrooms were prestige – not just coloured suites of exceptional quality, but patterned with fish and flowers and ferns, shells and shamrocks and sparrows. Some were patterned all over, some bordered and some with a single, delicate motif. They were works of art and almost collector's pieces.

Clive Phillips, the man who had built up the business from fairly humble beginnings, was coming to discuss ideas. Jane had been drawing ferns and flowers from every angle, and this was the morning Simon chose to accompany her to the office.

At London Bridge station, Jane bundled him into the Harrods bag and told him firmly to behave. He did. For about one and a half seconds. Then he stuck his head out of the top of the bag. It was as well that Jane had him firmly tucked under her arm, for his first sight of London traffic was terrifying and he had a first degree panic.

It would have to be a taxi. She could not risk a nervy Simon on walkabout in the underground.

'You're costing me money,' she admonished, as she climbed into the taxi with the struggling cat. 'No chicken livers for you this weekend.'

'I don't actually like chicken livers,' said the taxi-driver. 'But thanks all the same.'

Opening the boardroom door was child's play for Simon. He had mastered doors at an early age. He knew just when a little extra weight or sudden jerk would unfasten a tricky catch.

He leaped unhesitatingly onto the polished walnut table, stalked straight across the layouts and designs, and threw himself into Jane's arms, clawing and purring enthusiastically as if he hadn't seen her for years. Whereas it must have been all of fifteen minutes since she had shut him in the stationery cupboard.

'I do apologise,' said Jane, trying to untangle her long red hair from Simon's claws. 'This is my cat,' she added, stating the obvious.

'I hope this is not one of your bright ideas,' said Mr Kennedy heartily, attempting a joke to cover his annoyance.

'Oh no, cats don't like water,' she said.

'That's it,' rumbled Mr Kennedy, who had had a hasty breakfast and was suffering. 'A cat in the bath-tub! Cats don't like water . . . but they LOVE Phillips baths!

What do you think?'

Clive shook his head. 'No cats and no nudes,' he said. 'There are too many cats on television . . . cat food, cats on carpets, bags of flour – '

'No, that's little men in bowler hats,' Jane interrupted. 'But I do agree that cats are very over exposed,' she added, trying to push Simon under the table. His long fluffy tail stuck out above the edge like a flag.

Mr Kennedy detected an obstinate gleam in his new client's eye. 'We'd better stick to our original idea. Nature walked in with a Phillips bathroom. Show him the designs, Jane. Now how does that strike you, Mr Phillips?'

Jane had drawn some very pretty illustrations . . . fish and flowers and ferns; shell and shamrocks and sparrows, and a tree or two. But Mr Phillips did not seem particularly enthusiastic.

'Is this an attempt at the personification of nature?' he asked curiously.

'Er . . . yes. Well, no . . . not personification. Nature is, as it is, walking into one of your bathrooms,' Mr Kennedy explained, hunting for a dyspepsia tablet.

'Like a Triffid,' said Clive, peering closer. 'No thank you. No walking weeds.'

Jane could see that Mr Kennedy was somewhat at a loss. No nudes, no cats, no walking weeds . . . That about demolished Hill & Kennedy's current ideas for the Phillips account.

Simon chose that moment to introduce himself to everyone at the meeting and went on an extended walk-about. Mr Kennedy seized the opportunity to close the meeting.

'I think we'll need to toss about a few more ideas,' he remarked. 'Back to the drawing-board, so to speak.' He flicked some of Simon's long pale hairs off his trousers. 'And Jane, please remove your cat. He's not on the payroll.'

Everyone laughed. It was another joke.

'Yes, Mr Kennedy. Of course, Mr Kennedy.'

She bundled Simon out of the room and took him along to her studio, where she deposited him firmly on her drawing-board. She stood back and looked at him sternly.

'You're a very naughty cat. You practically ruined everything,' she scolded. 'Mr Kennedy is annoyed with me and I could lose my job. I'm still on probation, you know.'

Simon assumed an expression of total innocence. He was having a great time, except for being shut in the stationery cupboard. There was no fun in packets of paper and envelopes, though he reckoned paper-clips had definite potential.

A dark head peered around the doorway. Jane had not realised that Clive Phillips was so tall, having only seen him sitting down. And he looked younger now that his gold-rimmed spectacles were being put away in a pocket.

'Don't worry, Miss Foster. It wasn't your fault, nor your cat's. I just didn't like the ideas. I want something simple and a bit old-fashioned.' He smiled, and it was a nice, slow smile. Jane felt the merest stirring of her pulse, a fractional quickening that was strange and new.

'I liked your drawings though,' he went on. 'Watch out! Your cat! He's on the paint.'

Simon was taken home with a yellow-spotted tail and a blue blob on his nose. He travelled in a cardboard box with two small holes cut out for air. He was denied any view, being in disgrace. On the underground he managed to claw the holes large enough to stick out his front paws, and thus he travelled, two paws protruding horizontally out of the cardboard box.

'Is it alive or dead?' asked the guard.

'Alive,' said Jane. 'No train is safe.'

Like Dick Whittington, Simon kept returning. No matter what precautions Jane took, the wily cat managed to outwit her. Once he even got to London Bridge before her, having travelled on an earlier train by mistake. He then waited on the platform, confident of her arrival.

'Gor bless my soul, miss,' said a porter who'd been sharing his breakfast with Simon. 'You've got a rum 'un here.'

'Yes, very rum,' said Jane. 'Thank you for feeding him, but giving him food is only going to encourage this outrageous behaviour.' She pulled out the Harrods carrier-bag, which was now permanently in her brief-case.

'You should be flattered, miss,' said the porter, giving Simon the last cheese-and-pickle sandwich. 'The little chap's obviously devoted to you.'

'That may well be,' snapped Jane. Simon stepped into the open bag with the air of a conjuror's assistant partak-ing in a vanishing act. 'But he's costing me my job.'

Gregory Kennedy had surpassed himself with ideas for the next meeting with Clive Phillips. After days of agonising, he had come up with bathrooms from heaven with a Phillips bath descending gently to earth by para-chute.

Clive shook his head thoughtfully. 'Sorry, no jumps,' he said. 'I don't care for heights.'

'Thought you'd say that,' said Gregory Kennedy, toss-ing Jane's designs onto the floor. 'Then how about this one? This, I know you are going to like. Phillips bath-rooms are a gold-mine . . . stark contrast of a coal miner digging underground and finding – wait for it – a gleam-ing Phillips bath complete with gold taps.'

Gregory Kennedy waved Jane's drawing of a coal-mine triumphantly under Clive's nose. The bath glowed like a nugget in its sombre surroundings. Clive frowned.

'Mm . . . I'm not so happy about the coal-mining aspect,' he said. 'It would remind people of the days when they kept coal in their baths. It also seems some-what socially tactless. They might even start doing it again.' He shuddered at the idea. 'Definitely no coal-mines.'

'Diamond-mines? Gold-mines?' Mr Kennedy suggested desperately.

'You'd expect to find gold in a gold-mine,' said Clive logically. 'The point of the ad is then lost.'

Gregory Kennedy wiped the perspiration off his brow and closed the thick file of papers. He could see thousands of pounds' worth of business going down the plug hole.

'I suggest we break for lunch,' he croaked, even though it was only ten to twelve. 'See you all later.'

Clive stopped behind to help Jane collect her designs from the floor. He shuffled them into some kind of order.

'I like this little cloud motif,' he said, looking at the parachute idea. 'I might be able to use it on a bath.'

'You can't,' said Jane primly. 'I'm under contract to Hill & Kennedy.'

He followed her back to her studio, carrying the bulky portfolio. He was feeling conscience-stricken that she had done all this work for nothing, but she did not seem too upset by it.

Simon was lying exhausted in a filing tray. He had camped out all night near the station in order to leap into the guard's van the moment Jane appeared on the platform. He had had no breakfast. He had nibbled at a few pot plants in the studio, but they weren't up to much, and Jane hadn't had time to give him more than a saucer of milk before the meeting.

'So your cat's here . . . again.'

'Don't talk to me about Simon,' said Jane. 'He's driving me spare. Yesterday he went walkabout round the office and was missing for three hours. I looked everywhere for him. And where did I find him? Stuck in the lift, going up and down like a yo-yo.'

'Oh Simon,' Clive laughed, touching the soft furry dark head. 'You do lead your mistress a dance. Miss Foster, I know one shouldn't tell a lady that she looks frazzled, so I won't because actually you don't . . .' He was struggling for words. 'But I do owe you something for all the work you've been doing on my account. And

Simon certainly owes you a lot for sitting in your paint and leaving hairs in your filing tray . . . may we both take you out to lunch?'

The shy, involved invitation brought a sweet lift of longing to Jane's heart. She wanted to go out with him. She could see that it had been an effort for him to ask her. Clive Phillips was obviously unused to dating girls, far too busy working at his business.

'I'm sorry, but I can't,' she faltered. 'There's Simon. I can't leave him.'

'I don't think you quite understand. We're taking him with us. I know a restaurant where the chef dotes on cats. Simon will be entertained to a banquet in the kitchen. He'll probably get better service than we will. And, as I was once a boy scout, I always carry a piece of string . . .'

Over lunch in a pretty courtyard restaurant, where the white ironwork tables were screened from their neighbours by pots of peach trees, Jane and Clive talked about everything under the sun. Everything except baths. Simon strolled about on his piece of string, greeting luncheon guests and generally playing mine host. Then the smoked salmon was too much for him and he curled up in a patch of sunshine on the paving stones and fell asleep, content with his life commuting and working in an office.

It was Jane who brought up the subject of bathrooms; she really did want to help him, to find a way of promoting his product.

'I don't really want all these gimmicks,' Clive replied, watching the way the sunlight was playing on her red hair. 'My baths are good. They speak for themselves. I don't need parachuting nudes and cats in coal-mines, begging Simon's pardon. You do understand, don't you, Jane?'

'Oh yes, Clive, I know just what you mean,' said Jane, thinking that she had never seen such deep brown eyes in a man. 'But Mr Kennedy is so full of bright ideas.'

'I'd hate to take my business elsewhere.'

'Mr Kennedy would blame it on Simon, I know he would.'

'Then I can't, can I?'

Clive reached across the table, negotiating the vase of daisies on the way, and took told of Jane's hand. She looked down at their clasped hands, the one so broad and practical, hers so slim and artistic. They were perfect together, almost made for each other.

'We'll have to think of something,' she said, her eyes fixed on his face. They smiled at each other and neither of them was thinking about baths.

A few weeks later, when Mr Kennedy was on the point of a nervous breakdown, Jane did think of something. The answer came to Jane in a moment of calm happiness as she carried Simon to work in a newly purchased glass-fibre carrying box from which he looked smugly out onto the passing world.

Being under contract to Hill & Kennedy, and still on probation, Jane went straight to her employer.

'Phillips baths are so good,' she said. 'Why not let them speak for themselves?'

So the idea was born. The advertisements in the newspapers and magazines, and the commercials on television, centred solely on the bath, beautiful, delicate and elegant. No puff, no commentary, no gimmick . . . just the whispered words, the tiny print: 'They speak for themselves.'

It was so simple. The campaign worked and Clive was delighted. He was so happy that his courage grew and dating Jane became a habit he never wanted to break. Simon went with them everywhere. His wicker basket began to have that travelled look. Some days after lunch Clive took Simon back to his factory for a change of walkabout, and to give Jane a few hours off.

Simon looked at everything with interest. He decided that the tool-shop was too noisy, the paint-shop was fun, and the packing-sheds were a dream. All that lovely wood to scratch, and packing-cases to climb, and shreds of brown paper to leap about in. The factory workers were kind and made sure he did not get in the way or get hurt. They took to sharing their tea-breaks with him, and Simon really got hooked on tea-breaks.

Then at the end of the day, Clive would give Simon a lift to London to pick up Jane before their evening date. Simon even began to recognise the street.

As Clive reached across to open the car door for Jane, Simon would retreat tactfully to the back seat and stretch out for a snooze. It was a big car.

'Hello, darling,' said Clive, giving her a very discreet hello kiss.

'Hello, darling,' said Jane. 'Has Simon behaved himself?'

'Perfectly,' said Clive. 'No trouble at all.'

Simon allowed himself a small purr of congratulation. He hoped Jane and Clive would remain on 'darling' terms for a very long time. Wicker baskets and Harrods carrier-bags were all right in their way, but travelling in a Silver Shadow Rolls beat British Rail hands down.

# Flat Cat

She trod rapidly but warily over the cellophane tops of the preserve jars, right to the furthermost reaches of the long, dark wall-cupboard, curled herself up into the smallest possible ball and tucked her nose into her long, quivering fur.

She was hiding from the world.

Cindy did not understand what was happening. Suddenly she had been catapulted out of her secure five years of existence with Lisa into a vast alien world that simply terrified her with all its grotesque peculiarities. It was as if something had exploded in her mind and pitchforked her into another universe.

In the fog of her bewilderment she retreated into the darkest space she could find and hid her face in her fur. She was totally alone. It was very frightening.

And why? What had she done wrong? Was she being punished for some heinous sin? If so, she did not know what she had done. Had she sat on a book, knocked over some perfume, scratched the baby?

A kaleidoscope of distorted images swam round her brain: what were those tall rustling giants that swayed in the air? The thick, uneven walls of green bits that buzzed and hummed with flying things? That funny, spiky floor that bent when trodden on? And even more startling, the

288

enormous empty blue ceiling that stretched forever, making Cindy feel that the sides of her world had fallen outwards?

Then the place to which she had been brought: there was room after room, one leading from another. She had never seen so many rooms. She had crept through their strangeness, trembling, always expecting something new and terrible to happen round each corner. She hid under a table in the quietest room wondering if it was all a bad dream, and she would wake up soon within the safety of the four walls of Lisa's tiny studio flat.

'Let's leave her there under the table,' said the strange woman who had brought her to this place. 'Everything is so different to that London flat. She must be very frightened.'

The experience had begun in a very ordinary way. The woman had arrived at the flat, and Lisa had asked her in and made a cup of tea. Cinnamon Rhama had greeted the visitor with her usual party trick, a series of pretty rolls, a kind of floppy somersault on the carpet that usually elicited murmurs of admiration and did so again in this instance.

'Oh, she's really beautiful,' said the visitor. 'What a lovely cat. Gorgeous fur . . . is her colouring sealpoint? She's like milky coffee, and those lovely dark brown paws!'

'She's a tortie colourpoint,' said Lisa, turning Cindy's gentle flat-nosed face to one side. 'There's a little bit of tortoiseshell in her face, and see the spot of pure white on the top of her head?'

'What beautiful eyes . . . so blue. No, they're more a pale aquamarine. And those funny tufts in her ears!'

'That's the sign of a true Persian,' said Lisa, sitting companionably on the floor beside her cat. 'She's an almost perfect colourpoint. Her registered name is Cinnamon Rhama, but we call her Cindy.'

Cinnamon knew nothing about being a perfect colour-point. Her world revolved around Lisa and the baby and the restricted view from the studio skylight. She did not know that any other world existed. Even the birth of her two litters of kittens had been by Caesarean section, and her matings had merely been a necessary ruffling of her dignity and an affront to her ravishing beauty.

But maternity had suited her gentle nature, and she had loved her kittens, and the high-protein diet of stewed steak, minced chicken and brewer's yeast tablets. But the kittens were taken away and she had almost forgotten them.

The woman visitor did not pick her up or maul her in any way. She also sat on the floor and held out a hand for Cinnamon to sniff.

'I don't think I can bear to let her go,' said Lisa, her voice impassive. 'I love her so much.'

'I won't try to keep her,' said the other woman. 'She'll always be your cat. You can have her back whenever you say. I promise you that.'

'I really do have to go back to America,' said Lisa, more to herself. 'I really do have to go, me and the baby. We have to get away.'

'And it's only Cindy that's keeping you here?'

'Yes. I can't leave her . . . unless . . .'

'I'll take great care of her.'

'I know you will. You're the right person. I can feel it.'

When her wicker travelling-basket came out of the cupboard, Cindy knew exactly what to do. She jumped into it and curled round into a small fluffy ball. She did it so innocently, as if it were just a routine visit to the vet's.

The two women closed the lid on her and tied it with extra string.

'I don't want her leaping out in Victoria Station,' said the woman, with a nervous laugh. 'I think I'll carry it in my arms. I don't trust the handle.'

She lifted the basket, wanting to leave now, to cut short the painful scene, to make the parting easier for Lisa. There had been no last stroke of the long pale fur, no last kiss on that sweet face. They had simply closed the lid. It was cruel, but the kindest way in the end.

'You'll need a bag of litter,' said Lisa, suddenly practical as they were leaving. 'Cindy's a flat cat. She's never been in a garden.'

This journey's amazingly long, thought Cindy, curled up in her familiar basket. She could hear the woman's voice talking to her soothingly, and fingers stroked her through the slat in the wicker. Eventually Cindy went to sleep, lulled by the motion of the train. She did not know the woman was taking her to a new life.

The new life began with a series of sharp, horrendous shocks. She tore panic-stricken round the garden on the end of a lead, her heart pounding wildly as trees, grass, hedges, flowers, sky, birds, insects flashed across her eyes as distorted visions, sounds and smells. What was it? What were these things?

She shot back into the house, the woman close behind, knowing only the safety of concrete and bricks.

She roamed the rooms restlessly, looking for Lisa's flat, which must be somewhere inside this building. She sniffed for Lisa's divan, Lisa's tiny kitchenette, the baby's cot, the baby's pushchair . . . They had all gone.

Instead there were new things: furniture she did not recognise, flat white fingers that made a noise as she ran across them, a rocking machine with a round face that imprisoned water, a box with moving pictures. Part of the floor was broken into small pieces and put one above the other. This led to more rooms, and beds that had space beneath them.

She leaped up onto a windowsill and came flat against a glass pane. Outside was the same great vastness that frightened her. She ran trembling into a cupboard and burrowed her way to the back among the shoes and handbags, hiding herself from the terrible sight of the sky.

'She's hiding at the back of the wardrobe,' said the woman gently. 'Leave her. She obviously feels safer there.'

At first Cinnamon Rhama would not eat or drink. They put down tempting dishes and warm milk. But her appetite had vanished. The other cat, old, short-haired and sleek, her blackness tinged with ageing brown, finished it all up. The two cats eyed each other and hissed, but they did not fight. The black cat was old and beyond fighting. But her green eyes narrowed with hostility and her stubbly fur stiffened, despite the many strokes and reassurances from the family.

'This is Cindy. She has come to live with us for a while. You must try and be friends,' said the woman hopefully.

The black cat recognised youth and beauty, and sat with her long rope-like tail flicking with suppressed anger. This was her house, her garden, her family . . . The stranger was an enemy. She hated the woman for bringing her. But she was also old and loved food, and when she found herself being fussed over and given special tit-bits while the newcomer was in hiding, her resistance mellowed to the odd hiss.

It was during the night that Cindy found a way into the kitchen wall-cupboard where the woman stored home-made marmalade. Despite the cat's haste to find a new hiding-place, she was light-footed and only stepped into one jar. In the morning she heard their voices and the familiar sounds of tea being made.

'But where is she? She must have gone out. Did anyone let her out? Who opened the door? No? Then she must be here.'

They went round the house, upstairs and downstairs, calling. 'Cindy, Cinnamon. Cindy, Cinnamon.' The cat froze.

'I can't have lost her!' The woman was dismayed, her voice rising. 'Lisa will never forgive me . . .'

'Everybody look. She must be somewhere.'

'Supposing she's got out.' The woman was close to tears. 'Perhaps she's trying to walk back to her old home.'

Someone was opening cupboard doors, getting nearer. Cindy crouched back into the darkness, watching the shafts of light growing closer.

'Well, I never! Come and look at this!'

Faces peered at her from a distance, but they could not reach her. She was still comparatively safe.

'How on earth did she get there?'

'She jumped onto the working-top, then onto the dishwasher, and up onto the plant shelf. One of the cupboard doors must have been left open.'

'How are we going to get her out? If we chase her, she'll just run down to the other end. She could evade us for days.'

'Lisa told me that she's addicted to Munchies.'

It wasn't fair. They laid a trail of Munchies, each tiny biscuit a few inches further on. Cindy was hungry and she did love them. So this place had them, too. It was the first good sign.

She was tempted beyond her fear. She ate her way out of the cupboard, and the moment she was within reach, she was lifted down by firm hands.

'Make sure all the cupboards are shut in future. I can't have this palaver every morning.'

Cindy did not eat or drink that day either. But she did use the litter tray. She was a small cat despite all the fluffy fur and she could creep under almost anything. She hid under the music centre, squeezed herself between the desk and the wall, flattened herself under beds where only dust collected, burrowed her way into every cupboard. They spent the whole weekend hunting for a small, pathetic face and two baby blue eyes.

She then discovered a top shelf behind a barrage of plants. She sat there, eight feet high, safe and camouflaged, able to contemplate the people below.

For a while they fed her on the shelf, climbing up on the kitchen steps to leave saucers of milk and the odd Munchie.

The woman put the lead on Cindy's collar and took her

to the garden door and sat down on the top steps. The cat stood beside her, astonished by the outside again.

'This is the garden, Cindy,' said the woman. 'You'll love it when you get used to it. You'll be able to play in the garden and climb trees. It won't hurt you.'

Cindy was persuaded to sit for a moment, calmed by the woman's voice, just beginning to be a mite curious about this strange new outside. Then suddenly something alarmed her, and she dashed back indoors, dragging the lead, straight upstairs and into the depths of the wardrobe.

'I won't rush her. One step a day until she gets used to it. We'll see if that works.'

They went one step further into the garden each day. Sometimes Cindy stayed only a few moments before something frightened her: a bird, an aeroplane, a rustling branch, a butterfly . . .

They walked a few yards together. It was a token walk. Then Cindy tugged at the lead to go back into the house. She was eating now at an allotted place, just a few mouthfuls before climbing up to her hideaway behind the plants.

One day the lead disappeared. Cindy found herself sitting on the top step with the woman, quite free. It was a heady moment. She took a few tentative steps alone and sniffed at a plant. An ant ran across her path. A leaf fluttered to the ground. She retreated back into the house, still unsure.

The door to the garden was left open. She peered round it, looking, sizing it up. The woman was always somewhere near, watching patiently.

She began to follow the woman when she went outside. She sat and watched her weeding the flowerbeds; picking beans, snipping dead-heads. There was a garden table and Cindy sat on that, absorbing this new green world, the sun warming her fur, and slowly her fears went away . . .

But one day she went outside into the garden and the

shock tingled her spine right to the end of her tail. Confusion added to her distress. She bounced on the wet grass like a lamb. The ceiling was pouring water. Had they got taps up there? She peered through the wet leaves, expecting to see some gigantic gusher spraying the earth. But there was nothing, only moody grey clouds. She shook her paws fastidiously. She did not mind a bath now and again, but this amount of water was ridiculous.

'It's only raining,' the woman laughed, as Cindy sprang across the grass to come in. The cat shook out her fur and dried off on top of the boiler.

By now she had discovered the joys of the garden. There were games to play. The best was racing. Cindy would follow the woman to the far end of the garden, then the woman would turn and look at her expectantly.

'Race you to the house, Cindy!' she challenged. She set off running up the lawn towards the house, looking back at the still, indifferent cat. 'Come on, Cindy. Race you.'

When the woman was precisely three-quarters of the way up the lawn, the cat sprang into action. She flew through the air, light as wind, her long pale fur streaming, her paws bouncing off the soft turf. She shot between the woman's legs, the fur brushing her skin like thistledown. The cat leaped onto the steps and sank gracefully with a little humorous half-look, as if to say: 'Well, what took you so long?'

It was a game she played again and again, always winning.

In winter, the snow came; that was something else. It did not frighten her. She was losing her fear of strange things. Snow astonished her, then annoyed her. She shook her paws free with each long stride through the pesky stuff. When she found herself up to her chin in a drift, it was time to cut short her visit. They could keep snow, along with rain. They were only fit to be watched from the dry shelter of a windowsill.

She liked the car. 'Coming for a ride?' and she did not

need asking a second time. She often made the round trip to Caterham, either sitting on the driver's knee or the woman's lap, or stretched out on the back shelf, her nose on her paws, her bright eyes taking in all the new sights.

Cindy's Siamese call was strong, but she only used it when she had something definite to say. The old cat got caught in the tiled space between the two front doors and it was Cindy's call that brought the woman into the hall to see what was the matter. Cindy had not moved from beside the door.

'That was very clever of you,' said the woman, freeing the old cat. 'Thank you.'

Another evening a loud miaowing came from the kitchen, which the woman heard even above the television programme. She hurried through and immediately saw the cause. The stock-pot was bubbling and rattling on the stove, its contents boiling over.

'Sometimes I wish you could talk,' she said, lowering the gas. 'I'm sure you have a lot to say.'

Cinnamon Rhama had definite airs and graces. If she was told off (mainly for sharpening her claws on the side of a chair), she retreated in a huff and sat in a corner with her back to the room. But her nature was sweet and the huff did not last long.

She also understood that her long tail was a hazard and quickly forgave any clumsy human who stepped on it.

She grew to trust the woman; allowed her to bath her, groom her, put ointment in her eyes, special oil in her ears. She sat on her lap while the woman typed or read the newspaper, or tried to sew or knit.

The morning began with no hint that it would be a different kind of day. Cindy had taken to waking the woman in the mornings. The moment the kitchen door opened, she sprang off the washing-machine and ran swiftly upstairs.

She jumped up onto the duvet, sat on the woman and began to pat the woman's face with a gentle brown paw. When this had no effect, her maternal feelings stirred and she began to clean the woman's chin, or fingers or cheek . . . any exposed skin got the treatment. The woman had become an expert at dodging the rough little tongue.

The third stage was the nips. The woman kept very still as Cindy nipped her chin for she had seen the size of those strong teeth. But Cindy never hurt and there was never a mark.

'All right, Cindy. I'll be up soon. I've got a lot to do today. We've got very special visitors.'

Reassured, Cindy tucked her nose under the woman's chin and joined her for another forty winks.

The woman was busy. She did a lot of cleaning and cooking cakes. Cindy was not perturbed. This did sometimes happen. She sat in the garden, enjoying the sunshine, her pale fur tipped with its radiance.

A car drew up and a woman and small boy got out. Cindy recognised the voice, though she did not move. The knowledge of Lisa's arrival erased her time in the country in a flash. She remembered the studio flat, the tall walls, the skylight and its fleeting glimpses of sky. The memories came back strongly.

The small boy went straight to Cindy and tried to lift the cat.

'Take Cindy home now,' he said firmly.

Cindy struggled out of the awkward grip and landed on her four paws. Her face was a mask.

'Come on, Cindy. Do your victory roll,' said the woman, encouraging Cindy to show off her floppy somersault. But Cindy did not move. 'Come on, you funny thing. It's Lisa . . . don't you recognise her?'

'I guess she's being a little off-hand at first,' said Lisa, laughing. 'Because I've been away. She'll come round.'

Cindy disappeared down the garden as the visitors went in for tea. She climbed to her favourite place and contemplated the sky.

The woman was disappointed. She wanted Cindy to be her usual sweet and engaging self, to show Lisa that

Cindy had been happy living with her. But the cat was showing a stubbornly anti-social streak, and it was not like her.

Later, the woman fetched Cindy in from the garden, stroking her so that a reluctant purr started somewhere in her throat, but it soon stopped. She looked at the woman suspiciously.

'Come in and behave,' said the woman. 'I don't want Lisa to think you dislike it here.'

Cindy cat motionless in the middle of the room. Then she walked under the table and sat with her back to everyone in her huff position. She sat there for the whole of Lisa's visit, refusing to come out, refusing to be tempted by Munchies. The line of her back was one of disapproval and unco-operation. She would have nothing to do with anyone. The woman was at her wit's end.

'I simply don't know what's got into Cindy,' she said. 'She's not usually like this.'

At last the visitors rose to leave. The small boy crawled under the table and hauled Cindy out.

'Take Cindy home now,' he said.

'Oh no,' said Lisa. 'We can't take Cindy back to America with us. Besides, she has this lovely garden to play in.'

It was quite a few minutes before Cindy realised that they had gone. The car had driven away and the woman was clearing dishes into the kitchen.

Cindy went and sat at the garden door, waiting for it to be opened. The woman bent and touched the soft furry head.

'Did you think they had come to take you away?' she whispered. 'To tell you the truth, so did I.'

She opened the door and Cindy flew out, her fluffy tail like a plume. She sprang onto the grass, executed a few floppy somersaults, heady with the sense of freedom and joy under the blue ceiling of the sky. Then she looked back at the woman, expectantly.

'Race you,' said the woman, starting to run.

They ran down the lawn, woman and cat, exhilarated with the relief they felt. They were still together.

There was no need for words. The cat simply let the woman win.

# The Vanishing Act

She was born in a theatrical hamper in the chorus dressing-room at the back of the Royal Variety Theatre on a cold December morning. She could not help having the theatre in her blood from the moment the dancers found her among the costumes and reared her on a diet of milky coffee, cottage cheese and ham rolls.

No one knew how the little ball of silver fluff got there. The mother disappeared as silently as she had arrived. It seemed as if the kitten was the result of some tempestuous love affair that was quickly over, and once the kitten was born – the wrong side of the blanket – the mother returned swiftly to her old life.

The chorus girls knew little about pedigree cats. This one was a rare and beautiful long-haired silver tabby with large lustrous hazel eyes and clearly defined tabby markings on her dense and silky coat. The girls called her Silvikins.

The dancers came and went with the seasons, but there was always someone, perhaps a little homesick, who liked and would look after Silvikins. Babs was such a person. She was a tall, long-legged brunette, but perpetually in the back row because of her height. She was never quite going to make it, even though her dancing was slick and her stage smile as dazzling as any other.

'I wonder what it is about me?' she asked Silvikins, gently disengaging the cat's claws from the mesh of her black fishnet tights. She couldn't afford another new pair this week. 'I sometimes think I'm invisible. The director never notices me. The choreographer can't remember my name. I'm going to be in the back row until my hair goes grey and my teeth fall out.'

Silvikins sprang off the young woman's lap. She knew it was curtain-up soon, and then it was wiser to keep out of the way of all those high heels and hurrying legs. She prowled into the wings, keeping well back in the shadows. She looked up into the tangle of ropes and wires and acres of canvas in the flies. There were so many favourite places for Silvikins to view the show among the jungle of lighting equipment.

She was incurably stage-struck → every night she watched the jugglers, comedians, magicians and dancing girls. Her bright hazel eyes closely observed the scenery changes, quick to get out of the way if she was liable to be toppled from her perch.

She loved all the bright colours and the movements. Her paws twitched to catch the flashing silver balls as the juggler threw them into the air. She blinked at the magician's tricks, wondering where the bouquet of flowers had suddenly come from, how objects appeared and disappeared, and even more miraculously the vanishing of people from a big black cabinet.

The cleverest of the magicians was a young man called Monsieur Herriot. His real name was Henry, and somewhat like Silvikins, he came from a good family who had now disowned him for not going into the family stock-broking business. His magic act was particularly exciting to watch because he used a lot of white doves and tiny yellow canaries, and a white pom-pom poodle with a bow tied on its head. One night when Monsieur Herriot produced a moon-faced goldfish swimming round in a bowl from out of nowhere, Silvikin's mind was made up. All her latent ambition came rushing to the fore. She was going on the stage. She wanted to be part of the magic act.

But how? Henry had hardly spoken to her, beyond the odd pat on his way to the dressing-room. He had a black velvet jacket with lots of pockets and Silvikins wondered if she could fit into one of those pockets. She doubted if she could get down his sleeve. No, it would have to be the black cabinet. It drew her like a mysterious magnet. She would like him to make her appear and disappear, to hear the gasps from the audience and then those waves of applause. Silvikins knew she would be able to do it with far more showmanship than the dim poodle. And she wouldn't need a bow on her head.

The first bit of luck, if it could be called luck, was when Joyce, Henry's shapely assistant, slipped on the pavement outside the theatre, breaking the stalk-like heel of her shoe and her ankle, in that order.

'I'm going to sue,' Joyce howled in pain and dismay.

She wondered if Henry would let her hobble on stage with her ankle in plaster. But understanding as he was, Henry did point out that National Health plaster, however imaginatively decorated with gold spray, was not glamorous. And a magician's assistant had to be glamorous.

The second piece of luck was when he knocked, somewhat hesitantly, on the door that led to the chorus dressing-room. He hardly expected to find any of the girls in early. But Babs was there, feeding Silvikins a tin of pink salmon that cost almost as much as a new pair of tights.

'Hello,' he said. 'So you feed the cat.'

'Yes,' she said. 'We take turns, but it's nearly always my turn.'

'Tough.'

'I don't mind,' she said. 'I like animals.'

'Do you like doves, canaries, goldfish and poodles?' he asked.

'Yes . . .' she replied, bemused and still not recognising him.

'I'm the magician, Monsieur Herriot,' he said, introducing himself. He did not look much like a magician off-stage in his casual jeans and sweat-shirt, and rather quiet, shy manner. 'Henry to my friends.'

'I'm Babs. Back row, third on the left. Red feathers in the last number.'

'Very nice,' he said, at a loss.

'Don't try to make out you've noticed me,' she said, scraping out the last of the tin for Silvikins. 'No one ever does. I'm one of the perpetual invisibles.'

'Perhaps you're the very person I'm looking for, then,' he said instantly. He was very good at rapid decisions. It was all part of being a magician. You had to be quick, and he had noticed that she had a lovely smile and legs to match.

'I need an assistant tonight,' he said. 'Joyce has broken her ankle. Have you seen my act? Do you think you could do it?'

'Of course I can do it,' said Babs immediately, seeing herself at last coming out of nowhere into somewhere. 'Do we have time for a quick run-through of the sequence?'

Silvikins took a gulp of her salmon and followed them onstage. She knew that one of the first rules of the theatre was to be in the right place at the right time . . . you never knew who might notice you.

She watched Henry do a brief run-through of his act. She knew from his actions just when he was about to produce the white dove from a top hat, the row of wine bottles from a single container, the canary in a light bulb, the goldfish in a bowl . . . and then of course, that snooty poodle disappearing and reappearing in the black cabinet, not a hair unruffled.

Henry really did have magical powers, Silvikins was convinced. It was amazing. And now Babs was going to help him. Silvikins watched the show that evening with a small throaty purr of contentment as Babs handed him props with an elegant flourish and turned this way and that to milk the applause from the audience. She was born to it.

'You were absolutely stunning,' said Henry, after the show.

'It was fun,' said Babs. 'But I'd like to rehearse again tomorrow. I know I was a little slow at times and I want to get it quick and slick.'

'Yes, of course. But . . . I say, er . . . would you like to come out for a coffee and a hamburger?'

Babs lowered her stage lashes. She'd had dozens of invitations from men for after the show, but never one from a nervous young magician with a dove up his sleeve. It was rather touching.

'Thank you,' she said demurely. 'I'll get changed.'

Silvikins prowled the empty theatre, seeing off the mice that dared to sneak into the labyrinth of corridors in the basement. She liked it when she had the stage to herself. It was all so vast and exciting. She dreamed dreams, not quite sure what it was all about, but uplifted by all the waves of enjoyment and appreciation that came over from a happy, laughing audience.

Babs had an inventive mind and came up with a few ideas which Henry worked into his act. Silvikins liked seeing the professional way they worked together, and at one rehearsal she jumped onto the black cabinet and sniffed around. She really did wonder what vanishing was all about.

'Silvikins is curious,' said Babs. 'She wants to know how to vanish.'

'A pleasure to oblige,' Henry grinned. Silvikins sat in the small space, a little alarmed, wondering what was going to happen. If she was going to disappear, would she be able to come back? But she was not that frightened, because she could hear Babs' reassuring voice. Suddenly the blackness changed and she was sitting in the open cabinet looking out at the empty auditorium. Why, it was quite easy after all . . .

'Do you think it's possible to teach a cat anything?' Henry asked. 'I mean, well, it would be different.'

'No,' said Babs, shaking her head and lifting the silver tabby into her arms. 'Cats are much too independent. They do just what they want to do. Silvikins only co-operated today because she was curious and she wanted to know what was going on. But it might never happen again. They are not like dogs.'

'I suppose not,' said Henry, giving Silvikins a small tickle under her silvery chin. 'But she is a beautiful cat. She'd give my act real class.'

He saw the hurt expression flash across Babs' face. For all her glamour and harsh years in the theatre, Babs was as sensitive as any woman would be.

'Oh, I'm so sorry,' said Henry with a groan. 'I didn't mean it like that. You are a marvellous assistant and your ideas are terrific. I just thought that being a pedigree cat, she would . . . well, she's streets ahead of a canary. I could teach you some of my tricks if you like . . .' he offered.

'Yes please,' said Babs, before Henry could change his mind. 'How do you do the one with the linked silver rings? That's always puzzled me.'

'That's easy. You just need to be fast.'

Silvikins began to wash her ears. She was very fastidious and the inside of the black cabinet had been a little dusty. She sneezed in a refined way and they both laughed and said 'Bless you', which she thought very odd indeed.

She sat and meditated, front paws placed neatly side by side, while Henry gave Babs a lesson. She was very quick to catch on and resolved to practise and practise.

'Do you think I'll be good enough in time for the Command Performance,' she asked, hardly daring to voice the hallowed event.

'We'll see,' Henry promised. It was going to be a big occasion in his career. A Command Performance in front of Royalty; a big charity night to raise money; television cameras transmitting the show into millions of homes. He was praying a lot of prayers. Babs was quite lovely and intelligent, which added an extra zing to his act; she was not just a pair of long legs and a few sequins. But to let her do a trick . . . it was a bit risky.

Henry thought about it and hated having to disappoint her. The Command Performance was too big and too special. Babs took the news like all the other disappointments in her life, with a smile and a little tilt to her head.

'Another time, eh?' she said.

'Yes, another time.'

Everyone was nervous before the big night. The theatre had been searched for bombs and Silvikins had done her best with the mice. The Royal Box was decorated with garlands of flowers and draped with satin, and special brocade armchairs were put into place.

Silvikins sensed that something was different. The air was tense with electricity. It made her fur stand on end, and she licked it down with infinite patience.

The girls were all on edge with excitement, borrowing each other's make-up; in tears if something snapped; re-painting their faces till every blush was perfect.

Babs had an extra change of costume for Henry's act. He had lashed out on a gorgeous gold lamé outfit for her, and she was very touched.

The responsibility was making her extra nervous, and in her haste to give herself plenty of time to get ready, she forgot to bring in any supper for Silvikins.

'I'm really sorry,' she told the cat. 'Can you wait till after the show? Then I'll pop out for some fish and chips.'

She looked up to see Henry waving at her from the doorway in an agitated manner. She hurried over, pulling a thin wrapper round her flimsy costume. That was another thing Henry liked about Babs: she still retained a sense of modesty.

'It's the poodle,' he said. 'He's being sick. God knows what rubbish he found to eat.'

'Perhaps he'll get better.'

'I can't have him being sick on stage.'

'Scrap the trick.'

'But it's my best,' Henry despaired. 'You know it's my best trick. No one expects to see a fully grown dog suddenly appear.' His capacity for instant decisions seemed to have disappeared with his trick.

'Wait until the interval,' said Babs, hurrying back to the mirror to fix her headdress. 'At least you're on in the second act.'

Silvikins sat on the long dressing-table, being careful not to disturb the pots of powder and paint. She closed her eyes, blissfully content just to be where she was, among people she knew, to be part of all that was happening.

'There's the cat,' said Henry.

'No,' said Babs firmly. 'That time was just a fluke. She would never do it again and it wouldn't be fair to expect it from her. She's a cat not a dog.'

'I suppose you're right,' Henry agreed with a sigh.

Babs was too busy to see Henry again. The dancers had a lot of numbers and changes of costumes. By the time she was putting on the gold lamé outfit, Babs supposed that the poodle had recovered. They stood in the wings, their nerves in their throats, waiting to go on.

'Is the vanishing act still in?' she whispered.

Henry nodded. He was too uptight to speak. Suddenly their music began and Henry strolled on, tall and debonair in evening clothes, top hat and flowing opera-cloak. The act had begun.

It went very well. His new tricks were daring. The audience gasped at his ingenuity as doves and canaries appeared rapidly from anywhere.

Then it came to the vanishing act. Babs wheeled the mystical black cabinet forward to the centre of the stage. The drums began to roll. Henry began the routine of showing how empty it was, opening all the sides and whirling his magic wand around in the black voids.

Silvikins sat in the small cramped space, hungry and a

307

little puzzled. It was too tight a fit to turn round and her tail was twisted uncomfortably under her. The way Henry had sneaked into the dressing-room was puzzling too. She could hear a lot of noise, music and clapping. That was familiar enough, but it seemed louder and closer than she was used to. Still, she trusted Henry and Babs. Then something happened . . .

Silvikins was transfixed with terror. The blackness was suddenly flooded with light as powerful spotlights beamed in blinding and dazzling her sight. A primeval fear of werewolves, monsters and great beasts surged into her mind in a tumultuous rush. She saw great white eyes gleaming, lurking high in the dome of the theatre, growling, poised to pounce on her. Her jaws opened wide.

With a shriek Silvikins leaped out of the cabinet. She landed on a trolley, sending a chrome container flying, and dozens of bottles spilled from its inside all over the stage. She fled, knocking over Henry's top hat and bouquets of bright flowers sprang out in all directions. She skidded into a curtained box and a flurry of doves rose into the air, flying straight into the light.

The panic-stricken cat, still blinded and dazzled by the light, blundered about the stage, scattering tricks and equipment like some four-legged bulldozer.

Babs and Henry watched in horror as his set was demolished. Without a second's hesitation Babs ran to the five silver hoops which were still at hand. She tossed them into the air with a flourish, pressing the secret spring which would loop them together into a chain.

The cat heard the noise. The clinking sounded vaguely like the bracelets that Babs often wore on her wrists and Silvikins homed in on it, springing through the centre hoop with all the grace of a flying panther. It was a spectacle of utter beauty, her silvery fur sparkling like moondust in the light.

The audience rose on a wave of thunderous applause. Gloved hands clapped enthusiastically from the Royal

Box. Henry blinked, unable to believe his ears as he stood among the chaos on the stage. The camera crews were giving each other the thumbs-up. It made marvellous television.

In the wings, Babs and Henry hugged each other in a fever of excitement. They had to run on stage again because the applause would not die down. Their hands touched, and it was not just in the excitement of the moment. They had suddenly discovered something else.

Silvikins had escaped from the two-eyed monster. She sat halfway up the flies in the gloom of the fly floor among the counterweights, licking down her disarranged fur. She hoped Babs would remember about the fish and chips after the show.

They all knew it was a one-off trick, but Monsieur Herriot made his reputation on it. He never looked back, and when he got his own television series, Henry and Babs decided to make their partnership into a relationship.

Silvikins, however, refused point-blank to join them in their little mews house. The theatre was her home.

Besides, she had her eye on the new juggling act. She realised that she might have problems tossing the silver balls, but she reckoned she might manage to spin a plate.

# An Absolute Bargain

In a house the size of the Robinsons', it was difficult to understand why there was not room for one small kitten that weighed less than a pound. It was a weird scrap, all ears, with a tiny pointed face and a spotty patterned coat that made it look as if it had been smudged with a leaky Biro.

The Robinson house had a lot of rooms and they were filled with a lot of people, all doing their own thing. There was Mr and Mrs Robinson, three daughters – Priscilla, Augusta and Ermentrude – and two sons – James and Jonathan.

They were a family of talent. They were all so busy painting, writing, composing, dancing and sculpting that there had never really been any time for pets. And they did not see how one could fit into their household.

But Trudy, the youngest daughter, being as yet unformed in any direction, was the one person who thought there might be a corner somewhere for the small creature.

'Her name is Louella,' Trudy announced. 'She's from the Old Vicarage. They were going to drown her. They said she was retarded.'

Everyone looked at the kitten with more interest. They had never come across a retarded cat before. It was crawling between the pepper and salt on the supper-table with pathetic feebleness.

'How does one know that a kitten is retarded?' asked Augusta kindly. 'Are there tests?'

'Mrs Owen said she was the last one to be born and was slow to feed; therefore a weakling and the duff one of the bunch.'

'So why have we got it?' asked Mr Robinson, coming straight to the point.

'I thought it was a pretty hasty assessment at six weeks old. The poor little thing hasn't had a chance to show what it's made of. Believe me, I have a wide experience of unrecognised talent,' said Trudy with feeling.

'Did you pay for it?' asked Priscilla sharply. 'Mrs Owen is a professional cat-breeder.'

Jonathan choked on his chili con carne. Priscilla was not good at pronouncing her r's. He grinned at Trudy. He knew why she wanted the little misfit.

'Well, not exactly money,' said Trudy. 'But I did promise to do some gardening for her.'

'Does Mrs Owen realise that you know absolutely nothing about gardening and will spend most of the time up the nearest tree?' asked James.

'Why are you calling her Louella?' her mother asked, with a novelist's interest in names.

'Vicarage . . . parsons . . . straight and narrow . . . columns . . . the columnist, Louella Parsons. Neat, eh?'

'Classy, like all Robinson names.'

'And she's a lilac-coloured oriental tabby,' said James, who knew a little about everything. 'She ought to have a properly registered name.'

'Really?' said Trudy, impressed. 'How about Louella Parsons Robinson.'

LPR, as everyone else called her, was a weakling. She could hardly feed herself, and Trudy went straight to the chemist in the village to buy a baby's bottle and sterilising equipment.

'Expecting a happy event?' asked the chemist.

'The happy event has already taken place,' said Trudy haughtily. 'We Robinsons work fast.'

Mrs Robinson insisted that Trudy should take full responsibility for LPR; she was up to her writing neck trying to get instalments of a serial ready for an editor. Feeding the family had a great deal of random luck about it at present, without taking on a weak kitten.

'Can I have a lunch-box then?' asked Trudy, sitting on the kitchen table, the kitten asleep in her pencil-case.

'What's wrong with paper bags?'

'Paper bags are passé this term.'

Jonathan produced a Snoopy lunch-box, the kind designed for five-year-olds. Trudy took it to Augusta's studio in the garden, and bored a series of holes in the red roof of the lunch-box with some of Augusta's tools. It would do nicely.

Rumour swept round the school like wildfire that Trudy Robinson was feeding a baby behind the bicycle shed during break. She found herself surrounded by an open-mouthed audience, and fending off requests to feed/hold/play with the kitten.

'Go away,' Trudy pleaded. 'She's delicate and you'll frighten her.'

Louella sucked on the bottle, almost choking on her own small purrs of contentment. She was wrapped in Trudy's school scarf, and as far as she was concerned, the Snoopy lunch-box was home and Trudy her mum.

Trudy was not surprised when Miss Stewart, the head-mistress, sent for her. Trudy was tactically ready.

'Just one week more and then I'll be weaning her onto solids,' said Trudy, who had been reading up child deve-lopment. 'Then it'll be half-term. After that I should be able to leave Louella at home.'

'Very well,' said Miss Stewart, appearing to give in. 'One more week.'

She did not mention that her staff had been sending back signals about peaceful playground breaks. It was not surprising with half the school wedged behind the bicycle shed.

'Thank you, Miss Stewart,' said Trudy demurely.

The weaning of Louella was in fact quite a turning-point. Liver and bacon purée and apricot custard agreed with her. And the little baby tins were fun to play with. She grew into a remarkably handsome cat, elegantly oriental, with long legs and slanting eyes, the elusive lilac colouring giving softness to her angular shape.

The other turning-point was that, quite by chance, Trudy happened to be paying attention during a biology class; thus Louella had to tolerate an instant name change.

'Louella is now called Alphonse,' Trudy informed the breakfast gathering. 'APR instead of LPR.'

'APR,' mother nodded between mouthfuls of muesli and correcting a draft. She did not ask why. That was her trouble. She had to go to Augusta for help on the passages of purple passion in her novels.

The change of name also heralded a change of character. Whereas Louella had been weak, pathetic and possibly retarded, Alphonse was a cat of insatiable curiosity, endless vitality and a rock-like devotion to Trudy. But the curiosity, vitality, rock-like etc led him straight into trouble.

'That cat of yours has walked all over my Fort Stanley,' stormed Mr Robinson one morning. He was a naval painter. At present he was painting a Falklands scene; he was not yet onto the Caribbean.

The storm was quite unexpected, because Trudy's father was the most placid of men. 'Pawmarks all over it,' he glared.

'Couldn't you pretend they are penguin footprints?' Trudy suggested with some hesitation.

'Walking up the main street and along the harbour?' he said scathingly.

'Yesterday APR knocked coffee over chapter four and I had to type it again,' said mother, her glasses slipping off her nose.

'Ditto my current guitar composition, only it was

313

wine,' said Jonathan.

'I found my new poem shredded,' said James.

'And you should see my third best tu-tu,' cried Priscilla, near to tears. 'Ruined, absolutely ruined. That cat trampled all over it. The sequins were all over the floor. It'll take me hours to sew them on again.'

'I'm terribly sorry. I'll help,' Trudy offered, hushed. She turned to Augusta. Augusta was her favourite sister, as Jonathan was her favourite brother. Augusta had said nothing yet.

'Well, I did find that my piece called Earthquake had fallen over and was a bit chipped,' said Augusta reluctantly.

'It could have been the wind,' said Trudy.

Augusta nodded. 'Probably the wind . . .'

Trudy could read the writing on the wall. All that Robinson talent was not geared to cope with an inquisitive cat. Trudy felt her nose prickling. It seemed Alphonse would have to go.

Her practical streak to the fore, Trudy negotiated swopping Alphonse for an album of The Who. Her best friend, Jane, was smitten.

'Well, I don't know,' said Trudy reluctantly. 'He is a registered lilac-coloured oriental tabby.'

'And you can have my signed photo of Tony Blackburn,' said Jane, who really wanted Alphonse.

Trudy hid her unhappiness by playing The Who very loudly all evening. It was a very good album, much better than a half-grown cat with big ears that wrecked everything, she told herself. She put on a brave face. She hung photos of Alphonse round her bedroom wall draped with black ribbon.

'He hasn't died,' said Priscilla, peering round the door. 'He's only gone to live two roads away.'

'I didn't think you would understand,' said Trudy. Priscilla was wrapped up in her dancing, and her feelings were definitely centred in her feet.

Three mornings later Trudy heard a strange noise and

opened the back door. A lilac-coloured oriental tabby walked in and leaped straight into the Snoopy lunch-box.

'Alphonse, darling,' cried Trudy. 'You've come back.'

Alphonse turned round and round with difficulty, having outgrown the box, but the message was clear. He was home.

Trudy returned the record and the photograph. Jane's mother went out and bought a hamster.

Alphonse, clearly delighted to be home, had a tour of inspection of the house to make sure nothing had changed in his absence. The resulting chaos had the Robinson family signing a petition, which they presented to Trudy after she had finished her homework.

*'We the undersigned,'* the petition read, *'do humbly request you to remove the aforementioned APR, to the furthermost distance possible. Financial aid available.'*

'What does that mean?' Trudy asked suspiciously.

'It means we'll pay the fare,' said James, who had suffered the most during Alphonse's exploration of the study, and was still retrieving sheets of poetry from the vegetable garden.

'And what's aforementioned?'

'It's legal wording,' said Mrs Robinson.

Trudy found a new home for Alphonse some three miles away. The deal was finalised with the exchange of an unwanted painting-by-numbers set and an unopened box of chocolates.

'You can have Alphonse on Saturday,' said Trudy picking out her favourite coconut éclair. 'He's got to be briefed as to the new situation.'

Being briefed consisted of being walked on the end of a piece of string the whole of the three-mile route to the new home.

'Sniff, sniff,' said Trudy at intervals along the road. Alphonse obliged. It was a long walk, but he was with Trudy so nothing else really mattered. She had to carry him the last mile.

Alphonse stayed at his new home less than a week. The stay would have been even shorter, but he was a polite cat. When he reappeared on the Robinson doorstep, paw-weary but triumphant, Trudy hid her pride in his achievement behind a dramatic display of dismay.

'Oh no, oh dear, oh heavens, glory be,' she wailed, banging her head lightly on the kitchen wall. 'Whatever shall I do? I'm so sorry, everyone. Forgive me. Just give me time . . .'

'Encore,' said Jonathan, clapping from the doorway.

'It does seem a shame,' said Augusta, stroking the cat's pointed ears. 'Alphonse seems determined to live here.'

'And we are just as determined to get rid of him,' said Priscilla. 'You'll have to advertise, Trudy.'

Trudy could not return the chocolates or the painting-set, as she had eaten the first and almost finished the last.

'It's quite revolting,' said Mr Robinson, consigning the gaudy picture to the dustbin. 'I'll draw her another one and put in lots of numbers. I hope she likes ships . . .'

Trudy composed an advertisement to go in the local free newspaper.

'*Lilac-coloured oriental tabby for sale,*' she wrote. '*No reasonable offer refused. An absolute bargain.*'

Trudy, who rarely received any post, was delighted by the response. It was one way of getting letters. She began to wonder what else she could sell. Some of the replies were useless. One person thought Alphonse was a china cat and wanted to know if he was cracked; another mis-read tabby for hubby and wrote asking for a date, and please did he speak English?

It did not take Trudy long to arrange the sale. This time money exchanged hands. Trudy spent it on replacement typing-paper, manuscript sheets, sequins and a bottle of turpentine for her father. She couldn't think what to buy Augusta. It wasn't easy to buy rocks.

'You'll really like this family,' said Trudy, as they walked along the lanes that led to the next village.

'They've got lots of children. Perhaps you'll be able to play with their toys.'

Alphonse looked up, his oriental eyes inscrutable slits.

'Sniff, sniff,' said Trudy hopefully.

Alphonse stuck it for twenty-four hours. The children were unbearable and shrieked every time he went near their toys. He galloped across the fields, swift as a leopard, soaring over hedges, the dew clinging to his long spotted tail.

'He's back,' said Augusta, looking out of the window. 'He's sitting on the wall looking smug.'

'Do you think Alphonse is trying to tell us something?' said Jonathan.

Trudy stopped herself from rushing out to welcome home the traveller with a big hug.

'Perhaps he's just visiting,' suggested James.

'No such luck,' said Priscilla. 'I shall have to lock up my ballet costumes, and I don't want any more chewed ballet shoes.'

It was not easy to outwit Alphonse's investigations; it required pre-planning and the purchase of locks. Everything lockable was locked; the house began to look tidier. Fewer stories, poems, music, paintings, ballet shoes were left abandoned in rooms.

So Trudy's suspicions were aroused when one day she came home from school and found evidence of the household's customary chaos. Priscilla was sewing yards of frilly net all over the floor; father had a mural drying in the hall; Jonathan's best guitar was propped against the stairs.

'Where's Alphonse?' Trudy asked.

'Darling,' said her mother, putting an arm around her youngest daughter's slim shoulders. 'We've found Alphonse a lovely new home. They're very fond of cats and have a beautiful walled garden. I know APR will be well looked after.'

'Where is he?' Trudy was stricken.

'Oh, he's gone. They took him straight away. He was

ever so good going off in their car.'

Trudy felt a cold shock wave of anguish. He'd gone. Her darling Alphonse. Some strange people had taken him away in their car.

'Where have they taken him to?' she asked in a tiny, unrecognisable voice.

'Epping, darling. It's a very nice place.'

Trudy rushed from the room. There was an *A-Z* somewhere in the house. Her eyes were blurred with tears as she fingered the pages. There were so many streets . . . it was the other side of London. Page after page of streets and bridges and traffic-lights, and then the Thames. Alphonse would never find his way back. She didn't even know if he could swim.

The family were very kind to her that evening. Mother cooked Trudy's favourite baked-bean pie; father, Jonathan and James made up a foursome for Scrabble; Priscilla offered the last of her best bubble-bath. Augusta had carved a tiny oriental cat with pointed ears from a piece of rosewood.

'Thank you all very much,' said Trudy, rising to go to bed at the unheard-of hour of 9 o'clock. 'You're being most kind. I just hope Alphonse will be happy in . . . in . . . Epping!'

Trudy burst into tears and ran from the room. There was silence as they looked at each other.

'Perhaps we ought to get Alphonse back,' said Jonathan.

'We can't,' said Mrs Robinson. 'I don't remember their name and I didn't get their full address. Oh dear . . .'

It took Alphonse more than a month to cross London, or perhaps he took a circular route and by-passed the great metropolis. He arrived back late one evening, thin, dirty, one ear torn where he'd been in a fight over a scrap of food, but still inscrutably Alphonse. He walked in and leaped straight into Trudy's lap, his muddy paws printing his happiness all over her English essay, which she had already copied out twice.

'Oh my darling Alphonse, you've come home,' she cried, hugging him closely which he bore with dignity. 'All that way from Epping. What a clever, clever cat.'

It was necessary to have another family conference. Alphonse was present, and insisted on sitting in his Snoopy lunch-box with his long tail hanging over the edge.

'I think that Alphonse has earned the right to live here,' began Augusta. 'Just think what he went through to get back. Such determination. Alphonse has made his point.'

Everyone agreed. Alphonse had made his point. They would have to try to live with him. It really was as simple as that.

Trudy tried not to look too pleased. Alphonse might not have talent in the normally accepted sense, but he certainly had potential.

# Joint Custody

She swept into the police station like a gust of autumn wind. Her streaky brown hair flew about her small round face, rustling like leaves, her bright brown eyes flashing with indignation.

'I believe you've got my cat,' she said, with a touch of haughtiness that added inches to her five foot nothing.

Sergeant Brady was used to strange requests, and they often concerned lost or strayed pets. However, there was a difference in this case, for indeed they did have a cat, a large marmalade cat at present eating fish and chips from the police canteen in the comfort of cell number five.

'A cat, madam?' he said slowly, as if he had never heard of the species. 'Now how do we know if we have got your cat? Perhaps you would like to describe your cat.'

'He's beautiful with long fluffy fur and great big eyes and he can talk to you,' said Lisa all in one breath.

'Not much of a description to go on so far,' said Sergeant Brady, opening a ledger at a blank page. 'What colour would you say?'

'Russet . . . every shade from the deepest red mahogany to the palest creamy salmon.'

Sergeant Brady wrote down: '*One ginger cat.*'

'Excuse me,' said a firm, aggressive masculine voice. 'But that's my cat you are talking about.'

The owner of the voice was a tall young man, not a single ginger hair on his city suit, carrying a leather brief-case with brass hinges, very expensive-looking and executive style.

Lisa sniffed. He did not look like the owner of a large ginger cat. He looked more like a small dog person.

'I think you must be mistaken,' she said crisply. 'Rubens definitely belongs to me and I've come to take him home.'

'Although I'm sure you know whether you have lost a cat or not, Marmaduke is mine, and I've his travelling-basket in my car outside to prove it. We could match hairs.'

'Marmaduke?' Lisa scoffed. 'What a name.'

'No more unusual than Rubens,' the man said, dangerously cool. 'It is four weeks since I came home from a business trip and found that my cat had disappeared. I will not say stolen. Merely disappeared.'

'Fancy going away and just leaving your cat. Disgraceful.'

'Left in good hands, I assure you, with my neighbours. He may have been lonely, but he was not neglected.'

'It is true that I have only had Rubens for a few weeks, but when I found him, he was lonely, friendless, starving and longing for a little love and affection,' said Lisa.

'Marmaduke is a born actor.'

'I took him in and he immediately put on weight.'

'Starch, merely starch. Now if you don't mind,' said Stephen Randolph turning to Sergeant Brady. 'I'd like to take my cat home.'

'But how do I know who this cat belongs to?' said Sergeant Brady. 'You both seem to have mislaid a large ginger cat.'

'It's definitely Rubens,' said Lisa.

'Positively Marmaduke,' said Stephen.

'Would you care to identify the incumbent?' Sergeant Brady offered, coming round to their side of the counter. He led them down a green-painted corridor and took a key from his watch-chain and opened the heavy plated door at the far end.

'I always thought cells were in the basement,' said Lisa, following the burly back of the sergeant.

'Only in films, madam. Our cells are on the ground floor. Number five, if you please. Allow me to unlock the door.'

The marmalade cat was curled up on a blanket on a bunk-bed, the shades of his reddish fur warmly glowing in the electric light. He had opened one eye sleepily as he heard footsteps coming along the corridor. His new home with bars across the window was strange and he did not know why he was there. He was hoping that someone would tell him.

'Oh, it is Rubens,' said Lisa, with a cry.

The cat immediately leaped into her arms, hooking his claws into her hair, nuzzling under her chin, purring ecstatically. It was quite moving.

'There,' she said triumphantly. 'You can see he's mine.'

'That's Marmaduke,' said Stephen bluntly, clicking his fingers.

At the sound, the cat jerked his head round and began to struggle in Lisa's arms. He sprang to the floor and twisted himself round Stephen's ankles, arching his back and miaowing.

'Obvious, isn't it,' said Stephen.

They glared at each other, seeing nothing but the struggle for the ownership of a charismatic marmalade cat.

'I suggest you sort it out between you,' said Sergeant Brady. 'We only keep cats a short time and then we pass them on to the RSPCA. We're only waiting for the little fellow to be picked up by the inspector. Why don't you talk it over having a cup of coffee? There's a nice little café on the corner of the street.'

Lisa was seething with anger as Stephen steered her towards the cosy lights of the café. She crunched through the leaves scattered on the pavement, brittle red and gold under her feet. She tucked her hair into her collar and set her face determinedly.

'It's no use thinking that you are going to make me change my mind,' she said. 'I'm going to keep Rubens. He likes living with me.'

'I can well imagine that Marmaduke likes living with you. He adapts very easily,' said Stephen smoothly. 'But the fact remains that he began living with me, and he should return to me.'

They did not speak as they stirred the froth into their cups of coffee. The silence hung in the steamy atmosphere, clinging to the mirrors and curling advertisements on the walls.

Lisa looked at the man carefully through her lashes and through the steam. He looked tired, jet-lagged perhaps. She met his eyes. He had been looking at her, noting the bright defiance in her eyes that hid some kind of hurt.

'Did you notice the way Rubens began to talk to you,' she said at last.

'A noisy devil,' said Stephen, with half a smile.

'I like the way he talks. Makes me feel less lonely. I'm sorry if I've been a bit sharp this evening, but I'm not quite myself these days. Something happened . . . something personal . . . and Rubens has been a kind of life-line.'

'I'm sorry,' said Stephen, more gently, but not probing.

'You can have him back. He is your cat really. I guess he just strayed when you were away.'

'He seems to like you . . . a lot,' said Stephen, remembering the picture of the cat nuzzling in her arms, purring like a steam-engine.

They talked over second and third cups of coffee, and eventually, when the owner wanted to close, they wandered back to the police station. Sergeant Brady had his eye on the clock. He could go off duty in ten minutes.

'Well, whose cat is it?' he asked. 'What have you

decided?'

'Joint custody,' said Stephen. 'That's what we've decided.'

'One week Rubens will live with Stephen,' said Lisa.

'And one week Marmaduke will live with Lisa,' said Stephen.

'He's very adaptable, you see,' Lisa added.

Stephen put the cat's travelling-basket on the counter. 'If we could have our cat back now,' he asked. 'I'll give you both a lift home, Lisa.'

'Oh, you can have him the first week,' she said generously.

Stephen shook his head. 'I think you should have him. He'll need a lot of extra loving after his terrible experiences in the police cells.'

The marmalade cat awoke from his terrible experiences and wondered what was going to happen next. He allowed the sergeant to carry him out, leaving ginger hairs all over his uniform.

The two people he cared for most in the world were smiling at each other, and he recognised his travelling-basket. He stepped into it, full of fluffy dignity, handing them his life with implicit trust.

# Nine Lives

Lucinda Ward Barrington was an undeveloped cat lover. She had never owned a cat or lived with one, but she stopped to stroke every mangy stray on the streets even when it was raining.

Her parents had never bought her a kitten; her school friends were dog people; her work as a photographic model consisted of cat-less sessions under arc lamps or on exotic locations. Occasionally she was asked to pose with a greyhound (she was that kind of model) but never with a cuddly cat.

Though cats played no definite role in her life, she was nevertheless aware of them. She never passed a cat without a word of greeting; she always bought a cat calendar; the enchanting ways of a tiny kitten in a pet shop window practically melted her heart into her high fashion boots.

At this particular time in her life Lucinda was on an emotional see-saw, being courted, to use an old-fashioned word, by a man who wanted to marry her. She found the situation intolerable because she did not want to get married, even though she loved him as she did. Her freedom and independence were precious. She did not think she could live without them. It was hard to sleep at night with these thoughts chasing her dreams, all of which tended to create fragile blue shadows where blue shadows should not lurk.

'Darling, you're looking tired,' said Marc Lauritzen, the Danish photographer who used her regularly for glossy fashion photos. 'Have I been pushing the work too hard? You know how I get carried away.'

'These coats are hot and heavy,' she said, slipping a hand under the big collar of the long fur to ease it away from her damp neck. The spot lights and reflectors gave off a glaring heat. It was the middle of summer and she was modelling furs. It was a crazy world.

'Would you like to take a quick shower? I can be setting up the next shots. More fake whelk stalls,' he grinned.

The luxury furs were being photographed against barrow boy settings. It was supposed to be amusing. Lucinda thought it was tactless but then she only did what she was told and Marc only photographed as commissioned. He was very professional.

'Lovely,' she said, planting a small moist kiss behind his right ear. 'I'd love a shower.'

'Come back to me gorgeous and smelling of heaven,' he said extravagantly, all Danish charm and gallant confusion.

Marc's flat was on the floor over his photographic studio and dark room. Living above the shop, he called it. Lucinda went up the spiral staircase to his bathroom. She knew her way around his flat since he was the man she loved. He was sensitive, kind, funny and talented. He loved photographing beautiful things and beautiful women like Lucinda. She had strange and haunting eyes . . . large and luminous like green water, flecked with specks of gold. Her cheek bones were narrow and high as if an ancestor had been a Tibetan princess; her long silvery hair spun a halo of magic round her small face.

She was always graceful, with dignity and a sweet nature. It was not surprising that she was a highly paid and successful model.

Lucinda threw off the heavy fur coat, slipped out of her bikini pants and bra and stepped under the shower. Turning the dial to tepid, she tipped her head sideways so that her hair and make-up would not get wet.

As the water touched her skin, it was like an electric shock. She leaped back, cringing against the wall of the shower unit, her nerve cells tingling. The spray fell harmlessly from the nozzle onto her bare feet, but she cried out, moving this way and that to evade the water, curling her toes as spasms shot through her body, whimpering with terror.

Lucinda crouched away from the water, trembling, watching the curtain of hissing steam that, cutting off her escape route, sharpened her fear. It was a crawling feeling that touched all the nerve ends of her skin. At the same time she felt she was almost choked with a terrible premonition of drowning. She was so frightened that for a moment she almost fainted. But she had to get away. She had to steel herself to make a dash through the water. It never occurred to her to turn it off.

As she floundered through the stinging droplets, eyes tightly closed, gasping helplessly, she no longer thought of her hair or her make-up. She stood on the bathmat, shaking, her knees barely holding her up. She did not understand what had happened, but the sensation of horror had been real enough as the water swept over her skin.

It took several minutes to regain her composure. She grabbed at a big towel and began to dry herself, not merely patting the moisture but scrubbing her skin dry. She calmed down and decided that there must be fleas in the fur coat. That must be the explanation. There could be no other. Some microscopic insects must have been nestling in the fur, close to the warmth of her body. Well, she was not wearing that coat again. She slipped into Marc's bathrobe and went downstairs to the studio.

'Have you got enough shots of this coat?' she asked in a voice as near normal as she could manage. She slung the ocelot fur over the clothes rail, and it crouched like a leopard preparing to leap, one sleeve swinging like a feline tail.

'Plenty, darling. Are you all right? You look a little pale. Do you want to stop?'

Lucinda shook her head and found a smile. 'No, I'm fine. I'll just repair my face and hair.'

'I'd like to do the slinky evening dress and the Arctic fox fur cape. Just the right outfit for an evening at a whelk stall,' he grinned.

Lucinda posed for every angle, stretching her limbs, shaking the vinegar, popping a whelk between her glossy lips. They were funny little morsels of coloured fish; she had never eaten one in her life. The first slipped down her throat without her even knowing it. Marc moved round her . . . click, click, click . . . the shutter of his camera sounding like castanets.

'Lucinda! You've eaten the lot. You've eaten all my props! I didn't know you were a whelk gourmet. Perhaps I shan't have to buy you supper now.'

'I'm terribly sorry,' said Lucinda, perplexed. 'I just didn't notice myself eating them. Have I ruined the shots?'

Marc began dismantling his equipment. 'Of course not, darling. You are obviously starving yourself again, hence this charming air of abstraction. When are you going to let me look after you permanently and properly?'

'Oh Marc, please . . .' Lucinda was dressing rapidly in the little room allotted to his models. 'I don't want to talk about it, especially today.' The experience in the shower had left her nervous and disorientated. She began filing her nails with an emery board. They were long, filbert-shaped nails and she was proud of them.

'That's what you keep saying, Lucinda, and it's driving me mad. I must know some time.'

She came out of the dressing room in her street clothes, a vision in a hand-dyed cotton prairie skirt with glimpses of lace petticoat, her tiny waist emphasised by a laced-up antique bodice, a twisted scarf of rainbow colours threaded through her silvery hair.

Marc wrapped his arms round her, rocking her close, breathing in the elusive perfume of her skin and hair.

'Don't keep me waiting too long,' he groaned.

He took her to a well-known riverside restaurant that specialised in seafood. Lucinda shivered as she caught sight of the Thames flowing darkly past the terrace. She turned away from the river. She wanted to be somewhere dry and warm.

'Can we eat inside?' she asked, tucking her arm through his. 'I'm feeling a little cold.'

She ordered prawn cocktail and left the lettuce; sole bonne femme and did not touch the accompanying vegetables; strawberries and cream and ignored the fruit. Marc said nothing. It must be some new diet. Models were always dieting.

'Do you think I could have some more cream,' Lucinda said as the sweet trolley went by. The waiter, captivated by her smile, poured cream generously over the strawberries. 'Lovely,' she murmured contentedly.

She felt better after the meal and was able to dismiss the earlier experience from her mind. She curled up to sleep in her bed with Marc's kisses still warm on her lips.

But in the morning, when she turned on her shower, the same electrifying fear shot through her. She watched the water with horror although it was not touching her skin. It splashed harmlessly before running away down the hole. Nothing would make her go into the water. She wrapped a towel round her arm before darting her hand to the controls and turning off the water from source. She leaned against the edge of the washbasin, her head hanging, taking in deep breaths. She could not understand this fear. There were no fleas to blame it on this time. Perhaps it was an allergy. Seafood was always tricky and she had eaten rather a lot. She suddenly remembered the whelks . . . yes, it must be the whelks.

A damp flannel temporarily freshened-up her face and body. She discovered that if she used the cloth with slow, sweeping strokes it was not so alarming. She brushed and brushed her hair, not wanting to risk a shampoo.

That evening Marc took her to a first night at Drury Lane theatre. All the stars were there, but it was Lucinda who was turning heads. She looked ravishing in a 1930s slipper satin gown with trailing ostrich feathers, a diamanté band taking her hair back from her brow, long sparkling ear-rings hanging from her tiny ears.

She did not touch the vodka and ice that he bought her in the bar. There was something about its taste she disliked.

'Darling, I've rented a villa in Cannes for a month. Will you come with me? It would be a wonderful place for a honeymoon. Please think about it . . . you've been working so hard.'

Lucinda thought about it all through the first half of the musical. She sat in the dark, absent-mindedly filing her long nails. She did not want to make this kind of decision, even though she knew she loved Marc. But she needed her freedom and the space to breath. The idea of being tied, even to someone she loved so dearly, made her heart sink. It would be like a prison, taking away the independent spirit which she had always felt so strongly.

The lights went up for the interval and Lucinda blinked open her eyes. Had she fallen asleep? Marc took her hand.

'What a marvellous show. Would you like another drink? I left an order at the bar for your favourite vodka.'

'Could I possibly have an ice cream instead?' she asked.

'It could be wonderful in Cannes,' said Marc, as he kissed her goodnight. 'Swimming all day . . .' Lucinda shuddered involuntarily. That decided Lucinda; definitely no Cannes. 'And fishing for our supper, grilling our own freshly caught fish . . .' Now that sounded more interesting . . .

She could not sleep. She stood in the kitchen of her flat at 2 am, wide awake, her finger in a pot of crab paste. She licked her finger in a worried and abstract way. This aversion to water was beginning to make life difficult. Baths were totally out. She had leaped into a shower like a demented kangaroo, hating even that brief contact with water. She was using gallons of cleansing cream, and she had bought paper plates and cups to save doing any washing up. How strange her life was becoming and she could not understand it. Perhaps she ought to see a doctor. It could be her hormones.

After drinking a glass of milk, she nibbled at some raw liver she had bought to make pâté; then she went back to her bedroom. Only she did not go to bed. Instead she curled up at the foot of the bed and went to sleep under the duvet.

The doctor referred her to a specialist. He thought it was a psychological reaction to her work where the emphasis was on beauty and cleanliness.

'You are fighting against your own image,' he said, pleased with the neat phrase. He wrote it down for future use.

The clever words did not help Lucinda to adjust to this dread of water. One day she sat crouched on her fire escape in the rain, just tolerating the fine mist. Her face was hidden against her knees, rain dripping down her hair. A small soft padded paw touched her ankle tentatively. It was a little ginger creature, drops of rain on its whiskers like pearls, its bright eyes questioning and curious.

'Hello,' whispered Lucinda, her fingers stroking the wet fur gently. 'Isn't it a strange world, cat?'

The cat looked at her with unblinking concern. There was nothing it could do to help her.


'Wake up darling. You've dropped off again,' said Marc as he caught her napping for the third time in a morning. Lucinda yawned and stretched her spine deliciously.

'I've discovered I have the knack of dropping off to sleep for a moment and then waking up quite refreshed,' she said lightly. 'It seems perfectly natural.' She got to her feet from the studio floor and began to prowl round the set, then came over to Marc and nuzzled her face against her arm. 'Have you got any milk?' she asked.

'Shall I make some coffee?' he offered.

She shook her head, scratching her ear. 'I've gone right off coffee. Just milk . . . unless you've got some cream?'

'Gold top,' he promised.

She slept less and less at night and took to walking. She found she could see perfectly well in the dark with no need to take a torch, and she was never afraid. And her fear of heights seemed to have left her. One night she walked along the parapet of London Bridge without a qualm, with only the ghostly Tower Bridge and the steely HMS Belfast to witness her feat of balance.

She huddled against the stone lions guarding the base of Cleopatra's Needle on the Embankment. There were all kinds of legends about the tall obelisk, stories of hauntings and ghosts that returned to the place where they had leaped into the Thames. She wondered if the cold stone missed the warmth of sunny Heliopolis where it had once stood 3,500 years ago . . . her clothes felt hot and itchy and she longed to take them off, removing the leather belt of her coat and letting it slip to the ground. How tightly her shoes pinched her toes; they were heavy and she eased them off.

Marc had the opportunity to buy a week-end cottage with a marvellous view of the Mendip Hills. He could get it for a bargain price and his bank would give him a generous mortgage.

'But I'm not going ahead until I know definitely that we are going to be together,' he pressed.

'Of course we'll be together,' she said lovingly.

'I mean married,' he said, his mouth taking on a firm line. 'It's time we came to some decision, Lucinda.'

'Oh no, please,' said Lucinda. 'Please don't make me decide between you.'

'Between you? What do you mean? Is there someone else?'

'No . . .' Lucinda said unhappily. 'I meant you and my freedom, my independence.'

'You meant another man.' Marc was hurt and angry. 'Now I understand why you have been so difficult to pin down. I should have known. Perhaps there are dozens of men in your life.'

Lucinda was shocked at his unfair accusation and the grim, uncaring look in his eyes. She rushed at him with her nails drawn. He caught her wrists in mid-air, astounded at her sudden turn on him, and held her away in an iron grip.

'You little hell cat,' he rasped. 'Don't you dare use your nails on me!'

Lucinda wrenched herself out of his grip and ran from him. Marc had never lost his temper before, nor ever spoken to her so roughly. She did not know where to go to hide the hurt. Tears choked her as she fled into the dark streets, not caring where she went. The wind lifted her hair and she felt as if she was falling into a bowl of stars . . .

It was all becoming too much, these strange fears of water and her changing habits. How could she cope with this illness, and at the same time make decisions which would affect the rest of her life? She fought the tightness of panic . . .

Her vision blurred, her thoughts, confused and incoherent, seemed unable to recognise anything as familiar. The streets were longer and the buildings grew taller in the night air. She lost her way, blundering through alleys she did not know. Blindly she ran along the Embankment, stumbling over the uneven flag stones, scattering a beer can. It rolled away into the gutter with a loud clatter. Somewhere she dropped her handbag and the pretty things spilled onto the pavement. Somewhere near the tall looming obelisk, she just . . . disappeared.

It was in all the newspapers.

FAMOUS MODEL VANISHES

They printed photographs of her modelling the long ocelot coat with the lynx collar. They wrote snappy stories about her rise to fame and the pressure of a model's life style. The police found her handbag and some of its contents scattered near Cleopatra's Needle, and frogmen began searching the muddy water of the Thames. Some small boys found her leather belt when the tide went out.

Everyone came to the same sad conclusion. Cleopatra's Needle, shrouded in night mist, had a long history of suicides and mysterious, unexplained happenings.

Marc was stunned. He held a sombre farewell exhibition of Lucinda's photographs because there could not be any kind of funeral. Her lovely face gazed at him from the walls, the golden-flecked eyes and silvery hair more ephemeral than ever.

Marc went back to his work and tried to numb his mind with punishing schedules. His new model, Vicky, was hopeless. He could not get the right angles of light for her face. After several unproductive sessions, they agreed that Marc should phone the agency to send someone else.

He held open the door for Vicky to leave and in walked a thin silvery white cat, blinking brilliant green eyes. It walked straight in as if it owned the place, climbed onto the dais and began grooming its fluffy fur.

'Good heavens, what a gorgeous cat,' said Vicky. 'Is it yours?'

'No, I've never seen it before. It must be a stray, but it seems to know its way around.'

'It looks to me as if you are being adopted,' said Vicky, straightening the seams of her stockings. 'Don't you know about cats? They always choose their owners, not the other way round.'

Marc grinned briefly. 'Really? I didn't know that. Good-bye then, Vicky, and thanks for coming. I'm sorry it didn't work out.'

As he cleared away his equipment, he became aware of the cat staring at him with solemn eyes, watching his every movement.

'I'm going through a rough time,' he said conversationally. 'I can't seem to work without my darling Lucinda.'

The cat jumped down from the dais and wound itself sympathetically round Marc's ankles, its back arched gracefully, little paws so dainty and light, kneading the air.

'You're a pretty little thing,' said Marc, going down on a knee to touch the soft fur. 'Would you like some milk?'

A tiny throaty purr began to vibrate, and the sound was joyous and unexpected.

'Gold top?' he promised.

The cat stretched up, one paw on his knee, and nuzzled his face with a small, moist nose. It tickled and Marc had to laugh. The light from the studio arc lamps turned the cat's fur into a silvery halo, sparks of light shooting into space.

The artistic possibilities suddenly took Marc's breath away. This gentle, intelligent cat was the most beautiful creature.

'I think I'll call you Cindy,' he said, gently lifting the furry chin with one finger. 'Will you be my new model? I need you.'

The gold-flecked eyes deepened and gazed at him with unconcealed love. She had no more decisions to make.

# Arbuthnot Road

A senior official of the local council authority recommended that Arbuthnot Road should be demolished and its inhabitants, mostly elderly people, be rehoused. He thought it a good decision. Two years later he was in the Birthday Honours list and his wife bought a feathered hat for the presentation at Buckingham Palace.

The elderly residents of Arbuthnot Road did not go to Buckingham Palace. They were rehoused in small flats. It was argued that at their time of life they would appreciate modern heating and indoor loos. To some extent they did, but many pined for the old road and their diminutive gardens.

The bulldozers moved in and soon the area was a heap of rubble with shreds of faded brown wallpaper fluttering in the dust cloud, heavy old mantlepieces leaning drunkenly against splintered and smouldering timbers. Once the crashing of the demolition ball and collapsing brick walls had ceased, Arbuthnot Road died. The nettles grew in silence and pale pink lupins pushed their heads through the rubble from buried herbaceous borders like souls of the dead. Almost unnoticed, the new inhabitants moved in.

The first cats were not new to Arbuthnot Road. They were domestic pets abandoned because their elderly owners had been rehoused in controlled premises. These cats were shocked and withdrawn, used to living with people, they were not equipped to forage for themselves and did not understand why they had been left behind. They hung around their old haunts waiting for a miracle to restore everything to normality.

Into their nervous midst stalked a leader, a big black feral tom. He was a second generation feral and totally wild with a ferocity and cunning sharpened by a lifetime of self-defence. His mother had been thrown out by a family when they realised she was pregnant. They panicked, took the queen to a rubbish tip in a cardboard box and left her. She reared her kittens in the same box, but she too was used to living with man and pined away.

The strongest of her kittens grew into a lean and lethal man-hater. He was quiet unapproachable. He had lived in dockyard factories, and marshland near a derelict airfield; he dominated any colony he joined. He fought, he hunted, he killed. He fathered dozens of scrawny wild-eyed kittens. Savagely dangerous, the tom was the nearest to a wild beast that a cat could get.

Santa, on the other hand, was a Christmas kitten, passed around in the New Year like the unwanted present he was. The last of his new owners could not cope with a kitten but were too soft-hearted to say no and too squeamish to drown him. Twice he had been half way to a bucket. Santa decided he was not going to risk a third trip. When he simply disappeared, nobody cared.

A cross-eyed tortoiseshell had quite a different background. He had been encouraged to live in an old red-brick fever hospital. Both staff and patients fed him, and many an elderly patient partially owed their recovery to the therapeutic purring which kept them company on long lonely afternoons. When the hospital was closed down due to a Government cut, no one thought of their loyal vermin catcher.

'Whatever happened to old Loopy?' one of the porters asked as he packed the last of the patient files into plastic boxes for removal. No one knew. Loopy was at that moment, roaming the empty wards, puzzled, wondering where everyone had gone. When it finally dawned on him that his source of hospital meals had also vanished, he cleared off. He wasn't catching their mice for nothing. He was a strong cat, in good condition, and drifted into the colony growing in Arbuthnot Road. But he kept out of the way of the big tom.

This lack of understanding in their changed circumstances brought on definite personality changes in the domestic cats. The sleek grey had had a long and comfortable existence with a kind and caring pensioner who had talked to him constantly. His world became melancholy and silent when the old woman suddenly died. No one remembered her cat in the excitement and bustle of the police being called in to break down the door; the welfare organised her funeral after trying to contact uninterested relations. Tibbles sat outside the smashed door for days but no one noticed him. He was just another neighbourhood cat. Eventually he gave up waiting and wandered away. He sat on the fringe of the colony because there was nothing else to do. His life might as well have been over.

The most exotic cat in the colony was Samantha. She was pert and pretty, once a valuable Cream Persian. She had been abandoned when her owners booked a holiday in Barbados and had then found out about the boarding charges at a cattery.

'We need this holiday more than we need the cat,' they argued among themselves, shrill and guilt laden.

They threw her out of the car window on the way to Heathrow. She crouched, dazed, on the hard shoulder of the motorway until sheer hunger forced her to find food. After the big tom mated with her, she followed him like some kind of groupie.

Another, kinder family did take Jupiter, their seal point Siamese, with them to their new home, but they never ensured that he became familiar with his new surroundings before they let him out. They had so many things to think about. Jupiter was full of curiosity, went for a stroll and got lost; he wandered for miles with increasing confusion, unable to find anyone or anything that was recognisable. Eventually he reached what was left of Arbuthnot Road. The family put an ad in the paper but, of course, Jupiter could not read.

Nor were all the cats fierce. Thomas, a thin tabby, had spent a terrified kittenhood with a noisy and undisciplined family where the children pulled his tail, tied his paws with string and shot caps into his face. One day the husband left home. The next day Thomas did the same. It was the bravest thing he ever did. Everyone cried, but whether it was for the cat or the father, no one was a hundred per cent sure.

The Arbuthnot Road colony grew as the toms and queens mated and bred. The kittens were very wild and could not be touched. Some of the cats remembered their domesticated lives and would occasionally accept food from a quiet middle-aged woman who always took a short cut through the waste ground to her job at a supermarket. She began saving scraps of stale cheese, bacon and old bread. Sometimes there was a bit of mouldy ham.

'Here, here, here,' she called to the distant cats watching her from piles of broken bricks. The site had never been properly cleared. 'Puss, puss, puss.'

The ferals did not move. They had forgotten the meaning of puss, puss, puss, if they had even ever known it. But they did know that humans had a diminished sense of responsibility towards them. The drunks trod on them, swore and threw bottles. Youths chased them with beer cans and bricks. A clutch of kittens had simply disappeared when the site had been invaded by a swarm of school thugs with penknives and wire and boxes of matches. So the ferals were not moving for anyone.

'Puss, puss, puss,' the woman persisted. She was not called Martha Strong for nothing. She lived a street away from Arbuthnot Road. The demolition squad had stopped short of her house, though the work had not helped her outer wall and now it was shored up with timber.

Tibbles was the first to move, stretching his thin grey body as he walked nonchalantly towards her as if actually intending to go the other way. She was holding out a handful of cheese. He had once adored cheese. His mistress had always shared a cheese sandwich with him at bedtime.

'Full of protein,' she used to say. 'I'll never starve as long as I can buy a bit of cheese . . .' She little knew that cheese would not save her from falling out of bed and lying on the floor with a broken hip until dehydration and a heart attack finished her off.

Tibbles gulped down a few scraps of cheese, then bolted for cover. He did not trust her. Samantha darted forward, judging that she might as well have a piece of the action.

'Wicked shame,' said Martha, crumbling a bit of cheese for the dirty white cat. 'I reckon you could do with a good bath. Not much of a little beauty now, are you?'

The other cats stayed like statues. Santa watched the woman with narrowed green eyes. He knew she had food and he was hungry. She had a shopping bag that looked a bit like a bucket. He dared not risk it.

Martha straightened up and scattered the cheese on the ground. She supposed they did not mind a bit of dirt with it. As soon as she was out of sight, the cats swarmed on the cheese, biting and scratching for the scraps. The big tom snatched the biggest chunk and

337

growled at anyone who dared to challenge him for it. He slunk back to his domain inside a crushed water tank and chewed carefully. No one knew that his teeth were rotten and there was not much he could eat these days. His size and strength still made him the leader, but if he could not eat he would grow weak. There were several younger cats, lean and wild-eyed, waiting to take his place.

It began to rain. The cats shook themselves and ran to find shelter among the rubble. Thomas stayed out in the rain, sniffing among the earth to find sodden fragments of cheese left by the others. It was the only way he fed. He was so timid. The rain plastered his fur to his thin ribs; he was starving and looked it.

'Has it ever stopped raining this summer?' asked Inspector Alan Murphy, turning from the window to accept a cup of tea from Celia Hamilton, the young veterinary surgeon who had recently joined the league. She was a very business-like young woman with over-sized glasses and a severe haircut. It looked as if she cut it herself, unless the urchin look was high fashion.

'I don't believe it has,' she said briefly.

'Settle down everyone,' said Mrs MacKay, chairman of the league's working party. 'We've got a lot to get through. And this month we must decide what we are going to do about the Arbuthnot Road colony.'

'More complaints?'

'Dozens of them. Apart from the general nuisance of smells and dead cats, they are beginning to invade nearby houses for food. They knock over milk bottles, steal from kitchen tables, dig up gardens. It has become a very large colony and no one dares to leave a baby outside in a pram.'

'A cat wouldn't attack a baby, surely?' asked Celia.

'It's the milk around a baby's mouth that attracts the cat,' said Alan Murphy. 'The baby could get scratched.'

'Sounds like a horror film,' she shuddered.

'We must consider all the methods open to us,' said Mrs MacKay. She was a round little woman, almost cat-like in appearance, and she had spent thirty years working for animal welfare. It had begun with a small rescue centre for strays which she had run single-handed. Now she was in demand for committee work of various kinds, and she sometimes thought the paperwork exceeded the practical. She had so little time for looking after her own cats.

It was not a new situation for the league by any means. There were some 12,000 cats living wild in the 704 colonies which had been located in Great Britain. People did not believe Mrs MacKay when she told them the statistics. And obviously there were a lot more colonies undetected. It could mean a feral population of perhaps a quarter million.

Hospitals were a favourite spot for colonies to establish themselves, hidden in the heating plant, closely followed by factories and dockyards. Cats attached themselves to military camps, schools, caravan sites, rubbish tips, power stations, farms and prisons. They were not all a nuisance. As from their earliest history in Egypt, they were valued for keeping down rodents. In this way they were unlike many other species of wild animals, and it was for this reason that the league had developed different methods of containing a colony.

'There are several courses of action open to us,' she began, chiding herself for sounding like a trade unionist. These were real creatures whose fate they were deciding, brave and fierce, living as best they could in a foreign environment.

'Firstly, we could leave the colony alone and allow nature to take its course. That is, the survival of the fittest.'

'More dead and bedraggled cats.'

'Secondly, the complete eradication of the colony by trapping and killing.' To her own ears, she now sounded like a concentration camp commander.

'A bit drastic.'

'Sometimes if a colony has lost its source of food, say an old hospital has closed, then it is the most humane course. But in the case of Arbuthnot Road, probably another colony would form and we would have to do it all over again.'

'No, thank you,' said Celia, knowing who would have to do the wholesale killing.

'We could reduce the numbers by controlled culling, trapping and re-housing any suitable cats. This is the cheapest method but the result is not a permanent solution.'

'Fourthly, we could trap the entire colony, neuter and return to site. This does stabilize the life of the colony and improve general health. Or lastly we could try chemical birth control. Of these last two methods, we must consider the cost of such operations. Perhaps the local authority could be persuaded to fork up some money . . .'

The working party talked far into the afternoon about the future of the cats living in Arbuthnot Road. Inspector Murphy watched their new recruit with veiled interest. That brisk, no nonsense manner was hiding a rather insecure young woman, he decided.

Celia contributed only the briefest remarks to the discussion. She was frozen with fear. Suddenly she had forgotten everything she had learned at veterinary college; supposing she could not manage the sterilizations, the trappings, the injections, the euthanasias?

Alan Murphy leaned across the table. 'You won't have to do everything by yourself,' he assured her. 'You will have help.'

'Thanks,' she said. She was not sure whether he was laughing at her or not. She was unused to men, that's why she worked with animals. She turned away so that he could not see her face.

As the rain stopped, the cats came out to dry themselves. They were a matted and bedraggled lot with torn ears and eye infections. Some made valiant efforts to clean up. The really wild ones, although they had a cat's inborn habits, were less compulsive. There was too much fighting and foraging to be done. Grooming was way down on the list of priorities.

Two people came to the site and began walking about in welling-ton boots and climbing over the rubble with notebooks. The cats watched from afar. They knew nothing about the working party's decision.

'Trying to count ferals is impossible,' said Alan, helping Celia over a dangerous pile of planking. 'One is never quite sure, unless the marking is very distinctive. The same cat can get listed twice – or more.'

'There's no mistaking that big black tom, a ferocious looking brute, or that grubby white persian. I bet that's an abandoned pet. She's hardly chocolate box prettiness now, more like a squashed box of liquorice allsorts,' said Celia. She was feeling less of a new girl now that she was out of the meeting and on site.

'That sad looking grey might be quite friendly. See how he's watching our every movement while pretending to be quite disinterested. Rustle your paper bag and see what happens.'

'Yes, a definite twitch of the ears,' said Celia, amused. 'He's wondering if I've brought any goodies. Urgh, look at all this mouldy sliced bread. No wonder they get infected.'

They put down several dishes of food and retired to a distance to watch the behaviour of the colony. As they thought, the tamest ventured out first, but they were then quickly followed by the wild ones. It turned into a snarling scrap for every morsel, sharp teeth ready to snatch food right out of another's mouth.

'Look at that timid tabby, right out on the fringe. It's starving. You can see it never gets anything.'

'I suppose you are going to try and feed it separately, said Alan, reading her mind. 'You're a softie.'

'Perhaps. I'm going to have a go.'

She followed Thomas across the waste ground, inch by inch, calling encouragingly, isolating him from the main group of ferals. He was a pathetic sight with ribs showing through his short muddy coat. The first candidate for the humane injection, thought Celia, trying to be dispassionate.

She herded him further away so that the other cats were not within smelling distance of the food she was going to put down for him. She scraped out the last of the fish and put the dish among some tall couch grass which would give the timid cat some cover. She then placed herself between the main colony and the food.

Thomas sat watching these manoeuvres from the safety of a derelict pram. He was curious, but too frightened to move; he knew there was food. The smell was driving him insane. He forgot about the woman crouched some yards away.

He darted forward on shaky limbs, half expecting to be set upon by the black tom, or some of the other wild cats. But none came. He reached the fish in total disbelief. It was real fish, such as he had not tasted for many months. He gulped the food, swallowing flakes and skin without even masticating.

'Hold on,' Celia murmured. 'You'll choke.'

The fish was demolished in seconds. Thomas had a vaguely mesmerised look. He licked every wet shred from the dish, pushing it along the ground, determined that not even the smell would escape. It was then that Thomas saved himself from the humane injection. He began to purr, quite unconsciously, as he pursued the dish through the grass.

Celia wrote down a careful description of the tabby's markings. She would find this one a home.

By the end of the week Alan and Celia had identified a fair number of the cats and noted their condition. They had also met Martha Strong with her bag from the supermarket.

'Oh no, I couldn't possibly have a cat,' she said, alarmed and defensive. 'I'm out all day and the price of cat food is awful.'

'But you're managing to feed several cats now on the scraps you collect,' said Celia persuasively.

'But if it were my own cat, that would be different. I'd have to buy the food. Then there's the milk. I can't afford a pint of fresh any more. Anyway I wouldn't fancy one of these cats. They're full of fleas.'

'We'd make sure the cat was in perfect condition before it came to you. No fleas,' said Celia. 'And sterilized.'

A van appeared near the site. The men began to unload wood and wire traps. It was essential to trap the females first, and with Martha's help they had been able to pick out those cats she had seen pregnant or with kittens. For a few days a dummy trap was left on the site with food inside, so that the cats became used to it. The trap was padlocked to a rusty hulk of iron. Traps were often stolen. They made good rabbit hutches.

Alan decided to use a manual trap rather than the automatic type, even though it meant a long patient wait for the operator, but he could be selective. It was no use trapping a bold tom, if the pregnant female he really wanted was sitting inches away. Once the trap door had sprung, the female would be too nervous to come near it for weeks, if ever again.

The traps were mainly wood which cats preferred, with an open view all round. Inside were wire modules which could convert the trap into a crush cage so that Celia could work on a cat without being bitten or scratched.

Alan sat in the van, half reading a newspaper. The cord from the trap came through the window and was looped to the door handle. He had sandwiches and a thermos of coffee. He was prepared for a long wait.

342

He watched the plump white persian. She was definitely with kitten. She was filthy, scratching herself to distraction. Alan longed to use a very effective spray and solve one of her miseries.

He unwrapped his substantial sandwiches, ham, egg, cheese, lettuce and tomato. Being a bachelor, he believed in good plain food. That young Celia, now, she needed feeding up.

'I'll make her a Dagwood sandwich one day,' he chuckled.

They were soon to receive a batch of automatic traps that had spring loaded drop bars to secure the door. These could be put out, baited and left. Alan was not so keen on them. It was difficult to remove a cat from these without it escaping, and it was not possible to comb the cat to the end for an injection. The trap could be vandalized, with or without a cat in it. They were, however, inexpensive, and that today was a prime consideration.

Samantha was the first to be caught, beguiled by the bait of squashed minced chicken. Alan pulled up the slack cord, then went towards the trap, keeping it absolutely taut. Samantha flew into a temper when she realised she was caught, hurling herself at the sturdily welded steel mesh sides. Alan bolted the door, put the paddle down the centre slit and gently pushed her to one side so that she might settle down. She tried to evade the paddle by squeezing herself over the top of it.

'It's no use you trying to do that,' Alan soothed, tossing in a few crunchy cat biscuits. 'Now then, calm down.'

Samantha crouched at the back of the cage, spitting and hissing. She had once been addicted to cat biscuits, but they had been out of her diet so long she had almost forgotten them. The factory-made shapes slid under her paws as Alan loaded the trap into the van. She pounced and crunched.

Back at the clinic, Celia's routine was an anaesthetic injection, followed by the sterilization operation. Then the cat was injected with a long acting antibiotic and checked for fleas and mites. But as Samantha was heavily pregnant Celia decided to wait until the kittens were born. Meanwhile her coat was treated while she was still trapped by the paddle. Celia reached for the spray canister.

'This cat's absolutely crawling,' she said with a shudder as the fleas hopped out onto her sleeve. 'And her ears are infected where she's scratched like mad. Some people might say that a jab of phentobarbitone sodium would be more sensible.'

'But not you,' said Alan from the outer unit where he was disinfecting the trap before re-use. 'In a couple of days, she'll be a little beauty. We ought to try and find her a home.'

'You try,' said Celia. 'We'll have to keep her a few weeks because of the kittens.'

Tibbles, the melancholy grey, was the next to be caught. He walked right into it. He had always had a passion for boxes, baskets and sitting in paper bags. After sterilization and a thorough wash and brush up, he was returned to the site faintly bemused and dozy.

That evening Martha came along with her usual bag of goodies. She put her shopping basket on the ground and without thinking Tibbles got in and curled round on top of her library book and the evening newspaper, and went to sleep.

It seemed like an omen. Martha scuttled home, looking guiltily behind her. It seemed almost like stealing. Once in the seclusion of her small kitchen, she put down the basket and poured out a saucer of milk. Tibbles opened one eye.

'It's only dried,' she said apologetically. 'But a lot of people can't tell the difference. Of course, I could bring home a carton of fresh milk from the supermarket, now that there's the two of us. After all, it wouldn't go to waste. That is, if you decide to stay.'

Three days later Tibbles jumped onto her lap. As Martha slowly stroked his bony head, she felt almost happy. Tibbles was wondering if she knew how to make a cheese sandwich. He would take a chance on her breaking a hip.

The trapping went on slowly and cautiously. It was work that could not be hurried. But the big tom escaped all capture. He would dart into a trap, snatch the bait and be out again before the door could be shut. Alan swore to himself, mildly, as the big cat leaped over the rubble and disappeared from sight.

Gradually all the other cats were caught, sterilized, treated for fleas and their ears nicked for identification. A few old and diseased cats were put down. Celia hated doing this. She leaned against the table, feeling quite faint. The dead cat was a pathetic sight, mangy and sick. Alan saw how pale she was and quietly put the body into a plastic bag for incineration.

'Found a home for the white one yet?' he asked, changing the subject, though he knew quite well it was still being housed at the clinic. 'I see she's had her kittens.'

'Why ask me?' said Celia, sharper than she meant to be. 'I'm not a welfare officer. Why don't you have her yourself if you are so keen.'

'If I gave a home to every cat I liked, I'd be over-run with the creatures,' he said cheerfully. He was so much older than Celia, ordinary and uninteresting, he knew there was nothing he could do but keep his growing affection for her at a distance. It pleased him to help her in little ways, knowing the long hours she worked and the serious attitude she took towards her work. Those big glasses and severe haircut made her look plain, but to Alan she was just a scared young woman, trying to be grown up.

'I haven't seen the timid tabby come in yet,' said Celia, plunging her arms deep in hot soapy water. She was aware she had been short with Alan, and he was always so kind. 'Do you know the one I mean? The one that never gets any food.'

'I haven't seen it around lately. We've just the big tom to get now and we can call it a day at Arbuthnot Road. The new automatic traps have arrived so we could put a couple of those out and move onto the next job.'

'I'll put them on the site if you're busy elsewhere. I'd like a breath of air.'

Celia wanted to find out for herself what had happened to the timid tabby. She did not like the thought of the cat being holed up somewhere, perhaps injured or ill. She took some chloroform with her, just in case. She had to be prepared to give it a whiff straight away if it was beyond help.

As she parked her car at the lower end of Arbuthnot Road, she saw a movement of cats disappearing. And even that brief glimpse confirmed that the ferals were generally in better health. Stabilization of their numbers always seemed to have this effect.

Celia put a new automatic reinforced wire mesh cage in place and spread some strong smelling pilchards for bait. The hinged door had a release mechanism which dropped when the cat stepped on a contact plate at the rear of the trap.

She scrambled over the rubble, glad to be away from the clinic for an hour, to relax away from the responsibility of the work. Mrs MacKay and the committee were watching her all the time, evaluating her competence. Even Alan kept an eye on her. It was like working in a glass bowl.

She turned over unspeakable rubbish with a stick knowing that the tabby might be hiding in a very small place, too frightened to come out and look for food. She had saved some pilchards though she really expected to find it dead somewhere.

Thomas watched her from the depths of a rusty drain pipe. He had been alarmed by all the recent activity on the site. His eyes glinted moistly in the darkness. He was so thin he had no trouble squeezing himself down to the end of the pipe and then turning. He was shaking with nerves though he knew no one could see him.

Celia moved on, a tall grey figure on a grey afternoon, and soon she was out of sight. Thomas tucked his nose into what was left of his fur and tried to sleep, but the muscles of his hollow stomach gnawed and cramped. Sleep was impossible. It was a life beyond hope for Thomas. He thought of nothing.

After half an hour of searching, Celia gave up. He must be dead. She strolled back to her car, hands deep in her pockets, fingering the phial of chloroform.

Suddenly a piercing scream split the air. It was the most horrifying sound Celia had ever heard. She ran towards the unearthly shrieks. No human could make that cry . . .

The big tom had tried his trick again. But the new cage was much narrower than the old wooden manual type. He could not streak in and streak out without turning round, and in turning he had touched the contact plate and released the rod. He moved fast but so did the mechanism.

He was outside the cage, a writhing, seething, snarling black mass of animal fury, his back leg and tail trapped by the door. As he struggled to pull his foot free, so the weight of the door pulled closer. The bone was showing through the torn flesh and blood.

Celia was shocked and appalled. The tom was outside the cage so she could not use the grasper even if she could get it in through the small hatch. This tom, quite apart from being the wildest of the bunch, was incensed with pain. It was quite unapproachable, but then she could not leave it in pain while she went for help. She had to do something; there was the chloroform.

She took off her raincoat, intending to wrap it tightly round all that spitting, clawing hatred. Then she might be able to sprinkle some chloroform on a pad and put the cat out long enough to release the foot, push the creature back into the cage and secure the door with the drop bar. It might just work.

But she was dealing with 20 lbs of crazed wild animal. The big tom had years of fighting for his life behind him. The slim young vet, fresh from college, was no match for him. He sank his teeth and claws into her raincoat, ripping it out of her hands. A long scratch opened up on her forearm, welling pricks of red. As she reached for her coat, he leaped on her. She fell awkwardly, the phial of chloroform flew from her grasp and smashed on a brick. The cat was clinging to her legs, claws ripping her stockings and sinking into the soft flesh. She fought off the snarling teeth with her bare hands, gasping, trying to shield her face. She rolled back as the fumes from the chloroform started her coughing. She tried to crawl away, but the cat hung on. She was dragging the cat and the trap . . . the last thing she remembered as she passed out was that the cat's teeth were bad and her wounds would be infected . . .

It was Alan who found her. He would have driven passed her parked car if he had not noticed Thomas sitting by what looked like a pile of rags. He remembered that Celia had been asking about the timid cat.

She was lying unconscious, her face and hands and legs a mass of deep scratches. Thomas was sitting on her raincoat, licking the last of the pilchard from a torn pocket. He had not been afraid when he saw that she did not move or make a sound. But now as Alan approached, he fled into the undergrowth like the small ghost he was.

Alan lifted Celia gently and she moaned against his shoulder.

'Dear God,' he said. 'What a mess.'

Her glasses were broken and he removed them; her hair was matted with dirt and blood; her blouse was torn open and he saw that round her throat she wore a thin gold chain with a small heart-shaped pendant. It looked old as if it had belonged to a mother or grandmother.

His heart was moved with love and compassion and he bent and kissed the cold metal in the soft warm hollow of her throat. He felt he was entitled to one kiss in his life, to treasure the touch and smell of her skin. Even now he did not think of her lips as being for a man like him.

She was trying to say something, her mouth moving feebly. He put his head closer and caught the word ' . . . rabies . . .'

'Don't worry, darling,' he said. 'I'm taking you to a hospital.'

She seemed to smile and then slip away again into unconsciousness. He carried her to his car.

Alan went back in the evening and found where the black tom had dragged himself and the trap. The cat's foot was almost severed, and the feral was exhausted from fighting this ruthless steel foe. But his eyes were still blazing as Alan prepared a final injection.

When the Arbuthnot Road colony was considered sterilized, Martha was persuaded to monitor their welfare. She formed, with much hesitation, a cat committee which met regularly in her front room for coffee and biscuits to discuss the feeding rota and fund raising events. She enjoyed these meetings, making friends, with Tibbles sitting on her lap purring like a motorbike.

'This is one of them,' she would say proudly. 'You wouldn't think so now, would you, to look at him?'

Finding a home for Samantha, the white persian, proved difficult. She quite refused to be separated from her kittens and they grew into a large, playful, unmanageable family. One day a black postman and his wife came into the clinic. They wanted kittens for each of their children. They fell for the pure white cat and her brood. The black family came from Barbados. They thought she was really something and called her Sugar Ray.

Thomas did not have to be caught. When Celia came out of hospital she went back to the site and found him, so weak, that she could just pick him up. For several days she fed him baby cereal from the tip of her finger and milk from a dropper. She knew she was going to keep him; she reckoned she owed him her life. The first time that he came to her, timidly but of his own accord, was a moment of joy.

'I believe he had been trying to make up his mind for days,' Celia told Alan, 'but he just didn't have the courage. I can't describe how touching it was, Alan. It was such a tremendous step for him. The first time he believed in himself enough to trust another person.'

'I think I know how he felt,' said Alan, but he did not elaborate.

Perhaps, like Thomas, one day there would come a time when he would take the same step, when he believed enough in himself to go to Celia with what was in his heart.

In the meantime there was work, their mutual concern for cats, companionship and friendship. And as he watched Celia talking to her timid little tabby, scratching the angular furry chin, he was content to wait.

# The Great God Mau

In the calendar-less days before man, violent changes within active volcanoes threw rock into new mountain ranges and created immense ravines flooded with water. At the same time a new species of animal appeared. It was a small, short legged animal with a sleek body and a long tail. It was called Miacis. It was destined to found a family of mammals – the dog, the weasel, the raccoon, civet, hyenas and the cat.

When Man emerged, he hunted for food but he did not eat cats. He found them too useful merely to eat. He discovered that they could protect his precious stores of grain by keeping down the rats and mice. So the cat became the protector of granaries and in Ancient Egypt was as sacred as the Gods themselves.

The cat goddess was called Bast, or Bastet. She was also known as Pasht. She was portrayed as a tall, slim woman with a cat's head, holding a musical instrument, a shield and a basket of kittens. Her temple was built at Bubastis, east of the Nile delta and was more beautiful than any other temple.

The cat of Ancient Egypt was an elegant, strikingly marked spotted tabby, long of neck and shoulder, reddish brown in colour and altogether a handsome creature with great poise and presence. Cats were also kept to guard the family from poisonous snakes, and there were strict laws to protect them. To kill a cat meant the death penalty.

Mau was one such valued cat of Ancient Egypt. He was regularly taken to the vast temple of the cat goddess at Bubastis. The long journey was made in a gold boat from Thebes to the temple and Mau was accompanied by his own servants. The Pharaoh travelled in another boat and so did his Queen. They arrived with pomp and ceremony for feasts held in honour of Bastet.

Mau was always a little in awe of the splendour of the temple, but he did not show it. Towering red granite blocks dominated the great square, with canals on either side one hundred feet wide and in the centre was the shrine to the goddess surrounded by tall date palms. The walls of the temple were richly decorated in every colour with scenes of kings presenting gifts to the goddess. She was as important as the great god Ra.

Almost the same reverence was bestowed upon Mau. He was allowed to roam the deck of his boat, returning to his silken pillow to sleep. He wore a gold ear-ring in his large, pointed ear and he had a jewelled collar studded with emeralds to match his fathomless eyes. On special days he also wore a bronze chain and sacred pendant hung about his neck, and an amulet of the sacred eye which represented the solar eye of the god Horus. Mau tolerated the jewels, though he was always glad when they were removed and put away in a golden chest.

There was also a cat cemetery at Bubastis and many Egyptian families would bring the embalmed bodies of their pet cats for ritual burial. The small bodies were wrapped in linen or in simple cases made of straw. Some came in a casket or cat-shaped box.

Mau knew nothing of these burials. He was venerated by the Pharaoh and his Queen, and lived a life of luxury in return for the remarkable power which the great god Bastet could evoke against sickness and evil. But Mau was not worshipped as Bastet was worshipped, although to the Pharaoh, the cat was sacred and no one cared to dispute the fact.

Mau's sacred role began in this way. One day the Pharaoh and his Queen were hunting in the Nile marshes when suddenly the cat appeared among the reeds with three waterfowl. He had one bird gripped in his jaws and the two others held tightly in his claws.

The royal party were overcome by the sudden presence of Mau. It seemed to them that the cat was a re-incarnation of the cat depicted on the tomb painting of Pharaoh Thutmoses II and his Queen Hatshepsut, who had been gathering lotus blossoms in their light papyrus boat when a similarly remarkable cat had appeared to them.

It was taken as a special sign and Mau returned with them to the Pharaoh's palace and was proclaimed sacred. Not being born to such nobility, Mau insisted on a certain degree of freedom. The palace covered a large area and Mau spent his days inspecting the great halls and vast granaries. He knew every inch of the spacious courtyards, gardens and rooms, as if he had been the architect himself.

Each morning he went to the pool with its shady trees, where he could sharpen his claws and frighten the silly ducks. He watched the servants drawing water from the wells, then skirted the cattle yards and dog kennels. He did not care for the smells from these places.

His favourite part of the palace were the stewards' rooms next to the kitchens and food stores, for although Mau was fed with chicken and fish from a golden bowl at the Pharaoh's table, a little snack never came amiss. Here the servants gave him delicious nibbles and goats milk.

The Pharaoh never knew of these early morning visits and would often remark: 'How fastidious Mau is with his food. See how he picks only the best from the fish. How little he eats. A true god is fed from the spirit within.'

In fact the true god was rarely hungry for he also visited the Queen's suite and her womens' rooms where they teased him with sweetmeats and brushed his fur with silver brushes. They painted his nails with a shining coloured enamel, and Mau thought this peculiar and rather pointless.

At mid-day Mau strolled through the great audience hall to the Window of Appearances where the Pharaoh held his daily public court and gave gifts and rewards. Mau always appeared with him. He sat in the portico, long and elegant, quietly unmoved by the cheering crowds. The people thought it an excellent sign that he should be there. It meant that Bastet was regarding them with favour.

A servant was sweeping the floor between the two rows of columns in preparation for a great feast that was to be held. Mau liked the servant; his name was Thut. He was a simple but strong young man and he was kind to Mau, sometimes forgetting that he was a god and treating him as an ordinary cat. Mau appreciated this and he also liked Merya, the girl that Thut was always talking to in the kitchens. She had beautiful hair that rippled like silk.

Mau watched the broom of rushes sweeping rhythmically across the floor. He crouched down, his long black-tipped tail whipping from side to side. He would dearly love to pounce on that broom and send it skidding across the marble tiles. Thut realised that Mau was watching and gave the broom a few quick jerks to tease the cat.

Mau's whiskers twitched. He would not be able to resist it much longer. A small growl grew in his throat. The Pharaoh heard the sound and felt that Bastet must be displeased. He immediately doubled the gold he was about to give to an old steward who was leaving after many years in his service. The old man fell on his arthritic knees and mumbled his astonished thanks.

At night Mau was put to sleep on a gold silk pillow in a special shrine in the chapel. The pillow was slippery and uncomfortable, so he often toured the granaries at night, roaming the vast storehouses and inspecting the corn bins. Then towards dawn he would go to the servants' quarters. He knew the room that Merya shared with the other women and he would curl up at her feet, careful not to wake her.

'Oh Mau,' she whispered one night in a terrified voice. 'Something terrible will happen to me if I am caught sleeping with a god.'

When there were ceremonies in the Sanctuary, Mau awoke to the sound of the priest chanting hymns. He allowed them to bath him in perfume and put a wide collar of linked gold round his neck. Then Mau was carried in his boat shrine by a procession of priests to the outer court of the Great Temple. Granite statues of the Pharaoh towered above him, each toe the size of a table, and the great columns rose to the roof and into sunburst paintings of reeds and the papyrus flower and lotus buds. It was very spectacular and the endless singing was enough to send him to sleep. If he began to doze, the priests whispered among themselves, so Mau kept himself awake with day dreams of catching the painted birds that decorated the columns.

'We will go down the Nile to the Valley of Kings,' said the Pharaoh. 'I want to see how my work is progressing.'

Mau was quite happy to go anywhere. They disembarked at one of the landing stages and were led along a causeway to the foot of the cliffs. A large number of ramps were in place, and stones were being dragged on sledges up the slopes by lines of workers roped

353

together. There were thousands of workers drawn from the peasants who could not work in the fields when the Nile was flooded. Long conveys of barges had brought the stones from distant quarries and oxen had dragged them from the banks. The skilled masons were shaping and preparing the rocks and the noise was deafening.

Mau thought it all very dusty and noisy. He sneezed twice. So many people milling about . . . he was glad that Thut was among the servants carrying his gold food bowls. He watched the water being poured in front of the sledges to help them slide up the ramps, and tried to close his ears to the man beating time with clappers so that the strength of the workmen could be united. The men groaned and gasped under the hot Egyptian sun as they strained to drag the huge blocks of stone up the ramps into position.

Mau could not see the point of all this frantic activity when they could fish in the Nile or merely sit in the sun and doze. He made a pretence of lordly supervision for about ten minutes, but then boredom took over and he retreated to the shade of his boat shrine and went to sleep.

'See, the great god Mau is content,' said the Pharaoh with satisfaction. 'He is pleased with the work. He is meditating with the gods and leaves this great work in my hands.'

The workers cheered, believing him, though the Pharaoh had not touched one trowelful of soil. And the work went on.

One night some time later Mau was prowling among the granaries when he became aware of people hurrying. The fur on his back stood up – the atmosphere had changed. It was charged with something he did not understand. For a moment, he was alarmed, every sense alert.

'But where is the great god Mau?' they whispered among themselves. 'Where is Mau? We must find Mau.'

'Here he is,' said Merya, with tears in her voice.

A procession of boats left Thebes and went down the Nile. Mau lost count of the number of boats. He had never seen such a procession, each boat laden with rare carvings and statues, jars of wine and oil, pitchers of milk, chests of gold and jewels, papyrus scrolls and valuable ornaments. There were platters of fruit and bread, even live birds caught by the legs with twine.

354

Perhaps they were going to have a special feast, thought Mau, as they reached the landing stage. It certainly looked like it. He watched with interest as the birds fluttered helplessly. He was not hungry, but he always enjoyed a quick pounce.

A long line of priests and servants formed by the landing stage. They began dragging a boat-shaped sledge covered with lotus flowers. The Queen followed, wailing and weeping, throwing dust on her head.

The procession went first to the Mortuary Temple where rituals were carried out and jars filled with organs. Mau could not understand why no one would look at him, not even Thut. The priests then carried out the ceremony of Opening of the Mouth in front of the chapel and the sacred tablets were put on the eyes and mouth of the dead Pharaoh by his eldest son. Mau felt a cold shiver along his spine even though the sun was hot as the mummy was lowered down the shaft.

Mau found himself being carried through a narrow entrance into the rock and then along a dark passage. He did not like it, but could see from the flickering torches that the walls were carved with inscriptions and scenes from the Pharaoh's life – hunting and fishing and feasting. They passed storehouses filled with furniture and household goods. The procession went deeper and deeper into the heart of the rock and Mau could smell the dampness even though wells had been dug to drain away flood water.

They came at last to a small chamber where the mummy was placed in a great stone sarcophagus. The walls were covered with paintings and the scent of musk and spices was strong.

'I think it's cruel,' muttered Thut. 'The practice of burying the king's household was abandoned years ago, thank goodness,' he added, thinking of his own skin and Merya's.

'The great god Mau will ensure the safe passage of our dead king through the underworld,' said a priest. 'He will help him answer the questions of the forty-two animal and human-headed gods. Then the god Osiris will see that Mau is returned to us. You will see.'

Thut hoped he was right. He was very fond of Mau, god or no god. The cat had given him comfort and, in a strange way, a hope for the future.

Mau was sitting alert on his golden cushion, his pointed ears pricked for any new sound that would solve the mystery of the day's events. He was wearing the heaviest of his ceremonial collars and that was a bad sign. The collar rubbed on his shoulder bones and he hoped Thut would take it off soon.

They all heard a low rumble and then the chamber resounded with thuds as the work began of filling in the shaft with rocks and earth. The priests hurried through their last ceremonies although they were in no danger.

Thut put his hand briefly on Mau's head and touched the short reddish fur. 'Farewell, old friend,' he whispered.

The movement caught the attention of a priest. 'You dare to touch the great god Mau,' he hissed. 'You will be punished.'

'Only for luck, for luck,' the young Thut pleaded, bowing his head. 'I am humble before the god. I am his servant.'

'Out of the way,' the priests swept past and retraced their steps through the passageways and staircases to the main entrance of the tomb. They gave the command for the entrance to be sealed and hidden.

Mau did not pay much attention to his surroundings at first. He thought it a pretty odd game and waited for someone to come and fetch him. He knew where a mouse was hiding in the granaries and was keen to chase him out.

He sneezed as the dust settled around him, and the noise stopped echoing in the chamber. He had the feeling he was alone. He stretched his legs and jumped off the cushion. It was then he discovered that his collar was fastened with a length of chain to the ornamental carved stool on which lay his cushion. He growled at the chain and shook it angrily. He tugged and leaped this way and that but he was jerked back by the linked gold plates hard against his neck.

He crouched at the full length of the chain, his tail flicking with fury. But he was feeling his first tremors of fear. He had never been chained before. Again he attacked the chain, the stool, the cushion. He lay exhausted and slept.

When he awoke he thought he was back at the palace, near the gardens and shady tree-lined pool. Then he remembered from the darkness, the smell and the heavy collar that he was still a prisoner. He twisted and turned in the collar, flattening his ears and trying to

356

drag it over his skull. He began to scratch at the carved stool but it was a hard wood, and it seemed hours before his claws made even a small groove.

He cried out, a loud strident call that echoed down the passageways. The candles fluttered in deep pools of wax and the incense drifted away to the ceiling of the tomb. It was getting very cold.

As time passed Mau was racked with hunger and thirst. He knew he was getting weaker. He knew he must find food before he lost the strength to move. With a tremendous effort he dragged the stool across the rock floor, the collar biting into his neck and almost choking him. Many times he had to stop and rest. Then he knocked into one of the pitchers and it fell over, water flowing onto the floor and gathering in little pools. Mau drank eagerly, his parched tongue lapping in weak gulps like a kitten.

He found wide necked earthenware jars of corn and dates. His primeval ancestor, the Miacis, had eaten fruit. Mau chewed, not caring what he ate. Perhaps if he was very quick, he would catch a lizard. His neck was a mass of open sores from dragging the stool around. He grew thinner and the collar began to get loose, but still he could not pull his head free. The craftsman who had made the heavy gold ornament had measured him carefully.

Days and weeks went by. Mau was living in hell. He was constantly in pain from the festering sores. The corn and dates had long since gone and now he ate the candle wax from the dark pools. He had almost forgotten the outside world, but he clung to life. His dreams were confused, and his thin limbs twitched with memories.

He hardly heard the soft footsteps of the robbers as they crept stealthily and warily down the passageway. Their burning torches cast long shadows on the walls and it was this light that Mau first noticed through half-closed eyes. He kept quite still as the figures crept into the burial chamber. Mau trusted no one.

The men were dark-faced and in ragged robes. They were whispering and trembling with nerves. They touched the stone sarcophagus with awe at first, but they had levers in their hands and were soon seeking a crack. Mau lay in the shadows, watching them, his fluttering heart beating weakly against his ribs.

A flame spluttered and threw a brief streak of light onto Mau's collar. One of the robbers saw the gleam of gold. His eyes glinted.

357

'Gold,' he whispered excitedly. 'Look at this! It's solid gold.' He peered at the corpse of a dead cat lying in the gloom. His gnarled fingers fumbled at the heavy clasp of the collar and found the way to unfasten it. It snapped open. Mau gathered his remaining strength to emit a piercing howl.

'M . . . A . . . U . . . ' He yeowelled with ear-splitting clarity.

The robbers shrieked with fear, dropped their levers and fell over each other in their haste to leave the chamber. They ran, moaning with fear, their hands over their ears as Mau's cries rang through the passageways.

'Mau . . . the great god Mau,' they whimpered as they stumbled through the darkness. Mau flew after them, brushing through their legs in the dark, and the touch of his fur sent them into further paroxisms of terror. 'Ah . . . the god . . . the god. Save us, be merciful and save us,' they cried.

They clambered and slithered over the rocks that they had dug through at the entrance, their hands slippery with sweat. Mau smelled the fresh air and leaped in front of them, sensing freedom at last. He streaked towards the glimmer of light, unseen in the grey shadows, a great surge of willpower giving him strength.

He tumbled out of the narrow hole into the desert night. He paused momentarily, amazed at the brightness of the desert stars in the velvet black sky and the heady oxygen of the cool night air. Then he fled like the wind, not caring in which direction he ran, rejoicing in the feel of the balmy air that stirred through the wisps of fur on his sore skin and the sheer joy of being free . . .

The new Pharaoh had brought his own servants and all the former servants were sent to do other work. Thut had become a brickmaker and he worked hard making bricks from the mud of the fields after the annual floods. Merya spun cloth and brewed beer for the workers and they lived together in a small terraced house that had only a matting of reeds for a roof.

Thut was laying bricks in the sun to dry when Mau approached him. The cat had been walking for many days and his fur was matted with dust. At first Thut was frightened, like the robbers, but when Mau twisted himself round Thut's bare ankles, demanding attention, Thut realized that this was no spirit but Mau alive. He wrapped the cat in a piece of linen and took him to Merya.

'Look at his poor sores,' she said, tears in her eyes. 'And he's so thin. Bastet has sent him to us to be cared for.'

She fed him goats' milk and fish that Thut had caught in the river, and put a soothing ointment on the sores. Mau did not move as she administered the herbal balm. The matted hut was no palace but it seemed he still had his servants.

That night he curled up at Merya's feet, a deep purr of contentment throbbing and swelling in his throat. He would sleep now, with complete trust in the two humans.

'But if they know that we have the great god Mau, we will be punished,' Thut whispered to his wife, too distracted to sleep.

'Ssh . . . ' said Merya, stroking his thick dark hair as if he were a child. 'Who will know? One cat is very much like another. And who would expect to see Mau here? Of all places?'

She got up very early the next morning before it was light and took a file from her small box of precious possessions. Mau again sat quite still as she patiently filed away at his claws. It was ticklish and occasionally he twitched at the light sensation, longing to lick between his toes and be done with the pedicure.

Carefully Merya gathered every fragment of gold off his claws and put it away in a small pouch. Then she gently eased the heavy gold ear-ring out of his ear and put that with the gold dust.

'Now no one will recognize you,' she said. 'And we will spend the gold wisely when there is a time of need.'

Mau stretched and yawned then licked at her hand with his rough pink tongue. He shook his head delightedly. He had always hated that ear-ring.

Outside the sun was burning on the marshes, and Mau sniffed at the odorous air. There were wild fowl to chase and scare, birds to catch, fish to eat, mice to stalk and tease. He leaped out to begin a new dynasty.

BOOK THREE
# True Cat Stories

*To Cousin Edna*
*and the elusive Katie*

# Splodge and Tab

The strongly marked grey and black tabby was the wildest cat for miles around. No one could catch him or touch him. He prowled the neat Surrey gardens as if remembering the days when it was a primeval forest and ferals roamed in packs; or perhaps his ancestral memory went back to the century when huntsmen flew along the ridge of the North Downs led by their cruel king, a heavy man whipping his steaming horse.

Battles had been fought where there are now leafy suburban gardens, and a medieval cannon-ball had been unearthed near where the tabby sat, so still, like a statue, watching the family going about its tidy, methodical ways.

He did not know if he envied them, but something drew him to the family. It was more than curiosity. He was not starving. There were mice enough on the farm where he hung out. He needed this family but he was not sure why.

They tried to approach him but immediately his upper lip curled back in a ferocious snarl, a deep hiss coming from his throat. Then he was off like an arrow into the safety of the bushes. He watched from his hiding place as they searched for him, making soothing noises.

'Puss, puss, puss. Where are you?'

He stayed hidden. Eventually they gave up and went back indoors, but the woman returned with a saucer of milk, which she put down. He did not touch it.

She did not give up easily. She gave him a name.

'Tab, Tab, Tab,' she called now. But he made no move towards her. He came and sat and watched. If anyone came too near, he hissed, fangs bared.

She began to leave food. He had never smelt anything like it before. He could feel his resistance slipping as his salivary glands began to work and his stomach churned. How did she find such delicious food? There was none of it around the farm, only mice, dormice and moles. Sometimes he caught a squirrel, but their fur was so rough and harsh in his mouth. Once he had chased and pounced on a rabbit in the field behind the church . . . now that had been a feast. Perhaps this woman had been into the field chasing a rabbit . . .

He waited until she returned indoors, shutting the back door. She was watching from the kitchen window so he did not move. It was hours before he crept forward in the growing darkness and tentatively sniffed at the new food. It was good. He gulped it down and fled.

'Tab, here's your supper.'

She was there again the next evening with a saucer of food. It was not fair. Tab could not resist. But he did wait until all the humans had disappeared before he ate. This food was so much nicer than mice and so much easier to get. A plan formed in his mind.

One day he came to sit in the garden and watch, and he was not alone. He had brought another feral with him, a small black cat. She was a thin creature but her stomach was swollen with pregnancy.

It is thought that ferals always fight over food, but Tab allowed the black cat to feed first from the dish that had been left out. Then he finished off the remains. The female cat was too heavy to hunt now. Someone had to take care of her, so he had brought her to the family.

'Do you think it's his mate, or his sister?' they whispered. 'She's as wild as he is.'

'Perhaps they are just good friends.'

'I'll find a box and put it outside in the covered way. It's getting cold at nights,' said the woman. 'She may have her kittens here.'

Titch produced four kittens in the box . . . two grey, one black and a tabby. Tab grew more handsome in appearance despite his ragged cauliflower ear. The black markings were dense on his brown ground coat, the rings narrow and numerous; and his round face was fiercely protective. But he was affectionate towards the kittens and could be seen washing them occasionally.

Titch was a good mother, though she was even wilder than Tab. She reared her kittens well. But the road was a hazard she did not understand. As her kittens grew more independent she often left them to escape to the fields. It meant crossing the road. One day she did not make it.

Tab remained, thrown by the death of the female feral. He stood guardian over the kittens, disturbed to find that they were also disappearing from the box. They were being found good homes, civilised homes in houses with doors and windows and rules for cats. He did not know whether this was a good thing; it was not something he wanted for himself. He wanted freedom and life in the wild. But other cats seemed to like it and even thrived on domesticity. He had seen them cleaning their paws on doorsteps in the sunshine.

One of the grey kittens was a pretty long-haired fluffy creature with a fawn splodge on the side of its neck. The woman seemed to favour this kitten, picking it up and talking to it.

'Come along, Splodge,' she said. 'You're going to live with us. I think you'll like it.'

The kitten was quite happy with the idea. She liked the woman and the family of four children, and she took to living in the house with a natural grace.

Tab wandered back to the fields around the farm and

thought about this new development. Would the woman still put out those delicious saucers of food now that she had her own cat? Perhaps he would be back to catching mice and more mice. He roamed the North Downs wondering if the woman was catching rabbits for the grey kitten.

But he could not keep away. He came back and sat in their garden to watch the strange business of training the kitten. It required a lot of putting out and bringing in, and calling.

'Splodge, Splodge, Splodge . . . kitty, kitty, kitty.'

The woman pretended not to notice Tab though she was well aware that the feral was watching, almost camouflaged by the leafy shadows and ferns sprouting from the next door rockery. She was teaching the kitten to dig in the soft dry earth. Splodge was wriggling and rolling over in the dust on the garden path.

As they went indoors together, the woman looked over her shoulder, directly to where Tab sat immobile in the shadows.

'Hello, Tab,' she said. 'I'll put your supper out in a minute.'

He snarled and hissed though she was nowhere near him.

No one knew that Tab's eyesight was not as good as it used to be. He thought perhaps the world had gone hazy and that it was an atmospheric change due to the weather. He had always been able to roam and climb as vigorously and fearlessly as any feral; nothing was too high or too difficult.

There was a willow tree in the next door garden. He had climbed it many times. Sometimes he had climbed to the topmost branches so that he could see into the upper windows, watching the family at their curious activities.

This day he climbed to the top of the willow, leaping with ease from branch to branch, scattering the twittery birds and hovering bumblebees with a lash of his tail.

Perhaps today they would be gardening or washing the car; or the boys would be kicking a football around in some game in which he longed to join.

As he watched, he slowly noticed that this atmospheric change in the weather which was affecting his eyes seemed much worse today. He could hardly see what was going on below. Then he realised that he could not see the other branches of the tree either; that it was all a confused pattern of changing shapes and shadows that bore no relation to the tree which he had climbed.

He waited, hoping that the mist would clear. He sent silent distress signals into the air waves. But who would hear him? He had no friends.

Splodge was by now almost fully grown, a beautiful cat with a long silky grey and fawn coat and big amber eyes. She summed up the situation at once, and climbed the tree with the agility of youth. She came to within a few feet of the feral cat and miaowed.

Tab turned his head towards the noise. He vaguely saw the young cat, recognised its smell. It was one of those kittens, the one that went to live in the house. He had observed its antics as it was put out and called in. But it was the kitten of the black feral and therefore not alien.

Splodge miaowed again and moved along the branch so that the long swaying leaves made a noise. Tab realised that here was an opportunity to descend, even if only to one branch lower. He jumped.

The family watched from a window. They were amazed, calling to each other to come and watch.

'Just look at this. Splodge is helping old Tab get down the tree. I've never seen anything like it. Look, she's actually guiding him . . .'

It was true. Branch by branch, with infinite patience, the young cat was showing the feral where to jump, guiding him down a safe route through the swaying and rustling tree. Splodge jumped to the ground and looked back. Tab followed, feeling the earth beneath his paws with a wave of relief. The two cats looked at each other, and then with one bound Tab disappeared into the bushes and ran home to the farm.

The family made a great fuss of Splodge, with much stroking and patting and a saucer of cream from the top of the milk. She was a heroine.

'Clever Splodge. Well done, Splodge.'

'Old Tab didn't seem very grateful.'

'How can you tell if a cat is grateful?'

They wondered if Tab would now seek different pastures, but after a few days he turned up again. Still watching and waiting and eating whatever was left out for him when everyone had gone.

If there was a rapport between the two cats, it was unspoken. There was no obvious comradeship. But there was a degree of communication indiscernible to humans.

The woman was quietly ironing one afternoon by the window that looked onto the back garden. There was no one else about and she was making very little noise. Through the glass serving partition into the kitchen, she had a good view of the back door.

Splodge came in through the open door, hesitated and looked back. To her amazement, the woman then saw the striped front paws and flat nose of the wild feral. He peered into the kitchen as if into another world.

She expected him to immediately turn tail and race back into the garden, but Tab's long white whiskers were twitching with all the new smells, and curiosity overcame his fear. Splodge moved a few paces over the polished lino and looked back again. Tab followed slowly until the whole length of his body was over the step. But that was as far as he was going.

The woman held her breath. Splodge had achieved the introduction where they had all failed. The wild cat was actually in the kitchen.

Tab looked around with wide-eyed wonder at all the strange things – cupboards and kettles, sinks and saucepans. He had never seen such objects and had no idea what people wanted them for.

Splodge moved a few more steps and looked back as if to say, 'come on'. Tab followed Splodge into the sitting room, amazed by the softness of the carpet under his paws and the warmth from the fire. He saw the woman outlined against the window, but it was as if she was just another object. He was walking through a wonderland, treading carefully, unsure of everything, tense, but following Splodge like an open-mouthed tourist through a palace.

Splodge took Tab on a complete tour of the house. They went upstairs, into every bedroom, even the bathroom. There was not one nook or cranny that Tab did not peer into. It was the most amazing adventure of his life. He could not believe all that he saw.

But it was also quite overwhelming. There was so much that he did not understand, so many things that puzzled him. He looked at Splodge regretfully. This could never be his world. His life was the open fields, the wild and wet woods, the stream that threaded through the gardens, and the echoing barns around the farm. He could not stand four walls.

He finished the tour politely enough. No panic or mad rush to escape outside. He left as quietly as he had entered. Splodge sat down and began to wash her long pinky-tinged fur. She had done her best. She had been a good hostess, shown the visitor around, and when he wanted to leave, she had let him go.

The woman was speechless. She had never seen anything quite so moving between two animals . . . first the intelligent rescue from the tree, and now the guided tour of the house.

She held the beautiful, purring grey cat in her arms, thinking how strange it was that in a world full of bitter fighting and global tragedies, two cats, one wild and one domestic, could actually show some concern for the other.

Then Splodge disappeared. At first they thought that she was just being wilful and staying out all night. But night turned into the next day and she did not appear. Day one grew into day two and the woman was sick with worry. There was a busy blind-junction at the end of the road and she remembered little Titch. A stream of lorries came from the chalk pits that were being dug out of the North Downs. And not far away, behind an embankment, the new motorway thundered with vehicles day and night.

Days turned into weeks, then a month. Tab still came to their garden. He saw their distress, but how could he tell them anything? He was only a cat. He was powerless. He could not take the place of Splodge. He could only try with his continuing presence to give them some comfort, little as it was.

The woman continued to put out food for Tab in the cold and frosty December days.

'Here you are, Tab,' she called out, but her voice was without joy.

It was five weeks since Splodge had disappeared and it was Christmas Eve. Although they had searched around and asked neighbours and given the police a description, there was no news and they had given up hope. They could only cross their fingers that death had been kind and that she had not been stolen for her beautifully coloured coat.

School had broken up and the younger son was in the kitchen. He was looking out of the window, thinking of what he had yet to do for Christmas, when a grey shadow crossed his vision. A cat was strolling nonchalantly up the garden path, its long tail sweeping the stones.

'Mum, Mum,' he called out. 'Come here! There's Splodge, I'm sure. She's coming up the garden.'

The woman had never taken the stairs so quickly. She flew down them, her heart in her mouth. Could it be . . . could it be their Splodge, or was it just some other cat that looked like her in the gathering gloom?

Her son opened the kitchen door and the grey cat sauntered in, slightly overdoing the casual act. She went over to her chair, jumped up onto it and sat down as if nothing had happened.

It was Splodge, thinner, a little bedraggled, her lovely grey and fawn fur dirty and tangled; but it was the best Christmas present the family had ever had.

Tab sat outside in the garden, the frosty stars bright in the December sky. He had watched the cameo of the return and was satisfied that the family were reunited.

Only Splodge and Tab knew where the grey cat had been all that time. Perhaps Tab had taken Splodge on a tour of his world, through the acres of fields and woods. Perhaps Splodge had felt the stirring of her ancestors' blood and tasted the delights of freedom. Perhaps she had forgotten about the family in the heady joy of running wild.

It may have been the cold that drove her back to her chair and the fireside. The diet of mice could have palled and become hard to find. Perhaps she longed for a dish of chicken or liver.

Or perhaps Tab had brought her back. No one knows and no one would ever know.

# The Stowaway

(Adapted from an account by Mrs Janet Gadd)

The kitten was being brought home by car. He had never been in one before, and it was a highly alarming experience. He threw himself dramatically at the windows in an attempt to escape from this monster.

There was pandemonium. His tiny white paws clawed from window to window, accompanied by terrified mews. He had come from a semi-wild cat family owned by the village butcher. Some of the litter were too wild to be caught.

'Got him,' said Mum, throwing her cardigan over the kitten like a matador. 'He's as wild as a tiger. And he looks like one too. We'll just have to call him Tiger.'

So Tiger he became, but only by name and not by nature. Love tamed him and he matured into a friendly family cat, sharing the Roberts' home with another cat and four dogs, living in the beautiful seaside village of Penmaenmawr in North Wales.

He developed a penchant for sleeping next door. Many times Janet Gadd went to her front door to fetch in the milk and found Tiger asleep on the doormat or curled up among a pile of leaves that had blown into the porch. His favourite sleeping place was in the basket of a bike stored in the garage.

She had several bikes, for Janet and Harold Gadd are members of the Long Sutton and District Veteran Cycle Club. They own several veteran bikes, including a rare 1877 penny farthing.

In the middle of August 1985, the club was invited to ride and display their cycles at the annual Vintage Vehicle Rally at Rickinghall Inferior, Suffolk. The Gadds usually drive the three hundred miles overnight to avoid the heavy North Wales holiday traffic, but that Thursday evening the fuel tank was reading low and the nearest all-night filling station was some fifty miles away. They decided to postpone their departure, but packed their car and roof-rack with the bikes ready for an early start the next morning.

First their tent went on the roof in front of the extra-long rack. Then a canvas-covered bike went on the rack, with the penny farthing secured on top of the lot.

It was a clear summer's night when Tiger took his usual leisurely after-supper walk. He had had a lovely day playing with seven-year-old Stuart and now he was ready for a little snooze. He liked interesting new places. He nosed around the Gadds' garden, digging up a few bedding plants. He approved of the Gadds even though they did not have a cat. Perhaps that was why he liked them.

He explored a few of his old haunts but for some reason they all seemed boring. He fancied somewhere really new. Something a little out of the ordinary.

Janet and Harold left early on the Friday morning, one of those dewy-fresh mornings that make one wish for the incentive to get up at dawn every morning. They drove into the ancient town of Conwy, past the brooding castle and over the famous Telford bridge. The narrow streets were already traffic-jammed, and they stopped for petrol as soon as they could.

Tiger opened one eye. A red traffic light stared at him.

It was very strange. The lights began to blink, then moments later he was being jolted around and he dug his claws into some fabric to keep his balance. What on earth was happening? He hung on as he was carried away, the wind whistling through his fur. He gritted his teeth and shut his eyes against the rush of air, finding it difficult to breath.

He squinted sideways. Trees, houses, shops sped past. It was both terrifying and exhilarating at the same time. Tiger clung on, keeping his head down to reduce the wind resistance. So much was happening he could not take it all in. Up and down, this way and that way. He felt as if he were on a roller-coaster, only he didn't know what a roller-coaster was.

Daringly he peered about, trying to get his bearings, to make some sense. Where was he? He had vague memories of a journey once before, many years ago, when he had fought to get free, but that had been different, with walls he could not get through. Here it was all air – too much air, in fact. He was as free as a bird, but could he fly? The wind told him that he could, but a sense of self-preservation told him to stay where he was.

He sniffed, smelling salt in the air. He turned his head carefully, and there was an amazing sight before him. There were miles and miles of sparkling blue coming and going, breaking over the rocks and washing up on the shore. He had never seen such odd stuff, although he had sometimes smelt the same salt in the air at Penmaen-mawr. It was fascinating; all the little specks of white foam, begging to be played with. He longed to dip his paw in that tantalising straggling line of bubbles.

He was too absorbed to notice when they began to leave the sea road and turn inland. The scenery changed from blue to green and brown hills, then to red and grey. It was bewildering. He had never realised that there was anywhere else. He had thought the world began and ended in the village of Penmaenmawr. How wrong he had been.

They were slowing down now, circling in slow curves, but at the same time he could hear a growing roar. What could this noise be? It was louder than a tiger roaring in the jungle. The fur on his back began to tingle, to stand on end . . . it must be some enormous fearsome animal.

A vast grey path of asphalt stretched ahead, going far out of sight, and wider than anything he had ever seen before. It was packed with lines of cars and lorries, all travelling very fast.

As their speed increased, Tiger grew more and more alarmed. He dug his claws even further into the weave of the fabric and tucked his nose under his fur. There was nothing interesting to look at, only the roof-tops of cars, and besides, the great container lorries thundering by scared him stiff.

He felt he was spinning, disorientated, deafened by the traffic, speeding to some alien place where nothing would ever be the same again. Bridges rushed overhead, making his heart somersault.

'I could do with some coffee,' said Janet. 'And breakfast.'

'We'll pull off at the next service station,' said Harold. 'I'd like a stretch. We've done a hundred miles already so that's pretty good going.'

They turned off the M6 motorway at the Keele service station and drove slowly into the parking area, followed by another car. The passengers in this car were looking at them. Janet and Harold were used to this as their 1877 penny farthing always attracted attention wherever they went.

The passengers from the other car immediately came over to them.

'Do you know there's a cat on your roof?' they said.

'A penny farthing, you mean,' said Harold, blankly.

'No, it's a cat. Look for yourself.'

Janet got out of the car and looked at their car roof. She could not believe her eyes. Crouched among the bikes on their roof-rack was Tiger, their neighbours' cat.

His sweet tabby face peered down uncertainly. He was glad the jolting had stopped; that the rushing wind had stopped; that the world was steady at last. But he was still very wary.

He knew two of the people who were staring up at him in amazement. They lived next door. But there were a lot of other people, too, and he did not know any of them. He retreated further back among the folds of canvas.

'It's Tiger . . . Stuart's cat, from next door,' said Janet. 'I don't believe it. Good heavens, whatever do we do now?'

It took a combined effort to get Tiger off the roof-rack. He was obstinately reluctant to be moved from what now seemed a safe haven. Harold, who is not a cat-lover, tried to get hold of him from one side. Janet, who is shortish, was unable to reach him at all. The young men from the second car joined in the Tiger hunt. Tiger clung on grimly, determined to evade capture. At last he was dragged off the roof and bundled into the car. Janet went quite cold at the thought of Tiger charging down the M6.

'Now what are we going to do?' she said again.

Harold went into the service station shop to get a cardboard box, and Janet phoned home to her mother to get a message passed to the Roberts family next door.

'We can't come back with the cat,' said Janet on the phone. 'It's over a hundred miles. We'll have to keep Tiger with us for the weekend. We'll look after him the very best we can, but . . . you know, a cat in a strange place, and we're camping. And we've never looked after a cat before. There's a lot of problems and that's putting it mildly.'

'Are you sure you know what you're doing?' asked her mother, bewildered.

'Not really,' said Janet, running fingers through her tousled hair. 'But anyone ought to be able to look after one small tabby cat, oughtn't they?'

The news travelled round the car park like wildfire and

their estate car became the centre of attraction. The Gadds downed a quick breakfast while Tiger roamed around, restlessly investigating the back of their car.

As they sat in the front seats eating bacon sandwiches, a man came up to them. They wound down the window an inch.

'I believe you've found a cat,' he said. 'Would you like a box?'

They stared at him, unable to believe their good luck.

'I'm the driver of a removal van and I often have to move cats along with the furniture. There's a spare travelling box on the van. You can have it. I don't want it back.'

Tiger took an instant dislike to the box. He wanted to go back on the roof-rack. Why wouldn't they let him? It had been a bit precarious at times, but quite a thrill. He eyed Harold carefully, his wild-cat blood rising. Suddenly he saw his chance. He slithered through their hands like a furry eel and raced across the car park to freedom.

One of the helpful young men sprinted after him, cornering the cat with some fast thinking. Tiger growled.

'Oh no you don't,' said the young man, tucking the protesting tabby firmly under his arm. 'You've had enough adventures for one day.'

Tiger objected loudly to being put in the travelling box even though it was a good size. The car had to be repacked to make a space for it in the back.

'We'll have to stop somewhere and do some shopping,' said Janet raising her voice above Tiger's piercing miaows.

'I thought you'd done all the shopping before we left,' said Harold, putting the car in gear.

'Cat food!' said Janet with a grin. 'We've another mouth to feed.'

At Rickinghall, the organisers were preparing the site for the weekend rally. It was being held in a big field surrounded by trees and large enough to accommodate all the vehicles and tents.

'Hi there, Janet, Harold. Have a good journey?'

'You could say that,' said Janet. 'By the way, have you got a rabbit run?'

The organisers got asked for a lot of strange things, but this was a new one.

'A rabbit run?'

'Er . . . yes,' said Janet. 'You see, we've brought a cat with us.'

As their cycle club friends arrived, the search for some kind of cat run began. Tiger had to have some exercise without escaping. He could hardly live in their tent.

More friends, Nancy and Norman from Wisbech, arrived. They usually drove a small three-wheeler, but this weekend their son had brought them in his transit van.

'Oh, he's beautiful,' said Nancy, straight away taking him to her heart. She loved cats and Tiger knew it. 'He can live in our van. He can have the run of it during the day, and then sleep in his box in your car at night.'

Tiger settled to his new regime without a fuss, though he did a spectacular impersonation of a mad cat whenever they tried to put a collar and lead on him.

'He'll hurt himself,' they cried, abandoning the idea.

'Got a tiger in your tank?'

'Cat on a hot tin roof?'

Despite the jokes, Tiger enjoyed his celebrity status. Nancy made a fuss of him and he had a constant stream of visitors. He shared a fish-and-chip supper which the club organised as a Saturday evening event. It was bought from a little shop in the village and everyone saved him a morsel.

Sunday dawned cold and damp and the organisers of the rally eyed the grey skies with dismay. The thirty vintage cycles were given their final polish and oiling. The muddy field was going to be a problem.

Tiger heard his story being told over the Tannoy

system to all the visitors. He was an added attraction to the day, an extra dimension to the display . . . all those lovingly cared for vehicles from bygone eras and one small scrap of fur with an equal sense of self-preservation.

By mid-afternoon the sky had darkened and the drizzle turned to heavy rain. The club's cycles had been on display all day and members had taken part in an arena ride dressed in costumes suited to the year of their cycle. Now the crowds started to drift away, squelching over the mud.

Janet and Harold began to pack their bikes and camping gear, not forgetting to leave a space for Tiger's box. It was still raining hard and a strong wind was blowing. They needed all the help they could get to take the tent down and load it onto the roof-rack.

Tiger watched the preparation with curiosity. Was he going for a ride on the roof-rack again? He did not fancy the pelting rain, and the wind was already running cold fingers through his fur. But he trusted his new friends and waited to see what they were going to do with him.

Nancy gave him a big hug and kissed him, whispering into his ear all sorts of things that he understood perfectly. She would have liked to keep him.

'Come along, love,' said Norman, her husband. 'You can't adopt him.'

Finally Tiger was put into the travelling box and stowed away in the car. For once Tiger did not object. He was only too glad to be inside and not outside, watching the rain streaming down the windows. He enjoyed a service station stop for a drink and a stretch.

It was late evening when the Gadds drove into the road at the rear of their house.

Tiger had been dozing but suddenly he was alert. He leaped up, miaowing loudly, scratching, creating quite a commotion. As Janet opened the gates and Harold reversed the car into their garden drive, Tiger went wild. He knew exactly where they were. Hadn't he heard these noises a hundred times? Tiger threw himself about, pink mouth open in hoarse cries. He was desperate to get out, clawing at the wooden box.

The lights burned in the living room of the Roberts' house next door. They had spent an anxious weekend wondering if their pet would survive his camping holiday so far away. They had been waiting up and watching for the return of the Gadd's car.

Harold went to knock at the back door whilst Janet unlocked the tail-gate of their estate car and lifted out the box. She could hardly hold it as Tiger was throwing all his weight around in another exhibition of wildness. It would have been impossible to keep him in her arms.

As the Roberts opened their door, Janet lifted the wire mesh from the front of the box. Tiger shot out like lightning and raced across the garden, leaping over the wall in one high, effortless bound, straight into his house.

It was a beautiful sight. Janet felt a catch in her throat. That small creature had feelings. He was home. She could imagine the relief he felt after his strange adventure that weekend.

The Gadds went in next door for a cup of tea to tell the Roberts of Tiger's precarious one-hundred-mile ride on their roof-rack and the odd set of coincidences; stopping at a motorway service station fifty miles sooner than usual; the kindness of the removal-van driver; Nancy turning up in a much larger vehicle.

The next morning young Stuart woke up early. There was a familiar heaviness on his feet. Tiger was asleep at the end of his bed, nose tucked into his white bib, one paw curled over his face. The boy gave a wide smile. His cat was back, safe and sound.

Tiger refused to leave the house all that Monday. But come Tuesday . . . well, Tuesday was another day and there might be a new adventure around the corner.

# Nirvana

The man stood staring out of the window. She had been gone some months now but still her fragrance lingered in the house. It was so empty and quiet. He was used to the two cats chasing each other up and down the stairs, the scampering feet on the wooden floor, the mock fights and hissing, then the chorus of catcalls when his wife took their supper out of the refrigerator.

He missed them curled together on his lap, replete and sleepy, each trying to push the other off, striving for extra space even in sleep. The two Burmese had been delightful innocent witnesses to his disintegrating life.

They had been a present to her, so she took them along with her other possessions. Taking the cats had been a knife turning in the wound. He was lonely. He found it difficult to work. He was a fine print photographer and worked at home. He was used to cats around, helping him at his desk, sometimes providing inspiration with their fine eyes and ethereal beauty. He could not bear life without having a cat.

Many miles away in Bedfordshire, a tiny female lilac Burmese kitten stirred in milky sleep. She had been bred from Bathsheba, a queen of rare beauty. There were four kittens in the litter, two small bundles of pink and grey fluff, two of the palest milky chocolate. They stretched their tiny pin-pointed claws into the warmth of their mother.

The breeder wanted a home for the lilac female with someone particularly loving and understanding who would give her the kind of extra care she would need.

'I've got to find someone very special for you, little one,' she told the kitten, examining the tiny creature again.

She was expecting a visitor that day, a man who had telephoned earlier asking particularly for a lilac Burmese female. He sounded weary but was prepared to drive a long way to see her kittens. She tried to explain the circumstances but he seemed undeterred. It was almost as if he was not listening to her.

'We used to have two Burmese but my wife's taken them with her,' he explained somewhat incoherently. 'I can't blame her, of course, they were a present to her, but I miss them . . . I've . . . I like . . .'

'You like having a cat around,' she finished for him. 'Especially a Burmese. I understand. They are so affectionate and make good pets. But this lilac female kitten, as I was saying, I don't know whether I should let her go . . .'

'I'd like to come and see her anyway. Please.'

She heard the despair and loneliness in his voice. It seemed this was another marriage break-up that had included not only the loss of a marriage partner, perhaps children, but also beloved pets. People rarely thought about the impact of losing pets.

The man must have started the long drive soon after talking to her on the telephone. He was a small, stocky man, dressed in jeans, sweater and sneakers, the past few months clearly etched on his face.

'Hello. You're here already,' she said in the doorway. 'What a long way to come. I hope you won't feel it's a wasted journey. Of course, I've other kittens – but only the one lilac female. Will you come this way, please?'

She took the man into the garden room, where the newest litter were lying in a heap on the sofa.

The man sat down on the floor in a slow movement of tired limbs folding up under him, wishing he had his camera with him. The heap of kittens rolled over and the lilac female detached herself. She pushed her way out of her squirming brothers and sister, an unsteady puff-ball of lavender fur, tiny tottering legs trampling over the vast expanse of the sofa towards the man.

They held their breath. They had done nothing to encourage the kitten, or attract her attention. The kitten went straight to the man. It seemed like an abyss between them, an unequal descent to reach the man's lap. There was nothing tentative about her movements or her determination. She was set on her objective . . . the man sitting on the floor.

To a kitten of that size it was a journey of immense proportions. But she made it, kneading the warmth of his sweater, a throaty purr growing in the fragile bird-like throat, blinking mistily into his eyes. The man was enchanted.

'But she's beautiful,' he said, unbelieving. 'How can you say she's deformed? She's quite perfect.'

The kitten had done her choosing and, satisfied with her choice, she curled up on his knee, exhausted by the effort. She went to sleep, trusting, ready to devote her life to his companionship.

'She certainly seems to like you. Rapport at first sight. It's amazing. I always think cats choose their owners, not the other way round.'

The man looked content, stroking the kitten. Before her eyes the breeder could see him relaxing. Animals could be therapeutic. The kitten was already weaving a spell round the man that would last for years.

'I'd like to have this kitten,' he said. Then he murmured into the soft fur. 'Princess Esmé . . . you will have a crystal bowl to drink water from, and one day, when you are used to a collar and lead, you will sail on the Thames with me . . .'

'I do insist on you thinking it over for a night,' she said.

'Just to make sure that her defect isn't going to worry you in the future. I can't take any chances with this kitten. She has to go to a very special person. Please look at her foot.'

She turned the sleepy bundle onto its back and found the front left foot, pushing aside the pale lavender fur. The kitten had two shell-pink pads and two claws instead of the normal pad and four toes.

It was a strange sight on the kitten, a rare deformity. Perhaps it would put the man off; perhaps he would find it distasteful and take one of the other kittens.

'I knew there was something,' he said mysteriously.

'I beg your pardon?'

'We have a bond,' he said.

He held out his left hand, pushing up the sleeve from his wrist. He turned his palm to the light, showing the line of a surgical scar.

'I was born with two thumbs.'

She let him take the kitten. There was simply no question about it. They were soul-mates. Some divine instinct had led them to each other.

Perhaps the kitten would change the man's future, open new doors, point new paths, make things happen that in some way would restore peace and tranquillity to his life. She knew the kitten would bring him happiness. It was written so.

# White Tiger

Ebony was an ordinary black farm cat. He did not know that he was fated to cross the path of a white tiger cub, and that for a time they would live together.

The story really began ten years earlier when Dr Theodore Reed journeyed to India to escort one of the most beautiful and rare creatures in the world back to the Smithsonian Institution's National Zoological Park in Washington, DC.

Mohini, as she was called, translates as 'enchantress' and she soon became one of the zoo's greatest attractions. She bewitched people with her startling glacier blue eyes and her white fur with its glamorous greyish-brown stripes. She was a white tiger, a mutant from the better known orange Bengal tiger.

It was not surprising that such an outstanding beauty acted remote when it came to suitors. She did produce three cubs with Samson, but the only white tiger cub died of a virus.

Then she mated with Ramana and gave birth to a single female white cub. The zoo was ecstatic about the new arrival. The Indian Ambassador suggested a name for her, Rewati, meaning 'a pure mountain stream'.

It was as if Mohini knew that her tiny cub was precious and irreplaceable, very valuable and difficult to rear. She

385

began to lick the cub excessively and pace nervously around the cage, carrying the baby in her mouth. The zoo officials were worried. It was very odd behaviour. They felt the cub was in danger. The 420-pound tigress was normally a model mother, but the tiny bundle of 10,000-dollar fluff could so easily be crushed if Mohini was disturbed.

A decision had to be made.

Dr Reed took the cub home in his car. His wife, Elizabeth, was busy in the kitchen preparing a dinner party for fourteen guests. She was up to her elbows in stirring sauces and making dressings.

'Here's your new baby,' he said, putting the cub into her arms. 'We could turn one of the bedrooms into a nursery. She has to be in an incubator till she's stronger.'

Elizabeth looked at the small white kitten in her arms, totally bewildered. Incubator? Nursery? What on earth was she being let in for?

'But what are we going to feed her on?' she asked. 'Do we know about tiger's milk?'

'I can't find any information on tiger's milk,' said Dr Reed. 'The fat and protein content of the milk of big cats varies so much. We'll just have to use a commercial formula.'

Ebony watched the new arrival, his curiosity veiled with an aloof indifference. It was not unlike his own arrival at the house. He, too, had been smuggled up-stairs.

The black cat was born in a barn on a busy farm. When the Reeds were on a visit there, Maryalice, their ten-year-old daughter, pleaded to be allowed to have one of the kittens, but her parents said no. The girl was very quiet on the drive home and her father thought she was sulking. But Maryalice was up to more than that. She had one of the kittens tucked inside her coat, a scrap of black fluff with a white spot on his chest, just to take the curse off.

Elizabeth was unable to resist the kitten when

Maryalice eventually confessed. It was a bright, intelligent little thing and they could not possibly take him back. Dr Reed gave in. He knew when he was beaten. They christened the kitten Ebony and he quickly became Elizabeth's cat, following her everywhere.

He loved to be vacuumed. Whenever he heard the cleaner, he came scampering over, arching his back in delicious anticipation. Ebony had the run of the house and the yard, as well as the neighbourhood. There was never any evidence that he caught mice or birds, but the chipmunks in the garden decided to make a rapid and permanent exit.

Ebony listened to the cub yowling that first night. It was an insistent sound. He heard two pairs of bare feet hurrying across to the new nursery. Ebony stood in the nursery doorway, glaring balefully as Elizabeth went to tend the tiny cub. Rewati was howling for a bottle and a dry blanket. It was the beginning of a regular three-and-a-half-hour routine of feeds.

Ebony had no objection to this middle-of-the-night routine as long as there was some milk in it for him. He padded into the kitchen, where Rewati's feed was being made up.

'I haven't forgotten you,' Elizabeth yawned. She sat down for a moment, cradling her head in her arms. She was very tired. Ebony jumped onto her lap, pretending to be a kitten again. 'It's just for a few months, Ebony. I have to look after Rewati until she's strong enough to go back to her mother, and the zoo. Then it'll be just you and me again.'

A few months . . . How long was a few months, Ebony thought without enthusiasm. He felt threatened by the new arrival. He watched every move, every feed, trying to read the signs with suspicion.

Two days after Rewati arrived at the Reeds', her blue eyes opened and she looked in bright astonishment at the world around her. On the thirteenth day, she took her first wobbling walk on cotton-wool legs. On the twenty-second day, she began to play, shaking her towel, making miniature growling noises.

Ebony watched the cub's progress with caution. He sensed that the oddly striped bundle of snowy fur was something special. So special that everyone endured the round-the-clock routine without grumbling. Elizabeth was worried by the huge responsibility. So many people enquired daily as to the infant tiger's progress. And she was the one who the cub depended upon for its life.

At first it was difficult to find a compatible feeding formula, but by varying the commercial product, they gradually found the right mixture for a baby tiger. Soon Rewati outgrew the incubator and graduated to a box. The rate of growth astonished Ebony. He sat, meticulously washing his face and grooming his whiskers, but watching all the time. It seemed that with every feed, Rewati grew an inch. She became a bouncing bundle of energy, full of mischief, lunging and rolling about like a puppy.

The big black tomcat took no notice of these antics, but he was disturbed when the tiger cub began crawling in tight circles on the floor making small noises and dragging her hind legs. Ebony sensed that something was very wrong and he wanted someone to come quickly. He began to miaow loudly. Elizabeth hurried in.

When the zoo's veterinary specialist arrived, Ebony moved away to a distance, but they did not seem to know what was the matter with the cub. They talked in low, worried voices. They tried antibiotics, oxygen treatments, outside exercise lessons and a formula pepped up with brandy and egg. Ebony's nose twitched at the smell. He wondered if he would be fed any of that delicious yellow stuff if he fell about on the floor.

But in a week the panic was over. Rewati recovered and was running around her garden jungle again. She graduated to baby cereal and strained beef in a bowl. Rewati was a sloppy eater, leaving most of it on her nose and face. Elizabeth always had a clean-up job with a damp washrag. Ebony helped too by licking out the bowl when no one was looking.

The jungle was a paradise of shrubs for hide and seek, camellia bushes on which to sharpen her claws and a big red ball for Rewati to pounce on and attack. She roamed free in the house, much to the surprise of visitors, unused to being greeted by a hefty playful tiger cub with formidable teeth and claws.

By now Rewati was trying to be friendly with Ebony. She wanted a playmate, but the black cat was having none of it. He'd seen those sharp claws puncture the red ball. He did not want to be similarly deflated.

Rewati chose her moment. She crept up to the unsuspecting Ebony and gave him a playful nuzzle in a soft spot. Ebony leaped into the air and up onto the fence. He sat there, totally outraged, licking down his disarranged fur. He glared down at the cub, whose baby blue eyes blinked back so innocently.

'Rewati needs someone to play with,' said Dr Reed.

Ebony could not believe his eyes when a second tiger cub arrived at the Reed household. The zoo had bought an orange Bengal cub as a playmate for Rewati. This cub was called Sakhi, which in Hindi means a close and dear companion.

Ebony was disgusted. He told Elizabeth in no uncertain terms. Now he had two half-wild creatures romping round his garden. He thought briefly about leaving home, but he loved Elizabeth too much. The yard had once been his domain; then it became a jungle for one baby to play in; now it was out-and-out tiger country. It became necessary to plot a course for safety with a dozen escape routes. He wasn't black and canny for nothing.

Rewati loved company. If she was left alone, she would howl and scratch and get into mischief. But if she could see someone, even just Ebony, she felt secure and happy.

As she grew bigger she was moved into new quarters in the basement. Elizabeth forgot to warn the man from the electric company about the new arrangement when he came to read the meter. He took quite a while to recover from the shock.

Rewati liked Elizabeth's company in the evening. The cub would curl up on the couch beside Elizabeth while they both watched television. Even the most boring programme took on a new lustre in such élite company, thought Elizabeth, stroking the white fur. She could rarely go out now. But when she did manage to get a brave tiger-sitting friend to stay for a while, the rule was: 'If the house catches fire, grab the cub first!'

The cub was now worth 35,000 dollars.

At two months old Rewati weighed a solid fifteen pounds and was eating ground beef. She greeted everyone in the Reed household with enthusiasm and affectionate chuffing noises. Ebony kept his distance. The young white tigress was already something of a handful. Friends were less keen on visiting. The cubs were becoming a rough and rowdy pair with teeth and claws that could hurt.

Ebony sensed something was different on that last day. Elizabeth was rather quiet. The two cubs were romping as usual in the garden and Ebony suddenly knew that they were going. He thought of all the friendly overtures he had dismissed. Perhaps he had been a little too stand-offish. His icy reserve melted a fraction at the thought of their imminent departure.

Crossing the yard, he stopped, eyeing a thrashing white-striped tiger tail. The temptation was too much. For a few moments he batted the tiger tail back and forth with his paw like the kitten he was at heart.

Rewati turned and looked over her shoulder, blue eyes wide with surprise. Was this a game two could play? Ebony straightened his back slowly, recovered his dignity and stalked off into the shrubs without a backward glance. He never saw Rewati again.

Two weeks later, Sakhi also returned to the zoo. The house very quiet and empty. Elizabeth wandered from room to room, at a loss without her tiger cubs. Ebony curled himself round her ankles. Remember me, he purred.

Elizabeth scooped him up into her arms, old friends, and nuzzled his dark head. 'They've gone. Just you and me now,' she said. ' . . . until the next phone call.'

Rewati is never lonely now. She has all the company she wants: hundreds of thousands of children visit the zoo every year to admire the magnificent fully grown white tigress.

Life returned to normal for Ebony. His patience was rewarded and he regained his rightful place in the Reed household.

He no longer shares Elizabeth's lap with a frisky white tiger cub. The garden is his, and the vacuum cleaner. Peace has returned.

# The Uninvited Guest

It was not long after we moved into our house that I saw the black cat walk into the larder. The occurrence was unusual as we did not have a cat. I thought perhaps a neighbour's pet had come to inspect the newcomers.

I could see him quite clearly from the corner of my eye . . . a large handsome black cat with long curving tail and alert pointed ears.

For a moment I paused, not wanting to scare him. Then I went over to say hello.

There was nothing. Empty air. The larder was stacked with tidy rows of bottles, jars and tins, the bread bin, vegetable rack . . . but no cat. I searched the larder thoroughly but he had completely disappeared.

Puzzled, I shut the door. We had made the larder from a large walk-in cupboard under the stairs. It was ideal; cool and ventilated and a blissful size after our cramped years in rented accommodation. Everything about the house was a long-awaited dream come true. It was old, weather-beaten red brick, brimming with character and space, with a rambling garden made for children and animals. We had the children, two daughters, Linda and Janice, and I had promised them a cat and a dog as soon as we settled in.

I began to search the house. I had clearly seen that cat, and yet there was no cat. Odd.

'What are you doing, Mummy?' asked my eight-year-old curiously, as I peered under beds.

'Er . . . just checking,' I said.

'Checking for what?' she persisted.

'Dust,' I said.

I sat back on my heels, pushing the hair off my face. I must be tired, I thought. The move had been hectic and there was still such a lot to do, getting the house straight and redecorated as well as caring for the family. Perhaps it had been a shadow, a very dark shadow.

It was easy enough to tell myself this, but I didn't believe it, not for one moment. I know a cat when I see one.

'Mummy, isn't it nearly tea-time?'

I shrugged off the incident and returned to the world of tea, baths and bedtime stories, dismissing the cat from my mind. What did it matter anyway? It had obviously found a way out of the house.

That same evening as I stood in the kitchen making a late drink, I saw the cat again. He was sitting on the floor near the larder, looking straight at me. There was no mistaking him this time . . . a big black cat with his tail curled neatly over his paws.

'Hello, puss,' I said. 'Where have you come from?'

I was talking to myself. It was ridiculous, but there was nothing there. The cat had completely vanished. I made a brief search of the kitchen but there was no way he could have got out.

'I just don't understand it,' I said to my husband, Neville, as I went back into the living room with our two mugs of hot chocolate. 'I saw a black cat in the kitchen this afternoon. It went into the larder. Then just now I saw the same cat, sitting outside the larder.'

'So? You've seen a black cat. By the larder. Perhaps he's hungry.'

I shook my head. 'No, it vanished into thin air. That's

what's so strange,' I said. 'It was definitely there, and then it wasn't.'

'You're imagining things,' said Neville.

'Once perhaps, but not twice,' I said firmly.

As the weeks went by I saw the cat almost daily, but only in the kitchen, either disappearing into the larder or sitting near it. I often spoke to him softly, but soon learned that if I made any movement towards him the cat vanished instantly.

'Puss, puss,' I said coaxingly. 'Come and talk to me. I won't hurt you.'

The cat stared at me, his slanting amber eyes unblinking, thinking secret thoughts in a secret world. His coat was a furry blackness that I longed to touch, to feel its softness.

'Talking to yourself again?' said Neville, grinning.

'I was talking to the cat,' I said. 'Are you sure you didn't see it?'

'No. Nothing. Not a black cat in sight.'

Everything about the kitchen was so normal. The warmth, the delicious smell of a casserole cooking, sunshine streaming through the window, curtains moving with the fresh breeze. We were not far from the sea. It was all quite ordinary. There was no icy chill, no hush, no premonition . . . only a mysterious cat that came and went like a ghost.

I made some enquiries. There was no large black cat living in the neighbourhood; the previous occupants of our house had not owned a cat.

Linda and Janice knew nothing about the uninvited guest in our house. I did not want to frighten them, although they occasionally caught me talking to thin air.

'Mummy,' one of them would giggle. 'You're talking to yourself again!'

I was sure that the cat could see me. It had a definite expression in its eyes as it stared across the kitchen. There was nothing unseeing about those eyes. I could not describe the look. I tried to find the words . . . the cat looked contented, almost serene.

It was some seven months later, a warm day in early summer, when my daughter Linda called from the kitchen, her voice high with excitement.

'Mummy, Mummy, there's a black cat just gone in the larder! A big black cat. Is it ours? Can we keep it?'

The girls had been wanting a cat for ages and I had promised them a cat and a dog. There just hadn't been time to look for the right pets.

'Oh, really?' I said, going into the kitchen. 'I bet you can't find him in there now.'

Linda looked inside the cupboard under the stairs, clattering around, but she came out mystified, her innocent face looking puzzled.

'But he's not there,' she said. 'How funny. I saw him go in.'

'I often see this cat,' I said casually, as if I were talking about some mundane daily routine. 'But he's not an ordinary cat. He can disappear, just like that.'

The child laughed at my impersonation of Tommy Cooper.

'You mean a ghost cat?'

I nodded. 'I think so, but there's no need to be frightened of him. He means no harm. He's quite friendly in a remote sort of way.'

Linda did not seem in the least alarmed. She quite liked the idea of having a ghost cat. 'We'll call him Spooky,' she said.

Linda only saw Spooky occasionally, but I saw him often. I got quite used to the black cat sitting by the larder or walking into it. I began to wonder if the cupboard under the stairs had been used as an air-raid shelter during the war years and he was waiting to take cover; or perhaps his favourite sleeping place had been in some dark recess under the stairs. I felt sure he must have lived in the house at some time.

'Hello, Spooky,' I said, standing quite still and returning his gaze. Cat and I stared at each other. It was a strange sensation, knowing that when I moved, the cat would instantly disappear.

We had not mentioned Spooky to Janice, my six-year-old daughter. We thought she was a little too young to cope with such an unusual phenomenon, even a friendly furry one.

One evening in August, we were downstairs watching television. I was knitting and thinking about the new baby I was expecting soon. Suddenly we heard Janice calling from her bed.

'Mummy! Mummy! Mummy!'

I raced upstairs as quickly as my size would allow and rushed into her bedroom. She was sitting up in bed, her eyes wide with fright.

'Mummy, Mummy, there's a big cat on my bed,' she cried. 'Take him off, take him off. He jumped on me and frightened me.'

'Is he still there? Where?' I asked, for I could see nothing.

'Yes,' she said, calming down but still trembling a little. 'He's leaning on my legs. He's ever so heavy.'

She was obviously getting over the fright, for she put out her hand and began stroking the cat. I was amazed to see her hand making the movement of actually stroking a non-existent cat. It was to be the only time anyone actually touched or felt the black cat. And I was not surprised that it was Janice who was given this gift. For she was and still is quite mad about cats.

I almost expected to hear a purr as Janice stroked the air, but there was nothing except my daughter's cooing and coaxing voice, then the rustle of bed sheets as I tucked her back to bed. Outside the house, the summer breeze combed the long grass and whispered to the nodding leaves.

'Spooky,' I said quite firmly. 'You are not to go waking the children when they are asleep and frightening them.'

I think he must have heard me, for Spooky was never again seen upstairs. Perhaps Janice's first reaction had alarmed him. He returned to his old haunts in the kitchen and all three of us saw him often. But never my husband.

A year after we moved in, our son Bradley arrived and about the same time we got a cat of our own. She was the runt of a litter and not expected to survive, but with some hand-feeding and lots of care, she grew into a lovely little black cat with white nose and paws. We called her Snagglepuss, after the tatty old cartoon lion.

One day the girls were playing in the field opposite the house where there were some ruined farmbuildings waiting for demolition, when they found the remains of a black cat. It appeared to have been squashed flat by some old machinery, although that may just have been the appearance it gave after decomposition.

The girls were very upset and wanted to give the cat a proper funeral. They dug a little hole and buried it wrapped in silver foil like a spacesuit, shed tears and said a little prayer.

'Maybe this was our Spooky,' I said, picking some wild flowers to put on the little grave. 'Perhaps he's at peace now and won't visit us again.'

He did, but less frequently. The family were growing up and when Linda left school and began working, she brought home a stray kitten, a pretty little tabby female which we immediately adopted and called Twinkletoes, Twinks for short. Perhaps Spooky was beginning to feel crowded out in our household, for Brad was a normal, noisy eight-year-old and we also had a red setter called Crackers, short for Meadway Caractacus.

Twinks settled down with Snagglepuss and Crackers and she grew into a beautiful cat with gentle, loving ways. Spooky was part of our family too, but only females saw him, human females – or so we thought.

Brad was fifteen and getting ready for bed one night. He was on his own in the house as we were out. Suddenly he heard the most terrible racket coming from the kitchen. He hurried downstairs and on opening the door was nearly knocked flat by Twinks, who leaped out, eyes wild and staring, her black striped fur standing on end.

She flew upstairs into his bedroom and hid under the chest of drawers. She refused to come out, her eyes transfixed with fright.

Brad searched the kitchen but could find nothing amiss. Puzzled, he went back to bed, Twinks still crouched in the furthermost corner under the chest of drawers.

'Mum,' he said the next morning. 'You should have seen Twinks last night. It's a wonder you didn't hear her! There was a terrible commotion in the kitchen. What a racket! I went down and Twinks shot out of the kitchen and up the stairs, breaking the sound barrier, I bet. She got under my chest of drawers and refused to come out. I wonder what on earth got into her?'

Twinks was sitting on the landing, peering down the stairs through the bannisters. She looked most unhappy. I took it that she needed to go out, having been indoors all night.

'Come on, Twinks,' I said encouragingly. 'Out into the garden.'

She did not move. I didn't have time for playing games so I went upstairs and picked her up to take outside. As I reached the hall, Twinks stiffened in my arms. I went towards the kitchen, intending to open the back door. It was too much for Twinks. With a screech, she leaped out of my arms and raced upstairs again. There was no way that cat was going into the kitchen. She was obviously terrified.

'For heaven's sake, Twinks,' I said. 'What's the matter with you?'

But I had a shrewd idea. Twinks had met Spooky.

I eventually got her out of the front door. From then on she refused to go into the kitchen. She avoided all contact with the floor, using every available piece of furniture to walk on. She insisted on being carried to bed by Brad. Her eyes always had a staring, frightened look and any slight movement or noise sent her into a panic with her fur standing on end.

During these months Spooky was never seen. Perhaps Twinks' reaction had alarmed him too. Twinks is a very pretty female cat and it could be he longed for some cat company.

Twinks has slowly recovered but still leaps off the floor as if it is hot coals. She sometimes ventures a little way into the kitchen. The encounter – or whatever it was – has changed her. She is extremely nervous.

Now Spooky seems to have gone forever and I often wonder if it was the presence of the girls in the house that brought him to us. Perhaps he once belonged to a little girl in the past.

Laura, our two-year-old grand-daughter often comes to visit us. She's a sweet little girl with long fair hair and big brown eyes. She loves pets and shows no fear, playing with Twinks for hours.

I was sitting in the living room, sewing, the sun streaming in through the window. We have half a dozen finches now and are hoping to build an aviary in the garden. Twinks is sunning herself in a warm spot.

Laura is wandering about, going into the kitchen to fetch some toys left on the floor.

'Nice pussy,' I hear her say. 'Nice pussy . . .'

I keep quite still, listening. I wonder if I am imagining things. But no, her childlike voice is cooing and coaxing something.

'Puss, puss, puss . . .' she is saying.

Perhaps she is playing with her toys, or talking to Twinks through the window. Perhaps our strange visitor is back. Maybe one day she will ask me about a big black cat sitting by the larder.

# Lucky's Story

She sat on the roof of a lorry sunning herself. She liked sitting up high, looking over the world, out of the way of the traffic, pedestrians and hotel guests.

Not that she had anything against hotel guests. They were part of her life and made a fuss of her. But there were so many of them and they were always changing.

These people were on something called a holiday. But since they ate, drank, talked and slept in much the same way as on ordinary days, Lucky could not see the difference.

Lucky dozed in the sunshine, dreaming dreams, chasing fleeing thoughts of other places that must be somewhere. She knew the world was a large place; that there were streets beyond this street, perhaps even a town beyond this town. It was all there waiting to be explored.

'One day you'll be carried away,' said the woman, lifting Lucky down from the cab roof. 'You have been warned.'

Lucky put her claws into the woman's short and shining black hair that hung like silk on each side of her face. Lucky called the woman Lindiladi. She liked her a lot. It was a mutual feeling.

'Come on, you soft thing,' said Lindiladi, carrying the cat indoors. 'I've enough to do without having to keep looking for you.'

Lucky was nine months old, having grown from an adorable white kitten with a black tail into a big and elegant cat with thick white fur and piercing green eyes. The top of her head was also black, and looked like a superior Frank Sinatra hair-piece. She had three pink pads on her paws and one black.

She was an affectionate cat. She knew that Lindiladi had rescued her from the RSPCA kennels, where animals disappeared if they were not claimed. But she was also very independent. Lucky had her own ideas about a lot of things, as did Lindiladi. That's why they got on so well. Lucky often jumped onto Lindiladi's knee and put her small nose right up to the woman's nose.

'You must have Eskimo blood,' said Lindiladi, amused, stroking the thick white fur.

Lucky did not understand about Eskimos but she liked to hear Lindiladi's soft laugh. The young woman was always working, so was her husband, whom Lucky called Peterman. Having a hotel meant a lot of work and no time to sit on the top of lorries, decided Lucky, as she escaped again into the fresh sea air. She stopped and sniffed; the pungent ozone was tantalisingly full of the smell of fish and seabirds and great oceans. Inland she sensed the mountains of the Lake District. She had not seen an ocean nor a mountain and she wondered why she knew these things.

It was Sunday, 21 April 1981, though Lucky did not know the date. Lindiladi put Lucky out on the doorstep. A scurry of wind whipped the woman's short hair against her face, and ruffled the cat's white fur like a flurry of snow.

'Now please be good,' said Lindiladi. 'I'm going to have a very busy day and I haven't time to waste hunting for you. Just stay around here.'

Lucky arched her back and swished her long black tail

and tipped the end over into a raised question mark. Of course she would be good. She was happy to oblige. It was too windy to go exploring. She would just take a look around the warehouse and see what was going on.

Near to the hotel was an antique dealer's shop and warehouse. Lucky considered this one of her favourite places to play. It had a particular smell all of its own, of houses long ago shut up and deserted, of cats and dogs and mice from the past. She sniffed at the clinging aromas of cigars and beeswax, dust and decay . . . it was all so interesting.

The owner did not seem to mind if Lucky padded around inspecting things. There was a cabinet-maker who was kind and gave her an occasional saucer of milk, but he was busy.

Lucky prowled around the antique furniture: Victorian tables and button-back tête-à-tête chairs; old pictures in heavy frames with cracked varnish; pots and bowls and old china. She liked all the different woods: rosewood, fruitwood, walnut, and ancient oak, knotted with veins of dried sap.

There was a lot of activity in the yard for a Sunday. They were packing a large container for delivery somewhere. Lucky danced across the yard chasing a woodshaving, pouncing on it as it caught against a railing. This was going to be a fun day.

It was late that night when Lindiladi finally finished work and went outside to call in Lucky.

'Lucky-lucky-lucky.' It was the familiar call sign. The woman peered into the darkness. No white ghost emerged sideways from the shadows, casual and offhand as if just passing by.

'Lucky-lucky-lucky.'

Lindiladi was getting worried. Lucky always came when she was called. There was such a lot of traffic in Morecambe, and Lucky was only just past kittenhood. She did not have all her road-sense yet.

'I can't find Lucky,' said Lindiladi.

'Probably having a night out,' said Peterman. 'Don't worry, she'll be back in the morning.'

But she wasn't. Lindiladi was up and out early before her duties at the hotel got into swing. She searched the streets and gardens, and then went across to the warehouse. She knew Lucky played there sometimes. It was 8 a.m. A large container stood in the yard, sealed and ready for collection.

'Have you seen my cat?' she asked the men. 'It's a white cat with black on its head and a black tail.'

They shook their heads. 'No, sorry . . .'

Lucky heard Lindiladi's voice, so she knew her beloved mistress was not far away. This was reassuring. The woman always found her. She would this time, too. Lucky yawned. This place was airless and making her drowsy. She had had a lovely time playing among the furniture, but now she was tired. She found some brown paper that was warm and just asking to be trampled into a bed.

A sudden jolt brought her sharply out of her sleep. Something very strange was happening.

The world was being tilted. There were harsh, unrecognisable noises. Bolts clanged. Then an engine was switched on. Lucky was confused . . . was she sitting on top of a lorry? Was this the moment to jump off into Lindiladi's arms?

But she couldn't jump. It was dark, and the darkness was full of shapes. There was no room to move. Lucky uncurled herself and miaowed loudly, but the engine revs drowned her call. A first tremor of fear ran along her spine, a prickle of alarm. This was all quite new and she was unsure how to react. She knew Lindiladi would be along for her soon. She miaowed again as she felt the movement growing within the darkness and the rattling and jolting throwing her from side to side.

Lucky crouched in her small place; two piercing green eyes searching for a solution. If only she could understand what was happening, then perhaps she could do something.

She tried to sleep again, but was unable to settle because of a growing thirst; then hunger. She prowled, squeezing herself small, sniffing and exploring. There was nothing. Pangs contracted her stomach and she miaowed helplessly, but no one heard.

Life was no longer the Morecambe sunshine and the smell of the sea in the air; it was a dark nightmare of unexpected jolts and endless vibration. Suddenly that movement stopped and, after a pause, a new sensation of swinging took its place. Lucky was thrown from her weak precarious balance, sickened as she lurched into the air; she heard the grinding and grunting of machinery: a throbbing, deafening power that grew into a crescendo of noise.

Lucky was terrified. She was convinced she was about to be devoured by some huge monster with gaping jaws. But it did not happen.

She was tortured by hunger and thirst. She sniffed dust, chewed paper, wood. Her limbs were racked with pain. Then as she lay, weak and exhausted, waiting to die, a trickle of condensation ran down the metal walls and her small tongue licked at the moisture as if it were nectar.

She followed the trickles everywhere, wiping them clean, licking and licking until her tongue was sore against the metal. But it came again, the life-saving water, replaced by some miracle that she did not question.

She was beyond all thought. Home had faded from her mind like a sweet, almost-forgotten dream. That was all so long ago, misty and unreal. Time meant nothing, stretching into a long dark tunnel of misery. She became weaker and weaker, life ebbing from her bright eyes.

But she clung to some intangible thread. She dragged herself to the trickles of moisture, her once-soft mouth now dry and cracked. A tiny flame of spirit still flickered in her heart, but it had almost gone out.

She could hardly stir herself any more. She was drifting into unconsciousness, but then somewhere it registered in her mind that all was quite still. The endless movement had stopped. She could almost hear the stillness and the silence. Perhaps this was death. Perhaps she had died.

Light streamed against her closed eyes. It blinded her. Yes, this was death.

Lucky hovered in the twilight zone between life and death. She was not aware of the strange voices, the rough but gentle hands that lifted her, the exclamations of astonishment.

'Hell. A dead cat!'

'Are you sure it's dead?'

'Yeah . . . chuck it away. Poor thing. Must have starved to death.'

'Let me look at it. I think it's still breathing very faintly.'

'Aw, leave it alone. It's a goner, Gary. We've got enough to do.'

'I'm taking it to the veterinary surgeon. It deserves a chance. It must have been in that damned container near on nine weeks.'

In the days that followed Lucky knew very little of what was happening to her, and she certainly knew nothing of the frantic searching and newspaper advertisements as Lindiladi combed the streets and pubs of Morecambe for her cat.

Lucky found herself in an amazing place. Everything smelt quite different; everything was so big. As she looked around her for the first time, it was as if an explosion had taken place and the outside of everything had disappeared, blown away. Where was she? And where was Lindiladi?

In her confusion she slipped in and out of consciousness, but gained on each encounter with this new world. She was drip-fed, injected, massaged, cared for as if she was worth a thousand dollars.

Her first sip of milk was an unforgettable moment. She almost fell out of the man's arms in her ecstasy. It tasted different, but it was milk all the same.

'Hold on,' laughed the man, Gary Fingleman. 'Not so fast. It won't go away, and there's lots more.'

When Lucky was strong enough, he no longer had to feed her by bottle. In three weeks she was able to stand and sip from a saucer. This new place had lovely food. Lucky ate well and sat in the blazing sunshine, dozing in the heat. She spent her convalescence with the man she called Fingleman. Sometimes she sat on his knee and purred, but he was still a stranger.

Lucky had always thought there must be somewhere beyond Morecambe, and perhaps this was it. People spoke differently; the cars and lorries were hugely terrifying; Fingleman had a refrigerator the size of a small room.

She liked the climate, but she missed the birds. And she missed Lindiladi. Sometimes she asked Fingleman where her beloved mistress was, but he did not understand and would just scratch behind her ear and grin, and pour her some milk from a carton.

It was August and almost unbearably hot. Lucky sat on the man's lap while he drank a cold beer. The telephone rang.

'Is that Gary Fingleman of Houston, Texas?' asked a woman. 'I know this sounds very strange, but I think you've got my cat.'

'Oh?' he drawled. 'Why should you think I've got your cat?'

'Last April I lost my cat Lucky. She just disappeared. I've just met a man who works in the antique shop opposite where we used to live, and he said an American came into the shop to buy some more antiques and said thanks for the extra package. There was a cat in his last delivery, half-dead. A big black and white cat with a black tail . . .' Lindiladi got the words out in one big rush.

'Sealand's sitting on my knee now,' said Fingleman, stroking Lucky's head. 'But how do I know she's your cat?'

'Look under her paws. She has three pink pads, but her right paw pad is black.'

Lucky suddenly found herself upended on Fingleman's lap, her paws waving in the air. He grasped them gently but firmly. She wriggled frantically. Her paws were very ticklish.

'Three pink paws and one black. Then this must be your Lucky, and lucky she is to have survived the journey to Houston. Four thousand and five hundred miles, lady.'

Lucky did not hear Lindiladi weeping at the other end of the telephone, but she knew something was happening. Her fur crept and she ran under a table, nightmare memories of the container sweeping back.

'She was just bones when I found her, but she's putting on a little weight now.'

'But how on earth do I get her home from America?' Lindiladi asked, dazed.

'We'll see she goes home in style,' said Fingleman, knowing that he must let the cat go.

It was the media that got Lucky home. She had taken herself to America, but it was the combined forces of newspapers, television, local radio and British Caledonian who reunited Lindiladi and Lucky.

While Lucky grew stronger in the Texas sunshine, the wheels went round, forms were filled in, people wrote things, took her photograph.

She was used to the veterinary surgeon and his needles, and she thought no more than a fractional irritation when yet one more injection went into her flesh. Fingleman was holding her in a firm grasp, and looking at her with a strange, fond look. The last thing she saw before sleep overtook her was his kind, strong face.

She knew nothing of the transfer to Houston airport or the long flight. Her limbs twitched in a deep slumber; dreams tumbled through her mind: the wild, wet rain and the smell of the sea . . . the dry baking heat of the past few weeks . . . the terror of the remembrance of that other place, small, dark, endlessly jolting her towards death.

Someone was carrying her into a small room. Lucky yawned. She was dry and sleepy, barely awake, her mouth like sawdust. With a tremendous effort she opened one eye . . . Lindiladi was coming into the room with another young woman holding her arm.

'Lucky . . . Lucky . . . my darling Lucky.' Lindiladi held her for a few brief moments, tears pouring down her cheeks. Of course it was her Lucky, a very thin and skinny Lucky, but still her beautiful cat.

Lucky tried to purr, but sleep overcame her, washing her back into dreams. Her last thought was where had Lindiladi been all this time? It was all . . . yawn . . . very strange.

At the quarantine kennels in Blackpool Lucky had her first English press conference. A lot of people looking at her and expecting something.

'How do you know it's your cat?' snapped the reporters. 'How can you be sure?'

Lindiladi was asked the same thing over and over again, even though she had brought photographs taken of Lucky before she went to America.

'You can see it's her,' said Lindiladi. 'Look, the same black tail, the black head, one black paw pad.'

A man came into the back of the room, unseen.

'Lucky-lucky-lucky,' he called.

Lucky looked up instantly and turned her head towards the voice. It was an echo from the past. Her call-sign. It broke through the long nightmare and the unreal days that had followed in that foreign land. It brought back sunning on top of lorries, the hotel guests, the antique shop. She made as if to spring towards

Peterman, a cry of freedom caught in her throat as she thought again of smelling the ozone and hearing the shrieks of the seabirds.

'You see . . .' said Lindiladi triumphantly. 'She *is* my Lucky. That's proof.'

Lucky waited out the long, boring six months' quarantine with commendable patience, reassured because Lindiladi came to see her every weekend. Lindiladi brought tinned salmon and cartons of cream, which Lucky ate because they were gifts of love and not because she was hungry.

They grew to know each other again, and one day Lucky jumped onto the woman's lap and put a small pink nose up to touch Lindiladi's nose.

'My little Eskimo,' said the woman.

Nearly a year passed before Lucky at long last returned home. She found that they now all lived in a shop. She took the new changes very quietly, sitting sometimes with a remoteness that was impenetrable.

At first Lucky would only sleep on Lindiladi's bed. The nightmares came often and her body shook. Then she would wake suddenly, sit up and look around at the sleeping figure and the dark hair on the pillow, reassuring herself that she was home; she was safe.

Sometimes Lucky gnawed thoughtfully on a piece of wood, the taste of timber still lingering in her mouth. She did not wander far. She had done her travelling.

Then, amid great activity, the shop was sold and another hotel bought. A popular feature of the new hotel is Lucky's bar.

Lucky sits on the bar counter, Persil white, poised and elegant, her press cuttings and photographs on the wall behind her. She wonders about all the fuss. Why people want to have their photograph taken with the cat who went to America on her own. Anyone knows it's just the next place on.

# Churchill's Cats

Jock II sat at the foot of the stairs patiently waiting for the doors to open. It was then that the visitors would begin to arrive. He did not know why there were often so many people about, but few failed to give him a friendly pat.

At other times the Elizabethan manor house was empty and Jock II padded silently through the deserted rooms like another of its many ghosts. He saw nothing but he sensed them. The vibrations were frequently so strong that Jock would perk an ear, his whiskers twitching, alert for the merest whisper from the past.

'What a cute cat! Isn't he cute? My goodness, and did you say Winston Churchill had a cat just like this one?' enthused the American woman, eyes bright with curiosity for every detail of the great man.

'Exactly like this one, a beautiful marmalade cat. Jock was Mr Churchill's favourite cat,' said the guide. 'And they always fed him just here in the kitchen.'

'You don't say? Fancy that. Can we see Jock being fed? You know, like it was the same cat?'

Jock II moved into position. This was what he had been waiting for. He was programmed for it. The visitors, especially the Americans, loved seeing him being fed. Obediently he ate his breakfast from a dish put on the same spot as his predecessor's dish. He re-enacted the past with enthusiasm for a spellbound audience.

Time had stopped still in the house; the library, drawing and dining rooms, and the study were left exactly as they had been in October 1964.

Jock wandered out into the garden and sat on the paving stones to wash his face. It was a large garden, sweeping down to a small valley and rising to a wooded ridge. The sun glinted serenely on the surface of the lake, barely disturbing the ducks and swans that glided between the rushes.

Jock II knew he had been chosen because of his resemblance to Jock I. It gave him the strangest feeling as if he were acting in a play, taking the part of this earlier cat, acting out a previous life.

He did not know this other Jock, had never met him. He knew there had been lots of cats . . . Nelson, Smoky, Gabrielle, Tango . . . he had heard them spoken of many times. The great man had loved cats.

Jock II yawned delicately in the dappled sunlight and stretched himself. The visitors milled about the garden, admiring the views, the rose gardens that had been planted for Clementine, the ornamental pools, the brick walls. The other cats came and gathered around him silently, contemplating his sleeping marmalade form.

'I was here when he built that wall,' said the tabby at last. 'I used to sit and watch him. Slap, slap. He really liked bricklaying. It was a way of relaxing. Slap, slap. And he was good at it. He could lay a brick a minute. He used to tell me about wars in many distant places as he took a trowelful of cement and slapped it on a brick. Slap, slap. I think I was his favourite cat. You could say I helped him build that wall.'

'I knew him during a war,' said Nelson, a short-haired black cat. 'I lived in the war rooms in London. A marine gave me to him. He was very pleased. It was pretty spooky living underground. Everything was grey or khaki, and tin hats and gas masks lined the walls. I did my bit for the war effort; I caught mice down there. I was

411

only allowed out when the all-clear sounded, then I'd race across the road to St James's Park to chase the ducks!'

The cats yawned, scratched, and changed places by leaping over the slumbering cat.

'He had me evacuated,' Nelson went on. 'Perhaps I was his favourite . . .'

'Evacuated? Evacuated? What does that mean?'

'It was during the height of the blitz. Those sirens used to make my fur stand on end. There was a very bad raid one night; he got all the staff into the shelters. A bomb dropped and the kitchen of Number Ten was extensively damaged, so he had me sent into the country, where it was safer. I was evacuated to Chequers. He knew I was very frightened with all the explosions and bombs dropping. But it meant I didn't see him so often. He could only come some weekends and then I would sit on his knee and let him stroke me. He was very busy with the war.'

A beautiful long-haired black Persian sniffed and swished her tail imperiously. 'Poof . . . I was in the secret Cabinet war rooms in Whitehall too. I didn't let people stroke me! Oh no, except perhaps one lady who let me sit on her desk. I bit people. I laddered stockings – and they were very precious in the war, you know. You could say I was unpopular, but it didn't bother me. I had my own war going. But he liked me; he liked a cat with spirit.' Smoky sniffed again, her eyes gleaming with memories of the mischief she had got up to among all those telephones and maps and charts.

'But I don't think I ever bit him,' she growled knowingly.

The cats fell silent, thinking of the man in his siren suit, his fat cigar that puffed smoke into their eyes, the big coat with the astrakhan collar. They were unaware of another group of cats coming to join them. They approached unheralded, hesitant, wary, ears flattened . . .

There was one cat, half wild, not sure how to

communicate with these sophisticated, cosseted and domesticated felines. He dodged and danced about a little, remembering how he had to escape the hooves of horses trotting on the cobblestones.

'He was six years old when he made friends with me,' he said at last. 'I lived in the stables at Blenheim Palace and he was always there looking at the horses. I remember one day in April we were playing in the grounds. We were playing wars. He had been building encampments and pitched an umbrella for a tent. I didn't understand the game but it was great fun and the umbrella kept rolling about in the wind. I know I was not his favourite cat, but I may have been his first.'

A pair of thin grey tabbies twisted themselves around each other, grinning wickedly, ears pricked with enjoyment.

'Oh brother, he liked horses all right. He was fourteen when he and his brother Jack came to Banstead Manor, near Newmarket, for a holiday. They both went straight down to the stables, even though there was four inches of snow. He didn't know there were two of us, and we played such tricks on him!'

'Leaping out.'

'Rushing round corners.'

'Climbing over stalls.'

'When he discovered there were two of us, he laughed and laughed. It was a good trick.'

'And he had a good holiday, shooting rabbits and rats and skating on the pond.'

The cat from Cairo sat apart, pale and dignified. He had lived in the barracks of the 21st Lancers. The cavalry charge at the battle of Omdurman on 2 September 1898 had been a dreadful, gory day. Many of the cat's soldier friends did not come back, but one special young friend returned, weary, battle-stained, but triumphant.

'I was under fire all day and rode through the charge,' the man wrote to his mother by candlelight. 'Nothing touched me.'

The cat kept him company as he began to write his second book, an account of the whole Sudan campaign called *The River War*. He wrote all day, every day, and far into the night till his hands were seized by cramp. He would rub the pain out of his fingers, stroke the cat's soft fur, then go back to his writing.

The cat from Cairo wondered whether to tell the others these things and how well he knew the man as a young fearless soldier, but he did not think they would understand. It was all such a long time ago. So he said nothing.

Out of the shadows slunk a timid greyish-brown creature. It was half-starved, with ribs sticking out. Yet something kept its valiant spirit burning.

'He hated every minute of being imprisoned,' the cat hissed as he crawled along the ground. 'It was in Pretoria in 1899. He was caught by the Boers after an armoured train ambush. The prison was an awful place. He tried to make friends with me to take his mind off being a prisoner. I tried to catch the vermin but I was so weak. He gave me some of his food. I'll never forget that. When he escaped over the prison wall, I lost my friend. I cried for days and days.'

The other cats looked uncomfortable. They did not know anything about prisons and ambushes. It was out of their experience.

'He was never my friend,' howled a feral cat from Venice. 'I spat and hissed at him. But he only had eyes for his young wife as they glided past the palazzos in a gondola. He was on his honeymoon and they looked so round and happŷ, whereas we were starving and miserable, roaming the alleyways and bridges. What could I do but hiss? He didn't hear.'

Jock II stirred in his sleep as if a cold wind had blown through his fur, ruffling the russet layers on his back. His paws twitched in combat with some dream adversary, neither losing nor winning.

Gabrielle detached herself from the group, an elegant

cream and brown Siamese with slanting blue eyes. She surveyed the gathering with a haughty disdain.

'It was none of you. I was his favourite, of course. I was her cat, their pet. I didn't have to work for my living, or steal or fight. Pedigree cats don't work. My life was one of luxury and ease. I'm sure he had the fishpond put in just for me.'

'You were the destructive one,' said Tango, a long-tailed tangerine-coloured cat with amber eyes full of wisdom. 'You were the one that clawed the Coronation chairs.'

'I did not,' Gabrielle denied huffily.

'The claw marks are still there,' said Tango.

'He wrote home sending tender love to Clemmie and his little kittens, and he thought the Prince of Wales should fall in love with a pretty cat,' said Gabrielle, preening herself.

'He didn't mean you,' said Tango. 'He sometimes called his children the kittens, and his concern for the young future king is beyond your comprehension. He thought that young man too thin and too spartan.'

'You were jealous of my position in the household.' Gabrielle arched her back. 'Just because you are in a silly painting. Who'd want to be in a painting? I couldn't be bothered to keep still. No one could paint my unique colouring.'

'Sir William Nicholson put me in the painting because I didn't mind posing,' said Tango. 'I just curled up and went to sleep. It was their Silver Wedding picture so I knew it was something very special. Perhaps that makes me their favourite cat,' he added, knowing it would annoy Gabrielle.

'It certainly does not,' said Gabrielle, reacting furiously. 'You look like a bowl of fruit in that painting. You look like a bowl of oranges.'

Tango did not bother to argue with her. It did not worry him what Gabrielle said. He curled himself into a comfortable position and went back to sleep. He knew only too well how much he had been loved by the master.

'Tango? Tango . . .' he could hear the gruff voice calling him now. If only he knew where to go, he would follow. They had always been so happy together, had such fun. There was no need to wonder about favourites. It did not matter.

'But what about me?' asked a pert little tabby. 'After all, I was the only one he advertised for. He actually put a card in the window for me.'

'Heaven preserve us,' groaned Gabrielle. 'We've all heard this a dozen times before. Do we have to hear it again?'

'Yes, you do,' the tabby insisted. 'It's my story and it's a good story. I had been, well . . . a little naughty – '

'Very naughty,' Tango yawned.

'And I was put out—'

'After a good hard slap with a rolled-up newspaper,' said Gabrielle.

'So I ran away. Any self-respecting cat would run away after being slapped with a rolled-up newspaper. Sarah was seventeen then and she told her father that I had run away. He was very worried about me and he told his secretary that if she wished she could put a card in the widow saying: "IF CAT CARES TO COME HOME, ALL IS FORGIVEN." He said it in fun, of course, but wasn't it nice that he should think of me?'

The tabby pranced around, still hugely amused by the whole idea. But then other memories returned and her dancing stopped.

'And did you go back?' asked one of the strange foreign cats who had not heard the story before.

'Not until ten days later. They searched and searched everywhere for me. They found me with a snare round my neck. It was horrible. Everyone was so upset.'

An uneasiness fell upon the group of cats. They all knew about snares and traps and the cruel things that could happen to an unwary cat, even to a cat from the best of circumstances.

'But you were found and rescued,' said a magnificent marmalade cat, speaking for the first time. 'Think how lucky you were. He really liked cats. And he liked some dogs. Monty's two dogs, Rommel and Hitler, were friendly little things, despite their names. And remember how he drew sketches of little cats and pigs at the end of his letters to Clementine to amuse her?'

'Those pigs!'

'Pigs . . . urgh,' the cats chorused. 'How could he?'

'And his special name for her was Cat, not always Clemmie.'

Jock II nearly awoke with a start. He stared at the newcomer. He was seeing a mirror image of himself. A big marmalade cat with the same markings and proud head. It was uncanny. Surely this must be the original Jock, the most famous cat of all.

'I must have spent more time with him than the rest of you put together,' mused the first Jock. 'He had always been so busy with travelling and wars. But he was getting old and I used to sit on his knee in his wheelchair and they would wheel us around the gardens together. He slept a lot and I was allowed to stay on his bed. I knew he took comfort from me, for often in his sleep his hand would stray to my head and he would stroke me gently. I was with him, right to the very end.'

A hush fell like a shroud upon the cats. They stayed still and silent. Only Gabrielle arched her back and lashed her rope of a tail.

'I don't believe you,' she spat.

'Does it really matter whether you believe it,' said Tango wisely. 'Does it matter who was actually there, as long as someone was with him?'

'And I should know, shouldn't I?' Jock sighed. 'It was such a long time ago. And I grieved for him. I was sad for weeks and weeks, looking for him everywhere.'

Up the long sweep of the lawn a small black cat came

417

scampering with a rolling gait as if the earth was moving beneath his paws.

'Am I too late? Do you remember me?' he panted. 'I had my photograph taken with him for the newpapers! He was on board the Navy ship, the *Prince of Wales*, to meet President Roosevelt. It was in August 1941, during the Second World War. They had their photographs taken for all the newspapers; then as they were moving across the deck together, he stopped to stroke me. He had seen me among all those important people! A photographer snapped the shot. Me, the ship's cat! I was famous, too. A lucky black cat, he said. Perhaps I was lucky for him.'

Jock II growled in his sleep. He didn't like his dreams being disturbed. There were more cats invading the gardens, big ones, small ones, black, tabby, tortoiseshell, grey, brown, long-haired, short-haired . . . cats from so many countries, from all over the world, from an English garden party, from his constituency in Dundee, from Sidney Street, from nights of the blitz, from the banks of the Nile . . .

Suddenly Jock II could stand it no longer. He leaped to his feet and with a great bound he sent the cats scattering in all directions. Some ran into bushes, some shot up trees, some vanished straight into the lake. He chased them out of the garden, back into the mists from which they had come.

'Good heavens,' said a visitor watching from the bow-window of the study. 'Whatever's gotten into that cat?'

One of the lady guides came to the door with his supper dish. 'Jock, Jock,' she called. 'It's supper time.'

Jock II stopped in his wild tracks; the garden was empty now. He sniffed the clean Kent air. Then he slicked down his tawny fur and regained his composure before returning to the house for his supper-time audience. Chartwell was back to normal.

# The Highland Hunter

Towser lived in the still house. It is normally very warm, but in deference to her great age, she also has her own electric fire on twenty-four hours a day.

She emerges from her bed located under a big onion-shaped copper still and stretches herself, shaking out her magnificent tortoiseshell fur. She is a long-haired cat with orange and black fur, tabby markings on a sweet, gentle face, and a white bib. Her long white whiskers twitch in anticipation of breakfast.

She is totally unaware of her champion status and that her photograph is on the cover of the *Guinness Book of Records* for 1984 in full colour – and that it also appears on the back cover of this book!

Her life is spent prowling the dark wooden halls of Glenturret and the forested hills that surround the ancient distillery. Breathing in the whisky-laden fumes is as natural to Towser as inhaling the crisp Highland mountain air that blows down the slopes.

The huddle of two-hundred-year-old whitewashed stone buildings has been her home since kittenhood. She was born behind a wash charger, a big warm container that was the perfect hiding place for the four kittens. The stillman had been hunting for Colette, the mother cat, when he found the kittens.

As soon as she was big enough, Towser began exploring the rambling distillery, up and down stairs and steps, along the many passageways. Once she found a room full of grain that was nice and warm, but then she could not find her way back to her mother. She was completely lost. The same stillman found her.

'Are you lost, wee kitten?' he said, scooping her up in his big hand.

Transforming the barley into a smooth Scotch malt is a long slow process; it ages for fifteen years in the huge oak casks. The rich smells from the distillery promise a feast of top-quality barley for families of woodmice descending in droves from the heathery hills.

It was not long before the kitten caught a mouse bigger than herself. This mouse changed the direction of Towser's life.

'We need a really good mouser to help Colette,' said the stillman. 'We ought to keep you.'

So Towser followed in the pawprints of her ancestors, who had patrolled Glenturret since 1775 when the distilling of whisky began on the banks of the tumbling River Turret, near the Scottish market town of Crieff.

She would not dream of missing her daily dram of whisky. It was every drop as good as a saucer of milk. She loved the taste, curling her tongue round the last sip of vein-tingling golden liquid. It was always a fifteen-year-old malt, but no one thought it wasted on a cat. Towser earned her dram.

Towser thought it was a day like any other day. She sniffed the fumes of the 130-degree-proof malt and it went straight to her head. She prowled her domain in the sheds storing barley, purring and growling softly through her sharp teeth. There would be breakfast waiting for her in the canteen, but first she had work to do.

It was all too easy, almost like swatting flies. She sat as still as a statue until her long white whiskers signalled a sighting. She pounced. Victory! A mouse dangled lifelessly from her jaws. She went on a triumphal parade with her trophy, growling at anyone who might dare to take her catch away.

Charlie got out a sheet of paper and a pencil.

'One,' he said, marking it on that day's log.

For a number of weeks they had been keeping track of Towser's mousing. It began as a joke, but as the tally rose, the distillery workers realised that they had a potential champion under their roof. Towser was catching an average of three a day; but she also caught pheasants and baby rabbits when she escaped from the distillery and raced to the dark roots and wet mosses of the woods, her shaggy coat flying in the bitter Perthshire wind.

There was a workforce of six at this time so there was always someone who had an eye on Towser's activities. She pounced. Again!

'Another mouse. Aye, chalk it up, lad.'

Towser crouched in the shadows of the pipes carrying water, steam and whisky. She knew there was a nest somewhere near but it was well hidden. She decided to try a little subterfuge. She climbed up onto the pipes to take a nonchalant walk. It was a tricky balancing act, not made easy by the alcoholic fumes fuzzing her keen eyesight. But she was a sure-footed alcoholic, practically weaned on whisky.

She dived off the pipe, fast as an arrow, silent as a ghost; her paws cupped the mouse delicately in a death thrust.

'Another one. How many's that now?'

'Three. And all before breakfast.'

It was not long before word went round the distillery that Towser was onto a winning streak. The tally rose steadily . . . four, five, six.

'This is amazing,' said Peter Fairlie, the managing director as he made his morning round of the distillery. 'We've got a real champion here. It must be the fumes that keep her fit for the job!'

For Towser was now no young cat in her prime. She was already twenty years old and had been catching the Glenturret mice all her life.

She became aware that she was being watched. Visitors were nothing unusual for more than 70,000 people a year toured the distillery, enjoying the occasional glimpse of her orange and black fur. Towser was happy to be the centre of attraction, stroked by her admirers. Sometimes she sat in the picnic area, watching the arrival of the cars and coaches, unashamedly cadging treats from the picnickers.

This was different. She was being shadowed. The stalker was being stalked and it was an uncanny feeling. She peered over her shoulder. A pair of jeans were not far behind. She blinked in case it was the whisky. But no, she was being followed by a pair of jeans.

She was intrigued, mystified. She took them on a fair old dance, behind casks, under pipes and through gullies, clambering over mountainous sacks of barley, through fanlights, over roofs, and into every dark corner. Her yellow eyes brightened with a gleam of mischief. It was something to do with hunting, she felt sure.

She pounced on an idle dormouse. Wham! She hid her catch neatly under a pile of sacks. That was one they weren't going to know about.

The day's happy hunting continued. The blue jeans, obviously exhausted, were replaced by a pair of white sneakers. She took them on another wild-mouse chase. It was such fun. She was almost giddy with excitement. She was chasing around the distillery, fur rumpled, her long plume of a tail carried high like a flowing banner.

'That cat's tiddly,' said Mr Fairlie, as if it was the most normal thing in the world.

Towser came back, a little wobbly on her feet, growling a low throaty sound, another victim in her jaws. She laid it at his feet as a gift.

'Thank you, Towser,' he said.

'Fourteen,' shouted Hugh triumphantly. 'Fourteen mice in one day! It's a record.'

Towser grinned smugly. Little did they know.

She took the next day off. All morning she lay draped dangerously over a pipe, letting the frail sun warm her fur. Later she ran across the fields that rose from the cluster of buildings, through the trees and up rolling heather-clad hills into the Highland mountains, a bird's eye view above the still loch and swiftly running River Earn.

Her ancestors had lived wild in the hills, she knew that. The knowledge pounded through her veins. She ran like the great cat she was, shaggy coat flying, big paws hardly touching the ground, every muscle moving in perfect coordination.

Down below in the distillery, the workforce had their calculators out. They reckoned that Towser caught an average of three mice a day. It did not sound much as a bare fact. But some bright spark was multiplying that by her age and came up with the astounding total kill to date of over 22,500 mice.

'Twenty-two thousand mice? You must be daft.'

'Work it out for yourself. She's twenty years old. Multiply the number of days she's lived by three, and that's the answer. I reckon she's the world's top mouser.'

The world's top mouser yawned and blinked against the mountain wind and thought about a nice saucer of her favourite condensed milk. She did not know that they were contacting the editors of the *Guinness Book of Records*; that a new cottage industry was about to spring up, with tee-shirts and mugs, life-size posters and post-cards of the champion, newspaper interviews, TV appearances and a fan club.

She wandered down to the distillery. She wanted her wee dram, and the warmth of her electric fire on her back. She was beginning to feel her age.

Towser was billed as the greatest mouser on record in the *Guinness Book of Records*, and the 1984 *Guinness Book of Pet Records* acknowledged a total kill of 23,000 mice. Journalists came to get the inside story. Often she kept them waiting; then brought them a mouse as a peace offering.

In April 1985, Towser indirectly received a letter from the Queen. They had something in common. They shared the same birthday, 21 April.

The Queen's Private Secretary wrote from Windsor Castle saying that the Queen hoped that Towser, like herself, would celebrate the day with all possible happiness.

Photographers came to take birthday pictures of the grand old lady – Towser, not the Queen. Towser loved every minute of it. She was used to this admiration. And for a twenty-two-year-old (154 cat years), she was keeping her good looks. Her coat was still beautiful and fluffy, her prowess at hunting unimpaired.

But something was amiss. Earlier that day she had fallen off a steam pipe which she had walked safely every day of her life. She had almost fallen into a wash-back container. Hanging on by her claws, she managed to pull herself up. It was not the alcoholic fumes, for she was nowhere near the stills, and she had not had her daily dram. She was not in the least pie-eyed.

Towser righted herself and shook out her fur, pretending that she had intended to jump anyway. No one had noticed. She was aware of something wrong with one eye. Puzzled and blinking, she began washing carefully with a curved paw, hoping to wash away the irritating blur. Eventually she gave up. Nothing seemed to make any difference. Perhaps she would sleep, and when she woke up the mist would have gone.

Birthday cards arrived from as far away as America, Canada, Australia and New Zealand. That evening there was going to be a party in her honour. She wouldn't miss a party. She would keep awake for that.

It was a grand party, but Towser got a little carried away with high spirits. She jumped out onto a window ledge and along a gutter, then climbed the sloping roof to the top of the distillery. It was an exciting, mad birthday gesture. She was twenty-two years old! She wanted to admire the sky and glory in the magnificent Highland panorama.

It was very exhilarating, the wind streaming through her long fur, until Towser decided it was time to come down. It seemed far steeper going down than it had coming up. Somehow the roof had changed. Towser found she could not get down. Apprehensively she looked around for another route and sniffed the air. She could smell thunder in the distance, and already grey clouds were gathering overhead. There was going to be a storm.

She panicked and began yowling, loudly and insistently. People came out into the yard, talking and pointing upwards to where Towser was perched on the roof, silhouetted against the sky.

She heard the scrape of a ladder and a familiar voice saying: 'Okay, Towser. It's all right. I'll get you down in a minute.'

It was her old friend, the stillman. He clambered over the roof, put Towser inside his warm tweed jacket and took her safely back to earth.

Some days later she was patrolling her territory when suddenly she saw a mouse. She was after it like lightning, across the still house, out into the yard. A van from the *Strathearn Herald* swerved wildly and slammed on emergency brakes. The driver got out, shaking, while Towser continued in hot pursuit of her prey.

'I nearly ran over your ch–champion c–cat,' stammered Peter MacSporran, the driver. 'Why doesn't she look where's she going?'

'Because she's almost blind in her left eye,' said Peter Fairlie coming out of his office. 'When she runs from right to left she can't see what's coming. But she doesn't seem to know it, and keeps on mouse hunting with as much vigour as ever.'

'And I nearly ran her over!' Peter MacSporran had had a terrible fright.

'Come and have a wee dram to settle your nerves,' said Mr Fairlie.

Towser pounced on the cheeky mouse and held it down with one big furry paw. That was mouse number twenty-five thousand, two hundred and seventy-seven. They weren't the only ones who could count.

# Top Cat

There was such a lot of fuss about this thing called Christmas. Streamers he mustn't play with; presents he mustn't sit on; decorations he mustn't chew . . . Sammy was fed up with Christmas before it had even begun. He was used to being the focus of attention and now Christmas – whatever that was – was uppermost in everyone's thoughts. Was it another cat? If so, Sammy wasn't having it. There was only room for one cat in his household.

Sammy sat watching the driving rain from the comfort of a windowsill. The weather was appalling, even for December. He decided not to go out until it was a sheer necessity. If he was bored he would go and play with Danny's toys or stalk that spider that lurked on the landing. He might just have a little snooze.

It was dark when he awoke. Time for a stretch, a quick wash-and-brush-up of his long, elegant ginger and white fur, a flick of his long whiskers and he was ready for supper.

'I haven't had time to cook your coley,' said Christine. 'You'll have to make do with a tin. I've been so busy Christmas shopping.'

After his supper, Sammy wandered outside. The family were all preoccupied with what they were going to

427

buy for Christmas, make for Christmas, do for Christmas. This Christmas person must be very important, Sammy thought.

His thoughts were still bobbing around when he noticed that he had wandered further afield than normal. The houses were all strange ones and the streets smelt different. He circled warily, trying to pick up a familiar scent.

Suddenly a pair of yellow eyes confronted him; then bared, snarling long teeth. Sammy leapt back, adrenalin pumping. Another deep growl from behind froze him in his tracks. Sammy hissed, fluffing out his fur to make himself look twice his size, tail thrashing.

But Sammy wasn't fooling anyone. He was still only cat-size, and the dogs were big, dirty and hungry. They knew they had him cornered and they crouched, ready to attack, sharp claws rasping on the slippery paving stones.

Sammy made an instant decision. He fled. He cleared the nearest dog with one bound and ran for his life. He did not know which direction to take. The terrifying chase took him further and further from home. It was alien country. The dogs yelped at his heels, getting closer as their longer strides narrowed the gap.

Sammy found himself in a big yard. He was panting and tiring rapidly. He knew he couldn't go on much longer; he must find some refuge, preferably a very tall tree. Something huge was ahead of him. He had never seen anything so tall and dark and menacing. It soared into the sky like a tree, but it was a giant, branchless tree, its tip lost in the rain-laden clouds. But there was not a leaf in sight.

There was no time to wonder what it was; the dogs were almost upon him. Sammy took a flying leap onto the lowest rung of a ladder which was bolted to the side of the tall structure. His claws slipped on the wet rungs, but with supercat strength born of sheer terror, he hauled himself up out of reach of the snapping jaws.

It was a narrow, slippery perch, even for a cat. He

climbed a little higher, hoping for something rather more substantial. There seemed to be more than one ladder, each twice as long as a man, overlapping, and where they overlapped the double width of rung gave Sammy more of a pawhold. He settled on a double rung for the night, the rain pelting him from all angles, stinging his eyes. He tucked his nose miserably into his wet fur and wished he were at home. He felt the first pangs of hunger in his stomach.

The dogs were milling around below, sniffing, snarling, confident that their prey would have to come down. They barked noisily in the mill yard, intoxicated by all the new smells, eventually finding places to shelter from the cold and rain.

Sammy crouched, motionless, thinking about this massive, inhospitable, silent tree. No leaves, no frisky birds, no nice rustling sound; just an impassive giant planted in the ground by some super being from the sky.

He sniffed. He smelt soot and brickwork. Bricks meant a wall. It was a tall round wall. How strange. It was certainly not a house. He had never seen a house that had no windows or doors and reached up into the clouds. But at least the bricks accounted for the lack of branches and leaves. Soothed by that little bit of reasoning, Sammy closed his eyes again and tried to sleep.

It was a bitterly cold December night; when dawn eventually crept unwillingly into the frosty sky, Sammy's wet fur was stiff with ice-white crystals. His limbs ached with coldness. He stretched himself unsteadily, longing for a good leap and run across gardens, hedges and railings.

He saw the dark shapes below of the dogs lolling in sleep, yawning and scratching. There was nowhere to go but up.

Perhaps there might be somewhere, up there. His heart lightened and this encouraging thought spurred his climb. The round wall looked as if it went straight into the sky, but it might not. He passed a derelict bird's nest pathetically stuffed into a crevice. Nothing in it but a few old spiders. He didn't eat spiders; not yet anyway.

Some schoolchildren saw him first. They shouted and waved.

'Puss, puss, puss.'

'Poor thing.'

'C'mon, superman.'

Sammy took no notice. He was not feeling sociable. He climbed a few rungs higher.

The mill yard was coming to life. Workers began to arrive by car, on motorbikes, bicycles, on foot. By now Sammy was a ginger blob half way up the chimney. He was very frightened by all the noise and commotion below. He was hungry. He licked some of the moisture off his fur, longing for a saucer of warm milk.

He peered down. It was a very long way. People were blurs of muddy colours, all heads. He couldn't see the dogs; perhaps he would take a chance and go down. He turned stiffly, each paw placed with care on the cold, rusty rung. It was breakfast time and he had missed a late-night supper.

It was then that Sammy discovered he couldn't go down. It was nothing like a tree, he couldn't leap from branch to branch in a zig-zag route downwards. He squinted at the rung below, trying to puzzle out how to reach it. The blood rushed to his head and his vision blurred. It was impossible. The rung was flat, almost non-existent. He was stuck.

Fear raced through him. What could he do? He leaped a few rungs higher in his panic, vaguely aware of a wave of sound from the ground.

'Look! That's a cat! Half way up the chimney.'

'Cripes. It's stuck all right.'

'Call the fire brigade.'

'How about the RSPCA? They'd know what to do.'

'What about the steeplejack. You know . . .?'

'Fred.'

'That's him. The one that's on the telly. Fred Dibnah.'

Fred Dibnah was a television celebrity, made famous by his steepleclimbing programmes. Sammy knew nothing about all that; he knew nothing about the news cameras arriving, being flashed skywards and popping off photos of him; he knew nothing of the television lens being focused on the chimney and the commentator interviewing anyone who would say anything.

'It gave me a real fright,' said a girl, bright magenta hair gelled out to porcupine spikes. 'I looked up the chimney and I said to my friend: "Look, Grace, there's a cat up the chimney." That's what I said. I don't know how it got there."

'Have you any idea how it got up there?' asked the reporter, keeping to his basic line of questions. He whipped the microphone back to her glossy lips.

'No,' she said, shaking her head carefully. 'It climbed up there, I suppose.'

Luckily Fred Dibnah was already at the mill, preparing to start some scheduled chimney-repair work. He collected his tackle and strode through the crowd at the foot of the chimney. He could just make out a gingery blob about a hundred feet up the steel ladders, two thirds of its height.

'I hope it doesn't bite,' he said jovially, strapping on his harness.

By now Sammy was terrified out of his wits. He was not going to let anyone within scratching distance. Instinct made him take the only action left to him . . . to climb higher and higher, rung by rung. The wind combed fiercely through his fur; the ladder creaked and seemed to sway.

Suddenly there was no more ladder to climb. Sammy was amazed. He was at the top. It was another strange place. Cautiously he crawled onto a narrow ledge, stretching his stiff legs in their first real movement for hours. He inched himself slowly round the ledge, blinking against the gale that howled like banshees around the top of the chimney.

He was hardly able to appreciate the view of Greater Manchester stretching into the dim grey Lancashire distance. An endless vista of factories, power stations, housing estates, church spires and cooling towers became a blur. He peered tremulously over the inner edge . . . down, down into a black void that plummeted into the very core of the earth. Sammy shivered. It smelt acrid and stale. He knew its darkness was dangerous.

'Don't be frightened. There, there, there, puss, puss, puss,' called Fred encouragingly, peering up from the ladder below the top. 'Come along now, good pussy. Come to Fred.'

Sammy wasn't coming to Fred. He wasn't going to anyone. He was too terrified to move, crouched aloft, watching the man with fixed, staring eyes as if he was an alien creature from outer space.

'I've a nice bit of sardine for you,' Fred tempted. 'How about some sardines from the canteen? Come along, old boy. Come on, ginger.'

Sammy's stomach was gnawing with hunger, but his taste-buds acted on smell, not words. He could not tell what Fred was waving about. Fred had brought up a wire mesh basket, tied to his waist. Sammy did not like the look of it . . . baskets meant captivity and visits to the vet.

Fred proffered more tempting morsels from the canteen, wishing the cat would make up its mind. Conditions were very unpleasant, with driving rain and a fierce wind. Even with his skill and experience of high buildings, this was no picnic.

Sammy flattened his ears to cut down wind resistance and huddled into his fur. The day wore on; television crews came and went. Fred threw sardines around, most missing the ledge and dropping onto spectators' heads.

A cameraman removed a sardine from the peak of his cap. 'I know it rains cats and dogs in Manchester,' he said. 'But fish is ridiculous.'

As the light began to fade, Fred came down, shaking

432

his head. It was too dangerous now to stay aloft, or even try another attempt that afternoon. Sammy was doomed to another night . . . if he didn't fall off.

While millions of television viewers watched the drama of the rescue attempts on the news in the comfort and central heating of their homes, Sammy was slowly freezing into a hump of abject misery. Only his long fur saved him, and the pockets of warm air still trapped in its wetness. He pushed his nose into what little warmth he could find and tried to concentrate on not being blown off his perch by the bitter wind.

He had found a tangle of rope securing some tackle to the brickwork, and dug his claws into the fibres. It was the only thing he could cling to. His frozen spirit put him onto automatic pilot as he hung on through the long night.

When dawn of the second day came, the weather had not abated. The driving rain still stung, the wind still howled and buffeted the top. Even Fred queried the wisdom of attempting another climb in such conditions, but the plight of Lofty – as Sammy had been christened by the media – had caught the imagination of the country. He was front-page news in most of the national newspapers.

Fred did not like the thought of the cat slowly starving to death 150 feet above Bolton. He would have one more try. He fastened on his cumbersome harness and started the climb.

'Come along, Lofty, now,' he coaxed, holding out a morsel of cold chicken saved by the canteen staff for their most reluctant customer. 'Nice puss. You don't want to stay up here in this nasty old place, do you? Don't you want to go home?'

Sammy did want to go home, but by now he was frozen, both with fright and cold. A second night aloft had reduced him to a shaking bundle of confusion. He defied Fred's entreaties without knowing why. He refused food despite his raging hunger and thirst. He clung relentlessly to the rope, only once forsaking it – to retreat further round the ledge when Fred got too close.

Fred jammed his cap firmly over his tingling ears and began the descent. It was time to knock off for a bite to eat and a pint of beer at the pub. His hands were frozen and it would need nimble fingers to catch that cat.

'I can't make him budge,' he said sadly.

A crowd of mill workers gathered below the chimney in their lunch-hour. It was drama on their doorstep. They craned their necks to catch sight of the tiny silhouette of pointed ears just visible against the sky.

The weather was deteriorating even further. The whiplash rain soaked spectators in minutes. But they hung around, stamping their feet, waiting for something to happen. Gerry Rodgers stood silent among the crowd. It was his lunch-break from a nearby rubber factory. He liked cats. He hoped to see the ginger cat rescued.

He tipped his head back. The chimney was the tallest, blackest, most frightening thing he had ever seen. The ladders crawled up the outside, disappearing into infinity. It towered above him like a monster from some disaster movie.

Suddenly Gerry made up his mind. Steeling his nerves, he raced to the chimney and shot up the first ladder. He climbed quickly, allowing no time to think, no time to look down, keeping his eyes fixed only on the rung above. He climbed, hand over hand, with relentless determination.

Gasps went up from the crowd. Time and again his green wellies slipped on the wet rungs, but he clung on, using the strength in his wrists till he gained a surer foothold. Rain plastered his dark fringe to his forehead. His clothes were soaked. The howling wind filled his ears with unholy ferocity. All this, he thought wryly, for a scrap of ginger fur.

He caught his breath at the top, and heaved himself onto the ledge, panting. He was thirty years old, but at that moment he felt about ninety. He could see the cat, its fur flattened and sodden. It looked as terrified as Gerry felt.

'Puss, puss, puss,' he called gently, the wind whipping his words away to the distant grey hills. 'I won't hurt you.'

But Sammy was not moving for Gerry either.

'Come along . . . you can trust me. I'll get you down.'

For thirty minutes Gerry sweet-talked the cat to come near enough to grab him. But he was always just that bit out of reach. Gerry clung to the top ledge, so cold he could hardly think. He could not stay there much longer.

A sudden gust nudged Sammy along a few inches. It was a chance movement that brought him within reach of Gerry's long arms.

Sammy felt himself grabbed by the scruff of his neck. He was swung off his safe perch. He found himself struggling in mid-air, all four paws windmilling like fury. The rain lashed at his eyes and a blurred panorama of sky, brickwork and bearded man whirled before him. He went wild with terror. He was being carried down with an awkward, jerking movement. The man descended painstakingly, rung at a time, using only one hand to hang onto the side of the ladder, the weather-bitten steel rasping his skin.

The other hand held the cat in a vice-like grip. Sammy fought the hand and arm that held him, unable to realise what was happening. It was all part of the nightmare. His bedraggled tail waved in a furious question mark.

'Now, now, pussy. Don't struggle or you'll have us both off.'

They were forty feet from the ground when Fred came back from his beer break. He hurried to hoist the wire animal basket up to Gerry on a rope. Gerry bundled the cat, head first and upside-down into the basket and slammed the lid. He leaned back onto the ladder with relief. His wrist was numbed and aching with pain; he could not have held on much longer.

Sammy huddled into the swaying cage as it was

lowered gently towards the ground. He dug his claws into the wire mesh as he swung in the air. He felt horribly exposed. He saw crowds of people below; they were getting bigger . . . policemen, camera crews, reporters, factory workers. What were they all staring at?

A terrific cheer went up as the cage bumped onto the ground, then the crowd broke into spontaneous applause. Gerry felt his knees buckle as his green wellies stepped off the last rung and touched the firm yard beneath. He straightened himself, grinning, aware that he was shaking.

The police were waiting for Gerry — but not with congratulations. It was an offence to climb someone else's chimney, even to rescue a cat.

'We shan't charge you,' said the police officer. 'But you're an idiot. No insurance, no harness.'

'I saw the cat on the television last night,' said Gerry, as if that was reason enough.

'Were you scared?' asked a reporter.

Gerry looked back up at the 150-foot chimney and its dwindling rim in the mist.

'I tried not to look down,' he said with a shudder.

Sammy was taken to the RSPCA van parked nearby. Someone was rubbing him gently with a towel. They were pouring milk into a saucer. There was the delicious smell of food being unwrapped. Chicken, fish, liver . . . Sammy didn't care what it was.

As his tongue curled round the milk, he nearly choked in his eagerness. He lapped and lapped, knowing the delicious smells were all for him when he had slaked his thirst. He began to purr. He couldn't help it, because now he had his answer. Now he knew what Christmas was.

# Hamlet on West Forty-fourth Street

I am a New York City street kid on the up and up. And I don't just mean riding the old-fashioned elevators of the Algonquin Hotel on New York's Forty-fourth Street and Fifth Avenue, but in the company I was now keeping. Writers, directors, producers, actors and actresses of stage and screen, journalists and gossip writers . . . they were glamour and class and everyone a celebrity.

Their haunt is my haunt . . . no, my home. I am a personage of some distinction, but careful not to let my origins slip. Nothing escapes my notice in this haven of genial companionship.

I guess it's a dollar to a dime that I was born in a carrier bag downtown. The seamier streets were my scratching ground and I latched onto a gang of wild ferals that terrorised any paunchy dog that dared to set a reckless paw on our territory. Then some cat groupies reckoned I was fitted for a better life and hauled me off to the Bide-a-Wee Society for Stray Animals' rescue home. That was me rescued. Was I grateful? Not likely.

In a swift counter attack they de-loused, de-fleaed and shampooed me inside out. I was so clean, I squeaked. It was a big leap from streets to sanitisation, which I bore with much fortitude.

Then some inspired lady novelist between books comes along and transports me in her automobile. I clawed my way out of the box and leaped onto the passenger seat. I'd diced with death in half of New York's traffic and I was not going to be intimidated by a red Volkswagen.

'Calm down, buster,' she said as she drove towards Manhattan. 'You're going to a very nice place and I want you all in one piece. You're for the high life if you behave. This hotel is the tops in New York. It's the pulse of New York's literary circle.'

I didn't let on I had no idea what she was talking about. My old neighbourhood was grey with sleazy rooming houses that called themselves hotels. They paid giants to throw things at cats.

'Someone has seen a mouse in the vicinity of the Algonquin and it's a red-alert situation,' she went on.

I decided to stake out this hotel. It is in the heart of mid-town Manhattan. I was jaunty as a sailor on a forty-eighter as we went in through the front portals, below the fluttering Stars and Stripes. What a shock was in store. It took my breath away.

I knew immediately I was in some special, superior joint. The air of grandeur, the elegance, the antique porcelain lamps glowing from the dark pillars, the grand furniture and smell of good polish. I tiptoed over the thick carpet as the grandfather clock discreetly ticked away the silent minutes . . . it was an island of old-world calm that I never knew even existed. A very long way from the antiseptic Bide-a-Wee.

My racoon-striped tail began to tingle with excitement. A single-minded determination seeded and grew. I would own what I saw. I would brook no rivals, no mangy street cat was coming within a mile of my hotel. I would become an equal to the great. I would be a celebrity in my own right.

'This is your new cat,' said the lady novelist.

The exact nature of the hotel was at first mystifying.

Under the floor, the boiler throbbed night and day. People came and went, preceded or followed by bellboys carrying luggage of different shapes and sizes, sometimes escorted by the bell captain in his brown and gold striped uniform. I saw no purpose whatsoever in this daily parade.

Another puzzlement was the crowd of people who came regularly for cocktails at six in the Blue Bar. It filled with literary agents and editors in a migratory wave as their offices closed. They did not bring luggage, only manuscripts. But the ritual of going through the crowded oak-panelled lobby was a must, whatever.

Cocktail hour was the tops. I crunched my way through snacklets dropped or sneaked to me by a surreptitious hand. I was always ready for the odd shrimp or slice of smoked salmon. And I could retreat and observe the human traffic from my favourite spot half way between the elevator and the grandfather clock, tucked away under a low sofa.

I gained the reputation of being a big sleeper, but was I asleep? No. I was merely listening with my eyes half closed, an air of royal aloofness disguising my curiosity. The scandal was amazing. Sometimes I had to remove myself from it all and curl up on the special shelf over Harry's news-stand on a stack of copies of the *Soho News*. One can only take so much.

I had my own door to the kitchen, but some guy had put the wrong name over the flap. A little sign said 'Rusty' and it creaked of long ago cat. Sometimes I had this dream of Rusty, a tortoiseshell tom, and we had tricky and near the knuckle conversations about the hotel guests. I learned a lot from Rusty. We had this understanding.

Talking of kitchens, the food was five-star. Chicken and cream, prawns and puddings. Gourmet. When I think of the trashcan pickings I was brought up on! But I was still street wise. I drank straight from the tap, even in the best company.

There were three dining rooms in the hotel, the Rose Room, the Chinese Room and the Oak Room. I wasn't fussy. Once I took my own mouse into the ruby-panelled dining room but no one was grateful. The women shrieked and hitched up their skirts, painted faces reflecting their horror in the mirrored walls. The chandeliers tinkled in the hot-air thermal of gasps. The head waiter told me off with a wagging finger.

'No mice allowed in the dining room, Hamlet,' he said sternly, removing the offending corpse. I growled. I was outraged. I was only trying to help. I thought he was my friend. They were so busy in the dining room with a post-theatre buffet. Did they want me to eat on the hotel steps like a vagrant?

From that day, I was barred from the dining room.

'Tut, tut, Hamlet,' said the reception clerk kindly as my eye swivelled in the direction of soft lights and starched tablecloths. 'You know you're not allowed in.'

I flicked my tail haughtily. It was no skin off my nose. Not with a name like Hamlet. Shakespearean, I was told, but it still sounded half way to a pork and egg fry. Some name for a handsome white and grey lynx cat, with a large white head and sharp amber eyes that can kill at five yards.

So they thought I was a big sleeper; I was a big nipper and that was no mean rumour, buddy. I was really hung-up on a dainty curved female ankle that I could clamp onto with both paws. How I loved to creep up under a sofa and suddenly fasten my claws onto an unsuspecting ankle. I reckon the stocking trade ought to pay me an honorarium.

Male ankles were not so much fun. Females forgave me as I pretended I was sorry and purred into their hands. Men just swore. I soon discovered that there was a vulnerable two inches of pale hairless skin above short socks that was extremely vulnerable. I could spot an unguarded shin at a hundred yards; crawl towards it under sofas, coffee tables and chairs, silent as a spider as

440

they discussed and argued about the theatrical and literary world outside. Suddenly I would pounce on my prey. His sharp yelp could be heard well above the chatter. Heads swivelled in the electric silence, craning at the culprit. It was very satisfying.

Being famous didn't mean no certificate of exemption. An ankle was an ankle. I bit 'em in the order in which they walked through my royal domain; it was the price they paid.

Don't think I didn't pay my price. No more street brawls. No more nights on the town. No more stalking dark alleyways with my pals.

But the Algonquin was mine. Any time. All the time. I rode in elevators, snoozed in linen carts, and if I was sure no one was looking, jogged along the maze of corridors on the upper floors.

Otherwise my demeanour was dignified, a shade haughty, stopping to greet guests, to pass the time of day, to reassure a nervous newcomer, welcome an old friend, my tail pointing up and curling in an elegant manner befitting my surroundings.

I was ambassador to the rich and not so rich, to the famous and to those who had not made it yet. Sir Laurence Olivier, Burt Reynolds, Albert Finney, Erica Jong, Peter Ustinov, Jeremy Irons, Anthony Andrews . . . they were all good for a tickle under the chin, a scratch on the head.

The past was another ball game. They say that the *New Yorker* magazine was born within these walls. Dorothy Parker, Robert Benchley, George S. Kaufman, Alexander Woollcott . . . I could sense these literary ghosts still sitting on the plump velvet chairs. They formed what was called a Round Table of wits that met at the hotel, but I never saw any such table. And I kept my eyes skinned.

Critics say I'm a snooty cat but that's just sour Bourbon, and a lack of understanding of the feline character. I keep my distance, like any self-respecting cat. I've seen enough dogs that fawn and ingratiate at their master's feet like there was no tomorrow. I get interviewed for television. They write about me in newspapers from coast to coast. I'm filmed with the cast at the Algonquin for a movie. Guests send me postcards and souvenirs from all over the world, photographs and gifts. Some joker sent me a little bell for my collar. They don't do all that for no snooty cat.

The cocktail-set told me that Rusty used to sip his milk from a champagne glass in the Blue Bar. So what? That's no big deal. I got my own style. I'm no cheap imitation. Besides, I got perception. I can tell when a new fresh-faced actress from the woods has got that special oomph . . . I can spot a writer with excitement leaking out of his eyes, casting around the lobby for the right face to talk to.

'I got it just right today, Hamlet,' he'd say, bending down to tell me. 'Wish me luck.'

'Who's here today, Hamlet,' she'd whisper, stroking my ears. 'Who's casting around? What did they say?'

A couple of times a week I'd saunter into the managing director's book-lined office, enjoying the literary ambiance. If only I could share my thoughts with him. Mr Anspach looks up from his executive desk, a contemplative twinkle in his eyes. People are always writing to him about me.

'I wish you'd answer your own letters,' he grins, tweaking my tail.

I've been lord cat of the hotel lobby a long time now. It must be nearly ten, twelve, fourteen years. I can't count and I don't bite so good anymore. Time is mellowing my fierce nature. The old clock and I tick on, measuring the minutes, watching the flow of humans through half-closed eyes.

Who would guess that I nearly didn't stay on after that first Christmas at the hotel? I almost snuck back to the streets of New York City on a night that I will never forget.

True, they had some kind of party going on. There had

442

been parties going on and off ever since Thanksgiving Day. My friends from stage and screen were wining and dining, talking, laughing, having fun. I'd eaten so much I had roast turkey coming out of my ears. I could barely squeeze my huge bulk under my favourite sofa to sleep it off.

I was slipping down the hazy corridors of sleep, chasing pigeons over the rooftops of Manhattan with Rusty in my winter dream, when suddenly, as the grandfather clock chimed midnight, an ear-shattering pandemonium broke out in the hotel.

My fur stood on end.

The swing doors from the kitchens were flung back. A chain of shrieking white devils came writhing in a snakedance through the lobby, clanging and banging pots and pans in wild abandon. The sound was cataplectic; it shook the windows, split the air waves, woke the long-dead fossils entombed in the hotel's foundations.

I froze with terror, cowering back under the sofa, the din attacking my delicate eardrums until I could have screeched with the agony.

The devil spirits danced past me, white-faced masks grinning, their banging and clanging vibrating along every jagged nerve-end of my body. If I could have moved, I would have fled. All the way to Coney Island.

They told me afterwards, when they finally managed to drag me out from under the sofa, that it was only the waiters and bellboys dressed up with tablecloths over their heads. But I knew better. I was street wise. Hadn't I come up from the pits? I seen a devil or two before . . .

'Sorry, Hamlet old chap,' said Andrew Anspach, trying to reassure me. 'We forgot to warn you. It's an old Algonquin tradition on New Year's Eve. We have to make sure no evil spirits are lurking around the hotel that might cause mischief in the coming year.'

'It's a tradition you could well discontinue,' said a lady guest, nursing her bruised ears.

443

'We're afraid to take the chance,' said Mr Anspach with an amiable shrug.

It took several saucers of cream to calm my shattered nerves. Okay, I could deal with hotel mice, dogs, chase away wavering shadows that might scare a late guest creeping along to his room, but those New Year devils are something else. Each year I got to take cover, curl my tail over my nose, shut my eyes tight and make out I'm not there.

When the ear-splitting uproar and tour of the hotel rooms is over, and the festivities settle back into near normalcy, I come out of my hiding place, first making sure it's all clear. Not a devil in sight.

I shake out my fur and my tail, have a quick lick and brush-up, and then after several deep breaths, join our partying guests as if nothing untoward has happened.

And that's a cat acting, buddy. Straight off Broadway.

# Scraps

(Adapted from an account by Mrs Olivia M. Slobbé)

He was the tiniest kitten of the litter and the last one left, an ebony black scrap of humanity, clawing at the empty air. No one wanted him. He was going to be drowned.

They had never thought of owning a cat. They were staying with her brother prior to moving to New Malden to their first house. The kitten looked so weak and appealing that they took him home. Anton, who was Dutch, had been in hospital for two years after the war and had only just started a job in the City.

'We can't really afford to have a cat,' said Anton.

'But we could feed him on scraps from the table,' said Olivia, wanting the kitten. 'He's so tiny and helpless.' Cat first, furniture later . . . her priorities were in that order.

They took Scraps to New Malden in the back of the van, on Olivia's lap. They did not have a cat basket. The kitten slept all the way.

It was a glorious August day, hot and still. They put Scraps on the lawn while they moved their belongings out of the van. The garden was an enchanted place. All they could see of Scraps was the tip of his black tail as he tentatively explored the jungle of weeds and grass.

Olivia and Anton set up home with the bare necessities. They had two beds, a piano (a legacy from Anton's mother), a statue of Nell Gwynn, an alarm clock and a set of fish knives and forks. Now they also had a cat.

Scraps was supposed to be fed from scraps from the table. He did not know but he sometimes ate better than they did. It was 1948 and rationing was still in force. Nor did he think it strange that they ate from the closed lid of the piano while they were saving for a table.

He was so tiny he could hardly climb the stairs and had to be lifted round the bend onto the landing. They took turns during the night to fill the hot-water bottle for his bed. He grew into a fastidious cat; he would not use his litter box if it was dirty; he would only eat off a clean plate.

Eventually Olivia got a job and Scraps was always waiting by the door for her return. She would get on her hands and knees for a few moments of rapturous reunion.

'Has it been a long, long day?' said Olivia, putting her face into the soft, glossy fur, knowing he would never put out his claws. 'When you've been neutered you'll be able to explore the wide world. We'll teach you how to come and go through the fanlight. Then you'll be free to do as you please.'

They began to teach him with a piece of string how to get onto the shed and jump through the fanlight. It was a wonderful game and Scraps thought it great fun. He was taught to jump down onto a low cupboard inside and then onto the floor. It took some time for Scraps to master this involved route, but they were patient and he was bright and intelligent.

He was light on his feet. He sprang through the fanlight with the nimbleness of an Olympic gymnastic gold-medallist. It was a joy to watch the performance.

Till the day Olivia forgot to open the fanlight.

Scraps knocked himself out. He lay unconscious on the

floor, the world black and reeling, kitten-size stars before his eyes.

Olivia was horrified. How did one revive an unconscious cat? She cuddled him on her knees until he was less dazed, then gave him some milk.

He didn't forget. He regarded the fanlight with apprehension and it was some time before he could be encouraged to use it again. It was back to square one with the piece of string until he gained confidence. But he always made sure it was open first.

How they enjoyed that first summer in their home. They quickly became a close family, the three of them, playing hide and seek in the garden like children during the long light evenings.

'Where's Scraps?' they would call. 'Where's Scraps?'

A tiny black streak would tear out of the bushes, touch ankles with his nose, then bound off to hide again. The garden was one immense playground for Scraps. Anton built a trellis to hide the bottom of the garden, but they all secretly thought that the part they were hiding was the loveliest. It was a wild paradise of tangled blackberry bushes, fragrant apple trees, blackcurrant bushes and raspberry canes.

Whenever they took a walk down the local lane, Scraps came too. He did not want to be left behind. He was never far from them, yet never ventured anywhere on his own. Malden was already becoming a suburban estate, although the village itself was quaint and pretty.

Scraps developed a sweet tooth, but only for home-made cakes. He scorned shop cake. He sat on Anton's knee to share his tea; when he thought no one was looking he would swiftly hook his paw round a piece of cake from Anton's plate. Delicious. He liked queen cakes, and sponges, but shortbread was his favourite.

While he was still small he sat on Anton's shoulder for the morning ritual of shaving. Perhaps he thought the lather was a sponge mix. He liked to lick the lather from Anton's face.

'Leave off,' grinned Anton into the mirror. A small black, foam-smudged face peered back.

Scraps invented a marvellous game along the hall passage, a sort of cat ski-run. It was a Saturday and Sunday game, when Anton and Olivia were both at home and all three doors would be open.

He would take off from the front gate, gallop along the path gathering momentum, leap onto the runner and slide along the polished floor all the way into the kitchen and out of the back door. He could also do this in reverse, from the back door to the front garden. It was exhilarating. But also exhausting. After three or four runs Scraps would flop down, flaked out, panting like a dog.

Winter turned the passage into an icy blast and Scraps liked warmth. He stopped asking for the doors to be opened. There was no central heating in those days, and the game stopped.

They did not go out much as they were saving up to buy furniture. They couldn't go on eating off the piano lid forever. But one evening they decided to go to the cinema.

'The one-and-nines?' Anton suggested.

'How lovely,' said Olivia, fetching her coat.

Scraps sat alone in the empty house. They had gone out without him. How could they? He always went on their walks. How could he convey his utter disgust that they had deserted him?

He was too gentle a creature to actually cause any damage. It was not in his nature. But somehow he had to communicate the depth of his feelings. He wandered around the rooms wondering what he could do. It is not easy for a cat to get a message over to human owners.

Olivia loved flowers. They grew mostly vegetables but because it was spring and daffodils were cheap, she had treated herself to a dozen golden-headed blooms. They stood, glorious and glowing, in a vase on the piano.

Scraps jumped onto the piano and very carefully, with his head on one side, put his mouth gently round a stem and lifted it out of the vase. He moved delicately because he did not want to knock over the vase or spill water on Olivia's piano top.

He laid the extracted daffodil on the piano and went back for a second. It took him a long time to remove all twelve flowers. He laid them in a row along the top and retreated to the top of the stairs, feeling pleased with himself. He had made a statement. That would teach them for going out without him.

They came back late, laughing and talking about the film. Scraps sat at the top of the stairs, dignified and remote, not coming down to greet them as he usually would. Olivia was too happy after the unexpected outing to take much notice. She went to put the kettle on for a cup of coffee.

When she went into the dining room and saw the row of daffodils laid along the top of the piano, she knew why Scraps was looking smug.

'The young monkey,' she laughed. 'Anton, come and look at this. See what Scrap's been up to. He obviously didn't approve of our going out. Hey, Scraps, are you coming off your high horse for some warm milk?'

It was some weeks before they had the temerity to go out again. They had forgotten the daffodil incident, but Scraps hadn't. When he discovered that they had gone out without him again, he couldn't believe it. He roamed around the house, his thoughts in a turmoil. Perhaps they hadn't understood . . .

A recent purchase had been a second-hand table for the hall which Olivia had polished and polished until it shone. On it she had put a bowl of dried flowers. Scraps decided to make the same protest, but with a little variation.

When Olivia and Anton returned from visiting her parents they found a dried flower placed on each step of the stairs and Scraps sitting at the top awaiting their return, the same smug expression on his face.

'Okay, Scraps, we get the message,' said Anton, much

amused. 'How about putting them back in the bowl if you are such a clever cat, eh?'

They did not try leaving Scraps again. They even took him electioneering, delivering pamphlets door to door in the village. One woman asked them in. Scraps took a strong objection to the delay and sat on her doorstep howling like a coyote. They had to make a hurried retreat.

'That's no way to win votes,' said Olivia, shooing him down the path. His glossy black tail shot up in greeting. He had only wanted to see them. Even a few minutes' separation was too much.

Some Saturdays Anton went to watch Chelsea playing. Scraps always seemed to know on which train he was returning, for the cat would move from the fire onto the windowsill to watch for his arrival. It was Olivia's cue to put the kettle on, and Scraps was always right. Moments later Anton would walk in.

'Our Lord and Master returning home from his gallivanting,' said Olivia to the cat with a secret smile as they both went to meet him.

They grew into a devoted family, a threesome. Scraps hated being away from them for any length of time. They insisted that he slept in his own sleeping box in the kitchen, but relented enough to take him to bed for a last game of pictures on the wall.

They made shadow pictures of rabbits and dogs on the wall with their fingers. Scraps watched, fascinated, occasionally unable to resist a leap and a paw at the moving pictures.

'No more,' said Anton yawning. 'It's bedtime. Even yours, young Scraps.'

'The show's over,' said Olivia firmly, taking Scraps downstairs. 'No more television. You're a lucky puss; you have a television but we don't!'

Nor did they need an alarm clock, for Scraps woke them each morning with a gentle paw on each eyelid. He waited on a small ledge in their bedroom, watching the early morning birds flying past, wishing he could catch one but knowing instinctively that he would be reprimanded. He did not get told off for taking a nap in the airing cupboard, tucked away among the towels. He knew what he could do and could not do.

He could tell them when he was hungry and wanted to eat. They had taught him how to open the larder door by hooking his paw round the edge and pulling it open. Scraps would go in, take off the cloth that covered his plate of fish or liver and carry the cloth to Olivia, waving it like the trophy of some fierce jungle hunter.

'Thank you, Scraps,' said Olivia, taking the cloth from his jaws. 'Would you like your breakfast?'

He never took the food. After all, he wanted a clean plate. He was fussy.

One day when Anton and Olivia returned home from work, Scraps was not there to greet them. It was so unusual, they looked at each other with unspoken fears. He did not come home that night or the night after.

They searched the house and the garden and the nearby lane, becoming more and more frantic with worry. He had never stayed out before.

'I can't think of anything that would make Scraps stay away from us for even one night,' said Olivia, over and over again. She could not concentrate on anything. She kept thinking of their little black cat, so small and sweet, and how he must be feeling. 'Something must have happened to him.'

It was autumn and the weather was crisp and dry. They searched as far as they could go, asking everyone they met if they had seen a small, glossy black cat . . . A young couple, desperate to find the tiny scrap who had become so much part of their lives.

'He's wearing his medallion so perhaps someone will bring him back,' said Olivia, clutching at straws.

'He wouldn't have gone with anyone. He must have been stolen,' said Anton, chilled by the thought of people's cruelty. That lovely glossy black fur had a price.

Scraps had been very wary of anyone strange since the day burglars broke into their house. They had stolen Olivia's engagement ring and Anton's suit.

Scraps had seen it all, hiding beneath Anton's wardrobe. At first even Olivia could not persuade him to come out; for a long while he never left their side, following them like a black shadow. They shut the fanlight for a time and Scraps knew why. He had seen how the burglars got in . . . He had seen the boy wriggling through and knew something was very wrong.

'He would never have gone off with a stranger,' they agreed.

'I miss him so much . . .'

'We both do,' said Anton, comforting his young wife.

The next evening they were sitting in their dining room. By now they had saved enough to buy a dining-room suite and two fireside chairs, but that night they took no pleasure in their new furniture. They were worrying about Scraps and wondering what had happened to him.

Suddenly they heard a familiar sound. The tiny scratch, the light landing of paws, the creak of wood. It was Scraps coming in through the fanlight.

'It's Scraps,' whispered Olivia, hardly daring to hope.

He did not come through to them. They waited.

'Scraps?' Anton called. But he did not come.

They went out into the kitchen. Scraps was sitting on the back door mat, plastered from head to foot in thick brown mud. It had dried on him and his tail was as stiff as a board and sticking up like a beanpole. He looked utterly dejected and weary.

'Oh my poor, poor darling,' said Olivia, going down on her knees to hug the bedraggled cat, mud and all. She felt a quiver run along his tired body. Somehow he had got himself home.

He allowed himself to be shampooed in the kitchen sink, something which he had never let Olivia do before.

He knew he had to get clean, and he could not do it himself. Wrapped in a warm towel and cuddled in front of the fire, he began a low purr, which grew and grew as if he would never stop. He was home. He was really home with them again.

Scraps had obviously fallen into some stagnant pond. But there was no pond for miles around and the ditches were all dry. If only Scraps could tell them where he had been taken, but they would never know. When his fur was dry, Anton brushed him gently with an old army hairbrush, and put him to bed. He slept the sleep of the exhausted, but they took it in turns to creep down the stairs to look at him.

When winter came, they sat each evening by the coal fire. Scraps invented a new game. He would sit with his head in a paper bag. How he purred, loving the warmth. It was nice inside the paper bag and it shut out the electric light. He had got the idea at Christmas when Olivia and Anton were opening their presents and the floor was strewn with paper.

One of his Christmas presents was a piece of ribbon which Olivia would tie onto his tail. Rolling over and over, he could untie the ribbon and take it to them, asking to start the game all over again. The paper bag and the ribbon at the same time was a special party trick.

'If only we could take a photo of him,' laughed Olivia.

Olivia was the pianist of the family. Scraps knew what he liked. He liked 'When Irish Eyes are Smiling' and 'Peg of my Heart'. But if Olivia began to play the popular song 'Mares Eat Oats and Does Eat Oats and Little Lambs Eat Ivy', he would jump up onto the piano and march along the piano keys in a highly successful wrecking operation.

It had been two years of working hard and saving to get their home together, and the following year Olivia and Anton planned to take a holiday, their first.

They booked two weeks at a holiday camp at Bracklesham Bay, and left Scraps at a cats' home, kissing his sweet nose goodbye when they left.

'Now be very good Scraps and we'll soon be back,' said Olivia.

It was a wonderful holiday, all thoughts of the desert war, the pain, the years in hospital, began to fade into the past. They walked along the steeply shelving pebble beach, watching the waves pounding the shore, listening to the music of the sea. When they returned home, they immediately went to fetch Scraps. He came before anything.

The little cat went wild with excitement when he saw Olivia and Anton. Purring, climbing over them, nudging chins, kneading, burrowing deep into their arms, all with little cries of joy. But they were shocked by the change in their cat's appearance. He was desperately thin.

'He pined and wouldn't eat,' said the owner of the cats' home, shaking her head. 'We couldn't get him to eat at all.'

The happiness of their holiday fled, melting like butter in that summer's sun. They wished they had never gone. The taste of the spray was bitter now. They took Scraps home, tenderly nursing the sick cat all that night and the following day. But Scraps had been the tiniest and weakest of the litter. His heart, valiant and courageous enough to find his weary way home after being stolen, could no longer take the strain.

He was cradled in Anton's arms when he breathed a last sigh and was gone.

He died of a broken heart, believing that they had left him. The vet said this too.

Olivia cried and cried. Scraps had been like a child. She couldn't believe he had gone, that sweet, glossy black little cat. It was heart-breaking.

For weeks they could not bear to go back to an empty house. They walked about every evening and did not eat. Nor could they have him buried in the garden where they had spent so many happy hours playing with their little black friend.

The local police buried Scraps in the garden at the back of the police station where he would be safe forever. They never had another cat. Scraps could not be replaced.

# Rescue in Venice

It was late evening when the plane from England landed at Milan airport, and 1 a.m. before they arrived outside Venice. Thick fog swirled round the Piazzale Roma at the end of the causeway, turning the magical city into a strange, unwelcoming and eerie place.

Damp rose from the canals in the chill January air. Mrs Helena Sanders shivered despite her warm clothes. The Cornwall she had just left had been warmer. For a moment she wished she was back in her cosy house overlooking the estuary; then she stiffened her resolve. They were here on a rescue mission.

She and Miss Mabel Raymonde-Hawkins and her photographer were weighed down with luggage; two cat traps, a pile of collapsible pussy-packs and photographic equipment. They were well prepared for this second visit to Venice.

They huddled together, the fog blanketing them from the real world. Footsteps on the wet flagstones came and went but they saw no one. It was only too easy to imagine ghosts of long-departed Doges flitting through the narrow passageways . . .

'Let's find a hotel for what's left of the night,' said Mrs Sanders briskly.

'What a good idea,' said Miss Raymonde-Hawkins with relief.

Next morning they caught a water bus travelling the entire length of the Grand Canal to the small hotel where they had booked rooms.

The long chugging ride down the winding Grand Canal was a dazzling dream-like experience even in mid-January. The pink and gilded marble palaces glided by, two hundred monumental palazzos of the wealthy merchants and Doges, the sea lapping the crumbling green-mildewed landing steps and blackened piles. The wash from the boat splashed relentlessly against the ancient stone buildings. How beautiful it looked in the cold luminosity of the pale grey morning light.

Mrs Sanders sat back to enjoy these last tranquil moments before the fight began. She knew it was going to be a fight. She had no illusions about anything being easy.

It was nearly two years since her first visit to Venice, in the summer of 1964, and that long-awaited holiday with her husband had been ruined by the misery they saw.

Swarms of emaciated and dying cats lay everywhere. Starving and diseased, they infested the city. If Mrs Sanders saw ten dying cats on one side, she saw twelve on the other. And this was Venice, Queen of the Adriatic, city of sixteenth-century magnificence, city of glorious disrepair, slowly sinking, drowning in its own beauty . . .

She had thrown a piece of ham to a cat so starved that its ribs were sticking out. But it was too weak to eat.

The sights sickened her. It was a dying city, its buildings dying, its cats dying. She had to do something. But she lived in Cornwall. How could someone living in Cornwall rescue the estimated 68,000 feral cats living in Venice?

The first cats were brought to Venice by a Doge to keep down the rats that crept in from the canals. They were ownerless, municipal rat-catchers, deliberately introduced to control plague. They lived all over the place, in gardens, under bridges, in the squares, the markets, in cellars. They bred rapidly in the maze of peeling-paint alley-ways, beneath the festoons of washing hung from iron balconies.

The authorities turned a blind eye despite the usefulness of the rat-catching cats. They ignored the dying, the diseased, the maimed, the pitiful starving kittens. The cats were prisoners in Venice. They could not escape to the countryside. There are only two dry ways out of Venice; one by a very busy motorway, the other by train from St Lucia station – neither recognisable cat tracks.

As the water bus neared the landing stage at St Mark's Square, Mrs Sanders caught sight of a headline in the *Gazzetino*: 'THE WHOLE TOWN IS LAUGHING AT THE CAT SAFARI'.

She had been afraid they might get a bad press. One of the English tabloids had got hold of the wrong idea and printed a story saying that they were going to hire a gondola, put a big cage in it and pay old women a hundred lire to give them cats. It was ludicrous.

Later there had been a cartoon in the *Corriere della Sera* and a leader headlined: 'DANGEROUS TIMES FOR THE CATS OF VENICE'.

The impression given by the paper was that they wanted to kill all the cats because they hated them.

Mrs Sanders knew it was going to be uphill work to organise their mercy mission. They wanted to make a drastic attempt to reduce the cat population by euthanasia, neutering and spaying by authorised vets, as well as supporting the existing system of cat women to feed the cats.

'Helena,' said Miss Raymonde-Hawkins. 'Who are all those people on the landing stage? Is it some kind of riot?'

Mrs Sanders saw a crowd of people milling around. She hoped they were not who she thought they were. At the approach of the water bus, the crowd began to jostle for positions in the firing line.

'It's a posse,' said Mrs Sanders. 'A posse of journalists.'

The Italian press were lying in wait; so were journalists from many other countries.

The director of the Italian Animal Welfare Organisation, known as ENPA, was furious. He said he had mobilised all eighteen of his inspectors, cancelling all leave and keeping them on emergency duty. Later he admitted that this was not true.

'If Mrs Sanders ill-treats one cat she will have to face the full majesty of Italian law,' he announced to the media.

The journalists pressed in on the two women they thought were coming to massacre the cats. It was a frightening moment, but Mrs Sanders and Miss Raymonde-Hawkins were not deterred. They were not totally alone. They had friends in Venice. There were people who cared and had been trying to get help for some time.

The two women could hardly walk because of the press. Photographers lay on the ground to get shots; reporters harassed them with microphones held to their lips to catch every word.

'Can't you get rid of all these people?' Mrs Sanders anxiously asked two policemen.

The officer shrugged his shoulders. 'You are celebrities,' he said.

During their visit one of the Venetian supporters accused the director of the ENPA of not supporting the English cat women. The director complained to the police. The two women were summoned to appear before the head of the Aliens Department. For half an hour he shouted at them. It was very unnerving.

'Why do you come to this country to break the law?' he bellowed.

'In which country is it illegal to take a sick animal to the vet?' Mrs Sanders shouted back. She tried shouting some more but it had little effect. It was a difficult situation.

Eventually he calmed down, Mrs Sanders explaining

in Italian the real purpose of their visit to Venice. He called in the director of ENPA, who kissed their hands and showed them to the door. They were free.

As soon as they were safely at a distance from the police station, they collapsed in helpless giggles and had to lean against a wall. The next day they flew home.

It was not the end of their work; it was the beginning. They left behind an organisation of cat women: selected, trustworthy old women who gave their time and money to feeding the cats. They were given veterinary forms which said in Italian: 'Please sterilise/give veterinary treatment/put down.'

They made arrangements with an Italian vet who agreed to spay, neuter, treat or destroy for his usual fee. Gradually the cat women started to take cats to the vet.

There was no first cat that was treated; there were only swarms. Among the first was a dying cat, his eyes and nose congealed with discharge from 'flu. He could neither see nor smell and was unaware that a plate of food was beside him.

The cats in the Rialto fish market were so hungry they were eating the paper in which the fish had been wrapped. January was a bad time for cats. Most of the hotels were closed and that source of food was denied them.

The main priority now was to raise money. It came from many different people and organisations; just enough to keep paying the bills.

Mrs Sanders returned to Cornwall to find she had made the headlines in the *Western Morning News*: 'TRURO WOMAN ARRESTED BY VENICE POLICE' and 'VENETIAN POLICE FOLLOW TRURO CAT WOMAN' then later 'APPALLING CAT CRUELTY IN VENICE ALLEGED'.

Miss Raymonde-Hawkins, who was already busy enough running the Raystede Animal Centre in Sussex and was planning to work for the Irish tinkers' equines, hoped to hand over to the Venetians, but it soon became obvious they had no plans to continue the work. It was an expensive scheme because of the enormous numbers of cats.

A new horror emerged during their third visit, in October 1966. The authorities planned to spend £70,000 on poisoning the rats with phosphorus, a poison which burns up an animal. A cat eating such a poisoned rat would die an agonising death. Mrs Sanders and her friends rushed to Venice to appeal to the Mayor of Venice and to the newspapers to publicise this horrendous plan. But the press had lost interest in cats.

The day before they left for home, the plan was abandoned and the lorries, already in Venice loaded with phosphorus, were sent back to Milan.

The following day the disastrous 1966 flood deluged the area. It swept through Venice, drowning many cats. But rats also drowned and so the cats' food supply was further diminished.

Mrs Sanders immediately rang the Italian Red Cross to ask what they needed. She collected two tons of bedding and warm clothing for the people of Venice, and a thousand tins of KiteKat. She organised ten tons of free freight space and gave surplus shipping space to the Anglo-Italian Society for the Protection of Animals to accommodate supplies of calf food to the flooded Po valley. The Italian customs held up the consignment because of the donated cat food; a sympathetic Venetian paid the considerable duty on this.

It was obvious that the rescue group had to be properly organised. Mrs Sanders sent out eight hundred letters to lawyers, clergy, doctors and accountants in Venice; eight people replied positively.

On 1 November 1969, the documents inaugurating DINGO as a registered charity were signed. Dingo was the name of a little stray dog rescued by Gina Fieri, the painter, better known as Gina Scarpabolla. It was a word which could be pronounced easily by speakers of both languages.

For several years DINGO treated about four hundred

cats a year. Then in 1982 the work doubled. It was estimated that when their rescue work began there were 68,000 ferals in Venice; their number now is between 4000 and 5000.

Many of the cats are astonishingly tame. They like spaghetti. They stroll among ᵗhe tourists. They sit beside the busy canals, not afraid of being kicked in. They traverse the burnt-red roof-tops with familiarity, knowing the nooks for sunbathing and the crannies to shelter from the rain.

The cat women still feed the cats, take the sick and injured to the vet's, collect new-born kittens to be put down and where possible take cats to be spayed. Their dedication is not easy. They are liable to abuse, ridicule and sometimes even violence.

In 1985 the Venetian DINGO was formed. It was a thrilling moment for Mrs Sanders, twenty years after her first mission, to be in a Venetian lawyer's office, putting her signature to an Italian document transferring responsibility to Venetian DINGO.

It was a very hot day in May. There was a dinner in the open air, the gift of a gold chain and two long legal documents about the principles behind DINGO. She thought of the thousands of cats they had rescued and treated, and the current colonies now healthier and cared for. And all against such odds. They had come a long way from that foggy night in January 1966. She remembered the cold fog swirling round them and the hostile press. It had not been easy.

On 26 May 1985, a colourful ceremony was held in the mediᵉval heart of Venice. In the Church of San Moisè behind St Mark's Square, near the pink and white marble of the Doge's Palace, Mrs Helena Sanders of Truro, Cornwall, England, was made a member of the Order of the Knights of St Mark. It was a most distinguished honour.

She arrived again, with Miss Raymonde-Hawkins and

Peter Bluck, her photographer, at Marco Polo airport. This time they were met by animal-lovers with a car and bouquets of flowers.

Several Knights, wearing their white cloaks and the bifurcated blue enamel cross of St Mark's, were gathered in the ornate Renaissance church. Mrs Sanders was the first to be led before the Doge by her sponsor. She was taken in front of the congregation and the citation was read.

The Doge put the St Mark's Cross round her neck, saying: 'I admit you to the Knights of St Mark in the name of our Holy Patron. Be a good citizen.'

Then a lady Knight pinned on a buttonhole with a miniature badge and put the white cloak round Mrs Sanders' shoulders. She is one of the very few British people to be so honoured.

Afterwards there was Mass and a sermon, then a party with wine and cocktail snacks. It was very hot and Mrs Sanders was in some discomfort. Her feet had swelled and her almost new shoes were killing her.

Later she hobbled back to the hotel and kicked them off.

'No more tight shoes for me,' she said firmly.

After that she went round Venice in old bedroom slippers with a hole in them, anxious to see how her big family fared.

A colony of cats races up and down steps and over the city's hump-backed bridges, their black and tabby coats gleaming with health, eyes round with curiosity. They sit by the canals, watching the river traffic; the slow gondolas, the chugging vaporetti, the sleek water taxis, bows polished and gleaming, speeding noisily for the lagoon.

They regard the tourists with well-bred indifference, the swarms of pigeons in St Mark's Square with calculated tolerance.

They are Mrs Sanders' real reward.

# Cat in Court

Mijbil sat at the window of the small flat in Ryde, watching – entranced by the outside world. She was fascinated by everything that she could not reach . . . grass, raindrops, scuttling leaves, the scurrying clouds, birds sweeping the vast sky with such enviable freedom.

She was too well mannered to sigh but she longed for a garden to play in. It was difficult to play in the flat without colliding with something, either the two children or the new Abyssinian kitten, Simba.

Her mistress understood. The flat imprisoned her too. She often took the cats out into the countryside or to the woods on the Isle of Wight so that they could have a romp. It was so exciting, going in the car, then being let loose to sniff and stalk, to leap and bound about in abandon. They never ran away.

Mijbil had come to the family as a temporary guest, a small, skinny, flea-ridden little black scrap. All eyes and ears and sharp little pin-pointed claws, almost too small to survive. She was going to be a surprise for a neighbour's child.

But the little black scrap knew where she belonged. She followed the family everywhere, purring and vibrating with love, till everyone fell utterly and devastatingly in love with her.

She grew strong and brave and it was this bravado that earned her such a strange name. She was fascinated by water and loved to dabble her paws, breaking up the shimmering reflections.

The family were in a swimming pool, splashing about, and she wanted to join them; she ran round the edge, nearer and nearer, then suddenly she was in the pool, paddling her splayed-out paws frantically towards her mistress.

'Silly puss,' said the woman, swimming towards her and pulling the kitten out of the water. 'What do you think you are – an otter?'

So she was called Mijbil, after the otter in *Ring of Bright Water*.

Mij and Simba were used to being taken out on harnesses and leads, but Mij loved travelling in the car most of all. The back window was her favourite place for watching the traffic flashing past, the trees waving branches overhead, wobbly cyclists and thundering lorries. She would sit there, safe and secure, purring, not minding the bumps as the ancient Morris 1000 took them towards the countryside.

'Come along, Mij. We're going visiting friends. It's a lovely sunny day. We ought to be outside enjoying it.'

Mij needed no second telling. She leaped down from the windowsill and twisted her sleek black body round her mistress's ankles. She was sure the friends would have a garden and she could spend a long, glorious afternoon chasing bees and flies and those fluttering butterflies.

They sang as they chugged over the downs in the warm, dappled April sunshine. The children and their mother sang pop songs while Mij purred an accompaniment that lulled Simba to sleep.

The Morris joined the main road and approached a big roundabout. There was an orange car coming from the right, so they slowed and stopped.

465

Mij was curious. She was always curious about everything. She climbed over onto her mistress's lap and looked out of the window to see if it was someone she knew. She arched her sleek black back, her golden eyes bright with speculation.

She was a little disappointed that it was a stranger in the other car. A man in a dark blue uniform with a woman and child. He drove round the roundabout and went down a road in the opposite direction.

Their car started again and they drove towards their friend's home, unaware that fate was about to take a hand in the proceedings.

Oddly enough, the orange car reappeared. It was right behind them. Mij spotted it first, then her mistress saw the car in the mirror. The woman drove especially carefully now, aware that the old car was conspicuous by the very fact of its age. She kept to a steady 35 m.p.h. The orange car stayed behind them.

'Oh dear,' she said, beginning to feel apprehensive. 'What a nuisance. There's a policeman in the car behind me and I want to turn right and these old-fashioned indicators don't work.'

Everyone swivelled round and stared at the orange car that was still following them.

'I'll go really slowly, then maybe he'll pass me.'

But he didn't. He stayed a steady, regulation twenty-five feet away.

'Mummy, he's tailing us!' the children shrieked. 'How exciting.'

'It is not exciting. It's worrying.'

Mij was aware of the rising tension in the car but could not understand it. What was a policeman? The cat was more interested in a small insect that was trapped in a corner of the car, buzzing around helplessly.

There was a slight jolt as the car stopped. What was happening? Her mistress got out. The orange car pulled round in front of them and the policeman got out too. Mij tore her attention away from the bug to inspect the new arrival. She was always interested in new people . . . perhaps he had come to make friends.

There were further, harder jolts as the policeman kicked all the wheels of the Morris. No, he definitely hadn't come to make friends.

'I'll have to caution you for driving without due care and attention,' he said, scowling at the rusting bodywork.

'I beg your pardon?'

'Don't you know it's an offence to travel with animals loose in the car?' he went on.

Mij listened with faint surprise. She thought about all the dogs she'd seen leaping about in the backs of cars, not to mention children quarrelling and fighting and crying. Mij felt quite indignant. She was not a loose animal. And Simba was still fast asleep, a fat bundle of apricot-coloured fluff.

Mij, the kitten and the children enjoyed their visit to the friend's house, but the woman seemed deflated and dejected. She was obviously worried about the incident.

'Don't worry,' said their solicitor later. 'The sergeant will throw it out of the window and tell the constable not to be ridiculous.'

But he didn't. A summons arrived and their mistress was ordered to appear in court. A mantle of gloom fell on the family's happiness. The woman was worried. At the last moment she picked up Mij and put the cat in her travelling basket.

'Mij is involved so she'd better come along too,' she told their friend Pat, who was going to keep them company in court. 'The whole thing seems so ridiculous and such a waste of court time and money. They might as well see my lovely Mij, see the kind of cat they are complaining about.'

Mij did not mind. It was another outing. Another chance to see something new. This court place might be interesting with things to chase and new delicious things to sniff. It would be heaps better than staying in the flat.

cat and owner sat outside Newport court, their thought-waves of apprehension and panic almost bouncing off the walls. Mij's mistress was wondering if she had done the right thing in bringing the cat to court. Would it be thought in contempt? Mij had no such doubts. She was with her beloved mistress and that could only be right.

'You are a good, well-behaved little thing, aren't you?' Mij was asked.

'For a moment I thought you meant me,' said a friendly policeman sitting in front of them. He was dark-haired and good-looking. 'What are you up for?'

'I'm not really sure.'

'I'll find out for you,' he offered. He went up to the prosecuting officer and returned with a huge grin on his tanned face. 'You're up for Driving in an Illegal Position!'

Mij felt her mistress relax a little as she and her friend Pat laughed. She was very curious about the place to which she had been taken. There was not a pot plant in sight, let alone a garden.

The case began. The courtroom was packed. The dark wood of the raised bench where the magistrate sat seemed threatening. In front of it sat the clerk of the court, rustling through his papers.

Mij began to enjoy herself despite the nervousness of the two women. There were such nice people around her, saying sweet things to her in her basket. She peered around with interest, noting the high bleak windows, wondering when she would be allowed out to explore.

Police Officer Roger Blench was giving evidence in the box. Mij recognised him as the one who had kicked the wheels of the car.

'First of all I want to say that I could not fault the defendant's driving,' he began. 'I drew onto the roundabout on the main East Cowes road and I saw the cat with its forepaws resting on the front window ledge.'

468

'Excuse me,' interrupted Mr Francis Eade, the magistrate. 'Do you mean forepaws or four paws?'

Mij heard the laughter sweep through the room. Yes, this really was a very jolly place with everyone laughing.

'Oh, only its forepaws, sir – the cat was on the lady's lap as she drove her car. He seemed to be looking out of the window,' said PC Blench. 'I then noticed two children and a second cat in the car as well.'

Pat testified as to Mij's perfect behaviour in the car, then her mistress had a turn to speak.

'Mij is an experienced car traveller and she enjoys it,' she told the court. 'I have learned a lesson, and so have many other people I've asked who did not know it was an offence to have a cat on your lap while driving.'

The magistrate listened gravely, his thin, lined face expressionless. 'As I understand we have the culprit in court, perhaps we had better have a look at her,' he said.

Mij looked around alertly, ears perked, as she was carried to the Bench and put down in front of the magistrate. Perhaps this was when she would be allowed to start exploring? Mr Eade came face to face with Mij's golden eyes and their amber-flecked depths held him in a long gaze. Mij certainly knew how to behave. She rubbed her head against the wire front of the basket in a friendly way.

Mr Eade hesitantly put his finger through the wire and tickled Mij under her small pointed chin. She purred with appreciation and nudged him gently, asking for her ears to be rubbed as well. His face softened, a smile threatened to break the normal gravity of his expression.

'Ah . . . er, well . . . yes,' he said at last. 'She's . . . er, obviously a very well-behaved cat . . . but as the case has been brought to court, and if the situation had arisen where, er . . . .' His voice grew gruffer. 'Then Mij could have got in the way, causing an accident. It is, therefore, I'm afraid, necessary to fine you the minimum, nominal fine of £5. But do please keep her in a basket in future.'

'Yes. Thank you. I will.'

Mij added her thanks, quite reluctant to leave her new friend, to whom she had taken a shine. But the press were waiting and she realised by now that she was of prime interest to everyone – quite a celebrity, in fact. There was still a lot to be said for leaping and chasing ants and bumble bees and flies in the long grass, but Mij reckoned that her appearance in court was a totally unique experience for a cat.

That evening Southern TV ran the story. Mij was somewhat less impressed by this part of the proceedings. She did not even recognise herself on the box.

Outside there was a cloud that looked just like a bird hovering, ready to swoop on a prey. Mij ran along the windowsill, her eyes gleaming, whiskers twitching like radar, her long black tail held high. It might just be a bird and she might just catch it.

# The Siamese Traveller

He came as a gift from another tea planter's wife, a creamy scrap of wild spitting and clawing that fitted into her hand. There was a dog in the household and since Chinky had never seen himself, he decided early in life that he was of the same species.

'Chinky,' they said, exasperated by his dog-like nips and bites. 'If you are going to behave like a dog, then you are going to be trained like a dog. And there's no need to glare at us! The first word you're going to learn is NO.'

Chinky had no trouble learning; he just had to copy the dog. Sit, beg, come . . . it was easy. Chinky prowled restlessly. He wanted something to sink his fangs into, something to do that was bold and fierce.

In the tea country in Assam, acre upon acre of plantations and rolling hills are cut with neat rows of green tea bushes edged with virgin jungle. The low evergreen shrubs shaded by tall leguminous flowering trees were an ideal playground for Chinky. It was fun but tame. He was a full-grown cat now and sat among the lush grass, tail flicking, watching the men who were coming to tidy the memsahib's garden. They were simple and poor but with the natural grace of their people; the sweeping movement of their *kadhalis* caught his eye.

In the distance is the country of the Nagas, the short

471

stocky hill people who lived in the thickly covered and almost impenetrable ranges of great hills, beyond which is Burma and then the ancient land of Siam. It is one of the wettest places in the world during the monsoon, hot and humid in the day. But it has a cold-weather season when the days are misty and evocative of England.

Chinky watched the workers walking slowly up the hill; his eyes narrowed. Suddenly Chinky leaped out, back arched, legs stiff, claws unsheathed, an unearthly Siamese yowl coming from clenched jaws. His ears flattened back, and with his tail raised high, he began an elaborate sideways dance, moving in a circle round the terrified men. Their eyes widened with fright. They had never seen such a small, fierce creature. Perhaps it was a demon!

All work ceased. They dropped tools on the ground in horror. Chinky danced round them, the sun sparkling on his short creamy fur, his blue eyes flashing like brilliant gems. His teeth bared. It was an awesome sight.

'Yee . . . ow,' he screeched.

They backed away. They knew about tigers, but when they saw Chinky's unsheathed claws, they could not be sure that it was not a new and dangerous species.

'Now, now, Chinky,' laughed the memsahib, lifting him up into the air, not afraid of his windmill paws. 'That was very naughty and I'm ashamed of you.'

Chinky grinned smugly. He was not in the least ashamed. He would do it again if he got the chance. And he did, every morning, until the men were less afraid and grew used to his wild tribal dance. Then it was no fun any more.

He had an amazing uncatlike speed. Arrow fast, he could beat memsahib to the veranda even after hiding in the flower beds and giving her a head start to the veranda steps.

The Assamese girls, wicker baskets strapped to their heads, worked their way from bush to bush skilfully plucking just the tip and two leaves from across the dark compact bushes. They were used to Chinky's antics.

'Bulbac Billi,' they giggled to each other and covered their mouths with their colourful saris. They thought he was like a clown, so they called him a clown cat.

Chinky did not think he was funny; he thought he was fierce. This warrior spirit made him heedless of danger. Each snake hole was examined with an investigative paw. He caught one of the silly, wriggly things and brought it back to the bungalow, its shiny black body curling on each side of his mouth like a mandarin's moustache. The memsahib was definitely not amused.

'No thank you, Chinky,' she said firmly, wanting the snake removed quickly. 'No snakes today or any day. And certainly not indoors please.'

Chinky took his prize outside in a huff. Humans were peculiar. He relaxed his jaws and the snake slithered away into the undergrowth. Chinky growled deeply in his throat. He had to find bigger and more exciting prey. His nerves tingled with the excitement of a fight.

He had to go where the action was. He embarked on the first of his travels . . . not far by human scale but a long way for a small Siamese. He strolled through the hut village where the workers lived and the tea factory compound, past the Indian clerks' brick houses and the great leaf-withering sheds.

A big wooden barn loomed ahead. It was the rice godown. Chinky smelt danger. A thousand tiny eyes pierced the darkness. Chinky stiffened and then pounced. Got it!

For four days they searched for him, scouring the large garden and the tea estate, walking along between the rows of tea bushes, calling his name and peering underneath. They began to dread that he had been taken by a leopard.

The factory engineer found Chinky in the godown, surrounded by his kill of rats and mice. He was wild with hunting. They couldn't catch him. He evaded them like quicksilver, a streak of pale fur in the gloomy darkness.

Eventually they tricked him into a box and nailed the lid down.

Chinky spat and yowled continuously all the way home in the lorry. He was furious. How dare they? This was no way for a triumphant warrior to return, in a box. He demanded to be let out.

He was eventually let out at the bungalow, but despite the great fuss made of him, he was still spitting and scratching. Nailed down in a box . . . the indignity, the humiliation. He would have nothing to do with anyone.

'How on earth are we going to get Chinky back to England?' said the memsahib. 'None of our friends will have Chinky even as a gift. He's far too much of a handful.'

'If he thinks he's a dog, let's treat him like a dog,' said the sahib, producing a lead.

Chinky eyed the lead suspiciously. He already wore a collar, but what was this? They started walking him round the garden on the lead. They called it lessons. Again it was pretty tame. They took him on practice car rides as a passenger, but not caged in a box or basket. He refused point blank to travel in a basket.

He liked to roam in the car, exhibiting his superior power of balance as they bumped over the rough tracks, always watching as they drove along the edge of the true jungle. He really liked being a traveller.

They had bought him a basket with a hinged lid. He sniffed at it, smelling the human hands that had woven the cane. They were local prisoners from Jorhat . . . prisoners making a prison for another. Chinky treated it with caution.

There was a great deal of activity going on, packing cases and crates strewn with crunchy paper and wood-shavings. Chinky tried to help with the packing, exploring the boxes, getting in the way.

'Chinky, will you please get out of that box? You are not travelling with my best china.'

Tail high, Chinky retreated into the garden. Whatever

was going on, he wanted nothing more to do with it.

He did not know they were leaving India, his home for years. The word meant nothing to him. But he was interested in the drive from the Hunwal tea estate to Jorhat airfield. He stood with his paws on the dashboard, eyes agog at the new sights along the road – the water buffalo, the cyclists, vans and lorries jostling along the roadway, bright saris fluttering in the wind, the scent of the Brahmaputra river.

At Jorhat airfield, Chinky was almost speechless with amazement. But not quite. The great silver Dakota did not frighten him. It was only another kind of bird . . . another way to travel.

It was even more exciting than hearing a tiger dragging a water buffalo after the kill. When the plane took off, he viewed the dwindling land below with star-bright eyes, paws kneading the arm of the cabin seat in a kind of tribal rhythm. This was really living.

His behaviour during the flight was impeccable. The memsahib was relieved. She had imagined a berserk animal in the cabin, or having to keep Chinky shut up which he would have hated.

Chinky wore his disdainful expression. He had his own label and his own ticket. He knew how to behave. He was a superior cat, an oriental, a warrior, athlete, supernatural being, and now a sophisticated traveller.

The sophisticated traveller bit the memsahib's sister on the leg in Calcutta. He did not care for Calcutta. It smelt different; the poverty rose in a wave and hit his delicate sense of smell, used to the scent of fish and the moist green aromatics of his beloved tea country.

Calcutta was an endless pageant of peasants, bearded Sikhs, holy men and sacred cows, cars, bicycles, buffalo and rickshaws, oxcarts, trucks, taxis and beggars. It was groaning with the burden of its growing population; an astonishing, overwhelmingly noisy place, palled with factory smoke, the din of steamer whistles invading even the human clamour.

The memsahib stayed in Calcutta for fourteen days and dared not let Chinky off his lead. That was why he bit her sister's leg.

He was sorry afterwards. But it was too late to make amends. He breathed a sigh of relief when they took off again for the long flight to Rome. There were several refuelling stops and comfort stations for Chinky. They rushed him to any available plant pot or patch of desert; this was fun. Chinky enjoyed the challenge. He often spotted a dry plant or dusty digging bowl first.

The apogee of the flight was when he was taken on his lead up to the flight deck to meet the pilot. He behaved as if he was always being taken to flight decks. It was all a bit of a mystery but he showed a polite interest in the dials and little flashing lights and everyone thought he was wonderful. Which he was.

The weekend stop in Rome presented a few problems. They left an indignant Chinky locked in the hotel bedroom, and hung up the DO NOT DISTURB notice. He was furious. He wanted to explore. Later they took him for a walk on his lead. He guessed it was a new version of spot the plant, and instead found a drain in a cleaning room.

Chinky was intrigued by the view of London from the air but not so keen on Heathrow. An airport policeman and a man from the quarantine kennels boxed up the spitting Siamese warrior and took him away in a van.

The memsahib watched them take Chinky away. She wondered sadly how he would cope with confinement. He had always been so free.

'This is not just an ordinary cat,' said the vet examining Chinky at the kennels. 'This is a strong character, a very strong character indeed.'

Chinky glared at him, blue eyes gleaming, long cream tail whipping the air. He was straining with frustration and fury.

'You are perhaps a little too fierce for domestic life in England. No tigers to fight here, old chap.'

After being neutered, Chinky was one degree easier to cope with; he became companionable and affectionate, but only with the very few people he liked. To the rest of the world his attitude was exactly the same.

He settled to life in England but there were no snakes to catch, no rumbling or roaring in the night or beating of the drums. His paws itched to be off, and an hour after being let out of quarantine, he was off up a tree, the memsahib hanging onto his lead. Time passed and his fur darkened that first winter in England. When a special hutch arrived he had no idea that he was about to embark on the biggest adventure of all.

The SS *Uganda* left Tilbury early at dawn one morning in October 1957. Chinky was more than a little puzzled at his new quarters in the hutch secured on one of the forward decks. The train journey to the docks had been invigorating, looking out of windows and watching the rural countryside flashing by, but now this new place . . . a house on water? Chinky was cautious, reserving his options.

He soon made it quite clear, and loudly, that he had no intention of staying put in his hutch. Once the ship had passed through the Bay of Biscay, he was indignantly asking to be let out. He was not going to spend the entire voyage cooped up like some pathetic invalid when there were so many new things to see and smell.

He got very bad tempered, and when the purser put his hand into the cage uninvited, Chinky bit his finger. It was a protest on behalf of all hutch-haters.

'I suppose I'll have to take you out on your lead just to keep you quiet,' said the memsahib. Chinky stood patiently while she fixed his lead to the collar. 'Now don't let me down. Behave.'

Chinky smirked his Siamese smirk. It was not quite a grin. He knew how to behave. Hadn't he been trained? He took to the ship like a second home; he had four sea legs in no time. He went everywhere. Everyone knew him. He was someone. But the swimming pool puzzled him; he could see no point in people splashing about in that horrid wet stuff.

It began to get very hot in the Red Sea. He lay panting in the hutch, his fur like an extra heated blanket wrapped round his skin. It had been hot in Assam, but the breeze from the jungle hills had tempered the air.

The memsahib was worried. She spent a lot of time on her knees talking to him and taking him cool water to drink. She took him to her cabin, where he lay under a damp cloth. Perhaps she should have left Chinky in England – but who would have given a home to a half-wild Siamese? Who would have loved him? No, she had done the right thing bringing Chinky with them to Kenya, but at the moment it was far too hot for someone wearing a permanent fur coat.

The captain came to the rescue.

'It's far too hot here for that animal,' he said, stating the obvious. 'Move the hutch up to my deck where there's more breeze.'

Chinky spent the rest of the voyage on the captain's deck, which was, of course, his rightful place. He could have told them that.

Chinky had a splendid view of Fort Jesus, which commands the entrance channel to Mombasa harbour. Mombasa was built on an island, a coral atoll, with deep water north and south. He could see the old harbour with ancient curved dhows at anchor, the dense mass of Arab houses, and ahead the modern city that had sprung up with the port of Kilindini.

The cat was tense with barely contained excitement. This was a totally new place! They went over the causeway linking the island to mainland, past many-storeyed houses jammed together in narrow streets thronged with black-skinned people.

They began the 320-mile train journey to Nairobi, climbing through the coastal hills, then the long haul over undulating country, speeding through cuttings and embankments some over forty-five feet high. Chinky was convinced they were travelling inside mountains.

The memsahib scratched under his smooth brown chin as he darted this way and that, taking in all the new sights.

'Soon be there,' she said wearily. 'Not long now.'

Chinky could sleep. He could sleep anywhere. But the memsahib slept only fitfully, keeping half an eye open on Chinky and their luggage.

They crossed dry and scorched plains dancing with dust devils in the shimmering heat, another source of astonishment to the cat.

They drove along the main avenue in the capital city, a wide handsome road built so that a trek cart drawn by sixteen oxen could turn completely. Now there were new office blocks, hotels and shops shining in the harsh sunlight, each street a profusion of trees and flowers, jacarandas carpeting the ground with blue blossom, fountains of bougainvillaea spilling from balconies.

Chinky liked everything about Nairobi except the anti-rabies injection which he had to have before they journeyed further up-country. He spat and scratched the veterinary assistants, but it was no good. This was wild-animal country and one small brown and cream cat was no problem.

They soon left behind the gardened highway of the city and took to the unmade earth roads that crossed the Great Rift Valley. The weather-eroded grassland was dotted with acacia thorn trees and bushes, lakes where massed pink flamingoes strutted, and zebra and wilde-beeste grazing the dry grasses. Chinky saw buck and gazelle, heard hyenas, smelt leopard and lion, screeched back at the chattering monkeys swinging in the trees.

Chinky settled quickly to living in several bungalows, travelling everywhere with them to various tea gardens in up-country Kenya, picnicking with the family in the beautiful green and uncultivated country of the Nandi Hill district, where the tea plantations were just begin-ning to be planted out. It was a lovely land of green rolling hills and deep valleys, cultivated farms and native *shambas* with round thatched huts and sweet corn growing close by.

Chinky would still not tolerate any other animals except their own labrador, and even chased off a long-nosed ant-eater who ventured onto the veranda. The astonished creature had never faced a wild, spitting, arched-back Siamese warrior before. He took to his heels, leaving Chinky victorious.

It was possibly an insect that nearly killed Chinky. Suddenly he became so ill that the memsahib took him fifty miles to the nearest vet. Sickness and weakness made Chinky no more docile and the vet had difficulty handling him.

'I've no suitable drugs here,' he said despairingly. He could see the cat was going downhill fast. A raging fever clouded the intelligent blue eyes.

The memsahib took him home, cradled in his basket from Assam, stopping frequently to feed him milk and brandy from a dropper. It was one journey that Chinky never wanted to experience again.

Back home, he spent the days lying on the memsahib's lap or crouching in a cool spot by the bungalow's shade. He gradually recovered; he was never quite the same warrior, although the fierce spirit was still there.

Two crested cranes decided to live in the field next to their garden. Chinky did not like this at all. He did not want the two big proud birds living so close to him. He started to stalk them, crouching in the long grass, a low growl coming from his throat.

But the big birds were not afraid of one small cat. They began to dance round him, their great black and white wings outspread menacingly. Chinky stood his ground, spitting and hissing with his squashed hat look. He countered their attack with aggressive yowls, fur standing on end . . . .

Suddenly Chinky lost his nerve, raced back to the fence and fled to the safety of the garden. He was trembling, but not with fear. He was furious with himself. He had met his match and it was difficult to accept.

Three years later Chinky undertook his last long journey, the flight home to England. The regulations had changed and Chinky was not allowed to travel with the family. He boarded a special animal freight plane in a specially constructed crate. The memsahib was apprehensive, but what could she do? She could not argue with an international airline that Chinky was a seasoned traveller and better behaved than most.

No one knew what Chinky went through on that flight or what strange animal cries came from the other crates . . . wildebeeste, monkeys, lions . . . perhaps even an elephant. If he was terrified he did not show it. But when they visited him in quarantine in Folkestone, he got so over-excited because he thought he was being taken out, they decided it was not fair to visit him again until it was time to take him home.

It was a long six months. But Chinky did not forget them. He was overjoyed to see the memsahib again. They put on his collar and lead and he leaped without hesitation into the car. Thank goodness that's over, his look said. Where are we going now? But this time he was not going far.

His new home was a long sunny garden in Sussex, down a quiet lane shaded with leafy trees. He still defended his territory, but now there were only squirrels to chase off the strawberry beds and birds and butterflies and ants that scuttled over the warm paving stones. He missed the old adventures but he did not complain. He knew he was slowing down and memories of his great journeys were growing dim. He was content to sit and doze in the dappled afternoon sun and dream of his warrior days, occasionally whipping his long tail . . . still proud and fierce.

Give or take a few ship's cats, Chinky knew he must be the most travelled cat in the world: ten thousand miles or more with not a hair out of place. He yawned. It must be some sort of record . . .

Chinky died, aged eighteen, in his old cane basket from Assam.

# Cat Knievel

No one told me there was going to be an audition. Nor that I was the item being auditioned. How was I to know, as I munched my way through a man-sized breakfast, that today I was required to look sleek and athletic, and not like an over-stuffed ginger-banded bean bag?

I was aware of the air of tension in the kitchen as I polished off the leftovers in Hebe's bowl. Hebe is a black Persian queen with an appetite like a bird, which is just as well for me. I took me and my stomach to the windowsill for a tidy-up while I had the strength. My fawn paws worked overtime as I coaxed my thick russet and caramel fur into near perfect order.

'I must have been mad,' Val was saying, rushing around cleaning up the place. This meant we were having visitors. I knew the signs. 'I wish I'd never written to them. After all, I mean, what does it matter, really?'

'You knew they'd go for it,' said Robert. 'It's just the kind of thing they love. A performing cat and an idiot owner. They don't often get both at once.'

'I'm going to look a fool if Copper won't cooperate,' Val wailed. 'He'll probably sleep all afternoon and refuse to budge an inch. Oh no, we've run out of cat sweets. I'll

483

have to rush to the shops and get some. He'll never perform without his usual bribe.'

'Bribe?'

'Reward.'

By now I had the faintest suspicion that they were talking about me partly because my name is Copper and I am addicted to cat sweeties. I need my daily fix. Sorry, folks, that's just a joke. I'm doing what comes naturally, and if a little reward comes my way naturally too, then I'm not one to refuse.

'May I point out that Evel Knievel is at present looking so unhealthily fat that I doubt if he could jump over a pincushion if you gave him a hefty push,' said Robert as he left for work.

Val scooped me up into her arms. I purred hello, patted her face gently, tugged a claw through a tempting brown curl.

'He weighs a ton,' she said, her voice doom-laden. 'He won't be able to do a thing.'

That was true. I only felt like sleeping it off under my favourite forsythia bush at the end of the garden.

A young man arrived, sleek, smooth, trendy. I could tell from his voice that he was not over the moon about cats. His name was Martin O'Connell and he was a director. Director of what? But I was only marginally curious.

'Do you like cats?' I heard Val asking him.

'I can take them or leave them,' he replied, with a distinct lack of enthusiasm.

I settled back into the warm crushed grass of my hideaway. It was nothing to do with me. The pale March sunshine dappled my coppery fur and lulled me into an unsuspecting doze.

But suddenly it had a great deal to do with me. I was unceremoniously heaved out and cajoled into my routine. It was the same old stuff – sit, beg, lie down, shake hands. Years ago, for reasons she cannot remember, Val had decided to train me in basic obedience as one would a dog. I was very easy to teach, of course, being intelligent and an extrovert. I didn't mind the treats either.

'Paw.'

I held out my left paw. Always my left. It's something to do with balance.

'Down.'

I flopped down, full length. I went through it all, trying to maintain a matching lack of enthusiasm, reacting to Val's voice and hand signals with an air of casual sophistication. I was doing it all for Val, though I do quite enjoy it. The O'Connell man was looking at me without any expression. I could do that too. I stared back at him, unflinching. I do have the strangest colour eyes; they are the colour of the underside of a new leaf, like the clear green sea off Cyprus; like a piece of polished green onyx marble in a museum. They can be disconcerting to some humans.

'Well . . . how about this jumping over toddlers you say he can do,' the director went on, continuing his laid-back attitude.

'Yes, yes,' said Val, rapidly producing our own home-grown toddler, a two-year-old variety called Jenni, and a collection of toys to add to the line-up.

'Jump,' Val commanded.

I cleared toddler and teddy with one spring. I was certainly not at my best as I was carrying a lot of extra weight. But Mr O'Connell seemed marginally impressed.

'Could we add a few more toddlers?' he suggested.

For two hours I defied gravity, heaving my great bulk over various toddlers and objects. Not satisfied with toddler-jumping, the director wanted to see stunning feats of athleticism involving various toys and children.

'Could we get him to jump over a toddler pushing a pram?' suggested Martin with signs of interest glimmering in his eyes. 'What do you think, eh?'

Val looked at me dubiously. It had been half-day

closing at the shops so she was rewarding me with biscuits, most of which I politely declined. She could see that I was getting tired and bored.

'I could get some more toddlers tomorrow,' she said, frantically thinking of her friends' offspring.

Martin went into a deep directorial think. I began to slink off. There was a limit to what I would do for a biscuit.

'Okay, then. We'll call it a day. The filming will begin at ten o'clock tomorrow. Sharp.'

They let me sleep on their bed. This was a great treat and I spent the night happily tramping about, pawing, clawing, purring, first with one and then the other. Of course, I did sleep but I can purr quite loudly even when fast asleep.

'Get this cat off the bed,' grumbled Robert from under the covers.

'No, I want Copper in a certain frame of mind for tomorrow,' said Val, trying to sleep with me half sprawled over her pillow, my fur tickling her nose. 'I want Copper to be relaxed and happy.'

'Urrgh . . . tomorrow.'

Anyone would think they didn't sleep well. I don't know what they were grumbling about; they've got a lovely bed. Try sleeping in a cardboard box in the kitchen every night and see how they'd like that.

'Will you go out and buy a bribe, I mean, a chicken,' asked Val anxiously at breakfast time. 'I'd like to cook it before the film crew arrive. It's for Copper's lunch.'

Lunch? Whatever happened to breakfast? I wolfed down the meagre spoonful of Whiskas on my saucer and looked up expectantly. What was that? A sample?

'Sorry, Copper. No more breakfast for you. This is your great day. You've got to be a little peckish.'

Peckish! I was starving. I prowled around, wondering what I could find that was edible. Crumbs from under the high-chair? There were some congealed bits of boiled egg and soggy cereal. No, thank you. Whatever was going on? Overfed one day, diet the next. I looked for the Persian queen's dish but it had been whisked away. Now that wasn't playing fair.

Okay then, don't feed me, I thought. They'd be sorry. I sat aloof, grooming my whiskers and long striped tail as if I didn't care. I was looking thinner already.

Suddenly the place erupted as the film crew arrived. There were hundreds of them, at least seven. I fled, watching the commotion from a safe distance. Furniture was moved out into the garden (were the family going to live in the garden? What about rain?); tall things with white faces were installed throwing out a bright hot glare. Long black snakes slithered around the living-room floor and boxes of equipment filled every available space.

Spotlights, cables, cameras, microphones . . . I'd never heard these strange words before. And the noise! The house was full of people all talking to each other at once and stomping about. What on earth was happening? I looked at Val, but she too had caught this distraught look.

People were stepping over other people as a man fiddled with something in the hall; another wrestled with a stubborn camera in the kitchen. The house had gone mad. It was like a rabbit warren on a Bank Holiday.

I kept out of the way though my nose was twitching with curiosity. The director arrived wearing a rakish cap and carrying a clipboard of notes. He was telling everyone else what to do. My poor stomach was rumbling. I connected Val's breakfast lapse with this horde of people who had invaded our house. I slid off into the garden. They wouldn't miss me. Perhaps they wouldn't even notice my disappearance for days . . .

'Where's Copper?' asked Val.

Her voice was like a thin reed in the lull before a storm.

There was a stunned silence. No one moved. The director went white. Panic swept through the assembled crew. Even the cables twitched. They were ready to film and the star had vanished.

'Oh my God. The cat,' gasped Martin. 'Find the cat. Esther will be furious.'

The whisper went round like a word game . . . find the cat, find the cat . . . careful now, don't scare him.

'Ah, there he is,' said Val with the air of a magician. 'I've spotted his ginger fur in the bushes.'

I was brought back, limp, disinterested, but I was only pretending. I could smell chicken cooking in the kitchen. That was a good sign.

The equipment and lights had been positioned. There were a lot of extra toddlers and every imaginable kind of toy. Were we having a jumble sale? Perhaps we had become a nursery school?

'Now, Copper darling,' said Val, taking me aside. 'This is your great chance. You're going to be famous. You're going to be on *That's Life*! Isn't that exciting?'

I nudged her chin. *That's Life*? Never heard of it. What was it, for heaven's sake? I'd been on a windowsill, on the top of a car, on a flower bed, but I'd never been on a that's life.

For the next six hours they had me working like a horse. Sit, beg, lie down, shake hands, jump this, jump that. Every conceivable camera angle was trained on me and caught on film.

Jumping toddlers isn't that easy. They move . . . unexpectedly. An arm, a leg, and curly little head can suddenly catch me in mid-flight. Ouch. It requires precision, timing and a certain expertise to cope with toddlers. I'm no amateur.

Someone crawled on the floor with this black object called a microphone and put it in front of my mouth. They wanted to catch me purring. I shook out my back leg. It's what I do when I'm embarrassed, and my goodness, was I embarrassed. It was covered in dust too. I gave it a quick lick. Then they wanted to catch me cleaning myself. Invasion of privacy, I called it. But I didn't complain. Val was rewarding me with masses of chicken morsels and I could handle quite a few.

There was a break for lunch; it was hardly worth my putting in an appearance. I got a kitten-size helping of chicken. What was going on? No proper meals but rewards coming my way like it was Christmas. Not the balanced diet I was accustomed to. Val wasn't eating much either.

Martin O'Connell was no longer so laid-back and remote. He became fired with enthusiasm for new stunts. He invented more complicated obstacles for me to jump over . . . toddler pushing pram, toddler on rocking horse, a two-storey green-tiled dolls' house, rows and rows of squirming toddlers side by side on the carpet . . . I was beginning to see toddlers coming out of the wall.

'Wonderful! Wonderful!' exclaimed Martin. 'Come on, Copper, you can do it! That's my baby! Did you catch that expression on film? I want that lion look. Again! Copper baby, you're the tops!'

By now I was like a machine, a gleaming oiled machine of muscles and sinews, my russet fur glowing in patches and stripes like fire under the hot lights. I leaped through the air, effortlessly and gracefully, my long tail streaming, a powerful beast of the jungle, a leopard in flight, muscles rippling under the taut shining coat. I was ecstatic. I could jump forever and I could jump anything. I could jump over trees, clear the roof tops, take on the moon . . .

One evening they insisted that I came indoors to watch some programme on television. Val and Robert were eagerly waiting to see what would be shown of six hours of filming. It had been weeks ago, way back in March. I'd almost forgotten all about it.

The programme began. We waited. I yawned delicately and wondered if I could ask to go out. There was far more going on in the garden.

'And now to Copper,' said Esther Rantzen, grinning widely. 'Our pet of the week. The toddler-leaping cat!'

'Jump!'

I pricked my ears. I heard Val's voice giving me my command. What did she want me to jump? But she was chatting away to Robert, not even looking at me.

'Jump!'

Hang on, now. She was doing it without moving her lips. I sat up, prepared to jump but the command simply wasn't clear. Jump what? The Sunday newspaper on the carpet . . .?

My attention was directed to the television screen. I yawned again. I hardly recognised the splodge of ginger doing all those pathetic little stunts. You should see me now. Since then I have gone on to perfecting bigger and better jumps. Now I am magnificent.

That other stuff was child's play.

# Susie's Letters

Dear Auntie Joan,

You are so very good to me! You sent me my first real live letter – a true message of sympathy for my lost love – and then you made a special journey to see me and to bring me a gift of Mr Safeway's rabbit. It was delicious, thank you.

How can I ever make amends for my behaviour yesterday? I do love you, but please let me explain. The day began badly. I made my call to the garden much earlier than usual so that I would be ready for you, but I stopped to speak to two men delivering coal. How did I know that they were going to pat me? My white ruffle was black!

Mother grumbled and helped to remove some of the coal dust from my fur but I was disturbed by the incident. However, when you arrived, it was lovely. I was looking forward to being alone with you for a cosy chat in the afternoon. That's why I went into the garden while you had a peaceful lunchtime. And then! I got ambushed by two black and white cats for hours. They wouldn't let me move until you came out into the garden and then they chased me. Since Nelson went out of my life I have had no wish for further male friends. I hope I made that clear.

As you say, males are too fickle, especially when a puss like that flapper Snowy winks at them. She is only two and I am nine years of age, but let Nelson find out for himself that youth can be very deceiving.

Speaking of age, I want to tell you about the deep sadness of my life. The first human friend I had was Isabelle. She was ninety-nine and very poor. She had one armchair and a bed in the same room and she always let me choose which I fancied for my afternoon rest. Part of her pension was put into a box and saved to buy me a tin of best salmon or sardines. When my mother heard of it, she said she was ashamed of me, but Isabelle and I understood each other. She said I was the loveliest thing in her life.

She died. Mother said that a lady of ninety-nine was too old to live. I do not understand that; she was so young in heart and mind. I grieved for her for months, sitting on her windowsill every day.

My next friend was Daisy, a lady of ninety-three years. I did not often go into her house, because she was afraid of my getting under her feet. I went to her back door to chat to her, caught all the mice from her falling down coalshed, and every sunny afternoon I waited in the garden until she brought her chair. She would nurse me and we would spend the afternoon in sleep. We were good friends, and I mourn her too.

My last friend was Mr M., who lives across the road. Regularly he would be at home for a day to clean and mend his car. I spent the day with him. If it was warm, I sat on top of the car, but if it was cold and damp, I sat inside and we chatted through the window. When there was a shower of rain, he would come inside and sit with me. That was very cosy. He would say in his kind, gruff voice: 'Poor little Susan'. You can tell that he understood me.

One day he told me he was going to retire and that we would have many days together. Soon afterwards I ran across the road to him but two men were holding him. He had died of a heart attack. What sorrow.

My mother is sorry for me and does all she can to make up for the loss of my loyal friends, but you can see, Auntie Joan, how I need your love, and I shall always be your most affectionate puss-niece,

Susan

PS    Having scorned Nelson on one occasion, I relented today and spent four hours with him. But no kissing! When he came this morning, he looked thin, dirty and miserable with a lump out of his tail. My heart melted and so did Mother's, for she gave him a piece of chicken. Whether the friendship will continue, I do not know, but he seemed comforted in sitting with me, and that's what love is all about, isn't it?

Mitcham
20 April 1980

Dear Auntie Joan,

Another little letter to you because my 'affair' with Nelson and then the altercation with him made me forget to answer the most important part of your letter to me.

Thank you for your kind invitation. I would love to see you and meet your beloved puss-cat Kiwi, but I think that the journey is too long for me. Perhaps it is a law of nature that humans cannot chose friends for their cats. My mother learned that lesson the hard way.

Thinking that we would all have a cosy Christmas afternoon together, she carried me round to her friend Mildred, who has two cats, Nimmo (he bears a remarkable resemblance to the actor Derek Nimmo) and Sookie. It was a disaster!

Nimmo pranced around with back arched like a silly tom-cat and Sookie rushed behind a door and kept peeking out at me. How would you feel, Auntie, if Uncle Wally took you to a strange house for tea, and someone ran behind a door and peeped out at you? I was very disturbed and so I sat on a chair and swore continuously on one note, scarcely pausing for breath, until I was wrapped in a blanket and taken home again to spend the rest of the afternoon alone. I needed that solitude to regain my equilibrium.

My mother tells me that your surname is 'Toy'. What a lovely name. (I adore my toys, especially Sally and Tommy, whom I suckle or kick according to my mood.) What better name could you have? My only other choice for you would be 'Rabbit' or perhaps 'Smoked Haddock'. Not so special as Toy, but two of my favourite dishes.

Nelson is still poorly, with a lump out of his tail. It looks very sore. Mother would like to take him to the vet to have his health checked and then adopt him – but I say no, very firmly. The pangs of jealousy would be too great for me to bear, Auntie, and I would have to leave home.

The other black and white male is still trying to force his charm upon me and the other night upset me deeply. Being put to bed is a personal and intimate occasion. I am cuddled and lowered gently into my basket and left with a kiss and a little prayer. That old moggy sat the other side of the door and listened! How rude and insensitive can you get? He is a good-looking, dapper little fellow. Just the type that you can never trust.

When I write next, Auntie, I would like to tell you about my early life. It began very happily but did not progress according to plan. In my case, my foster-mother had to become my mother, and I lost a whole family at one blow. But that is a long story and will take at least two letters to relate.

All my love and purr-rr-rr's to you,
from your puss-niece
Susan

Mitcham
Written from my favourite
chair in the sitting room

Dear Auntie Joan,

I am writing to tell you that for a few days I have been a
very sad puss. My little human girl friend, Jane, took me
to her home just round the corner, and there in a garden I
saw my one-eyed Nelson kiss Snowy, a pure-white
coated cat. (There is nothing else pure about her.) She is a
pert little flirt but my Nelson has yet to find out how
worthless she is.

Of course, I am not so broken-hearted as I was over
my first and real love, Tibby-Tabs. We spent part of
every day together and, when I was ill, he visited me
twice a day and watched me through the window. I lost
him three years ago from an attack of 'flu.

My only companions now are Tom and Jerry – two
growing kittens who live two doors away. I hate them.
You may remember that I had a ginger neighbour,
Freddie, who disappeared one evening. He was my hero
and taught me three things – to swear, to spit and a third
device which is too indecent to mention to you (you will
be pleased to know that I have dropped all use of it). I
employ the first two skills to keep those conceited kittens
in their place.

All my purr-purrs,
Ever your loving
Susie


Mitcham
10 May 1980

Dear Auntie Joan Toy,

Thank you for your letter. I am indeed lucky to have
such a devoted auntie, and although I like Mr Purr, the
butcher, I still think that Toy is *the* most wonderful
name.

Thank you also for the cake that you sent home on my

mother's last visit to you. Did you know that I like your cakes? It has to be your own make, of course.

On Wednesday mornings a lady named Ruby comes to help us, and this time Mother gave her a piece of your cake. I *made* her share it with me. I know it is not good manners but the scent of the cake is so delicious that I cannot resist pushing and scratching until I am given a share.

Yes, Auntie, I do think that cats have 'nine lives'. It is because we are very wise and we can act quickly and cleverly in most difficult circumstances. Also we are shrewd in judging human character and we soon learn whom we can trust – and ways of watching cruel or careless people. Of course, we vary in character and intelligence, as you know, but given reasonable care, I am proud to say that our brains are superb and we know how to use them.

In my last letter I said that my life had not developed as planned. I will now begin to tell my story.

My mother was a lovely little puss called Mina. She had only one eye (perhaps that is why I like Nelson) but she was the best mother a kitten could have, and she taught me my good manners. One day she told me and my brothers that it was time for us to think about leaving her and making our own way in the world. We all cried but she told us to be brave, because her human mother was kind and would try to find us happy homes.

That afternoon a gentleman named Mike arrived with a little girl, Sharon. He chose one of my brothers, but Sharon held on to me and would not let me go. She pleaded with her daddy until he agreed that I should be taken to their home. It was a long journey. I had never been in a car and I clung to Sharon and cried all the way.

When we arrived home, I found a lovely human mother, Pat, and another little girl, Michelle. They all made a great fuss of me – I was very pretty with a little kitten body and a beautiful fluffy tail. I was so happy, Auntie. They let me do just as I liked and I slept with

Sharon every night, until I found out that Mike danced professionally and did not come home some nights until two o'clock in the morning.

I used to hide in the bushes when I was called in the evening and play in the street until Mike came home. We would sleep together downstairs so that we did not disturb the family upstairs.

When I was about a year old, a puppy named Brandy joined the family. He was great fun and we chased each other round the house in the day and sometimes in the night until Mike shouted at us to be quiet. Then others joined the family – a parrot (I never spoke to him), rabbits, chickens and lots of pigeons. I can never understand that human phrase 'put the cat amongst the pigeons'. I was always with them and the rabbits and the chickens. We all played together and nothing ever happened to us.

There was one incident, but it was not my fault. Little Flora Fantail was one of Mike's special favourites but she was a dim-witted pigeon. She fell down the chimney of my present mother's house along the road and got herself stuck on a ledge. Fred, the ginger cat, and I rushed into the house, sat either side of the fireplace and talked to her. She answered but would not come down. All the neighbours tried to help.

On the third day, the RSPCA inspector arrived. He called the fire brigade, but they could not get old fantail. The next day he called an old-fashioned sweep. A little old man came with brushes and rods and fixed them up the chimney. Nothing happened!

We thought Flora had died, but just as we were all having a sooty cup of tea (sooty milk for Fred and me), she hopped onto the brush and was rescued with a lot more soot. She was quite composed and haughty, as if it was her usual habit to sit in chimneys. Mike gave her away to a gentleman living in the country, but she refused to stay and came back to sit on the chimney. How could anyone be so dim?

There was one other happening. Old Robert Pigeon fell down my friend Daisy's chimney. She was frightened and would not let me in. I had to watch everything through the window. My present foster-mother called the emergency gas officer to unfix the gas fire, and there was Rob in the grate. He was looking very poorly so she put him in her bath. She intended to give him a little brandy, but her hand slipped and she gave him a whole spoonful. She thought she had killed him, but no, he was quite drunk and snored all night in the bath. In the morning, Mike cleaned him and put the broken leg in a splint, and as far as I know he is still living.

Lots of loving purrs,<br>
your puss-niece<br>
Susan

Mitcham<br>
27 May 1980

Dear Auntie Joan Toy,

Another piece of your special puss cake! How clever of you to know the exact number of currants I like in each portion. Do you think of me as you count them into the cooking bowl?

I thought today that from the cosiness of my mother's bed (my special cover is on it, of course), I would continue my memoirs.

When I was two and half years of age, Mike took me aside and explained to me that he was what humans call 'black'. (I had not noticed any difference because I too am mainly black.) He said that he had a dear mother far away across the sea and she would like to see him. He could not take any animals, so would I live with a foster-mother for five weeks? What could I say, Auntie? After a little cry, I agreed, because I knew the lady who was to be my foster-mother.

The day of departure came. I was carried along to house number sixteen from house number ten, and put into the arms of my foster-mother. Auntie, my life changed suddenly. I had to learn a new word: 'discipline'. No running round the streets at night, or hiding in the bushes till 2 a.m., eating and sleeping where I liked. No! I could play in the street until 9 p.m., but on the stroke of the clock I had to be indoors. After an hour of playing up and down the stairs, I was put to bed in my own basket in my own room and left with a goodnight kiss and a prayer for my safety while my family was away.

Sometimes my foster-mum would call out in the night: 'Are you all right, Susie?' and I would mee-ee-eeow: 'I'm lonely.' She would come and carry me back to bed with her for the rest of the night. That was lovely. She would have had me every night but, not being disciplined before, I wanted to play and have a snack in the middle of the night. It was too disturbing, she said.

Time passed pleasantly. The only trouble was Fred! We were supposed to share our foster-mother, but I soon learned that Fred never wanted to share anything. I tried every ruse and wile I knew. I tried creeping up and kissing him while he slept, but he would wake in a great fury and swear abominably. I chased him, played with him, scared him by hiding behind the curtains and doors. (I could hear my foster mother say: 'Careful, Fred. She's hiding somewhere.')

Nothing would coax him, and then one day, my patience exhausted, I terrified him. I chased him into the drain and held him there until my foster-mother found us . . . Fred crouched on the grating, and me sitting on the side above him with my paw raised menacingly. Fred was rescued and given some cream. I was scolded and slapped, and after that we ignored each other. If we met accidentally, we passed with a spit and a hiss, until the day, years later, Fred disappeared. I will tell you that story another time.

After a long, long time my family returned and everyone came along to carry me home to number ten. We hugged and kissed each other. Brandy and I rushed around the house madly. All discipline was forgotten (except Mike noticed how well-behaved I was at first), and life was normal and happy again. I thought forever, but it was not to be.

All my purrs, dear Auntie,
Your loving puss-niece,
Susan

Mitcham
June 1980

Dear Auntie Joan Toy,

I am continuing my memoirs quickly, because I have a puss foreboding that something is going to happen in my life. A change that makes my spine quiver and my tail twitch.

Pat, my human mother, was always looking after the children, feeding them, putting them to bed, getting them up again, and bathing them. We kittens were taught to attend to ourselves at a very early age, but I did have an unexpected human bath once.

My foster-mother has a bathroom downstairs. She leaves the window open and by jumping onto the shed (it is my shed, with a cat door and a basket in case I get caught out in the rain), I can fix my back feet onto the window frame, slide my front paws half way down the bathroom wall, and then make a clever leap and land between the bath and the toilet seat. I then curl up on the mat until the door is opened and she says: 'Hello, come in, Susie.'

One particular afternoon, I was just about to follow this procedure, then to my surprise I saw her in the bath. Her warning: 'Careful Susie, the wall is wet' was too late. My front paws slid too far and I somersaulted into the bath with my foster-mother. What a splash! There was I, soaking wet, sitting on her tummy. Before you could say 'tails and whiskers', I was wrapped in one towel and she was wrapped in another, sitting in front of the fire trying to dry ourselves. I had hot milk whilst she had hot tea and we were none the worse for our adventure.

The only other time that I had a bath was very unfortunate. My foster-mother has a goldfish pond at the bottom of her garden. Fred spends hours on the side and sometimes he catches a fish, which he brings over as a gift to my foster-mother. (She never looks very pleased.) One day I thought I would try fishing. I sat there patiently for a long time, and then Fred must have crept up behind me because all of a sudden I felt a paw on my back. I lost my balance and felt myself drowning. Freddie sat there smirking, whiskers twitching, while I scrambled out and rushed in to my foster-mother. Once more I was wrapped in a towel and given hot milk, but she would not believe that Freddie had pushed me. She said that she did not listen to such tales, and so he never had the scolding he deserved.

But, dear Auntie Joan, then something really dreadful happened to me. The family found another house, not far away, and Mike said that it would not be safe to take me. I would have to live with my foster-mother always and not keep visiting from one home to the other. I cried and cried, but it all came to pass. Life was never the same. I used to sit on the windowsill of my old home, just hoping, but my foster-mother would come along and cuddle me and carry me home. So I had to learn to accept her as my mother. She told me that the only place my surname would be changed was on my sick record card at the vet's.

Next time, dear Auntie, I will tell you what happened in my new life.

All my purr-purrs for a little while,
from your puss-niece,
Susan

Dear Auntie Joan Toy,

Sometimes I too get a poorly head and I am so sorry for you. I wonder if you bang yours against the wardrobe as I do. Some of our furniture stands on polished lino and I love to chase a ball around the bedroom, but I go so fast I cannot stop myself, then bang! that's my head hit something. A dangerous game, Auntie. Please do not play it too often, because it will worry my mother if she knows that both of us have a sore head.

When Freddie knew that I was going to live here, there were terrible scenes. His temper was uncontrollable and his language unprintable! He came to meals as usual but would not share my place-mat. He insisted on having his meals on top of the fridge and then sleeping on the plate-rack of the cooker.

One night I thought that I would try sleeping on the plate-rack. It was exciting. You could stand up and look into the kitchen next door. When Fred came in for breakfast, I thought he was going to explode!

He spent quite a lot of time under the bed too. Mother and I would pop upstairs and take him a little cream.

She would say: 'Never mind, Susie. He can't help it.' She was upset really, Auntie, and felt that her house had been taken over by two uncivilised cats.

Occasionally we would make a pact to give up washing ourselves for a week, or hide at night when we were called then ask for the door to be opened about 4 a.m. This was life for the next two years.

Then one foggy October evening, Fred disappeared. When Mother called us, the fog was very thick and Fred did not come. He never missed a meal and we knew that something was wrong. All the children in the neighbourhood joined in the search. For weeks the postman, the milkman, the window cleaner and everyone looked for him, but he was never seen again. Poor dear Fred! We cried for him.

I missed my own dear family very much. How much I did not know myself until later that year. My next letter will tell you.

My love and purr-rrs,<br>Your puss-niece,<br>Susan

Mitcham<br>June 1980

My dear Auntie Joan Toy,

A sad little puss-niece is writing to you today because my old home at number ten is empty again and I cannot get in to look in all the corners. No one knows why I go to all the corners. It is a secret that I keep to my own puss-self.

After that, all the cats of the neighbourhood came to sympathise with me. Then my life became very peaceful. I played in the garden with the children next door. They shared their sweets with me until I was sick.

One night I was naughty and stayed out with my own special puss, Tibby-Tabs. He had a bad cold and the first thing I did when I went into breakfast was to sneeze. Mother was upset and gave me some cod-liver oil and malt, but it was no good. I was ill and had to go twice to the vet.

Tibby-Tabs was not well and a week after that he died. I had a relapse and was very ill indeed. Mother kept me in my bed with a fire night and day. The vet gave me injections and pills, but I was just fading away.

One day Mother remembered how clever her friend Richard was and asked him to help. He understood and explained to her that I was not trying to get better. Although I knew that my old family loved me, when they left their home empty, I felt that I had been abandoned, and in my weakness, I had lost the will to live. Mother was distressed. She used to get up in the night and tell me that I was loved and wanted. Then I would purr for her softly but I could not eat.

One morning I knew that I was fading away – the vet could do no more for me – and so Mother took my paw and kissed it. She said: 'All right, Susie, if you want to die, I'll let you go, and hold your paw.' Suddenly, Auntie, I knew that I could not leave her, and so I dragged myself to the edge of the basket and took a little milk and brandy. I began to get better from that moment.

The vet was so envious that I was being fed on chicken and jelly and cod in butter sauce, he said he would come and live with us when he was not well. I am glad that he did not come because I would not like to live with a man who was always taking my temperature and looking in my ears and mouth and feeling my tummy every day.

One winter evening I heard men's voices over the wall of some waste ground. It used to belong to the LEB, and then it was quite safe to visit the staff, to run up the fire escape of a stores building. After they left I was told never to go over the wall, but my curiosity got the better of me and that night I went to see what was happening.

The men got hold of me and put some nasty smelly stuff on my head and round my neck ruffle. Now one of my tricks is to lie very still and pretend I am not going to move, and then because I am double-jointed, I suddenly twist my body and I am off like a streak of lightning. I practise this trick on Mother sometimes.

My trick worked and I managed to get away and run home. Mother wrapped me in a towel and the next morning rushed me to the vet's. I had to stay in hospital for two days while I was cleaned and part of my ruffle was cut away. It was a terrifying experience, and please tell your own puss Kiwi about it so that she is warned. Sometimes men put this green thick liquid on you before they carry you off to be sold. Even in the few years that I have lived here, several cats have been lost for ever.

Mother has been in a search-party looking for them,

but she will never let me help. I am very carefully guarded when strangers are around. Only once I did get into the milkman's van and nearly got carried off to the depot, but he would have brought me back safely because he knew my name.

I will write soon and finish my memoirs, for I am wise and sensitive in my age, and I know that there is a great change coming to me for future years. I am sure that Mother would not let anything hurt me and so I must be happy and patient and await my new life.

With lots and lots of purrs,
from your puss-niece,
Susan

Mitcham
Still June 1980

My own dear Auntie Joan Toy,

Thank you for your loving letter. It was just what your puss-niece needed, for you have heard about my return to my family and the mixture of joy and sadness for me and my foster-mother.

A lady with a great big Airedale dog came to live at Number 10. He had a loud deep voice, especially when he saw me. I watched him at a safe distance every day, and then one day when my mother was out shopping, he broke down the fences, ploughed through the gardens (all the plants went flying into the air) and tried to attack me.

After that I was too frightened to ever go out again, even in the arms of my mother, who tried to comfort me and make me brave. My nerves were shattered. Nelson came regularly to see me. He sat on the kitchen window-sill and Mother would lift me up to kiss him and talk to him but I was afraid all the time.

My first mother, Pat, has been to see me and I am going back to live with her and Mike. Foster-mother has been doing my packing for me. Such a lot I have to take!

My basket, bed and rug, my bean-bag bed, which I like
to use during the day, my brush and comb, my cat basket
in case I have to go to the vet's, my toys, my night tray,
my rabbit saucepan, my packet of biscuits, three tins of
Whiskas and a bag of turkey-fido.

This is my last letter to you, dear Auntie, because I
cannot write from my new address. I was four and a half
years with my family, then four and a half years with my
foster-mother, and I expect to be another four and a half
years with my family again. My life has been turned into
a complete circle, but that is not the end of me, Auntie.
When cats just sit and gaze quietly, they are looking into
eternity. My foster-mother knows that and talks to me
about it. We all have to die, but there is no 'death' as
humans sometimes think, for all life returns to God who
gave it, so one day I will be with you again, dear Auntie.

Until then, all my purrs,
from your own dear puss-niece,
Susan

PS from Susan's foster-mother:

I would like to add 'Amen' to Susan's last letter. She is
now happily settled in with her original family, behaving
like the wanderer returned, demanding attention and
generally taking command of the whole family.

I miss her intensely and shall for the rest of my life.
There can never be another Susan. Thank you, Joan, for
being her dear Auntie Joan Toy. (How she enjoyed your
cake!)

# Star Struck

The deputation waited at the end of the lane, vague shapes moving in the moonlight, as mist rolling up from the Thames enveloped them, obscuring their dimensions. They were not there by chance. They met her every night. They knew what they were doing.

As a car approached the lane, their yellow eyes lit up and glinted in the sudden light, jewel bright.

'Hello, my darlings,' she called. Excitement stirred through the group and they clustered round the car so that the driver could not go on. Then habit reasserted itself and Dimly, their leader, turned towards the cottage.

It was after midnight and ten plumes of tails waved in the headlights as the car proceeded at a cat's pace along the lane, the deputation leading the car and welcoming their mistress home.

For some people, perhaps, ten cats might seem to be a bit over the top. But for Beryl Reid it is as natural as breathing. She collects cats as other people collect certain china, brasses or seaside souvenirs. She has lost count of the number of cats there have been in her life, but she has not forgotten their names: the eccentric roof and bridge dweller Lulu; one-eyed Emma; gorgeous Georgie Girl, who lived for twenty years; childhood Jumbo and

Hamish; beloved Footy, another twenty-year-old; Cuppy, a theatre cat who was more like a puppy following her around; the eighteen-pound Fred . . . They were shadows mingling with the current cats that wove around Beryl in the chilling river mist. No cat ever really left her. They stayed in her memory, long years after they had left this earth.

Dimly stretched his long black back and arched his spine. He was the only black among the current cats, who were predominantly ginger. There were four short-haired ginger cats, one long-haired ginger, one Olde English tortoiseshell, an enormous grey tabby and two brown tabbies. Dimly did a quick count. Did that make ten? He thought it did and yawned.

She was very late that evening. He had no idea where she went so regularly every day. She left at the same time in the afternoon and returned late in the dark. She was a night creature like them.

He did not know what being Beryl Reid meant. He understood nothing about theatres in London or her star billing. She was Queen Bee to him. It was the cats' name for her. Her father had called her Bee, which confirmed that the cats' choice was exactly right.

They were a motley crew. Bee's cats came from all walks of life.

Elsie was a nervous creature, unsure of how to behave after living with an Asian family in Bristol. She was acquired during a run of *Born in the Gardens* at the Theatre Royal. She was called Elsie because that was the name of the unseen cat featured in the play. But the real Elsie was a hell-cat.

Dimly was not around when Elsie first came to Honeypot Cottage, but he heard that she flew at Bee, clawing her legs till they bled. This went on for weeks until Bee said one day, in a voice that meant business: 'Elsie, how do you fancy a one-way trip to the vet's?'

Elsie did not know that Bee was an actress, nor that she would never have taken such a drastic step. But the threat worked. Elsie had a change of heart and became quite a push-over for affection.

Ronnie, at thirteen the oldest cat in the clan, was found by Bee dying of cat 'flu in a barn on a farm in Langley. Dimly had heard the story a hundred times.

She was in the country on location, filming *No Sex Please, We're British*, with Ronnie Corbett, when she discovered a tiny four-week-old kitten dying in a barn. A vet was on the set because there was a pig in the film, and Bee got him to have a look at the kitten. He said he would give it a 'flu injection and nine pills for Beryl to administer, but he did not hold out much hope.

'It won't live, you know,' he said.

'I really can't leave that little thing here,' she said.

The vet had not reckoned on Bee's determination. She got those nine pills down the tiny kitten and now Ronnie is a big butch cat, a beautiful golden-ginger colour with thick fluffy trousers.

She called him after her fellow actor, and every time she sees Ronnie Corbett, she tells him: 'Your child's doing very well.'

Dimly's own beginnings were through the RSPCA; he was one of an unwanted litter of three that arrived at the cottage on Bee's birthday in June. They became Sir Harry (named after Sir Harry Secombe), Muriel and Dimly. Sir Harry is a huge tabby with a penchant for children; Muriel is the Olde English and looks like a shaggy sheep; Dimly is the black-as-midnight cat.

Clive and Billy also came via the RSPCA and Bee has taught them to sit and stay. She believes that cats can be taught in the same way as dogs, though Barbara Woodhouse did not think this was possible.

The two newest kittens, Tufnell (called after one of Irene Handel's characters) and Paris (who slew Achilles and brought about the siege of Troy when he eloped with Helen), were also acquired from the RSPCA. Their staff thought of having a direct line to Honeypot Cottage.

The latest arrival is Jennie, a mature brown tabby in the

throes of cat grief. She had lived with an old lady who died, and was left without a home. Again the RSPCA knew who to ring for help; they knew who could coax a depressed puss back to the land of the living.

Dimly has no doubt about his Queen Bee's ability and vigour. She works hard, has dozens of engagements and little time off; she entertains and cooks wonderful meals for her friends; she also cooks for the cats – heart, liver, chicken and breast of lamb. She tries to remember which cat likes to eat what even though it is easy to get confused, especially the morning after a very late return home from the theatre.

He heard that she once fell in the river trying to rescue Footy. He was the cat who always tried to sit on her feet. He had strolled along the trunk of a willow tree, quite far out over the river. No one sitting in the garden actually saw the rescue operation, but the next minute Beryl appeared, soaked to the skin, pretty dress dripping, hair in rat's-tails, face streaming.

'I've fallen in the river,' she shrieked. 'My hair's like a Mars bar. And look at that cat!'

Footy was returning nonchalantly along the same branch. He sprang onto the lawn, unaware of all the fuss.

Bee is always saying that Dimly ought to have been called Brightly; he got his odd name in a very strange way. Some friends were staying at the cottage and looking for Beryl. One of them, Olivia, looked over to the carport and said: 'I think I can just see her moving dimly.'

After that, Beryl had to have something called Dimly to move.

Dimly does not mind what he is called. He loves the cottage, the garden, the river moving so mysteriously close by and the little noises it makes lapping the banks; he loves the other cats, particularly Elsie. They are the naughty pair. He also likes the foxes.

The cats often commune with the foxes. Bee goes to Berwick Market for rabbit to cook for the cats. What is left over she puts out for the foxes, though young Billy is a great one for seeing the foxes off.

But some nights the cats sit in a circle with the foxes. It is an amazing sight. Beryl watches from the windows of the cottage. Sometimes when the weather is very wintery, her garden becomes a haven in the snow for wild creatures – water-rats, seagulls, voles, mice, the habitual garden birds and the cats – all feeding together, sharing the food she puts out.

Early, very early, one morning, Dimly thought he would help Bee with the shopping. It involved quite a bit of manoeuvring, particularly getting it through the cat flap. Dimly sat under the bureau with his offering, looking sleek and velvety, purring with pride.

Beryl got up to go to the loo in her nightdress. She was confronted by Dimly, guarding an enormous live rabbit under the bureau.

She knew she had to deal with the situation firmly but tactfully. She did not want a slaughtering on her carpet.

'Oh Dimly – what a clever boy; goodness, gracious me, what a lovely rabbit!' she enthused. She hadn't won a Tony Award for nothing.

Dimly did a victory-growl through gritted teeth, his eyes glinting with pleasure. Beryl acted swiftly. She scooped the rabbit up into her arms, turning on her heel. There was no time to stop and dress.

She marched barefoot, nightie floating around her, out into the garden and down the lane, all ten cats following like the Pied Piper; they were wondering where she was taking their breakfast or if this was a new game.

'Oh, what a lovely rabbit! Clever boy, clever Dimly,' she kept saying, but Dimly wasn't fooled.

He ran ahead, miaowing. He loved her, but what was she going to do with his rabbit?

She had to walk quite a long way to find a flat piece of ground with nearby cover. Her feet were wet; her nightie trailed damply, clinging round her ankles. The early morning breeze was cool and she shivered.

'I know it's difficult for you to understand, Dimly,' she said. 'But I can't cook this wild rabbit for you. I'll go tomorrow and buy you a proper rabbit from the market.'

She put down the rabbit, who couldn't believe his luck and shot off into the woods. Then she made a great fuss of Dimly. She did not want him to feel hurt or that his gift had been tossed aside.

Dimly knows Bee will do anything for her cats. He knows about the time Lulu decided to live on the roof and Bee had to climb a ladder several times a day to feed her. Lulu was definitely a little eccentric. When it was snowing, she slept snuggled against the chimney, glad of its warmth.

When Beryl's neighbours had their pine trees chopped down, it became apparent that these trees had been Lulu's access to the roof of the cottage. Lulu promptly disappeared in distress.

This was worrying, so Beryl got a man from the Forestry Commission to cut down a branch of the willow, and they built a little run up onto the roof for Lulu, with slats in the branch for her claws to get a grip on.

But by then Lulu had gone off living on the roof. She had taken up residence elsewhere but couldn't get home because of the stream. So Beryl built a cat-bridge, heaving concrete blocks and wooden planks with her own hands. Now Lulu comes across the Bridge Over the River Kwai for her meals and a talk and a cuddle.

When she is doing this thing called filming, Dimly knows that Bee has to get up very early. The cats don't mind at all. Breakfast at dawn is always acceptable.

But there are so many of them and they all like to eat different foods. Bee usually finds herself tripping over their tails as they mill around the kitchen, desperately trying to remember what each cat is fed on.

'I know you think I'm stupid,' she says to them. 'But I am having to force my brain to work at a very early hour. I suppose Billy and Clive want some red meat. My butcher's making a fortune out of you. It costs more to feed you cats than it does to feed myself.'

They did not like it when she went away filming in America, or doing a play on Broadway. Did she really have to go away to play? There were plenty of bent twigs and little balls of Bacofoil to play with at Honeypot Cottage. She didn't have to get out those dreaded suitcases and pack.

When she went away for a long time to do *The Killing of Sister George*, they showed their displeasure by refusing to come into the cottage when she returned. They sat outside, stiff with disapproval and hurt. It took Bee a long time to win back their trust and love. One by one they gave in to her patient coaxing and returned to the fold.

Dimly often sits on the window seat with Bee when she gets out all her shoes; he loves to play with laces and straps and buckles.

'I have to find the right pair,' she explains to him. 'Before I get into a character, I have to have the right pair of shoes.'

Not being a shoe-wearer, Dimly does not really understand. Bee uses lots of words he does not understand . . . films, plays, theatre, television, parts, scripts, engagements. He just knows she is always busy and always going away. But she has lovely infectious laughter and dimples at the corners of her mouth that go in and out like sunshine.

Dimly is the adventurous one. He obeys the command 'sit and stay'; he will retrieve a Bacofoil ball and bring it back. He caught his leg in a trap and had to have eleven stitches, but he was the perfect invalid and endured the inactivity with dignity.

When he disappeared Beryl became very worried. It was so unlike him; Dimly always came when he was called. He was a lovely cat and they had a special rapport. It made her feel sick to think of something happening to her midnight cat.

She called and called but Dimly did not appear. She searched for three days. She began to feel desperate; she was up at 5 a.m. on the Sunday morning, looking everywhere and calling.

About midday she gave up searching and called a friend in Chatham who is a clairvoyant.

'It's something connected with water,' her friend said after a while. 'He's shut in. Is there a boatyard near you?'

'Nobody's there just now,' said Beryl. 'I don't think he could be shut in there.'

She phoned her friend again on the Monday morning because Dimly had still not returned home, and by now she was distraught. She had hardly slept.

'Get dressed, Beryl, and go round to the boatyard now. I'm quite certain that's where he is.'

Beryl hurried round to the boatyard, followed by Sir Harry and Muriel. She had not wanted them to come because it meant going along a main road. But they insisted. The two cats were miaowing all the time, as if they too were calling for Dimly.

'Oh do be quiet,' she told them eventually. 'Because I won't know if I hear Dimly.'

She searched in all the boats and then looked into a locked shed. There among the shadows was Dimly. He began to cry, a thin pathetic mew as he recognised her voice.

She talked to him all the time as she wondered how she was going to get him out. The door was padlocked; the glass had metal bars and chicken wire behind it. Breaking the glass would not help.

Dimly heard her, so near and yet so far. He could not understand why she was not letting him out. He clawed at the door, his nails rasping.

Beryl was determined. She was going to get her cat out somehow, even if she had to take the shed to pieces. She found an iron bar and with a strength born out of desperation, she levered up the bottom of the door. She is not a big woman and it took every ounce of her strength.

514

She could feel perspiration breaking out on her face as she strained against the strong door.

Dimly's head appeared through the gap. She gasped with relief, holding the gap open just long enough for a much thinner Dimly to slither out. There was much rejoicing. They all hurried home, Dimly racing ahead; he was starving. But every now and again he stopped to see if Bee was following.

'I'm coming, I'm coming,' she called, getting her breath back, suddenly aware how dry her mouth had been and how her heart had been pumping.

They made a triumphant return to Honeypot Cottage; to its circular rooms and gardens that sweep down to the Thames; to the welcoming committee of cats waiting around for them, tails waving, purring in unison.

At the Lyric Theatre, Shaftesbury Avenue, sat Fleur, a skinny pink-and-brown-patched short-haired cat. She sat at the top of the stairs that lead down to the dressing rooms, ignored and unloved. No one ever took any notice of her. There was a streak of Abyssinian in the bony head and pointed ears; her eyes were wary as if she had once been booted down the stairs or out into the streets.

Fleur did not know that a star was coming into her life who would change it. A woman who would bring her cooked food fresh from home; who would send out for turkey sandwiches, break them up and feed them to her from an ashtray; who would let her sleep safely on the divan in her dressing room.

Dimly could have told the thin theatre cat that all this would happen when *Gigi* opened in London, and she would soon become one of those fortunate creatures – a member of Bee's family of cats.

# Cloud Eight

It was a forbidden place. A cold white box with the faint hum of machinery. But it held a fascination for Victcha. She often sat outside its door, waiting patiently, knowing it housed all sorts of delicacies – chicken, liver, milk, cream, cheese, trifle, butter . . . Victcha almost drooled in anticipation. Even her favourite Whiskas used to live in there if she happened to leave any – which was not often.

Victcha was not sure of the sequence of events that gave her access to this holy of holies, but perhaps someone left the door open or the catch slipped. It was about five feet high, free standing; it was easy to miss a small black and white shape crouched on a back shelf hopefully impersonating a carton of juice. Then someone shut the door without seeing the cat.

It was very dark inside and the hum was louder now. Victcha explored the shelf. It seemed to be almost empty. Only some bottles and boxes. Where had all the lovely food gone? She sniffed expectantly. But everything was covered up.

It was also cold inside, a fact which did not bother Victcha at first. Her coat kept her warm. She huddled, flipping her tail over her nose. The tips of her ears were paper thin and beginning to feel cold. It was a sensation she did not like.

She curled herself into a smaller ball, wishing the cold would go away. It was not such a nice place after all. She grew restless and scratched at the door, miaowing. No one heard.

Sleep was coming over her in waves. Instinctively she fought off the sleepiness, knowing that this was not a normal sleep.

'Victcha . . . Victcha . . .'

She heard her name, very faint and far away.

She was trembling now, an ague over which she had no control. It was becoming difficult to breathe as the cold began to paralyse her muscles. She could not fight the overwhelming sleepiness.

She was floating. It was a strange weightlessness, as if she was made of air. She did not question her new state because it was not frightening and she felt very un-curious.

There were dreams in her mind. It was like spinning back to when she was a kitten and the world was very new. Images floated in and out of her consciousness, vague but recognisable, comforting and not in any way a threat.

The cold was something she had never endured before, but it no longer mattered. She had gone beyond the point of feeling the cold; she was frozen; but the pain had gone.

The mist was a strange colour now; lavender, rose and blue, very blue . . . it was the sky, a vast endless sky, above, below and all around her.

'Her heart has stopped beating,' said the vet, Dennis Archer. 'It's not surprising. How long was she trapped in the fridge?'

'We're not sure. But she was missing for up to twenty-four hours.'

'There's not much hope, then.'

'Can't you try? Please try. There could be a chance,'

urged Dorothy Wozniak. Her little black and white cat was the joy of her life. 'Please do something.'

Mr Archer tried to find the heart-beat eight times, but eventually gave up. Victcha remained icy cold. There was an odd gasp from the still form.

'I'm sorry, but she's technically dead of hypothermia.'

Dorothy was heart-broken. Her lovely little cat. They left Victcha lying on the vet's table, thinking they would never see her again.

'Look,' said Mr Archer. 'Her temperature is too low to record. But I will give her an anti-shock injection, and put her in a kennel with warm blankets and an infra-red light. If there's no change in the morning, then I'll make all the arrangements to dispose of the body.'

He always hated this part but someone had to be practical. Sometimes a grieving owner preferred to take their pet back to a familiar garden; others did not want a painful reminder.

The young art student went home with her family. They would never know how Victcha had got shut in the fridge. They could not forgive themselves for allowing it to happen. But the refrigerator was the last place they had thought of looking for Victcha when she went missing.

What a pity, thought Mr Archer, preparing the injection. It was a nicely marked cat with a sweet white face and big patches of black above the eyes and under the jaw. The cat would not have known much about it, or suffered. It would have got progressively colder, then simply gone to sleep. But he did as he had promised and left the cat under an infra-red lamp.

It was another busy day at the surgery; cats and dogs of all shapes and sizes came and went. Mr Archer was called out several times.

It was seven hours after Victcha had been brought into the surgery when a veterinary assistant, working late, heard a funny noise. The black and white cat had thrown off the blanket and was getting unsteadily to her feet, looking around in a dazed manner. Victcha shook her head, wondering where she was. She stretched her stiff limbs and began to stagger to the edge of the kennel.

'Good heavens,' exclaimed the assistant. 'She's alive! It's a miracle.'

Victcha began to miaow feebly. She was feeling hollow and hungry and still cold. The tips of her ears were tingling like ice.

The assistant heated some milk and Victcha lapped the warm drink gratefully. She was emerging from the strangest dreams. She could not make out what was real. They were fading now as the world became a familiar place again. The assistant wrapped her in a blanket and stroked her.

'There, pussy. You have had a strange adventure.'

'I can't believe it,' said Mr Archer, examining the cat thoroughly in the morning. 'That cat was technically dead. No heart-beat. Temperature too low to record. The odd gasp. Nothing. Somehow she's come back to life. As you say, it's a miracle.'

The Wozniak household was wrapped in gloom. They were all upset about the fate of their little cat. Victcha had meant a lot to them.

'I think I'll just ring the vet's, once more,' said Dorothy.

She listened in amazement, hardly able to believe her ears, trying to take in what the receptionist was telling her.

'It's Victcha! She's alive after all. She suddenly came back to life and started staggering around. She's all right now and we can go round and collect her any time.'

Dorothy's eyes filled with tears of joy. Her prayers to St Francis of Assisi had been answered.

Victcha came home to much rejoicing, though she did not understand what had happened. She had gone to sleep in one place and somehow woken up in another. It was all very peculiar.

She has fully recovered but is a little wary of the refrigerator now. Despite the memories of lovely food inside it, she knows it holds the cold hand of death.

# Ad Infinitum

The two new kittens, Clover and Rufus, did not get into a story, despite persistent cajoling. They were among the dozens of cats that did not quite make a story of their own. Big, small, funny, brave, strange, sad . . . each cat an individual character and special to its owner.

'Please do something,' the provider urged. 'Anything so I can use you. After all, I do know all about you. I ought to be able to write a good story about you two.'

'We're trying, we're trying,' they chorused.

'I did get stuck up a tree,' said Clover, the tortoiseshell kitten with a mascara-smudged face and two clown's teardrops under her big dark eyes. 'I was terribly frightened.'

'It was a very small tree and you were only stuck up it for about five minutes. I'd hardly call that a world-shattering event.'

'But my mistress also got stuck up the tree trying to get me down,' Clover went on. 'Surely that's worth a line?'

'Okay, a line. A line. But that's all you're getting.'

A brown black and white tabby called Corgi from Horley was rescued from a fire in a burning flat in Fulham. Somehow his half-burnt vaccination book survived the fire too. Corgi is now a massive twenty-pound twelve-year-old with a penchant for playing badminton and climbing into upstairs bedrooms via a handy fir tree.

Since 1981 Corgi has had diabetes and endures regular insulin injections. He is quite used to the routine and at the same time each evening sits on a dining-room chair waiting for his injection.

And the rescue from the fire? Only Corgi knows the details of that terrifying experience.

A brave cat called Smokey killed a snake in New Guinea, while Pepsi survived fifteen minutes in a washing machine and lived to produce her own kitten later.

From long ago comes the story of Pongo, the sea captain's cat who shared his master's cabin. In Alexandria Pongo took extended shore leave and the ship had to sail without him. A year later, in Cardiff, the captain was walking along the docks when a cargo vessel berthed. On board he saw his cat, Pongo. The mutual delight of their reunion can be imagined. Had the cat been searching for him, in the only way he knew?

Do cats cry? It seems that some do. A cat sat by the grave of a kitten crying for five minutes.

A cat called Sooty had to have a passport, pawprints and full description, before flying out of Aden. Another cat, Ponsonby, knew to the day when its owner was returning from a month in Japan.

Percy is a ginger cat who was brought up with a cat flap, but when the family moved, there was only a door with a letter box. Percy soon learned to use the knocker on the letter-box to ask to be let in. It became a family joke to send visitors to answer any knock at the door.

'They're lovely stories,' said Clover. 'Look, we're both sitting in your shopping basket, impersonating the cover on a calendar. Don't we look cute? Does that make a story?'

'No, sorry. Get out.'

There's an eccentric cat called Twit who once went swimming in engine oil and had to be bathed in the sink to get it off; he also sits under the village bus until rescued and swims in the bath.

Victoria is a cat who likes Ovaltine and whisky. She walked into the house and stayed eighteen years, a black and white Persian who can definitely play the piano.

A little tortoiseshell called Streaky was accidentally locked in a TV delivery van and driven away, but somehow travelled back the six miles to her home on her own over totally unknown main roads.

Billy, an active twelve-year-old living in Chesterfield, disappeared unaccountably one evening. Eight weeks later the mother and son in the family separately heard his special mew, asking to be let in. Though they searched the yard and the garden, Billy was nowhere to be found. They did not say anything to each other, hiding their disappointment. But years later, talking about Billy, they both mentioned the mewing they had heard that evening.

It made them wonder if Billy was trapped by cat thieves and the calls they heard so clearly were when their cat died.

There's a happier ending to the story of Basil, who swallowed a diamond engagement ring and had to have a £95 operation to remove it.

'I didn't mind about the loss of the ring. It was Basil I was worried about,' said his owner.

At this point, the kitten Clover curled herself round the provider's ankles. 'We eat all sorts of strange things,' she purred hopefully. 'Raw cake mixture, chocolate, sultanas, Christmas pudding.'

'We must be the only spinach-eating cats in Great Britain,' said the solemn kitten Rufus, speaking for the first time. He's a wise cat, this tawny fluffy lion with sleepy yellow eyes. He seldom wastes time on talking, except when climbing up the provider's leg to see what she is chopping for their supper.

'That's it. That's definitely worth a story,' said Clover, dancing away to chase a bumble-bee over the rockery, her thistledown mind already on something else. 'Spinach and liver. I love spinach and liver . . .'

There are countless tales of cats returning to their old homes when the family has moved to a new house. Tabs, a Portsmouth pussy, made such dreadful wailing noises night and day outside her old home that the neighbours had to call in the RSPCA to catch the homesick cat and return her to her owners. She was so cold and hungry that she decided to make the best of the move and rarely ventured out again.

Many owners believe that their cats speak to them. Fluffy, of Aristotle Road, London, seemed to speak quite clearly. He was a long-haired stray with the exotic make-up of a ballet dancer, whose gaze showed compassion, humour and an analytical approach to everything that went on around him. His owner is sure that there was some mental telepathy between them.

The cashier cat lives on a farm in north-west Yorkshire. The farm sells free-range eggs to passing motorists. On one occasion, as a customer held out a pound note to pay for eggs, the big ginger cat reached out from a bench, got hold of the note in its mouth and ran inside the farmhouse with it. The cat gave its trophy to the farmer's wife and went back to its seat in the porch.

Nor was it the first time. Some weeks previously Ginger had fished a £5 note out of the handbag of a customer who was trying to find some change.

A tiger tabby called Sir Henry fairly froze with astonishment when he saw a near life-size coloured painting of his owners newly hung on a wall. He looked in amazement from the painting to his owners and back again, investigated the frame, in and around it thoroughly. Reassured that they were not really hanging on the wall, he has totally ignored the picture ever since.

Sir Henry wheedled his way into the life and home of a pilot who was in Bomber Command in World War II, despite the fact that they were not a cat family and had never had a cat before. Sir Henry decided he was going to stay at April Cottage and proceeded to clear the area of all other strays.

He was knighted with a breadknife for his work among the mice. The local vet said he was pleased to have so distinguished a cat as a client.

A Swindon family had three highly intelligent cats, Albertine, Moppet and Flopsy. Albertine had hidden a damaged kitten and would not let anyone know where it was.

Her owner said: 'Oh Albertine, why don't you bring your kitten down? It's so cold up there for a baby.'

Albertine looked earnestly into her face, then ran upstairs, returned with the kitten in her mouth and dumped it onto her owner's lap, as if to say: 'Okay, she's all yours.'

Moppet could not stand her owner singing, particularly high notes and 'Silent Night'. This carol made her react quite fiercely. One night Moppet died and the next morning at school the music teacher chose for assembly . . . 'Silent Night'.

Flopsy had impeccable manners but once attacked the radio when a previously undiscovered musical instrument was demonstrated on Radio 3. The cat went wild. It was an April Fool's Day joke on listeners, but Flopsy had not been fooled.

A true music lover is the phantom cat of the Ohio Theatre, Columbus. This sleek black cat insists on joining in with the Columbus Symphony Orchestra, miaowing in time in an eerie soprano.

So often cats seems to be sent by some divine purpose to help in a situation. This is a beautiful story, almost spine-tingling. A strange tortoiseshell and white cat jumped in a window on a Saturday and made itself quite at home. The two sisters were surprised but pleased to see the cat for its presence comforted them. Their mother was terminally ill and she died the very next day.

The cat stayed with them night and day. When they

returned home from the funeral, the cat had gone, never to return.

The sisters hunted for the cat but without success. Two months later they saw an advertisement about a tortoiseshell cat that had been found. They hurried to see the cat, hoping that it would be the one that had visited them in their time of need, but it was not. However, she was a beautiful lost creature and they took her home. Taff gave them fourteen years of pleasure and they still have Nob, one of her kittens.

One morning Mrs Poole was washing dishes, looking out of the window at the peaceful Wimbleball Reservoir in Somerset, when she saw what looked like a can of baked beans on legs. Four legs. The can was progressing unsteadily across the garden. It was their cat, Tiger, a magnificent tabby, with his head stuck in a tin.

She tried to remove the tin but Tiger had his head hopelessly wedged. She rushed the cat and tin in the car to find the senior warden and another warden. With great care the two men were able to remove the can with a pair of snips.

Tiger made the national newspapers and became a local celebrity.

Tubby is an acrobatic cat who likes nothing better than to be wheelbarrowed round the room on his front legs; he also likes tea, Ovaltine and a tiny drop of Cherry Brandy. He turns his nose up at coffee.

Blackie, the family's other cat, enjoys the daily ritual of sitting in the front passenger seat of the car and being driven into the garage. He likes to eat fruit cake, salty biscuits, dry cornflakes and health-food fruit bars.

A colony of feral cats were inherited by new residents in Via Aschenez in Reggio di Calabria in Italy. On their first morning in the flat, the husband and wife found the ferals sitting outside, expectantly waiting in a semi-circle.

It was a problem – how to feed what amountd to a private zoo. They grew fond of the ferals, but the cats often disappeared or became ill. A female feral brought them her kittens for inspection then took them away. One they called Nelson, a fierce one-eyed creature, was untouchable. But years later, on the day that he died, he lay on top of their wall and allowed them a single stroke. It was probably the only time he had been touched by a human in his long, embattled life.

Lilian, actually a male black cat, lived in the home of the Senior Commissioner of the Gambian Protectorate in Bathurst. This cat's party piece was to be found sitting on the Governor's chair at the head of the table each time there was a formal dinner party. He liked to stroll over the dining table and drink the water from the flower bowls of bougainvillaea and zinnias.

He also loved to chase the house bats that flew down from the roof of their house-on-stilts. Lilian could leap as high as a standard lamp.

He went on safari with the Commissioner and his wife up the Gambia river, and was fast asleep in a thatched wooden guest house when a hoard of warrior ants came out of the jungle. These fierce creatures tunnel their way through everything, attacking and eating all in their path.

Lilian was saved by a boy watchman who lit fires to stop the invading ants and diverted their onslaught. They would have eaten the sleeping cat if they had not been stopped.

'Absolutely fascinating,' said Clover, walking over the provider's typewriter with little dancing steps. 'But you haven't put us in a story yet. Aren't we sweet and funny and amazing? And we eat beetroot, tomatoes, chocolate cake and raisins. We're nearly vegetarians.'

Rufus blinks his amber eyes wisely like an owl. 'Remember how we form a queue for supper? That's well-trained, isn't it?'

'What about when we first arrived and Cindy, our Colourpoint Grandmother, was jealous and ran away?' Clover said, prancing around on top of valuable papers.

'She only ran away as far as next door. We could see

her sitting there all day with her back to us,' said the provider, removing the now reconciled fluffy cushion on legs from a pile of typing paper.

'And she went on hunger strike for four days,' Clover reminded her. 'Who went crawling around under furniture with saucers of milk to tempt her?'

'Er . . . yes, well, we won't go into that,' said the provider.

'What about when I fell in the bath?'

'I fell in the frog pond,' Rufus yawned pinkly.

'You certainly did! I didn't expect to have to give you a bath at 1 a.m. in the morning. Green slime everywhere. Urgh.'

The kittens began washing each other's faces. A lick here, a lick there, totally innocent, intent on cleaning up.

'We help you tidy up, don't we?' said Clover, not giving up easily. 'Put things away.'

'You mean hide anything that takes your fancy, like ball-point pens and emery boards. I suppose it could be called tidying up. By the way, where's the top of my new pen?'

'And I'm helping in the garden,' Clover went on. 'I'm bringing in all the rhododendron leaves and taking them upstairs.'

'Thanks a bundle. We don't want the entire garden indoors. Why not try taking them down to the compost heap?'

The kittens ignored the suggestion; that would turn play into work, the last thing they were interested in.

'How about the sweet way I pat your face when you blow on my paws,' says Clover brightly, her little smudged face alight with love.

'Dear baby, that doesn't make a story . . . but thank you for trying. The moment I finish this book, you'll both do something amazing,' said the provider, scooping them into her arms, a gloriously soft mixture of black tortoiseshell and tawny marmalade fur, eight paws waving in the air, two pink noses burrowing into her neck.

'At least I can have the last word,' Clover purred.

'Definitely almost the last word,' agreed Rufus, drawing his huge foxy tail carefully over his eyes and drifting into sleep.

# Acknowledgements

With many thanks for so much encouragement and help to Mrs Barbara Bristow, Mrs Janet Gadd, Mrs Marion Porter, Dr Theodore Reed, Mrs P. Knight, Miss Linda Thomas, Miss Grace Hamblin, Mr Peter Fairlie, Mr Andrew Anspach, Mrs Olivia Slobbé, Mrs Helena Sanders, Mrs Jane Froud, Mrs Judith Malet, Mrs Val Andrews, Mrs Joan Toy, Miss Theodora Croucher, Miss Beryl Reid, Miss Dorothy Wozniak — and all those who contributed to the 'Ad Infinitum' chapter.

# A Selection of Arrow Bestsellers

| | | |
|---|---|---|
| ☐ The Lilac Bus | Maeve Binchy | £2.50 |
| ☐ 500 Mile Walkies | Mark Wallington | £2.50 |
| ☐ Staying Off the Beaten Track | Elizabeth Gundrey | £5.95 |
| ☐ A Better World Than This | Marie Joseph | £2.95 |
| ☐ No Enemy But Time | Evelyn Anthony | £2.95 |
| ☐ Rates of Exchange | Malcolm Bradbury | £3.50 |
| ☐ Colours Aloft | Alexander Kent | £2.95 |
| ☐ Speaker for the Dead | Orson Scott Card | £2.95 |
| ☐ Eon | Greg Bear | £4.95 |
| ☐ Talking to Strange Men | Ruth Rendell | £5.95 |
| ☐ Heartstones | Ruth Rendell | £2.50 |
| ☐ Rosemary Conley's Hip and Thigh Diet | Rosemary Conley | £2.50 |
| ☐ Communion | Whitley Strieber | £3.50 |
| ☐ The Ladies of Missalonghi | Colleen McCullough | £2.50 |
| ☐ Erin's Child | Sheelagh Kelly | £3.99 |
| ☐ Sarum | Edward Rutherfurd | £4.50 |

Prices and other details are liable to change

---

ARROW BOOKS, BOOKSERVICE BY POST, PO BOX 29, DOUGLAS, ISLE OF MAN, BRITISH ISLES

NAME................................................................

ADDRESS.............................................................

....................................................................

....................................................................

Please enclose a cheque or postal order made out to Arrow Books Ltd. for the amount due and allow the following for postage and packing.

U.K. CUSTOMERS: Please allow 22p per book to a maximum of £3.00.

B.F.P.O. & EIRE: Please allow 22p per book to a maximum of £3.00

OVERSEAS CUSTOMERS: Please allow 22p per book.

Whilst every effort is made to keep prices low it is sometimes necessary to increase cover prices at short notice. Arrow Books reserve the right to show new retail prices on covers which may differ from those previously advertised in the text or elsewhere.

# Bestselling Non-Fiction

| | | |
|---|---|---|
| ☐ Everything Is Negotiable | Gavin Kennedy | £3.50 |
| ☐ The Cheiro Book of Fate and Fortune | Cheiro | £2.95 |
| ☐ The Handbook of Chinese Horoscopes | Theodora Lau | £3.50 |
| ☐ Hollywood Babylon | Kenneth Anger | £7.95 |
| ☐ Staying Off the Beaten Track | Elizabeth Gundrey | £5.95 |
| ☐ Elvis and Me | Priscilla Presley | £2.95 |
| ☐ Maria Callas | Arianna Stassinopoulos | £4.95 |
| ☐ The Ulysses Voyage | Tim Severin | £3.50 |
| ☐ Something Understood | Gerald Priestland | £3.99 |
| ☐ Fat is a Feminist Issue | Susie Orbach | £2.50 |
| ☐ Women Who Love Too Much | Robin Norwood | £2.95 |
| ☐ Rosemary Conley's Hip and Thigh Diet | Rosemary Conley | £2.50 |
| ☐ Intercourse | Andrea Dworkin | £2.99 |
| ☐ Communion | Whitley Strieber | £3.50 |

Prices and other details are liable to change

---

ARROW BOOKS, BOOKSERVICE BY POST, PO BOX 29, DOUGLAS, ISLE OF MAN, BRITISH ISLES

NAME.....................................................................

ADDRESS..................................................................

...........................................................................

...........................................................................

Please enclose a cheque or postal order made out to Arrow Books Ltd. for the amount due and allow the following for postage and packing.

U.K. CUSTOMERS: Please allow 22p per book to a maximum of £3.00.

B.F.P.O. & EIRE: Please allow 22p per book to a maximum of £3.00

OVERSEAS CUSTOMERS: Please allow 22p per book.

Whilst every effort is made to keep prices low it is sometimes necessary to increase cover prices at short notice. Arrow Books reserve the right to show new retail prices on covers which may differ from those previously advertised in the text or elsewhere.

# Bestselling Fiction

| | | |
|---|---|---|
| ☐ Hiroshmia Joe | Martin Booth | £2.95 |
| ☐ The Pianoplayers | Anthony Burgess | £2.50 |
| ☐ Queen's Play | Dorothy Dunnett | £3.95 |
| ☐ Colours Aloft | Alexander Kent | £2.95 |
| ☐ Contact | Carl Sagan | £3.50 |
| ☐ Talking to Strange Men | Ruth Rendell | £5.95 |
| ☐ Heartstones | Ruth Rendell | £2.50 |
| ☐ The Ladies of Missalonghi | Colleen McCullough | £2.50 |
| ☐ No Enemy But Time | Evelyn Anthony | £2.95 |
| ☐ The Heart of the Country | Fay Weldon | £2.50 |
| ☐ The Stationmaster's Daughter | Pamela Oldfield | £2.95 |
| ☐ Erin's Child | Sheelagh Kelly | £3.99 |
| ☐ The Lilac Bus | Maeve Binchy | £2.50 |

Prices and other details are liable to change

---

ARROW BOOKS, BOOKSERVICE BY POST, PO BOX 29, DOUGLAS, ISLE OF MAN, BRITISH ISLES

NAME. . . . . . . . . . . . . . . . . . . . . . . . . . . . . . . . . . . . . . . . . . . . . . . . . . . . . . . . . . . . . . . .

ADDRESS . . . . . . . . . . . . . . . . . . . . . . . . . . . . . . . . . . . . . . . . . . . . . . . . . . . . . . . . . . . . .

. . . . . . . . . . . . . . . . . . . . . . . . . . . . . . . . . . . . . . . . . . . . . . . . . . . . . . . . . . . . . . . . . . . .

. . . . . . . . . . . . . . . . . . . . . . . . . . . . . . . . . . . . . . . . . . . . . . . . . . . . . . . . . . . . . . . . . . . .

Please enclose a cheque or postal order made out to Arrow Books Ltd. for the amount due and allow the following for postage and packing.

U.K. CUSTOMERS: Please allow 22p per book to a maximum of £3.00.

B.F.P.O. & EIRE: Please allow 22p per book to a maximum of £3.00

OVERSEAS CUSTOMERS: Please allow 22p per book.

Whilst every effort is made to keep prices low it is sometimes necessary to increase cover prices at short notice. Arrow Books reserve the right to show new retail prices on covers which may differ from those previously advertised in the text or elsewhere.

# Bestselling Fiction

| | | |
|---|---|---|
| ☐ Saudi | Laurie Devine | £2.95 |
| ☐ Lisa Logan | Marie Joseph | £2.50 |
| ☐ The Stationmaster's Daughter | Pamela Oldfield | £2.95 |
| ☐ Duncton Wood | William Horwood | £3.50 |
| ☐ Aztec | Gary Jennings | £3.95 |
| ☐ The Pride | Judith Saxton | £2.99 |
| ☐ Fire in Heaven | Malcolm Bosse | £3.50 |
| ☐ Communion | Whitley Strieber | £3.50 |
| ☐ The Ladies of Missalonghi | Colleen McCullough | £2.50 |
| ☐ Skydancer | Geoffrey Archer | £2.50 |
| ☐ The Sisters | Pat Booth | £3.50 |
| ☐ No Enemy But Time | Evelyn Anthony | £2.95 |

Prices and other details are liable to change

---

ARROW BOOKS, BOOKSERVICE BY POST, PO BOX 29, DOUGLAS, ISLE OF MAN, BRITISH ISLES

NAME. . . . . . . . . . . . . . . . . . . . . . . . . . . . . . . . . . . . . . . . . . . . . . . . . . . . . . . . . . . . . . . . . . . .

ADDRESS . . . . . . . . . . . . . . . . . . . . . . . . . . . . . . . . . . . . . . . . . . . . . . . . . . . . . . . . . . . . . . . .

. . . . . . . . . . . . . . . . . . . . . . . . . . . . . . . . . . . . . . . . . . . . . . . . . . . . . . . . . . . . . . . . . . . . . . . .

. . . . . . . . . . . . . . . . . . . . . . . . . . . . . . . . . . . . . . . . . . . . . . . . . . . . . . . . . . . . . . . . . . . . . . . .

Please enclose a cheque or postal order made out to Arrow Books Ltd. for the amount due and allow the following for postage and packing.

U.K. CUSTOMERS: Please allow 22p per book to a maximum of £3.00.

B.F.P.O. & EIRE: Please allow 22p per book to a maximum of £3.00

OVERSEAS CUSTOMERS: Please allow 22p per book.

Whilst every effort is made to keep prices low it is sometimes necessary to increase cover prices at short notice. Arrow Books reserve the right to show new retail prices on covers which may differ from those previously advertised in the text or elsewhere.

# Bestselling Humour

| | | |
|---|---|---|
| ☐ Carrott Roots | Jasper Carrott | £3.50 |
| ☐ The Art of Course Office Life | Michael Green | £1.95 |
| ☐ Rambling On | Mike Harding | £2.50 |
| ☐ Sex Tips for Girls | Cynthia Heimel | £2.95 |
| ☐ Sex Tips for Boys | William Davis | £2.95 |
| ☐ Tales from a Long Room | Peter Tinniswood | £2.75 |
| ☐ Tales from Whitney Scrotum | Peter Tinniswood | £2.50 |
| ☐ Why Come to Slaka? | Malcolm Bradbury | £2.95 |
| ☐ Football is a Funny Game | Ian St. John & Jimmy Greaves | £3.95 |
| ☐ The Bedside Book of Sex | Rolf White | £2.95 |
| ☐ Palace | Neil Mackwood & Bryan Rostron | £2.50 |
| ☐ Tim Brooke-Taylor's Cricket Box | Tim Brooke-Taylor | £4.50 |

Prices and other details are liable to change

---

ARROW BOOKS, BOOKSERVICE BY POST, PO BOX 29, DOUGLAS, ISLE OF MAN, BRITISH ISLES

NAME.................................................................

ADDRESS............................................................

......................................................................

......................................................................

Please enclose a cheque or postal order made out to Arrow Books Ltd. for the amount due and allow the following for postage and packing.

U.K. CUSTOMERS: Please allow 22p per book to a maximum of £3.00.

B.F.P.O. & EIRE: Please allow 22p per book to a maximum of £3.00

OVERSEAS CUSTOMERS: Please allow 22p per book.

Whilst every effort is made to keep prices low it is sometimes necessary to increase cover prices at short notice. Arrow Books reserve the right to show new retail prices on covers which may differ from those previously advertised in the text or elsewhere.

# Bestselling War Fiction and Non-Fiction

| | | |
|---|---|---|
| ☐ Passage to Mutiny | Alexander Kent | £2.95 |
| ☐ Colours Aloft | Alexander Kent | £2.95 |
| ☐ Winged Escort | Douglas Reeman | £2.95 |
| ☐ Army of Shadows | John Harris | £2.50 |
| ☐ Decoy | Dudley Pope | £2.95 |
| ☐ Gestapo | Rupert Butler | £4.50 |
| ☐ Johnny Gurkha | E.D. Smith | £2.95 |
| ☐ Typhoon Pilot | Desmond Scott | £2.95 |
| ☐ The Rommel Papers | B.H. Liddel Hart | £5.95 |
| ☐ Hour of the Lily | John Kruse | £3.50 |
| ☐ Duel in the Dark | Peter Townsend | £3.95 |
| ☐ The Spoils of War | Douglas Scott | £2.99 |
| ☐ The Wild Blue | Walter J. Boyne & Steven L. Thompson | £3.95 |
| ☐ The Bombers | Norman Longmate | £4.99 |

Prices and other details are liable to change

---

ARROW BOOKS, BOOKSERVICE BY POST, PO BOX 29, DOUGLAS, ISLE OF MAN, BRITISH ISLES

NAME. . . . . . . . . . . . . . . . . . . . . . . . . . . . . . . . . . . . . . . . . . . . . . . . . . . . . . . . . . . . . . . .

ADDRESS. . . . . . . . . . . . . . . . . . . . . . . . . . . . . . . . . . . . . . . . . . . . . . . . . . . . . . . . . . . .

. . . . . . . . . . . . . . . . . . . . . . . . . . . . . . . . . . . . . . . . . . . . . . . . . . . . . . . . . . . . . . . . . . . .

. . . . . . . . . . . . . . . . . . . . . . . . . . . . . . . . . . . . . . . . . . . . . . . . . . . . . . . . . . . . . . . . . . . .

Please enclose a cheque or postal order made out to Arrow Books Ltd. for the amount due and allow the following for postage and packing.

U.K. CUSTOMERS: Please allow 22p per book to a maximum of £3.00.

B.F.P.O. & EIRE: Please allow 22p per book to a maximum of £3.00

OVERSEAS CUSTOMERS: Please allow 22p per book.

Whilst every effort is made to keep prices low it is sometimes necessary to increase cover prices at short notice. Arrow Books reserve the right to show new retail prices on covers which may differ from those previously advertised in the text or elsewhere.

# Bestselling Thriller/Suspense

| | | |
|---|---|---|
| ☐ Hell is Always Today | Jack Higgins | £2.50 |
| ☐ Brought in Dead | Harry Patterson | £1.99 |
| ☐ Russian Spring | Dennis Jones | £2.50 |
| ☐ Fletch | Gregory Mcdonald | £1.95 |
| ☐ Black Ice | Colin Dunne | £2.50 |
| ☐ Blind Run | Brian Freemantle | £2.50 |
| ☐ The Proteus Operation | James P. Hogan | £3.50 |
| ☐ Miami One Way | Mike Winters | £2.50 |
| ☐ Skydancer | Geoffrey Archer | £2.50 |
| ☐ Hour of the Lily | John Kruse | £3.50 |
| ☐ The Tunnel | Stanley Johnson | £2.50 |
| ☐ The Albatross Run | Douglas Scott | £2.50 |
| ☐ Dragonfire | Andrew Kaplan | £2.99 |

Prices and other details are liable to change

---

ARROW BOOKS. BOOKSERVICE BY POST. PO BOX 29. DOUGLAS. ISLE OF MAN. BRITISH ISLES

NAME...................................................................

ADDRESS................................................................

........................................................................

........................................................................

Please enclose a cheque or postal order made out to Arrow Books Ltd. for the amount due and allow the following for postage and packing.

U.K. CUSTOMERS: Please allow 22p per book to a maximum of £3.00.

B.F.P.O. & EIRE: Please allow 22p per book to a maximum of £3.00

OVERSEAS CUSTOMERS: Please allow 22p per book.

Whilst every effort is made to keep prices low it is sometimes necessary to increase cover prices at short notice. Arrow Books reserve the right to show new retail prices on covers which may differ from those previously advertised in the text or elsewhere.